KATHARINE GRANT is (as K. M. Grant) best known for her prizewinning deGranville Trilogy. *The Marriage Recital* is her debut novel for adults. She was brought up in Lancashire, England, amid the ghosts of her ancestors, one of whom was the last person in the United Kingdom to be hanged, drawn, and quartered. She lives in Scotland with her husband, and is a Royal Literary Fund Consultant Fellow.

Praise for *The Marriage Recital*

A *New York Times* Editors' Choice
Longlisted for the 2014 Desmond Elliott Prize

"A tale of seduction, sex, love, death, and music, [*The Marriage Recital*] pulsates with pain but also with a wicked sense of humor that sometimes arises from the smallest details.... Grant never paints in strokes of black and white, of good and evil.... A subversive and thrilling gothic tale, it will keep you up all night. It's the sort of novel you say you'll read for only ten more minutes because it's already way past your bedtime. Two hours later, your light is still on."

—*The New York Times*

"One of the most delightfully contrary novels I have met.... A tease of a novel...I found myself irritated enough to throw the book at the wall several times, but then intrigued enough to read the whole thing twice.... Extremely impressive...A wonderful read from a born storyteller."   —Chris Cleave,
New York Times bestselling author of *Little Bee*

"Witty, dark...Grant eschews period clichés in favor of sharp, unsentimental storytelling that evokes the era with zest and authenticity. Her London, like her characters, is both flawed and fascinating. The novel's epigrammatic voice—'London was never so lovely as when you were about to leave it'—is another of its delights, detached in tone but delivering what are often dark ironies with memorable brevity and cleverness."

—*Publishers Weekly* (starred review)

"This is one of those precious novels. The kind that book-worms burrow inside to devour with relish from cover to cover. The kind you'll secrete behind all the other books on your shelves in case friends steal it and somehow 'forget' to give it back. The kind from which you'll read chosen snippets to your offspring when they're old enough. An induction into the magical unruliness of words. Not a dull or superfluous page . . . Grant at times writes like Jane Austen on crack cocaine or Dickens sating himself at an orgy—drawing freely on the literary posturing of past greats, but entirely, refreshingly modern, entirely herself. . . . She makes you gasp and laugh and reread, in order to relish again a paragraph or a full page. Her style is a triumph of wit and brio." —*The Scotsman* (Edinburgh)

"Packed full of colorful characters and with an unexpectedly poignant coda, this is an original, winningly imagined tale of the ties that bind (and some very naughty pianoforte lessons)." —*Daily Mail* (London)

"A provocative story of seduction and romance, lust and violence . . . A tale of nineteenth-century female insurrection, set to a tune of Bach piano inventions, *con brio*." —Kate Manning, author of *My Notorious Life*

"Late-eighteenth-century London is the well-detailed setting for this fun, lascivious gambol through the lives of women and men with decidedly carnal appetites. . . . Intriguing . . . The plot and characters are handled with grace and precision. Suggest to fans of Sarah Dunant and Sarah Waters." —*Booklist*

"Original and dark...[Grant] manages to be carnal without being graphic, detailed without being anatomical...aided by her narrative style, which bristles with dark humor and refuses to treat the past with the po-faced reverence it so often attracts. [*The Marriage Recital*] is not just about sex, although it is good on female passion.... The plot grows, like the music, to a staggering climax, and Grant happily subverts the clichés of the heaving bosoms and seductive Frenchmen. She writes as Alathea plays the piano—with wit, verve, and not a little mischief."

—*The Times* (London)

"Grant has rambunctious fun...but she studs it also with high seriousness.... The final set piece, the concert itself, plaits together comedy and tragedy with sly skill.... There is phrase-making here of high order, wise and funny arrangements of words that linger in the imagination."

—Jonathan Barnes, author of *The Somnambulist*, for the *Literary Review* (London)

"A startlingly good read. Grant, a skilled writer, makes each of the characters distinctive. She immerses the reader in late-eighteenth-century London.... A wonderful story."

—*Historical Novel Society*

"A wicked romp...Saucy."   —*Daily News* (New York)

"Bawdy, atmospheric...If Katharine Grant's adult debut... needed a subtitle, *Girls Gone Wild* would be ideal.... A tautly plotted novel of gender politics and sexual awakening, in the vein of Sarah Waters and Sarah Dunant."

—*The Bookseller* (London)

"[A] bustling, gritty, wheeling and dealing London reminiscent of Daniel Defoe's and James Boswell's worlds . . . compellingly edgy language . . . beautiful evocation of emotions through music."
                                                                    —*Library Journal*

"A fast-paced, sexy, historical read about the intriguing tutor/student relationship . . . Grant's girls are vividly described: funny, witty, melancholy, rowdy, elegant and kick-ass, each learning the skills to be the mistress of their own destiny."
                                                                    —*Marie Claire* (London)

"The grooming of five young Englishwomen for the marriage market goes wildly off the rails in a debut that, although Austenish in outline, takes some surprisingly saucy turns. . . . Grant's atmospheric evocation of London—seething with crime and grime—includes unexpectedly libidinous developments. . . . fresh and spirited . . . 'Girls shouldn't be puppets,' asserts this cleverly seductive romp."
                                                                    —*Kirkus Reviews*

"This subversive novel is a real page-turner: audacious, fast-paced, and sexy. . . . Dickensian in its energy and breadth . . . The pianoforte at the center of the narrative is a character in itself, and the music of Bach—ordered and disciplined—is a counterpoint to the emotional maelstrom which threatens to engulf the human characters in this compelling and twisted tale."
                                —Sally O'Reilly, author of *Dark Aemilia:*
                                A Novel of Shakespeare's Dark Lady

"As dark and deceitful as it is gloriously bawdy, the beautiful bastard child of Choderlos de Laclos's *Les Liaisons dangereuses* and Sarah Waters's *Fingersmith*."   —*The Observer* (London)

"A thumping debut filled with sex, manipulation, and a dash of romance. Wickedly dark and provocative... a bold reminder that the thirst for power and status remains unquenched over the ages."   —*BookPage* (April 2014 Top 10 Pick)

"A wicked, delicious romp through eighteenth-century London, written with the telling wink of an author whose affection for *Tom Jones* and *Tartuffe* sparkles throughout. I stayed up far too late devouring this rollicking tale of sex, intrigue, marriage, revenge, and the sordid side of the pianoforte. Bach's wig must be curling in his grave."   —Katherine Howe,
New York Times bestselling author of
The Physick Book of Deliverance Dane and
The House of Velvet and Glass

The Marriage Recital

A NOVEL

Katharine Grant

PICADOR

HENRY HOLT AND COMPANY
NEW YORK

THE MARRIAGE RECITAL. Copyright © 2014, 2015 by Katharine Grant. All rights reserved. Printed in the United States of America. For information, address Picador, 175 Fifth Avenue, New York, N.Y. 10010.

picadorusa.com • picadorbookroom.tumblr.com
twitter.com/picadorusa • facebook.com/picadorusa

Picador® is a U.S. registered trademark and is used by Henry Holt and Company under license from Pan Books Limited.

For book club information, please visit facebook.com/picadorbookclub or e-mail marketing@picadorusa.com.

Designed by Meryl Sussman Levavi

The Library of Congress has cataloged the Henry Holt edition as follows:

Grant, Katharine, 1958–
    Sedition : a novel / Katharine Grant.
        p. cm.
    ISBN 978-0-8050-9992-8 (hardcover)
    ISBN 978-0-8050-9993-5 (e-book)
    1. Fathers and daughters—Fiction.   2. Marriage—Fiction.   3. Piano teachers—
Fiction.   4. London (England)—History—18th century—Fiction.   I. Title.
    PR6107.R369S44 2014
    823'.92—dc23   2013031100

Picador Paperback ISBN 978-1-250-07171-2

Our books may be purchased in bulk for promotional, educational, or business use. Please contact your local bookseller or the Macmillan Corporate and Premium Sales Department at 1-800-221-7945, extension 5442, or by e-mail at MacmillanSpecialMarkets@macmillan.com.

First published under the title Sedition by Henry Holt and Company, LLC

First Picador Edition: November 2015

10   9   8   7   6   5   4   3   2   1

To William, for never doubting,

and to Michael Schmidt, for never saying he was too busy,

though he was.

LONDON, 1794

*L*ATE WINTER DAWN. THE WET NURSE SUCKLES a baby; the monk shivers through lauds; warm cow greets cold milker. Late winter dawn. Thief grins over sleeper; dead coals drop; the hangman, a novice, checks his rope. The day begins to stain.

Midday is different. By midday, the wet nurse is sore, the baby unsatisfied, and the monk willing to trade salvation for a hot dinner and a drop of restorative. The thief counts his takings and dozes. The hangman dampens the fire in the little brick house he has built under the walls of Newgate Prison. He checks tomorrow's ropes. One is chewed. Bloody dog. The executed don't pay for rope—a crime in itself. They seldom even tip, and a soggy rope won't sell as a souvenir. He's chosen the wrong profession. He'd give it up, except that would prove his father right. And now this: summoned to cut down some wretch who's hanged himself near the Bank of England. He sticks a knife in his belt and pulls on thick gloves. What a cheek. Death is his job. He feels robbed of his fee.

Out into the mud, he grinds the barrow through sludge and bumps it over knobbles of frozen dung. The February cloud is low and dense. Horses are lost in clammy steam. Urchins use fresh droppings to warm their hands, poor sods. It's the usual struggle through Cheapside—God alive, why do women have to gossip in gaggles? They part as soon as they recognize him. Bad luck to touch the hangman. Bad luck to touch his barrow. He pushes on through Poultry. Nothing at the Bank, but a hubbub at the top of Threadneedle Street. The hangman hoists his barrow onto the wooden pavement and heads for the crowd. As he reaches the Virginia and Baltick coffeehouse (formerly the Virginia and Maryland), a man barges into him, swears, then kicks at the coffeehouse's stout oak door until it opens. The man vanishes into a fecal fug and a girl emerges.

It was a month after her mother died that Alathea Sawneyford's father first took her to the V & B. At the sight of her, Mr. W., the proprietor, sucked in his cheeks. Children irritated customers. But Mrs. W. simply set a small chair below the counter to shield Alathea from the pictures Mr. W. favored for the walls. He called them "artful." Mrs. W. never thought of turning the little girl away. With no children of her own, she had love to offer—rough love, maybe, but love all the same, and although Alathea has long since outgrown the small chair, Mrs. W.'s welcome has never been withdrawn. Mr. W. can suck in his cheeks all he likes; it pleases Mrs. W. to encourage Alathea to look on the Virginia and Baltick as a haven, and occasionally Alathea chooses to do so, particularly when giving the slip to the stalkers set on her trail by her father. Never certain whether the surveillance is for her protection or his, it's nevertheless always a pleasure to identify the wretch so keen to be unidentified. As Alathea closes the V & B door, she spots today's tail—a poor specimen, exuding furtiveness. He might as well carry a sign.

Alathea sees the crowd and makes her way over, reaching the front at the same time as the hangman. A young woman is swinging from a gantry. She is quite dead. Alathea pokes the corpse with one finger. "Wire," she says, with a nod toward the girl's neck. The hangman bangs his barrow down. Unasked, Alathea holds the dead legs firmly and nods again. The hangman climbs onto his barrow, levers the wire from the gantry, and lowers the body. The crowd shuffles forward to have a look. Alathea settles the girl's skirts and contemplates her face.

"Desperate, your friend," the hangman says.

Alathea doesn't contradict, though she's never seen the girl before and wonders about desperation. The girl's hands are quite relaxed, her fingers spread as if to press a final chord on a keyboard. There is certainly evidence of pain in the bloated cheeks and bulging lips, but to Alathea physical pain is something to be squeezed out and wiped away. Despair, being more entrenched, is more worthy of note. She bends as though to look for signs of it but instead removes the corpse's shoes and tries them on. They don't fit so she returns them. "Pity," she says. Then, "Kiss her."

"What?" says the hangman.

"Kiss her," Alathea says. "Like this." She kisses the hangman full on the lips. It's not the unexpectedness he remembers, it's the feel of her tongue. He feels it from top to toe.

"If a hangman kisses a suicide, God forgives both," Alathea says. "Do it." Before the hangman can refuse, Alathea is gone, and though their acquaintance has been short, he feels her loss like a view suddenly revealed and as suddenly cut off. He rakes the crowd with his eyes. She is nowhere to be seen. A gloomy day seems gloomier. As he trundles the corpse to its paltry grave, the only thing that cheers him is a notice tied to a horse post just outside the Bank. It's a call to arms, brothers. Tax the rich! Power to the people! He counts six signatures. That should be six hangings this year at least. If all done at once, the authorities may ask for a discount. He'll be damned if he gives one.

ONE

Upstairs at the V & B, three men were in close conversation at a small round table. Their coats steamed and their faces were shadowed, Mr. W. favoring cheap tallow over expensive wax candles. Nor could the V & B steal light from neighboring shops, situated as it was between Gadhill the barber, who kept his lights low, and what had been the gunpowder office, now a storing, roasting, and grinding shed for the beans Mr. W. insisted, for quality's sake, must be kept in the dark. Even when a few rays of sun managed to twist down the street, the crust on the V & B's windows was as good as plate armor.

The men were waiting for the fourth of their party and looked to the door as he stamped in clutching *Spence's Penny Weekly*. A coffeeboy fed up with the V & B's poor gratuities and spoiling for a fight called out "Good news then, Mr. Brass?" since it clearly was not.

Gregory Brass turned on him. "Good news? Can't you read,

boy? Votes! Tax! We'll all be ruined. Spence and his like should be hanged for traitors. Hanged and then quartered."

The coffeehousers were momentarily distracted from bills of lading and tide calendars. "Spence's already in prison," said somebody mildly.

"Prison! Bah!" Brass banged his fist on the counter. "A public lynching's the thing. That'd teach him. I mean, the poor can't eat the vote or fornicate with it, so what use is it to them?"

Laughter. Brass whipped off his wig. "You think it's a joke?" He squared up.

Archibald Frogmorton rose, grasped his friend's arm, and would not be shaken off. "For God's sake, Brass, stop brawling and come and sit down. I'm not bailing you from Newgate again."

This last remark had some effect. Brass followed Frogmorton and threw himself into a chair. "It's a disgrace, I tell you." He waved the penny weekly in Frogmorton's face.

"Enough." Frogmorton seized the newspaper, folded it, and used it as a wedge to stop the table from rocking. "We haven't got all day. Let's turn to the matter in hand." Brass, still muttering, subsided. Chairs were pulled in and coffee called for.

The four men's chief interest was cloth, liquor, furs, leather, timber—anything that could be bought low and sold high—but it was domestic husbandry, not trade, that had drawn them here today to sit at a private table rather than the long trestle in front of the fire. Archibald Frogmorton, Gregory Brass, and Sawney Sawneyford each had one living daughter and Tobias Drigg, at forty-three the youngest of the men, had two. With Marianne Drigg eighteen at her last birthday and the other girls close behind, the time had come to find the girls husbands.

Trade in its own way, though the four fathers were not after money: they wanted grandchildren of a certain kind and were willing to pay.

Worldly success offered acquaintance, not friendship, with the rank of people these men had earmarked for their daughters: landed people, titled people, "the quality," as Mr. Drigg's father-in-law called them. Yet no matter how large the profits engineered by these four—and the profits were substantial—and no matter how significant Archibald Frogmorton's elevation to Alderman of the City of London, commercial gratitude was laced with social distaste. True, the Duke of Granchester did inquire after Georgiana Brass's health and Everina Drigg's talents, but these were simply polite precursors to inquiries about the ducal investments.

The water urn blew its lid. The coffeeboys cheered. "The girls must all be wed this time next year," Frogmorton declared, frowning at the noise.

"Yes, yes, that's right. By this time next year," Drigg agreed. Drigg's fatherly affection did not blind him to the fact that his daughters were too like their mother for complacency. Currently, Marianne and Everina were soft and plump. Soon they would be tough and fleshy—more likely to pick up a butcher than a baronet.

"Wed this time next year," echoed Sawney Sawneyford softly. He was the only widower among the four, and his tone was both agreement and disagreement, a confusion he cultivated. Marriage talk unsettled him. The others saw silken grandchildren behind unassailable social ramparts. Sawneyford saw his daughter sweating under Tamworth-pink flesh. Was that worth a coronet? Was it worth a rampart? Was it worth a dead candle? Sharp against his buttocks were three diamonds he liked to keep secreted in the lining of his coat: tiny things, the first gems he had ever touched. His eyes swam. Diamonds suited Alathea. What was he doing here? He didn't want Alathea to marry at all.

"This year's all very well, but we mustn't sell the girls short." Brass, still prickling, purposefully irritated Frogmorton, who had suggested no such thing. Brass was conscious of being the handsomest, his nose less bulbous than Frogmorton's and his ears neater, his eyes less fishlike than Drigg's, his chin round against Sawneyford's rapier. He had a powerful physique that always needed feeding, not necessarily with food. Losing his temper whetted his appetite for his new French *belle amie*. He drummed his fingers.

"Apply your minds, gentlemen," Frogmorton said. "Our daughters need some very particular attraction, an accomplish‑ment beyond the accomplishments of others. All are pretty." He gave a superb smile. Having fathered a beauty, he did not have to worry about Everina's unfortunate teeth, Georgiana's hipless‑ness, or Alathea Sawneyford's—what was it? He felt a clogging in his throat. That girl. He tried not to think of her. "As I say, they're all lookers in their own ways, but that's not enough. All young girls of a certain age are lookers." He wiped his forehead. The fug made him sweat. "Most girls can draw and some can sing. It strikes me that we must find our daughters something else to make them enviable and envied—something spec‑tacular."

There was talk, none of it conclusive. Finally, Drigg coughed. "Do you think we could perhaps make something of the rivalry between the harpsichord and these newfangled pianofortes?" The others looked at him with surprise—even Sawneyford. Drigg liked the attention. "It's the talk of St. James's Street, and the pianoforte, I'm assured, will soon be a feature in every home. If our girls were to master it before other girls, they would be at a distinct advantage."

Brass was openly derisive, which made Drigg more determined than was wise. He had no idea of music. There had been none in the Foundling Hospital in which he and Frogmorton, the latter superior because his mother had left him with a name grander than her own, had been raised. There had been none among the lighters on which Drigg spent five years coal heaving before he pulled a drowning Frogmorton out of the low-tide slime of the Thames, a rescue that set him on the road to riches. When he spoke, as he did now at some length, about the differences between harpsichord and pianoforte, his opinions were at least secondhand. He knew he was overpersuasive, goaded by Brass's sneers. But he did not stop and Frogmorton, initially sceptical, was soon quite taken with the picture Drigg painted. Encouraged, Drigg began to elaborate until somehow the notion of a concert party at which the girls would perform in front of potential husbands took shape.

After a while, Frogmorton raised his hand. "You speak of a grand pianoforte, Drigg. It will be large, I assume. Our girls must be seen. Will they be visible behind it?"

"Everina certainly will," said Brass with a snort.

Drigg snorted back. "Georgiana may vanish entirely. Mrs. Drigg wonders if she's quite well."

"Mrs. Drigg can save her wondering. Georgiana's well enough to bang a few keys." Brass was not worried about his daughter. Skinny and fey she might be, but she was musical. He was certain of that. She must be or what was the use of her?

"Do you think it a good idea, Sawney?" Frogmorton asked.

The others stopped talking. Sawney utterances were rare enough to be overvalued.

"Your plan seems good enough." Sawney picked at fraying cuffs.

"*Our* plan, Sawney. It's all of ours," rapped Brass. He thought, why does Sawney wear rags? He could buy a whole tailoring business. Or get that disturbing daughter to do some mending.

"We have a plan," repeated Sawney. "Why not?" Alathea already had a pianoforte but he kept that, as he kept many things, to himself.

"Well then," said Frogmorton. "Are we agreed on the principle?"

Nobody demurred so he turned to Drigg. "We must purchase an instrument," he said. "Drigg, you can see to it."

"Oh, I don't think so," Drigg said, suddenly alarmed. "It's a big purchase. We should all go."

"Nonsense," said Frogmorton. "If we go as a group of City men, we'll be fleeced. You must go alone. Don't you agree, Brass?"

Brass, keen to increase Drigg's alarm, agreed. "Then we can blame you if it all goes wrong."

"Sawneyford?"

Sawneyford didn't care who bought the thing, or if nobody bought it.

"That's settled, then," said Frogmorton.

More details were hammered out. Since the Frogmortons' Manchester Square house was the grandest, the pianoforte was to be delivered there, and through the pianoforte dealer, Drigg was to employ a tuner-teacher. Frogmorton would pay this music master every week and the full bill would be divided among them at the venture's conclusion. The girls would be chaperoned by Mrs. Frogmorton as they took lessons and when the music master was satisfied the girls were ready, invitations would be sent out and the girls would perform.

As the clock struck three, the men's minds turned to their offices. Clerks would be waiting. They pushed out their chairs, found their coats, and went to the counter, where Mrs. W. noted down each man's dues. She accepted few notes of credit but she trusted these four to pay at the end of each quarter. So far, prompting had not been necessary and Alderman Frogmorton could be relied on for a good tip.

TWO

HE GIRLS WERE NOT CONSULTED. HAD they gone to the workshop of the pianoforte maker at Tyburn, things might have been different. As it was, Tobias Drigg made his way to Vittorio Cantabile's workshop without the girls knowing anything of their fathers' plan. Drigg did not choose Cantabile: Cantabile was the only pianoforte maker of whom he had heard, and he could find his way easily enough. Ten years after hosting the last wretch's execution, the Tyburn gallows remained, even the destitute superstitious about chopping the famous arms for firewood. Today Drigg wished he could not find his way. He wished he had not been so assertive. He wished he had never mentioned the pianoforte. He wished he was back in the V & B discussing plundered ships and the muleishness of Yorkshire jaggermen.

One of the gallows' arms pointed to the right, and after a brief meander during which he seriously contemplated aban doning his commission, Drigg found himself in front of two square stories of black brick, the sullen hub of five narrow warrens. Lean-tos would have softened the workshop's appearance, but nothing touched it apart from the cartwheels that habitually clipped the corner stones of the three sides where the road passed very tight. On the fourth side, the road was wider, and a wooden pavement had been attempted. The building marked a boundary for local robbers: on the east side, official thief-takers and Bow Street Runners; on the west side, devilry. The window and the door were on the east side, as was the attempted pavement. It was a good place for the alehouse it eventually became.

Drigg rat-tatted on the door. No answer, except for jeers from a crowd of beggars. Drigg pushed the door open and took a moment to shut out the street. For a second, he could have been in the V & B—that tallow tang—then his eyes readjusted and he found himself contemplating a scene of destruction. Of the fifteen or so instruments in the workshop, few were whole. Two single-manual harpsichords had vomited their innards and from a spinet, a spew of shriveled veins. Another, skeleton cracked, had lost two legs and was frozen in a crippled buck. Others were covered with shrouds. Over the lid of a lion-footed clavichord, keyboard missing, implements to pluck, hit, squeeze, stretch, and force were spread in the manner of an orderly torturer. Directly in front of Drigg was a large desk, a stool behind it. Set in the right-hand wall, a fireplace, fire unlit.

Drigg shuddered. Overlaying the smell of tallow was a smell much more fungal—an undertaking smell. He ventured past the desk, dodged the shrouds, and was further unnerved by the drafts that caused a permanent whispering and twanging, as though a concert was either finishing or just about to start. He stiffened his spine. "Hulloa! Hulloo there!" He could feel dust spores in his throat and his nose prickled.

From somewhere emerged the proprietor, balding, thin as drawn steel and draped about with wire and ivory, felt and pivots, jacks, stops, mutes, and pins. His hammer was poised for a burglar.

Drigg blurted, "I wish to buy a pianoforte."

Cantabile at once recognized a City creature, a coffeehouse man. Which coffeehouse? Lloyd's? No Lloyd's man came this way. Garraway's? No banker's sheen. Batson's? Possibly, though the man lacked sawbones' smuggery. Cantabile kept the hammer raised. The Bedford? A man who shouted "Hulloa!" supping with poets? No. The Virginia and Baltick. That was it. Plain as plain. A V & B man. Cloth and furs. Thick thread and dead animals.

Cantabile did not see himself as a vendor of keyboard instruments. He was a musical craftsman like his late father and, also like his late father, he had achieved renown in their native Milan but no fortune. London had promised more discerning customers but in this Cantabile had been disappointed. Sales had been good—his reputation preceded him; it was the customers who appalled. He found it painful to part with creations over which he had crooned and labored, to imagine them under the thumbs and fingers of buffoons, money grubbers, and imbecile girls. He drove harder and harder bargains. Shortly before customers refused to buy from him, Cantabile refused to sell. Only when starvation threatened did an instrument depart. Cantabile did not care who saw him weep.

Starvation threatened today but he moved sideways and gently closed the lid of the pianoforte he was currently refining. This pianoforte was not a work of art, it was a work of genius. Under-dampers of brass and a sounding board of seasoned beech achieved resonances beyond anything Broadwood or Erard could boast. Innovation, materials, and the dexterity of a master combined with uncanny precision so that every grain and splinter, block and hammer, string and pad, screw and hinge was perfect. Cantabile had gilded the small rose in the middle of the sounding board as tenderly as an artist paints roses in a woman's cheek. He loved this instrument without reserve. It contained more of him than his child. It was, indeed, the child he should have had. He stroked it with spread fingers. Not a wisp of the V & B should taint it.

Drigg gave the piano no more than a glance, since it was brown and unattractive. Cantabile saw the dismissal and took umbrage. This beauty, this divinity, passed over as nothing by a V & B man! He reached for the pistol under the counter, then stopped himself. He had a better weapon at his disposal. "Annie, Annie," he thundered.

His daughter materialized. Drigg was knocked backward. Under her cap, Annie boasted lustrous chestnut hair. From wide forehead to sculpted nose, she was pretty. Below the nose, catastrophe. A harelip created a whole new gummy feature in her chin and Annie gave Drigg the full benefit.

Ah, Annie. She was beyond price. Cantabile had vomited when she was born and ordered her swilled away with the afterbirth. His wife objected. The baby was a baby, she said, her baby. In a moment he everafter counted as cowardice, Cantabile gave in. He had had no peace since. He had not gotten over his daughter's deformity as his wife had. The stabs of tenderness that caught him unawares mocked him when he looked at her face: a book with split pages, beauty above, monstrosity below. And ridiculously unstable. Annie's mouth drifted. He could not stand the smudginess of it. It tore at him, what the girl might have been and what she was. When Annie was three, he had sought help, but surgeons were afraid of adding to the damage. A harelip was not dangerous, they said. Dangerous? Of course it was not dangerous! It was horrible. Was that not as bad? Cantabile took her home again, a small, solemn, lisping child, who would learn to eat facing the wall.

She did have her uses. With Annie in sight, Cantabile could leave a pot of money in full view of the street and as soon as she could sit at the keyboard unaided, he set her to play in the window, a display that had helped custom fall away so satisfactorily that the show was soon no longer necessary. Instead, Annie buried herself in the brick fortress, absorbing music and the craft of instrument making as other children absorbed fairy tales and the craft of pickpocketing. Her presence agitated Cantabile, yet he could not do without her. When her mother took ill, Annie turned nurse and she worked harder on the instruments than any apprentice, playing better even than her father. He might have been jealous, but as she grew, the lip grew more prominent and kept her meek. Father and daughter lived like porcupines, prickles up, Cantabile's sharp with aggression, Annie's blunter, for defense.

The effect of Annie on Drigg, however, was not what Cantabile expected. The fool was too mannerly to stare and leave. At last, Cantabile was forced to say, "Annie, this—this gentleman wants to buy one of our instruments."

Annie stood boldly upright, tilting her chin, which, as anybody who got past her lip might have noticed, was dimpled. She did not smile—her smile made even her mother blench. Apart from not smiling, Annie faced the world headon. Her mother thought this brave. It was not. Despite everything, Annie was a dreamer. Some girls might have dreamed of physical correction, but Annie's dream was far more intoxicating. In it, she played her father's most sophisticated pianoforte to a public audience. This dream audience gawped at first, then it listened, marveled, and stood to applaud. In the audience was her father's only friend, Monsieur Belladroit, met in Paris on Cantabile's journey to London, a regular correspondent and occasional visitor, and in her dream, when the concert was over, Monsieur took Annie's hands in his, knelt at her feet, and loved her. This was the intoxication and this future audience was why she waited patiently for the man in their shop to find the words of farewell he was politely seeking and why, when such words eluded him, she made herself pleasant. This man might take a concert ticket. If he stared now, he would not stare then. Anyway, she did not share her father's horror of sales. Something must pay the rent and for the medicine needed to ease her mother's lesioned lungs. "Are you familiar with pianofortes, Mr.——" she asked, wiping grimy hands on a large cambric handkerchief tucked into her belt. She had been scraping wood.

"Er, Drigg. Tobias Drigg." He could not look away.

"Were you thinking square?" Annie took a lamp and led Drigg from the dingy front showroom to dingier storage where the heavy structural work was done. Bony frames and belly rails clattered together. "Watch out!" Drigg ducked too late. His hat and wig were swept off. He retrieved them and followed Annie more closely. There were no windows. Drigg had only fleeting impressions of ivory sheets, bunched quills, and the dull sheen of half-polished lids. So many unfamiliar shapes. So much unsilent silence. His shoulder caught on an iron hook. He pulled free, overbalanced, and stubbed the toe of his boot on a pile of curing leather. "God's teeth!" he muttered. "Is there to be no light?"

Annie lifted the lamp. Immediate transformation. The place was an ordinary workshop again, filled with ordinary instruments.

"These are very popular," Annie said, pointing to three harpsichords. "Many people find them highly satisfactory. All have cypress soundboards—my father follows the Italian way—and two choirs of strings. Listen." She made her way to the nearest instrument and rippled out the scale of D major with her left hand. "Try one yourself."

"Pianoforte, not harpsichord," Drigg said at once. "That's what we want."

"Really?" Annie lowered the lamp and padded over to a bigger square instrument sitting on its own. Drigg followed. Annie raised the lamp. Drigg's eyes locked back onto her lip. Annie kept the lamp high. Now he wished she would not. "Here's a pianoforte," she said. "May I know the color of the room in which your instrument will live?"

"Color? Green, I believe," said Drigg. He peeled his eyes away.

"Well then," said Annie, her voice low and pleasant, her lisp not unattractive. "This maple would do very well. As you can see, we don't go in for painted frames. Appearance should never take precedence over sound. You may like to know that we sold one of these only yesterday to the Duke of Granchester for his daughter Blanche to play." She lied easily. She was a good saleswoman.

The mention of the duke had exactly the effect Annie sought. Mr. Drigg calmed himself. "The Duke of Granchester," he repeated.

Annie put down the lamp and lit a bright candle. "Yes. Just look at the quality of the inlay." They both looked. "Lady Blanche is not a fine player," Annie confided, spitting slightly. Mr. Drigg curled his fists. "Your daughter will be more accomplished. If I'm not mistaken, your daughter is the person for whom the pianoforte's intended?"

"Two daughters," said Drigg, trying to move inconspicuously away without bumping into anything. "But not only for them. I am purchasing a pianoforte for all our daughters—I mean to say my two, Marianne and Everina, and for the daughters of three friends. They have a daughter each." His sudden loss of color had nothing to do with Annie and all to do with the weight of his responsibility to these friends and all their daughters.

"Five girls," Annie said.

"They're to play at a concert."

"A concert!" Annie echoed. "My, sir, they must be accomplished." The candle dripped and Annie, shielding it, curtailed the light. Drigg felt Annie was a nice girl. She would help him do the right thing. "They *are* accomplished. They're to play for potential husbands at a concert party. That's why we need a good pianoforte, one that can fill a large drawing room, or perhaps a saloon. We may have the concert at home, we may have it elsewhere. We really need what I think is called a 'grand.' We want our girls to have the best. Our girls deserve the best." His confidence grew as he spoke. Why shouldn't his idea be a success?

"Of course, sir," Annie said. Her voice grew wistful. "If your girls want love to flourish, what better way than through music?" Annie did not usually betray her soul's romance except at the keyboard, but she felt there was romance in what Drigg told her and she was happy to encourage it.

Drigg was happy to be encouraged. "Love?" he confided. "Between you and me, I don't think they know much about that. It's not a consideration. Getting on's the thing."

"Love's a good way of getting on, at least in music," Annie said. "To make good music you must know about love." She believed this utterly.

Drigg was indulgent. "My dear, I suppose girls like you set great store by love, since, as they say, love is blind. But you see, that's not the way our girls look at love. They've no need." He closed the lid of the pianoforte with a thump.

"Thank you," said Annie, her tone colder. She could see the proposed concert now. This man's satin-skinned daughters, their rosebud lips, the fluffy playing, the false adulation, the offers, the ring, the wedding party, and the faultless children to follow. After a long moment, she said "Come" in her shop-keeper's voice. "I see now that you need quite a different sort of pianoforte." She blew out the candle, lowered the lamp, and led him into darkness.

In an alcove apart was a large instrument. Annie swept off the covers. Its brutally handsome frame bore no trace of the experiments with detachable hitch pins, gut lift rails, and skin-packed hammers to which her father had subjected it. Inside, although everything was fixed, nothing was quite mended and, as a result, the pianoforte was unpredictable as a nervy car-riage horse. The keys, when depressed, sometimes clanged, sometimes made no noise at all. Strings were always bursting and scraping over their fellows. This pianoforte was destined for butchery. Even Cantabile agreed.

"This, sir, is just the pianoforte for your purposes," Annie said. "We've been waiting for that very special customer. It was too expensive for the Duke of Granchester. But you, sir, with your marvelous girls so anxious to get on, won't begrudge the money. Would you like to hear it?" She did not wait for a reply.

Annie knew this carriage horse. She alone knew how to coax it, drive it, steady it, and, more important, how to weave its percussive hiccups into the counterpoint. Under her fingers, it would bend its head and accept a rein meant for a harpsichord. This was the pianoforte Mr. Drigg and his dreadful girls deserved. Annie chose to play Maria Barthélemon's sonatas, works her father had come to admire after meeting the lady herself. He had sent Mrs. Barthélemon his compliments. Mrs. Barthélemon had sent these, with a dedication.

To warm the instrument, Annie spread a chord and executed two quick runs in thirds and sixths. Drigg clapped his hands over his ears. "Mary have mercy! The noise! The clacking of those keys will bring the house down."

Annie put her hands in her lap. "You wanted a grand pianoforte," she said. "This is the sound they make." She half got up.

"No—no," said Drigg, removing his fingers from his ears. "Sit down. I was only surprised. I've never heard one"—he did not want to confess to "ever"—"so very close." He stepped back.

Annie started again, the Larghetto, not the Allegro. She concentrated. If the music was to work its magic, she needed more from this pianoforte than a grudging acceptance of her instructions. She scolded; she flirted; she ordered; she cajoled. After fifteen bars, the pianoforte submitted. Together, they set to work on Drigg.

Once he grew accustomed to the sound, dimmer and more clinging than the sharp pluck of the harpsichord, there was no sham in the trembling far beneath the skin, a trembling that increased to a nostalgic twitch as the music revived memories of Mrs. Drigg on their wedding night. How shy she had been. The tone changed. Now he was reminded of Marianne's childish ringlets—sadly long gone—and the tiny eyelashes of his poor dead son. His mouth opened slightly. Through some trick of memory, he could hear a mother sing. Perhaps it was his own. His eyes pricked.

When the music stopped, he cleared his throat. One thing was certain: if Marianne and Everina could play this instrument as Annie had done, so moving, so pure, there would be offers for them before the concert had finished. He spoke as soon as he was able. "A glorious instrument, my dear, and after that first shock, how well it sounds. Shall we return to your father?" It was dark. Annie may have smiled.

"I'll have the large pianoforte in the back, Mr. Cantabile," Drigg said, rhyming "Cantabile" with "crocodile." He took a part-printed bank note out of his pocket. "You know. The one too dear for the Duke of Granchester. Oh, and I'll need the name of the person who taught your daughter. She plays with great skill. How much shall I write?" He unfolded the note and picked up Cantabile's quill. He was in a hurry.

Vittorio Cantabile ignored Drigg. He eyed Annie up and down. "That black piano, eh?" Annie stared straight back at him, for once father and daughter rather than aggressor and defender. Cantabile thought, she's a wily one, this Annie of mine. Why not let the black devil loose to do its worst? Annie thought, don't deny me this small revenge, Father; surely even to you I'm worth more than this City creature. Cantabile offered the tiniest of nods. Annie felt as if he had embraced her.

"And a teacher?" Cantabile asked. "Can't your girl play,

Mr. . . . ?" He had not cared to remember the name. "Not much point in having a pianoforte, and certainly not that black one, if she can't play."

Drigg bridled. "Of course my daughters—as I've just told your daughter, I have two girls—can play. All the girls can play. Naturally, they'll need help moving from harpsichord to pianoforte and I've heard that these instruments need to be well regulated. A teacher is skilled in that too, I believe."

"All the girls?" Cantabile's face turned to stone. Like Annie, he saw a parade of girlish perfection. Where was the justice in that? Annie took Drigg's note and removed the lid from the inkwell.

"The instrument is to be shared," said Drigg, fiddling with his wig. "Although perhaps my Marianne and Everina could have special tuition, at home, on our present instrument, as well as on this one, just to, well, to help perfect their technique?" Harriet Frogmorton's trim beauty and Alathea Sawneyford's troubling charms loomed. Marianne and Everina must be best at something. "The girls are to give a concert, you see," he said in tones he thought commanding.

Mr. Cantabile watched Annie smoothing Drigg's note. "If you want a good teacher, why not take Annie herself? There's no better player and she can keep a pianoforte up to scratch. Believe me, you'll need her for the black demon she's sold you. She could help your girls at home and direct the concert from the stage. What do you say to that?"

Drigg dropped his wig-ends. "Oh," he said, "I'm not . . . I'm not sure . . . I'm not . . . you see, they're . . . well, they're . . . and your daughter is . . ."

"My daughter's what?"

"She's . . ."

"Yes?"

"Well, you know what I mean. I mean—oh dear—I mean if she perhaps could cover herself up? Then it might be possible, Mr. Cantabile?" Again pronounced wrongly.

"Why should she do that?"

Drigg silently appealed to Annie. She was as stony-faced as her father. "Our name is Can-ta-bi-lé," she said. "The end does not rhyme with 'vile.' It has two syllables: *i* and *é*."

Drigg felt he had doubly insulted her but how could he apologize without saying rather more than he meant?

"I'm willing to teach your daughters," Annie said, "if you're willing to have me." And how I'll teach them, she thought. I'll teach them their just deserts. Her eyes almost sparkled.

"But we cannot have you," Drigg cried. "You must see." He could not look at Annie; he looked straight over her head.

Cantabile waved his hammer. "I don't see at all. You'll get no teacher as good as she and you'll get used to the lip." He cackled. "Useful thing, in fact! If you've sons, there's no need to worry." He glanced slyly at Drigg's crotch. "No one will ever want Annie in that way, eh!" He lunged forward and peered at her. Realizing he had hit a nerve, he gave a little crow. "Annie a wife! Why not? I suppose you'd be happy with a blind man?" He turned back to Drigg. "Do you agree, sir. I mean, if a blind man heard Annie play at a concert, he might imagine that only a beautiful girl could create such a beautiful sound. But oh, the horror of a kiss! Like kissing an oyster."

All sparkle was extinguished in the flood of Annie's flush. That earlier silent communion with her father over Drigg had been a trap. She should have known. Her concert dream tottered. Her belief that her music could triumph over her deformity began to shrink, her vision of Monsieur kneeling before her to fragment. She tried to blot out her father and bolster her belief, reminding herself that when she was twelve, Monsieur Belladroit had arrived at the workshop worn-out and sad and she had played from Herr Bach's *Well-Tempered Clavier*. After, Monsieur had kissed her like a grown-up. Not on the lips, to be sure. Nearby. Eyes open. Certainly, Monsieur had not been back to London since then, but that had not stopped Annie's concert taking real shape. She knew what she would play and in what order. She knew what she would wear. She knew what she would say to Monsieur as he took her hands.

But no matter how hard she fought to keep her dream clean and clear, her father, with his guess, had poisoned it. Even as she struggled, she knew she would never again dream without his tainting intrusion, never again imagine Monsieur's words of love without hearing her father's mockery. Monsieur would never kiss her. She stopped struggling and stood helpless as her dream darkened and soured.

Drigg blustered into the silence. "Of course Annie is—of course such a girl would be—of course there's no question." He was out of his depth. "Now, look here. You must understand. Sorry as I am for your daughter, Can-ta-bi-lé, and really, her, er, her, her *affliction* is hardly that bad—I see worse, far worse—almost every day. But we need everything to be perfect. We simply cannot have her."

"Well then, you cannot have the pianoforte!" Cantabile twirled the hammer and shot Annie a bolt of pure malice.

Annie leaned hard on the desk. She was barely aware of making a decision, but a decision was made. There would be no tremor in the floor as she crumpled, because she would not crumple. She went straight to her father's pride and joy.

Cantabile, quick to understand, tried to slam the lid. Annie thwarted him with a shoulder strong enough to unbalance. She sat down. Haydn's Capriccio in C major sprang from her fingers, spirited, charming, ruthlessly in time. Cantabile righted himself and tried to push Annie off the stool. Drigg, emboldened by the music, rushed forward and knocked the hammer from Cantabile's hand. The men seized each other around the neck and rocked around the instruments, grappling and grunting. Drigg was short but strong. Cantabile, randomly flailing and kicking, wasted himself hurling abuse. In the end, and without much trouble, Drigg neatly crushed Cantabile's arms together and they stood locked in a wrestler's embrace.

All the while, Annie played. It did not matter that Cantabile continued to shout. The music drowned the man. Through the grunts and groans, Drigg listened with new wonder. This sound, this particular sound, was exactly what he wanted. Brighter than the black pianoforte, less smoky, less troubling, this pianoforte caused shudders, yes, but nothing discomfiting— more like shudders of joy. What had he been thinking? He almost blushed. Compared to this instrument, the other was improper. He saw that now. A narrow escape. This pianoforte was the one. It sang like a bird, flowed like water, fortified like wine, and its virginal innocence was just the thing for virginal girls. How could two instruments called the same name be so different? No matter. As Annie's fingers drew everything from the brown pianoforte that it had to give, the pauses in the music teasing and tantalizing, Drigg dismissed the black pianoforte. Forget that one. This was the ship sailing into harbor, the path up the splendid aisle, the investment paying out.

He let go of Cantabile, who rushed at Annie and slammed

the lid almost on her fingers. Drigg said, thinking to be placating, "This is a pianoforte, a pianoforte indeed!"

"Quite right, sir," Annie said with some animation as she slid past her father and returned to the desk. "It may not be as handsome as the other, which is why I thought it wouldn't appeal. I apologize. This is the best pianoforte in London, possibly the world. With the other instrument, your girls would amaze. With this, they'll astound."

"This piano's not for sale. You can't have it." Cantabile poked the hammer at Drigg. "Nobody can have it."

Drigg ignored him. "We can pay," he said. His note had fluttered to the floor. He picked it up and imagined himself telling Frogmorton, Brass, and Sawneyford that he had secured the best pianoforte in the world. "We'll pay top price."

"And so you should," Annie said, picking up the quill. "You'll not get such a chance again. This piano has six octaves and the pedals—well…"

"Six what? Never mind. How much?" Drigg blew sawdust from the note.

Mr. Cantabile was a dervish between them. "I've told you. It's not for sale."

Annie opened the inkpot. "There's no fixed price, sir. You take the pianoforte and I'll send you my mother's doctors' bills."

Drigg balked. He did not want that kind of a bargain. It was not what he was used to.

Cantabile was beside himself. "The girl has no authority. The pianoforte's not hers to sell! If you lay a finger on it, I'll have you for theft."

"The best pianoforte for your concert; the best husbands for your daughters; the best treatment for my mother. Is that not fair?" Annie asked, the quill held out.

"I'd rather just pay." Drigg tried not to hear the increasing violence of Cantabile's threats.

"That's the bargain. Take it or leave it." Annie laid the quill down.

"Well, I'm—"

"You'll not have it! You won't!" Cantabile's hammer whistled past Drigg's nose.

Drigg suddenly hated him. "We'll have it," he said to Annie. "We'll damned well have it on any terms."

"You won't," shouted Cantabile. "This pianoforte goes nowhere."

Annie locked eyes with her father. His were burning. Hers were cool. "My father speaks ill of the king," she said, enunciating each word carefully.

"What?" said Drigg. "Everybody speaks ill of—"

Annie interrupted. "My father has French pamphlets. Here in London there are groups of foreigners who are no friends to England—"

"Be quiet!" shouted Cantabile. "I'm not French. I've no sympathy with the chicanery going on over the sea."

Annie leaned forward and whispered into Drigg's ear. She straightened up. Her father opened his mouth and closed it. "The pianoforte goes with you," Annie said to Drigg.

"Shall we say next week for delivery?" Drigg crammed his hat on. He had heard not a word of Annie's whisper, if, indeed, she had whispered anything. He wanted only to get out.

"Certainly," Annie said.

"I'll pay a lump sum." Drigg seized the quill and scribbled an amount onto his banknote, then, for want of more paper, turned the note over and scribbled down Frogmorton's Manchester Square address, glad not to be writing his own. He did not want Cantabile turning up outside the Drigg establish-ment. He blotted the ink firmly and made for the door. With his hand already on the door handle, a noise caused him to turn. Cantabile had his mouth open. For a moment, Drigg wondered whether the man was having some kind of seizure. Cantabile was laughing. Drigg shook his fist. Cantabile held up his hands in mock surrender. "I won't have my pianoforte played badly at your concert. You do need a teacher."

"We've been through that."

"Not Annie. Forget her. You need a true master. I know just the man."

The door was already open. Escape! Drigg tossed caution to the wind. "I accept your offer, Mr. Cantabile. We'll pay your man so long as he produces the desired result. Now, if our business is concluded, I really must go. Good day to you both." He threw the door wide and was assaulted by the scrum of the street and a chorus of "Watcha, Frenchie! Fuzzy-wig! Fuzzy-wig!" He walked fast, without looking back. Thank God that was over.

The second Drigg closed the door of the workshop, Canta-bile slapped Annie hard across the cheek. "What did you whisper to that man?" Annie said nothing. Cantabile slapped her again. "Blackmail is not pretty in a woman." He spun away from her, opened the lid of the pianoforte, and blew gently over the keys. He closed the lid. He would not look at it again.

Grabbing a bottle from one shelf and a dirty glass from another, he poured wine and set the bottle on the desk with a thump. "I'm going to send them Claude Belladroit as teacher," he threw out. Annie slipped Drigg's note into her apron pocket. "I'll write to him today. He appreciates beautiful girls, *fully appreciates* them"—Cantabile's lip curled—"and even ugly girls if they're rich." He gulped his wine. "Do you know, I believe I might persuade him it's time he settled down with a wife. Why shouldn't he marry one of these concert puffballs, then leave her when the money runs out?" He drank some more. "Wait! Why doesn't Claude seduce them all while he's about it? That would be a pleasant task for him, and the girls' ruin would be some revenge for my pianoforte." He finished his wine and crunched the glass until it splintered, a favorite trick. "Claude Belladroit with those girls. Dream about that, Annie." He laughed as he headed for the stairs, but Annie knew he would sob for his darling pianoforte tonight. Once in her own bed, she did not dream about the girls: she thought about them, wide awake, and did not close her eyes until dawn.

THREE

THE GIRLS WERE TAKING TEA AT STRAT-
ton Street, Everina Drigg their giggling
hostess. The room was opulent: maroon
velvet, lime-green silk, pink brocade,
two sofas plump as the girls sitting in
them, and half a dozen squat plaster chickens (why chickens,
Agnes Drigg had thought many times, I mean, why *chickens*)
among other geegaws, none of which had any connection to
one another or anything else imaginable. Small tables with
barley twist legs were scattered about; a rectangular walnut
desk lurked in a corner. The decor was both designed and not
designed. Agnes had drunk three glasses of brandy before she
greeted the decorator with "color, happy to pay"—not at all
what she meant to say, but this often happened to Agnes and
it was, nevertheless, an accurate précis of her husband's instructions. The decorator, anxious for his fee, complied. Two weeks
later, the full horror was exposed. Tobias Drigg said "Excellent job, Mr. G." Agnes Drigg said "So homely" and fled to

the comforting stink of her father's eel stall and the three-legged stool she had sat on as a child. She never felt at home in her own house again.

The girls had been singing, and when they sang, the pleasure in their eyes, the stretching of their necks, and the rise and fall of silk-covered breasts softened their defects. This softening was particularly necessary for Everina, whose teeth had been expensively and unsubtly replaced when her real ones became painful and discolored. But Everina was not alone in needing help. No amount of ribbon or skill could fatten Marianne's disappointing hair, and although it would probably do no good, Harriet Frogmorton, who, by age, came between the Drigg sisters, was right to clip her nose with a clothespin every night since its roundness spoiled an otherwise lively face atop a neat body. Of the other two girls, Georgiana Brass's defects were difficult to pinpoint—since she had given up eating, it was difficult to see much of her at all—and Alathea Sawneyford was, as Mrs. Frogmorton and Mrs. Drigg often remarked, purely and simply an astonishment. It was hard to pick out a single extraordinary characteristic. Her dark hair was remarkable only because it was cut short and her skin, compared to Harriet's and Georgiana's, was sallow. Yet one thing was certain: men saw Alathea and wanted her, as men eating eggs want salt. In the eyes of Mrs. Frogmorton and Mrs. Drigg, this was a defect nothing could soften.

"The tea is ready, Alathea. Come and sit with us." Harriet aimed her remark straight at Everina, who was being particularly slow with the kettle. Alathea left the harpsichord from which she had been accompanying the singing and settled herself on a chair.

"For goodness' sake, Everina! You don't even make tea properly. Look at it. Slop water!" Marianne sniped at her sister.

"That's all tea is, expensive slop water." Everina was quite unabashed. "You said so yourself when Mama told us how much it cost."

"At least I manage to pour properly. Look at the mess you've made." Marianne pointed at extensive puddles and drips.

"What does it matter?" Everina tossed back. "We don't have to clear it up."

"Oh, be quiet, both of you," said Harriet, her patience giving out. "Are you going to give us some of this tea? I don't care if it's slop water."

Everina distributed dripping saucers. As soon as she'd drunk her tea, Harriet felt better. She turned to Georgiana Brass, sitting next to her on a sofa. "I've bought a shade I think suits me."

Along with her nose, Harriet had recently begun to worry about her lips. She found them too thin and was a keen experimenter with lip color, sometimes to comical effect that she was not above acknowledging. She had at her feet a basket filled with powder and paste as entertainment after the music until the carriage should call to take her home. "I know it's bright, but lips should be bright." She put down her cup, picked a pot from her basket, smoothed on some of its garish contents, made a large *O*, and laughed at her reflection.

Sulky Marianne was quick with her opinion. "You look like a doll. Lips should be natural." Marianne disapproved of Harriet's new interest although she herself used rouge every day, Everina, with sisterly slyness, assuring her that whatever their mother's warnings, the look was sophisticated.

Georgiana Brass dipped her little finger into the pot Harriet held out. Unsure what to do with the paste, she wiped it over the palm of her hand. Rouge would have improved Georgiana. In repose she comprised only a wave of corn-colored hair and a pair of empty eyes. There were bones inside her clothes, and little else. When the girls were together, she always chose to be near Harriet because Harriet's stance on everything, from allocating singing parts to cutting fingernails, was reassuringly practical. Harriet, who was sometimes impatient with Georgiana's inability to decide even the best way out of a door, nevertheless always made room for her, for which Georgiana was grateful.

Everina called for more tea. "Bring cake too, Sam," she said to the mulatto waiting-boy. "The vanilla one with the cherries." The boy vanished and came back laden.

"Look," Harriet said. She twitched up her skirt and nudged Georgiana. She had been waiting for the right moment to show off a pair of new shoes. To Harriet's disappointment, Georgiana appeared not to hear. Georgiana saw only the cake and heard only the imploring of her stomach. She could attend to nothing else. Food was the enemy. She must not give in. No cake. No cake. She could not remember why she had given up eating or when. She knew only that she must not start again because if she did, she would solidify into a person and she had no idea what kind of person she could possibly be. She waved away the plate Sam offered and he took it to Alathea, who plucked out a cherry, held it between two fingers, and licked it.

When Alathea's tongue was out, it mesmerized. In terms of years, it was still a novice. In terms of imagination and experiment, it was quite advanced. Before the age of thirteen she had worked out that the tongue, the physical tongue, that is, not the wordy tongue, was a woman's unsuspected weapon, attracting and repelling, drawing in and excluding, and all without even touching an opponent—Alathea classified most people as opponents. Servants like Sam were dull experimental subjects, though. Not like the hangman, the thought of whom made her smile. Her living flesh must have contrasted warmly with the dead.

Harriet could wait no longer. She took off a shoe and thrust it into Georgiana's hand. "See, Georgiana! Straight from the foot of a noble Frenchie. Aren't they fancy."

Georgiana forced her attention onto the shoe. A small garden scene had been painted on the heel. "How do you know they came from someone noble?"

"It was picked up at the guillotine, silly. There's lots of shoes like this to be had from France right now. Father gets them, though he tells Mother they were made in London. You know how she is about foreign things."

"Can you walk in them?"

"Why on earth would I want to do that?" Harriet slipped the shoe back on. "They're for parties."

"Let me see." Marianne peered over. "Is that blood on the toe?"

Harriet whipped the shoe back off. "Oh," she said, nonplussed.

They all inspected the stain.

"Blood, for certain," said Everina.

"It'll wash out," said Harriet uncertainly.

Alathea reached for the shoe and sniffed it. "A young girl's blood," she said. The girls shivered. True or fabricated or somewhere in between, Alathea's tales added spice to otherwise dull days. She never spoke about herself. They were never invited to her house. All they knew for certain was that under that dark halo of hair, Alathea could seem saintly and demonic at the same time.

"Take the tea away, Sam," Harriet ordered the boy. "Go on! Quick!" She never worried about assuming command, even in somebody else's house.

The boy collected the tray and slunk out, casting a last glance at Alathea. She blinked at him. For a second he was in heaven.

"Now, Alathea," Harriet said. "Go on. Tell us about the girl."

Alathea picked up a dropped crumb. Catching Georgiana's eye, she crushed it between her teeth. "A girl like you, Georgiana. I expect she was stripped to her petticoat before she faced the guillotine."

"Honestly, Alathea," said Harriet, uncomfortably. "Do you have to?"

"She'd have been wearing her best petticoat," Alathea said, her face completely straight. "Remember I told you of the dead girl I passed in the City the other day? She was in her petticoat. It's obviously the fashionable thing to wear for death." It was a lie. The dead girl had been fully dressed.

"It's unseemly, you wandering about the City alone," said Marianne. "Our mother would never allow it."

"I don't have a mother."

Marianne reddened. How stupid to present Alathea with an opportunity to remind them. "Father, then," she said.

"What had happened to that poor girl?" Harriet frowned at Marianne, who mouthed "Well, it *is* unseemly."

Alathea waited until all eyes were focused on her again.

"Her story's clear enough," she said, sidestepping Harriet's last question.

"Is it?" said Everina with a shudder. "Most stories don't end with a hanging."

"A garroting," corrected Alathea. "That was the end she chose, and who can blame her?" Alathea drew her knees under her. "Her story's sadder than the guillotine girl's. She was an only daughter, much beloved of her parents. They lived—her parents still live—in a big house in Lincoln's Inn Fields. Her name was Raphaella and the house was full of people and music and everybody was happy. It could have lasted forever, except that a man came, a musician. He played many instruments, but when he touched a keyboard, everybody wanted to listen. And he was beautiful to look at—young and strong, with the kind of body you see in books on anatomy."

"You've seen books on anatomy?" Harriet, startled, could not help herself.

"Of course," said Alathea. "Don't you want to know how men are made?"

"I—I," stammered Harriet, "I don't think about them," she said lamely. Alathea raised an eyebrow. Harriet raised one back.

"I once saw Sam relieving himself against the garden wall," said Everina. "It was—"

"Don't be coarse, Everina." Marianne was at her most reproving.

"You looked too," retorted Everina. "You said—"

"That's enough," Marianne barked.

Alathea shrugged. "All I'm saying is that if you'd been Raphaella, you'd have wanted him."

"You mean, fallen in love with him," Marianne contradicted.

"As you like," said Alathea. "Anyway, he and Raphaella began to play duets together. They were marvelous, and Raphaella soon found the two hours the musician spent at their house each day were the only hours that meant anything. But though she waited and waited, he never asked her to marry him. At first she wondered whether he ranked himself too far beneath her. But he always came through the front door, never the servants' entrance. Then she wondered whether he had too little money for marriage. But his clothes were respectable and his horses shining. Then it came to her: he didn't know she loved him. She hadn't made it plain, so she plucked up her courage and told him straight. And he did something terrible." She left the words hanging for a moment. The girls were agog. "He laughed."

Marianne sniffed. "That doesn't seem so terrible."

Alathea said, "She told him he was everything to her. She told him she would abandon family and friends for him. She told him she loved him more than music. She offered herself to him body and soul. And he laughed. He might as well have stabbed her in the heart with the heel of one of Harriet's new shoes."

Harriet scrutinized Alathea's face. Was that a tremor of real pity or a tremor of contempt at their gullibility? Harriet was never sure of anything about Alathea.

"Did she slap him?" Everina was asking. "I'd have slapped him."

"She didn't touch him," Alathea answered. "She felt the fault was hers. If a man who could make such music with her didn't love her, she couldn't be loved by anybody, so she cut a string from her harpsichord—it was bass A, a mournful note, don't you think—and when the musician left, she followed him into the City. At the top of Threadneedle Street, he turned and saw her. They exchanged glances. The musician raised his hand. He raised it high. Then he waved good-bye and ran away. That's when she twisted the wire into a noose, borrowed a flower girl's stool, slipped one end of the wire over the arm of a barber's sign, and—" Sam returned for the cake stand as Alathea raised her chin in imitation of the girl. Alathea's chin dropped. "Snap," she said gaily.

FOUR

No. 23, Manchester Square, March creeping in. The pianoforte materialized out of the morning, shrouded in blankets on an undertaker's cart. The complanatory vibrations were loud enough to alert servants and mistresses all down Spanish Place and into the square itself. There was a pause for gawping amid discussions about the removal of winter drapes.

Grace Frogmorton stood at her own window (whatever the temperature, she removed neither winter drapes nor woollen petticoat until May). She patted a new hairpiece and frowned. A bald turnspit dog, recently retired from kitchen duties, whined to be picked up. "What's this, Frilly," Mrs. Frogmorton said, bending stiff knees to oblige. She had been expecting the pianoforte for the past four days and now she was mortified. An undertaker's cart! Typical of Drigg.

She often wished it had not been Drigg who had rescued her husband when Archibald's early apprenticeship with a corn merchant had ended abruptly. One moment sweet, dusty corn; neat figures in the ledger; a tutorly finger explaining the balance sheet; two oat-fed daughters to ogle. Next, a roar, a club, a charge of short shrifting, a smash and grab, yellow corn peppering black mud, the mob swirling and shrieking, the corn merchant's daughters swirling and shrieking, the corn merchant blustering, begging, and finally hanging from a gallows made of his own rigged scales. Frogmorton and two other apprentices were lucky only to be tossed into the Thames. Drigg's strong arms had hauled Archibald out, and it was true that Drigg's eyes and ears at the docks had proved indispensable to her husband's ventures. Nevertheless, Mrs. Frogmorton had never thought much of him. She hoped the servants at That Place, as she called Spanish-occupied Manchester House, were not looking, or, worse still, The Spy, as she called the Spanish ambassador himself.

Neither Alderman nor Mrs. Frogmorton knew anything of Annie Cantabile or her father. Drigg had meant to disclose everything next time the men met in the V & B but had lost courage, and declared only that he had bought a pianoforte and that the cost had been eighty pounds—slightly more than quoted but less, he asserted, than the pianoforte's true worth. A teacher would present himself in due course. Long friendship brings trust. Drigg's story had been accepted without question.

Since nothing had been said of a man coming atop the instrument, Monsieur Belladroit's elegant dismounting took Mrs. Frogmorton by surprise. She drew back and would have declared herself out if a maid had not already indicated she was in by calling her name. She must go down. On her front doorstep, Monsieur seized her hand and kissed it delicately before raising a face finely boned with remarkably straight eyebrows and shoulder-length hair tied in a plain brown bow. Frilly commenced a monotonous bark. Mrs. Frogmorton pulled the dog closer, reducing the bark to a yap and two marble eyes bulging out of her bosom. "I was not expecting a man," she said.

"Just the pianoforte tuner and teacher, madame. Excuse me." He hurled a torrent of incomprehensible invective at the kite tail of urchins behind the cart, produced a pistol, and fired. The urchins fled except the one Monsieur managed to bring down. The boy howled and hopped, spraying blood. Monsieur wiped the pistol's barrel. He turned back to Mrs. Frogmorton. "I shall unload."

Mrs. Frogmorton was both impressed by his marksmanship and alarmed by his accent. A foreigner. "The boy," she said.

"What boy? I have not brought a boy."

Mrs. Frogmorton raised her hand to indicate the shot boy and found a beribboned note pressed into it. "Claude Belladroit. My credentials." French—that was it, thought Mrs. Frogmorton. Those *th*'s hissed into *z*'s. Those rolled *r*'s. This man was French. She felt quite flustered. He must be a Catholic, and probably part of the nonsense going on over the sea. Yet it was those neat, straight eyebrows that now gripped her attention. She had never seen such eyebrows. Had they been plucked into shape? And his lips quivered, as though waiting for her permission to smile.

"Madame?" He appeared anxious for her approval.

Mrs. Frogmorton stood straight. She understood that she was being charmed. That was what foreigners did. She resented it. The man did not seem to notice her resentment. A quick flash of small, even teeth, then a sharp berating of the muscle hired to shift the pianoforte. They must hurry since Madame Frogmorton had emerged without overshoes or cloak, Monsieur said. Quick quick now. Mrs. Frogmorton was startled. Her husband would never have noticed if she was cold. Monsieur ran up the steps and Mrs. Frogmorton could only follow as he zealously inspected the downstairs rooms. In the street, the pianoforte was dismounted, body first, the mechanism groaning.

As the pianoforte was brought indoors Monsieur verbally beat the muscle without cease. "This is a home, you clowns, not a warehouse! Take care of the statuary. Mind the pillars. Do not brush the paint. Do not displace a speck of dust on any of this big brown furniture, should we find dust in this home, which I doubt. Get on! Do I have to carry the instrument myself?" Once the pianoforte was safely in the hall, he ran out and threw the carter a tip like a slap in the face. He ran back into the house. "Upstairs?"

Mrs. Frogmorton meant to expostulate. Instead she said, "Upstairs on the right. The harpsichord has been moved to accommodate."

The only flaw was the fuss Monsieur made over the instrument's exact placing in the drawing room. Mrs. Frogmorton wanted it under the chandelier, sideways to the door, the centerpiece to a room whose furniture, however she placed it, was never elegant, and whose welcome, despite a generous fireplace, never convinced. Monsieur wanted the pianoforte in the corner farthest from the fireplace, tail toward the middle of the room. Mrs. Frogmorton could never remember how Monsieur won, nor why she forgave him. She only knew that she was being ushered out politely but firmly so that Monsieur could "bed the pianoforte in"—a phrase Mrs. Frogmorton had never associated with musical instruments. Foreigners, she thought. They turned even plain English upside down.

Harriet arrived home just after midday. The other girls visited later to be told of the concert plan. Marianne and Everina Drigg were quick to say that pianofortes had not been thought well of by the Misses Lee at the Academy for Young Ladies, where the sisters had been expensively educated. Marianne also declared that as the oldest of the girls and the one who knew most about music, she should have been consulted. Harriet had been dismayed at the thought of effort. Georgiana Brass had just been dismayed. Alathea had been curious, though she had not asked to know more. It made people uncomfortable if you found out things for yourself.

The following afternoon the girls and the three mothers were gathered in the Frogmortons' downstairs parlor, a room as unsuccessfully put together as the drawing room though decorated more lightly, with chinoiserie on a pair of blue-veined marble-topped tables, and on a third, a clock with a camel feature that Mr. Frogmorton had received as a present for a favor he did not care to recall. The settles, solid and English, had come from the sudden sale of another Manchester Square house, the paneling too. Mrs. Frogmorton had spotted the bailiffs from her bedroom window. There was velvet wallpaper above the panels, plain cushions, striped curtains, and a fireplace that kept most of its heat to itself. Mrs. Frogmorton never sat in this room when she was alone, preferring the little antechamber attached to her bedroom. There was a small stove in there that, once she had closed the door, she often tucked beneath her skirts.

Agnes Drigg was troubled by the fire. It told her she had

made a mistake ordering the Stratton Street drapes taken down. The drapes should have stayed up because in Manchester Square it was still winter and Manchester Square was never wrong. Mrs. Drigg knew better than to look to Elizabeth Brass for reassurance since Mrs. Brass had no notion of drapes or anything else. Stuck in a poky house in Covent Garden for the convenience of Mr. Brass's membership of Bedford's gaming club, Mrs. Brass, like her daughter, found daily life a series of unanswerable questions, whether it be breakfast eggs or moving, which she longed to do, if only to stop the ladies of the night earning their money in her porch, some of it from her husband. The last question Mrs. Brass clearly recollected answering was Mr. Brass's proposal of marriage. She realized soon after that her own judgment must never be trusted again.

All the mothers were conscious of a pang. "This will signal an ending of sorts," Mrs. Frogmorton had said while the girls were still upstairs, ushered up by Harriet to admire a music box she kept next to her bed. "Our girls will fly away."

"Surely we'll be welcome at their new hearths," Mrs. Drigg tried to comfort.

"Of course, Agnes, but we'll be encumbrances. Mothers are. At least, mine certainly was." Mrs. Frogmorton could already see doors closed, secrets kept, grandchildren steered away.

"At least Alathea will be, well, you know," said Mrs. Drigg.

They nodded in deep understanding. None of the three had known Mrs. Sawneyford. As a consequence, her looks and character were a regular subject of speculation, particularly as Alathea grew older and more bewildering. Mrs. Frogmorton and Mrs. Drigg thought the girl should want a mother. Alathea did not want a mother. That was perfectly clear. They thought she should want to be embraced. She did not. They thought she should want to confide. Not a word. Yet ignoring her would be unchristian. So she grew with their daughters, tolerated but never liked, included but never truly welcomed.

"We'll treat Alathea as if she were our own," said Mrs. Frogmorton with some effort.

"We'll try," said Mrs. Drigg, also with some effort. A mutual nod accompanied a mutual sigh.

Summoned downstairs, Harriet, Everina, and Marianne sat primly on the settle, their skirts jostling, Harriet once again wearing the bloodied shoes that her maid had made an attempt to clean. Alathea draped herself over a high-backed chair. On Marianne, spotted calico would have looked dull; on Alathea it created an intriguing map of curves. Georgiana, on another high-backed chair, had arranged her bones in a tent of figured silk through which her neck stuck like a flagpole. She had agonized over the choice of gown and now realized she had dressed for an entertainment, not for an introduction to a music master. Her miscalculation consumed her.

Mrs. Frogmorton, conscious of her hostess's advantage, moved about the room like one of her husband's larger freighters. "You will be taught separately in the following order: Harriet, Georgiana, Everina, Marianne, and finally Alathea. Sunday is—"

"Surely I should be taught first," Marianne interrupted.

"Why?"

"I'm the oldest."

"What difference does that make?"

"I just think—"

"For goodness' sake, Marianne, we're not deciding an inheritance."

"I didn't say we——"

Mrs. Drigg fell into a twitter. "But actually, Grace, isn't that a good idea? Marianne and Everina will need to come in the carriage and their father will want to get to the City afterward, and although they could walk——"

"Walk!" Marianne was outraged.

"No, of course not. Oh dear. I wish we lived here, Grace. It's so nice in this square. When we moved to Stratton Street it was with the best intentions and now we're surrounded by Jews. Jews! Think of it! Better to have Catholics." Mrs. Frogmorton frowned. "Or perhaps not," said Mrs. Drigg hastily. "I never quite know. What do Catholics actually do in their houses, I wonder. What view do they take on winter drapes, for example? Not that winter drapes are important. Though of course they are. Too early, yes, too early." She subsided.

Mrs. Frogmorton and Harriet exchanged a familiar look. "I think," said Mrs. Frogmorton before Mrs. Drigg could start again, "that Stratton Street is hardly the end of Christendom. Still, if Marianne's so keen, I'm sure nobody minds if she has the first lesson."

"I don't want to go after her," said Everina. She feared any comparison with Marianne's self-professed musical superiority. "It will hardly wear out the carriage to make the journey twice."

Mrs. Frogmorton grew impatient. "As you wish. This is the order: Marianne, Harriet, Georgiana, Everina, Alathea. Is that agreeable to everybody?"

They all nodded.

"Good. We'll leave it to Monsieur to suggest the number of lessons in a week. What about clothes? Do you think pianoforte playing requires a new type of garment, Elizabeth?"

Silence. "Yes, I thought you might," said Mrs. Frogmorton, "though I'm not sure you're right."

This was how conversations with Mrs. Brass were always conducted. Mrs. Frogmorton and Mrs. Drigg had long agreed between themselves that since Elizabeth seemed incapable of answering for herself, they would answer for her. It was a pact meant kindly and had become one of the bonds uniting the three mothers, bonds that were born of their husbands' close connections and grew in strength when Grace Frogmorton, disregarding the danger, billowed into Stratton Street when Everina Drigg had the pox, kissed Mrs. Drigg, and held Everina's hand; when Elizabeth Brass sent a note, smudged, unsigned, and saying only "weeping," to Grace Frogmorton after that first stillbirth; when Grace Frogmorton sent a tiny lace gown for Marianne Drigg when her own little girl (the second before Harriet) had, once again, needed only a shroud; when Elizabeth Brass turned up at Stratton Street, a weal across her face and her eyes glazed, and Agnes Drigg offered unquestioning shelter. Compared to the deep bonds of birth bed, marriage bed, and deathbed, the mothers' daily mutual irritations were only a scab. That all three could remember each child the others had lost, however brief its flicker of life, was indissoluble glue. When particular anniversaries came around, something, perhaps a little cake, perhaps a posy, would arrive. Every year, each husband asked what for. The mothers felt wounded by their husbands on those days. Those wounds were bonding too.

"Tea midlesson?" queried Mrs. Drigg. "How big a fire should be made? Is an hour's tuition too long? Can the girls practice on their harpsichords?"

Mrs. Frogmorton began to answer. Mrs. Drigg begged to disagree, or agree, or both.

Alathea raised her voice. "What are we to play?"

Cut off midstream, Mrs. Drigg thought, "Why does Alathea always sound so knowing? Why can't she chat and giggle like the others?"

"I expect Monsieur Belladroit will decide," Mrs. Frogmorton said, thinking the same as Mrs. Drigg.

"Let's ask him." Alathea unfolded herself.

"Sit!" Mrs. Frogmorton felt proprietorial. This was her house and Monsieur Belladroit had, for the day, been hers. She would introduce him. "Are we ready?" she asked. They nodded. Mrs. Frogmorton rang the bell.

Nobody heard his footsteps but Monsieur was among them at once, in gray breeches, dark stockings, short jacket, and shoes with no buckle, his demeanor absurdly deferential—not at all the jaunty cove who, earlier, had left Mr. Cantabile's. Harriet, Marianne, and Everina offered haughty greetings. Georgiana stared at her feet. Alathea's lips twitched "well, well, what's this."

Monsieur was delighted with the variety of young womanhood: the soft, the elfin, the solid, the nervous, the— He could not quite categorize Alathea, which was unusually delicious. Cantabile was right. He had said the job he had for his dear Claude would be a pleasure, and it would be. Monsieur would steal the girls' virtue and be away before the new husbands discovered the cherry picked, the goods secondhand. He quite envied these husbands. What a favor he was doing, enabling them to ditch the wife as sullied but keep the marriage settlement. Should he demand a cut? Unnecessary if he took

Cantabile's bonus for marrying one of the girls himself. An odd man, his old friend Cantabile. He was tight-fisted, yet wanted to pay over and above the fee the fathers were paying. But I'm an odd man myself, Monsieur thought.

This was nothing but the truth. With his penchant for varied personal histories and his inability to settle in one place, he was not quite as others. He had welcomed the revolution in his native France not for its ideas but because it made everybody as restless as himself—at least those not sent to their rest by Madame Guillotine. Monsieur had seen two executions—parents of pupils. It was not the blood that appalled him, or the mob. It was the tipping of the headless bodies into muddy holes of permanent dark. When he died, he wanted to be burned and scattered in the wind. Cantabile's invitation had come at precisely the right time. It took Monsieur's mind off those dark and muddy holes to be in London and to be considering marriage—a laughable consideration since he could bear neither landlady nor lover for more than a month.

Yet if he were to marry one of these girls, which would be the most profitable? His eyes flickered around the room, assessing the furniture, the drapes, the appalling clock. My goodness. Fancy coming home to this. Nevertheless, the house was solid, the fathers City men. But one thing at a time. Marriage was for after, if at all. Seduction was first.

Monsieur would deflower any girl from fifteen to fifty—perhaps not fifty—but he had his standards, one of which was that whatever the age and ugliness of the girl, he would never resort to rape. He disapproved of it. Even more, he feared a charge of it. Voluntary capitulation was the thing. That, so he had learned over many years, was what stopped girls tale-telling to parents—or at least stopped them telling before he had disappeared. He imagined they felt complicit. He encouraged them to do so. Not that it mattered if his conquests did tell. Wise parents covered up their daughters' indiscretions as was only sensible, and in France, at least, many husbands did not care if their wives were shop-soiled. Englishmen must be ridiculously fastidious, otherwise Cantabile would not have concocted this romp. He felt flattered to be the conductor. He had never seduced an English girl before. Getting these creatures to capitulate would be a charming exercise. He would, however, lace determination with caution.

"Mademoiselles!" He took each of the girls' hands in turn and peered at their faces. Why did portraitists depict women as flat skinned with pearly teeth and red lips? Women were not flat, or pearly or red. Women's skin was like the wood of a pianoforte frame: the little whorls, knots, and faults gave or withheld beauty and their lips were as notched as a man's bedpost. Take this one. (It was Harriet.) Her lips were thin. Smooth, they would be nothing more than a gash. Notched, with perhaps five tiny bee-sting swellings, they offered all manner of treats. Portraitists should try harder. He was much amused when Harriet snapped her wrist away. He was not to know that she took his lingering on her lips to be a deliberate focus on what she considered her worst feature.

Monsieur moved to Marianne. Oh dear. Skin pitted like an orange; mole like a slug on her left cheek. Freckles. Miserable hair. No neck. Portraitists had a point. It would be foolhardy to tell the truth.

Everina submitted with little shrieks. Those teeth, thought Monsieur with well-hidden shock. A cartoon. A creature of puff, poufs, and pom-poms. Still, her hands were plump, the fingernails clean, and she had plucked her eyebrows into the semicircles of fixed surprise favored for mannequins. It was unappealing but showed attention to detail.

Georgiana, trembling like a sinner before the priest, seemed too insubstantial to scrutinize. Gently, gently with her. She was a nervous dove.

Alathea held out her right hand voluntarily. On her thumb was her mother's wedding ring. Sawneyford would have buried it with the corpse but Alathea had clung so hard that Sawneyford had removed it. At that time, the ring had been too big even for Alathea's thumb. On her first visit to the V & B Mrs. W. had helped secure it with a bandage. As Alathea grew, it fitted better. She became accustomed to the feel of it on her thumb and had taken it off only twice, both times for a goldsmith to refit. Monsieur guessed nothing of this. The only lady he had seen wearing a thumb ring would not have been welcome in Mrs. Frogmorton's drawing room. He dropped Alathea's hand and found his own taken for inspection. He cocked his head. Well, well. Even without the ring, this girl was unusual: dark skinned, dark eyed, dark haired—not black, if you really looked, more the tarry coppers and russets of the inside of a volcano. He withdrew his hands with a quick "Mademoiselle." He would think of her later. "You will want to know our program," he said, giving the mothers a quick onceover. Portly, dumpy, skinny. Mothers, but not enough of them. Two girls must be sisters, or perhaps one or two were without mothers? It did not matter. "I shall teach these lovely girls easy madrigal accompaniments and simple ditties," Monsieur said. "They can sing and play. It will be charming."

Mrs. Frogmorton jolted. "Easy madrigals and simple ditties? The pianoforte up the stairs is not for trifles, sir. Attracting husbands is a serious business. Madrigals may do for bank clerks and milliners but they won't do for us, will they, Elizabeth?"

Monsieur waited for Mrs. Brass to answer. When she did not, he carried on. "In that case, what are your thoughts, mesdames?"

Mrs. Frogmorton made a magnanimous gesture. "Marianne? You're something of an expert, I gather?"

"I believe the *cognoscenti* admire music by a man called Bach," Marianne said, stressing the Italian with a smug nod at Mrs. Frogmorton and a slight simper for Monsieur.

"They do," Monsieur agreed.

"Does Mr. Bach write for the pianoforte? Could he compose something specially for us?"

"I doubt that." Monsieur Belladroit fanned his fingers.

"Is a commission from us not important enough?" Marianne was at her most superior. "If that's so, I think Herr Bach overestimates himself."

"Herr Bach, good ladies, is dead, and has been for some time."

Mrs. Frogmorton hid a smile. Everina giggled. Alathea bit her lip.

"Herr Bach may be dead," Marianne declared, flushing, "but his music lives on. We could learn preludes, fugues, or"— she struggled only for a moment, then dug the phrase out and sent it swinging—"suites de pièces."

"I see now what you are after." Monsieur's tongue peeped from the corner of his lips. Alathea noted it. "You want drama, you want thrill, you want arabesques, canons, sarabandes, the adagio arioso, the dotted gigue, the rondo alla Turca." He flourished the terms like a box of treats.

"They want husbands," Mrs. Frogmorton said bluntly.

"You want to show your girls at their most delirious?"

"Desirable," said Mrs. Frogmorton and Mrs. Drigg together.

"As I say, delirious," agreed Monsieur. Mrs. Frogmorton and Mrs. Drigg clicked their tongues but let it pass.

"What to choose. What to choose." Monsieur placed a finger flat against his cheek. "The pianoforte, you must understand, is an upstager. It upstages the little harpsichord as a river upstages a stream."

"Rivers don't upstage streams," said Marianne. "They're entirely different things."

Monsieur narrowed his eyes. "I bow before higher knowl-edge of waterways. You perhaps already know Mr. Handel's *Water Music*?" He hummed and waved for her to join in.

Marianne looked sour. "I don't hum."

"Oh, but you must. I shall teach you. You just press your lips together—such pretty lips—press them together—"

"For goodness' sake!" Mrs. Frogmorton glared at Marianne. "Never mind this nonsense. What are they to play, Monsieur?"

"Madame, you must understand several things. The piano-forte is a garden waiting for a gardener."

"What?" All the mothers stared at him.

"It is an instrument waiting for music," Monsieur explained.

"Monsieur Belladroit," said Mrs. Frogmorton, accentuating his name. "Never mind about the pianoforte waiting. We're waiting. What music are the girls to play? It's a simple ques-tion."

Monsieur flexed and unflexed his fingers. "I think I have it." Eight female faces were expectant. Should he try his luck with the mothers too? Old meat could be tasty. "The girls can perform a sonata each by the lovely Mrs. Barthélemon." He laughed to himself. Cantabile would find this amusing.

Mrs. Frogmorton sounded a ship's horn. "Music by a woman?"

"Women also write music, madame."

Her voice rose. "I daresay they do, but we can't have a woman composer for our girls. Music's a man's thing, Monsieur, and a man's music is what we want. There must be something suitable."

Monsieur pressed his fingers to his lips. Mrs. Barthélemon was a nice idea. He dismissed her reluctantly. The matrons leaned forward. "What about," Monsieur said at last, "an aria with diverse variations."

"An aria?" said Mrs. Frogmorton. "We've already told you about ditties. Our girls are not simpletons."

"Madame, the work to which I refer could not be played by simpletons. When played on the harpsichord for which it was written it is a work of the utmost difficulty. On the pianoforte, it is a work almost of impossibility." A groan escaped Georgiana. Monsieur softened his voice. "Do not worry, mademoiselle. Under my tuition and with a little rearrangement of the music, the difficulties will be overcome. That is *my* forte."

"Does it have a name, this rearranged aria with variables?" Mrs. Frogmorton asked. "It would be easier if it had a name."

"The name? It is called, I suppose, a *Clavier Übung*," Monsieur replied.

"*Clavier Übung?*" Mrs. Frogmorton was doubtful. "Sounds French."

"German," said Mrs. Brass unexpectedly.

She speaks, Monsieur thought, and she was once pretty. "Quite right. German," he said. "In France we call what I shall teach your girls something different." Mrs. Brass looked up. Ah, she was not so dozy, this silent one.

"And in English?" Mrs. Drigg was anxious to relieve Mrs. Brass of the pressure of saying more.

"Keyboard Practice."

"Oh dear! Not very romantic," Mrs. Drigg exclaimed.

"For goodness' sake, Agnes," said Mrs. Frogmorton. "We're talking about marriage."

"Of course, I just thought—"

"I daresay," Mrs. Frogmorton snapped. "Monsieur, which man wrote this—this variable thing?"

"Herr Bach," Monsieur told her, "about whom we have been speaking."

"I think we'd all prefer a piece by an Englishman. Doesn't have to be dead."

"You find me a suitable piece by an Englishman, madame, and I will be happy to oblige."

"Alathea?" said Mrs. Frogmorton, conscious of trying to include her. "Do you have any suggestions?"

Alathea shook her head.

"Marianne?"

Marianne, unable to think of any English composer, dead or alive, blustered, "Will this aria attract husbands for us?"

"Herr Bach himself described this work as 'prepared for the soul's delight.'" Monsieur was flexing his fingers again. "What could be more apt? You girls, like the piece, are already delightful. Your delight will add to the delight of the music. The occasion will be delightful. Never will there have been such delight."

"Are you mocking us?" Mrs. Drigg burst out.

Monsieur grew grave. "I offer an important work, a serious work, a holy work. Matrimony is an important undertaking, a serious undertaking, a holy undertaking. When music and matrimony themselves are married, the marriage is the music and the music is the marriage. I have the only copy of this serious and holy work in London, perhaps the only copy anywhere. Who would dare to mock?"

He confounded them all except Alathea, who continued to gaze at him in silence. A bead of sweat trickled down Mrs. Frogmorton's neck. Just above the gauze fichu, it veered to one side and started a new course. She felt Monsieur's eyes follow it into the chasm of embonpoint that, today, Frilly had abandoned in favor of fighting with his replacement turning the spit.

"Now," Monsieur said in more normal tones, "do you wish your girls to play this music or not?"

Mrs. Frogmorton felt another trickle of sweat and a surge of misgiving, which could not be so easily swatted away. This musical notion seemed suddenly foolish. Mr. Frogmorton should have brought it up for discussion at breakfast, over a cup of tea, not at dinner, over wine. Two decanters that night. She had been too easily persuaded. "Mesdames?" said Monsieur with some impatience.

"If it's suitable, the girls will play it. If it's not suitable, they won't," Mrs. Frogmorton said. "I would have thought that obvious, Monsieur."

Monsieur clicked his heels. "Very well. We have chosen the music and with my help, all the girls will ..." He searched for the precise word. "They will startle," he said.

"Startle?" It was the first time this word had been used in Mrs. Frogmorton's parlor. The Frogmortons were not people who "startled."

"We begin tomorrow," Monseiur said. "No time wasting. Please ensure that the girls wear suitable garments. Tomorrow I will hear them each in turn. After that, they will each have a lesson twice a week and practice for three hours every day including lesson days. If they do not reach my standards by practicing three hours, they will practice four." He bowed and vanished.

Immediately, Marianne and Everina were clamoring. They did not want to "startle." Nor did they want to trail to Manchester Square twice a week for something as dreary as a lesson. They refused, refused, refused to practice for three hours a day. Half an hour had sufficed on the harpsichord at the Misses Lees' Academy for Young Ladies. "I don't like this Monsieur," Marianne shouted with childish pique. "None of us wants to play holy music." Georgiana was teary, Harriet annoyed. Only Alathea appeared unmoved.

"Enough!" Mrs. Frogmorton barked, and sailed over to berth next to Mrs. Brass. Mrs. Drigg stood behind. Mrs. Frogmorton spoke loudly. The girls would do as they were told. They would learn from Monsieur. They would play. They would startle, secure husbands, and be done with it. Harriet knew her mother in this voice. Complaining was a waste of effort. She dug Marianne and Everina in the ribs. "When we're married," she hissed, "our mamas will do as we say. When they knock, we'll not be at home." Mothers and daughters glowered over the red Turkey carpet. Upstairs with the pianoforte, Monsieur's eyes were bright. He stretched and bent slowly to touch his toes, legs straight, an athlete limbering up. The morning would come soon enough. He was ready.

AT THE V & B, the fathers were easy, slurping from coffee bowls without ceremony, breaking wind without apology, stretching, and mingling pipes and legs with their usual familiarity. The die was cast; they could relax, though Brass had been stirring things, asking what would happen if Harriet married a duke and Marianne a baronet. Would one set of grandchildren have to bow to another? And what would happen if one girl was left unwed?

"We can't arrange for them all to be of the same rank," Frogmorton said. "We must take what we can get." He cared nothing for the distinction between dukes and earls. As practical as his daughter, Frogmorton admired any family whose forefathers hacked, trampled, and murdered their way to the top of England's tree, and stuck there. Strong blood was what he desired for his grandchildren and in that regard, Harriet's marriage constituted less a social aspiration and more a place of safety. To find such a place, Frogmorton thought, was every father's duty.

"And they'll make no distinctions in private, surely?" Drigg could not bear the thought.

Brass flexed a leg. "It might do my Georgiana good to be top of the pile. Give her a bit of body."

Drigg seized the opportunity to snipe. "If you want my opinion—"

"I don't."

"Georgiana's figure is unnatural," Drigg said.

"Like Everina's teeth?" Brass mocked.

Drigg flushed. Everina's dentures, so expensively, glaringly white, were an uncomfortable running joke. "At least we can get those fixed. You can't buy Georgiana a pair of hips."

Brass pushed back his chair, veins bulging, fists clenched.

"Gentlemen, please!" Frogmorton raised his hands. "Drigg, apologize. Brass, sit down."

Frogmorton was fed up with Brass, a perennial exasperation. Brass had started out the luckiest of the four. His parents owned a brewery before being carried off by cholera.

The chief brewer, sorry for the boy, offered home comforts and even love but Brass was a thankless charity. Sullen and thuggish, he fought and scowled his way out of the brewer's affections and was quickly apprenticed in a silk factory, where he encountered Sawneyford. The brewery was sold, and with his inheritance Brass had bought a fighting dog. Sawneyford was useful because he knew how to sharpen its teeth.

"Tell me again how the pianoforte's different from the harpsichord," Frogmorton said. "I suppose we should know."

"Well, you make the tone by, em, touch. It's very subtle," Drigg replied.

Frogmorton frowned. "You're sure it's quite decent?"

"More than decent," Drigg reassured. "It's perfect for our daughters." A vision of Annie briefly surfaced. With some effort, he obliterated it.

"Good. Now, Sawney. We haven't heard much from you. Are you still happy with the plan?"

"I suppose so," Sawneyford said.

Outside, the light was beginning to fade and the coffee-pots arranged on the hearthstone in strict height order (Mrs. W.'s little foible) cast dwarfish shadows. The cat who liked to warm his behind on the coffee urn's lid had gone hunting. Mrs. W. was piling up discarded papers, bowls, and pipes before the evening rush.

Brass raised his coffee bowl for a toast. "Here's to the con-cert, and since you suggested it, Drigg, I'll hold you responsi-ble if Georgiana ends up an old maid." He drank the dregs and grimaced. Ottoman beans. Looked like tar, tasted like tar. Frogmorton and Drigg drank too. Sawneyford picked up his bowl, half raised it to his lips, and put it down again.

The men pulled on their coats. In the street, Frogmorton

waited for his gig, Drigg had his usual difficulties hailing a chair though there were plenty about, and Brass sidled off on foot to sniff out a cock fight.

Sawney Sawneyford was last to step back into London's sticky spread. He was the child of the commercial City of London, that square mile of wheeling and dealing, speculating and calculating, as well as the child of the broader city. Indeed, much more their child than the child of the jostling, poking brother and crying sister who physically brought him into being. The City was the womb through which his world reverberated. How he arrived at the silk factory in which he had met Brass was of no interest to him, just as he had no interest in an uncle/father press-ganged and drowned at sea, or an aunt/mother still crying, or the whore who had cut the cord after servicing a customer—you're in a hurry, sir, extra for that, sir, three pence and a pint of ale to wash out the taste, sir—and who, on a whim, had decided not to dash his head against the cobbles but to push him through the pavement boards, where he was found by a human rat living underneath. The rat, drunk, mistook Sawneyford for her own. The mistake forever unrealized, she sold him at four: agile fingers were valuable to the factory loom. Sawneyford was quick: he kept his fingers and his place. At ten, he met Brass. At twelve, Frogmorton and Drigg. At thirteen, his first bet of over a penny. At fourteen, three successful betting scams. At fifteen, a deal. At eighteen, a banking account. At twenty, a house. At twenty-one, a living wife. At twenty-six, a dead wife and Alathea. A-la-thee-a. She had offered Sawneyford something quite unexpected and he had taken it. He headed toward a tannery for sale in Bermondsey and considered the pianoforte without enthusiasm. He reassured himself: Alathea might be no good at it. He kicked out. Who was he fooling. She would be good at it, damn her, she would.

At Tyburn, Annie and her father observed an uneasy truce. The gap left by the pianoforte remained unfilled and every time Cantabile passed, he shed a tear for Annie's benefit. Annie took no notice. Her mother was bad. Spring was the most dangerous time. Nature softened, and its softening suffocated the weak. Annie never knew whether to close the curtains around her mother's box bed for warmth or leave them open for air. The concert girls were pushed aside for the moment, as was Monsieur. Annie had seen his coat and heard his voice but they had not met. She had barely left her mother's side.

Now she was anxious for the doctor, expected imminently. It was a relief that Drigg's money had made the man more willing. It was also a relief that her father refused to have anything to do with the stacks of coins Annie collected from the bank and stored where she alone would look for them. The coins would last for months. Their clink was a kind of music and she did not underestimate its value.

For hours she had been laying cloths on her mother's forehead and tripping to and fro with pans of boiling water. Steam helped her mother breathe more easily. Francesca Cantabile murmured thanks and stroked Annie's hand. Annie murmured back. Enough steam. Time drifted. Only when her mother's breathing eased did Annie's mind turn back to Manchester Square. At first she imagined the pianoforte. The image changed. She imagined the girls' rosebud mouths. She imagined them crushed against Monsieur's, their white teeth nipping his tongue. She dabbed her mouth. Bile had sprung upward, stinging her lip.

A shout from below. At last! She ran to let the doctor in. He had seen too many deformities to notice Annie's lip. He pushed past her up the stairs to listen and poke, advise and ruminate, turning Mrs. Cantabile over as though she were a ragdoll. The news was not good, but not the worst either. He took his money and left. Annie straightened her mother's night-clothes, smoothed the pillows, and sat quietly, holding her mother's hand again until they both dozed off. Annie woke an hour later, cold and stiff. She checked her mother's pulse, then closed the bed curtains as the doctor had advised. Mrs. Cantabile's eyelids flickered. "Thank you, my Annie," she whispered. "You're a blessing to me."

"Sssssh, Mother," said Anne. "You're a blessing to me."

"We're blessings to each other." Mrs. Cantabile smiled the sweet smile Annie should have inherited. Annie pressed her cheek against her mother's as she had done since she was a little girl. It was an accommodation they had come to: an acceptable kiss. It made Annie want to howl.

FIVE

T HALF PAST EIGHT, MRS. FROGMORTON WAS already a cumbersome presence in her drawing room. She kept the drapes shut through some notion of secrecy, though the room was too high for peeping Toms. The lamps hissed. She stood on a chair to turn them down. No need for waste. The fire, stacked high, shed light enough and there were four three-candled candelabra on the piano-forte itself. Monsieur arrived, in brown again, workaday. He gazed with renewed disgust at the room, whose furniture, all depressingly resistant to woodworm, cast shadows as bulky as his employer's. An old suit of armor hanging between two of the three long windows hinted at a baronial past, the effect rendered comic by the greaves, not a pair, and the helmet stolen from a dressing-up box. A screen embroidered with Chinese dragons nodded to the privacy of the lesson, though Mrs. Frogmorton had ensured it did not completely obstruct her view. The floor was highly polished—no carpet. Monsieur was, for a moment, tempted to skate across it as he had skated on the river when a boy. Instead, he padded over to the pianoforte, removed two of the candelabra, and murmured his condolences to the keyboard. Mrs. Frogmorton stared at the instrument. Square tailed, with pedals angled like a bowlegged girl, it seemed unlikely that such a thing could attract a husband for Harriet. Monsieur Belladroit was soon busy under the pianoforte lid, twisting, tightening, prodding, dusting, stroking. Mrs. Frogmorton sighed. As chaperone, she was stuck here. She gathered Frilly to herself, rang for more coal, and plunged her needle into a small piece of tapestry. She would be bored. She was used to that.

Marianne arrived. Monsieur set to work. Had Marianne any skill at the keys? Of course, she replied. Then she should play something for him, so he could judge how best to progress. Marianne stopped after two bars of Couperin. "This thing doesn't make what I call music," she declared. "It's all uneven, and so dull. My harpsichord's much better."

"The pianoforte does not make music for you, mademoiselle," Monsieur agreed. "That we must acknowledge."

"Why can't I just play my harpsichord—or Harriet's? It's over there."

"With a harpsichord everything you say is the same. With a pianoforte, you may say many different things."

"I don't want to say different things. I'm supposed to say 'marry me.' Isn't that the whole point?" She bashed out the *Barricades Mystérieuses*.

Monsieur considered the unmysterious noise she was making. This girl was, and would always be, no more a musician than Mrs. Frogmorton's dog was an orator. If she played in time, that would have to be enough. As for seduction, yesterday's anticipation had been optimistic. There could be no pleasure here. Marianne lacked not only delicacy in feature and limb, she lacked any vestiges of girlish charm and her breath was still fuzzy from breakfast. Still, he told himself firmly, she had swellings in the correct places and assisted by silk, lace, and some decent brocade, a clever dressmaker was keeping her just short of impossible. When the time came, he could always close his eyes and hold his nose. He nudged the piano with a sympathetic knee. With luck, Marianne would be the worst. She ground out the final chord.

"B-flat major is a pleasant key, yes?" said Monsieur.

Marianne snorted. "You music masters! It's just a key, like the others. Let's get on. Where shall we start? I don't want to be here forever."

"Indeed not, mademoiselle. That would be intolerable." He gave her exercises. She copied them badly. He could not bring himself to care.

Harriet was next, in high-waisted, short-sleeved pale blue—rather too smart for a pianoforte lesson, Harriet well knew—with a long cherry-colored sash. She greeted Marianne at the door and dawdled across the room. "It's very dark," she said, picking up one of the discarded candelabra and placing it back on the pianoforte so that it shone directly on her. "That's better." She sat with learned grace, hands carefully in her lap. She studied the keyboard.

"This concert has been dreamed up by our parents," she said, sotto voce. "I'm not against it, but—"

"Dreamed up or not, we must make the best of the hour and instrument your parents are so generously providing."

Harriet poked middle C with her index finger. The note responded softly. She frowned. She rolled a chord. She rolled the chord again, more carefully. "It sounds peculiar." She bumped a toe against the pedals.

"The notes are struck, not plucked," Monsieur explained. "It makes the sound a little cloudier than you are used to. And you have bumped your toe on the pedals."

She regarded the pedals. "What are they for?"

"The right-hand pedal sustains the notes, the left-hand hushes them. It is the modern way."

Harriet looked faintly disbelieving. "Monsieur Belladroit, can we be frank?"

"Of course."

"I know I must be married," Harriet said, "and indeed, I want to be married. I will be married. I've decided to marry Mr. Thomas Buller. He lives next door and he'll marry me without any piano playing. I know he will."

"You are already engaged?" Monsieur cocked his head.

"Not exactly, and please keep your voice down. He was kind to me when we first moved here, so I know he likes me, and he's rich. I really don't have to bother with any of this. The servants tell me his father's considering buying an earldom."

Monsieur was amazed. "People still buy such things? Do you not see what goes on across the sea?"

Harriet laughed. "Oh, Monsieur, they're all foreigners across the sea! We're *English*."

"Well," Monsieur said, collecting himself, "even the English cannot buy the soul of Herr Bach."

"Oh, come!" Harriet faced him. "Of course they can. Isn't that precisely what we are doing? We're buying his aria, or whatever it's called, and using it to attract customers. It's no different from buying and selling cheese."

Monsieur was taken aback. He had no real liking for Harriet's type: too neat, self-conscious, pale; too contrived; too English. Yet a prickle of whip and leash. If she had made up her mind to grab this Thomas, the boy would not escape her. "You speak nothing but the truth," Monsieur said. "Perhaps you will be wasted as a wife. You should rather be a husband."

"Are you saying I'm bossy?"

Monsieur was humble. "I beg your pardon, no. I simply observe that you would be a good lady of business."

"I think that's a compliment?"

"Indeed."

"I like it."

Monsieur laughed. "Let's to the music, mademoiselle." He rearranged the exercises on the stand. "To play Herr Bach properly, the fingers must be dexterous. Do you have dexterous fingers?"

"My father says I play perfectly."

"Is your father always right?"

She tilted her head and flashed him a look, then leaned into the music. First finger, third finger, second, then fourth. Up the keyboard she went. Her father was not right in this case, as Monsieur and Harriet could both see. She began again. "Careful of your wrist, mademoiselle. Do not let it drop. Listen." He played with wrist raised and again with wrist sunk. "Can you hear a difference?"

She looked surprised. "Yes. That's extraordinary."

"You try."

She tried. "Goodness." The lesson progressed. After a while, the future Mrs. Thomas Buller worked with some pleasure, and when she gave up her seat to Georgiana, she and Monsieur were humming.

Georgiana Brass was late. Dressed by a well-meaning servant, she was so tied up in stiff damask and whalebone that she hobbled like a trussed goose.

"Suitable clothes, mademoiselle," Monsieur said reprovingly.

Georgiana had seen her mistake before he spoke. "I'm sorry," she stammered, her speech as impeded as her movement. "I didn't know what that meant." Her tears dripped as she attempted to sit down. Behind the screen, Mrs. Frogmorton was whispering to Frilly. Georgiana, certain the whisper was criticism, crumpled further.

Monsieur Belladroit hastily mopped her tears with a silk handkerchief Annie had given him years ago. He settled the whalebones. When Georgiana stopped crying, he perched beside her. "Dear mademoiselle. What can I do? Your papa does not wish you to be miserable."

"I don't know what he wishes, Monsieur."

"He wishes for you to marry well and be happy. We shall do our best to oblige."

"Yes. Our best." The notion of "best" nearly set her off again.

Monsieur tutted. "Mademoiselle, please do not cry. It is bad for your skin. It is bad for the pianoforte. It is bad for my nerves. What I say to you during our hours together will not be to criticize. It will be to help toward your concert performance." He paused until she had control of herself. "So. We have already established that it is impossible to play music in such clothes as you are wearing. To play the pianoforte you must be able to move freely. Let me advise. Tomorrow, wear muslin; wear gauze; wear silk; wear satin; wear ribbons; wear pearls; wear flowers. These will suit you and our lessons very well." He raised the handkerchief to her cheek, to mop up the last of the damp, as a father might. He spoke about the pianoforte, explaining the touch, pointing to the pedals. He played a little Mozart. Her eyes were gray pools. Monsieur had never seen anything so gray. Even the pupils were gray, as though constant tears had washed the color out. "This instrument sings," he told her, "and tomorrow, little dove, when you are dressed more softly, it will sing for you."

He bent down, as if to check the pedals. Yes, she had satisfactory ankles and her feet, encased in blue leather with tiny buttons, were enchanting.

The hour with Everina dragged the most. She blasted her way through the *Barricades*, stamping on the pedals as though crushing beetles. She never inquired about their use. The only thing in Everina's favor was greater accuracy than Marianne. Once she had finished the piece, she hammered through a Giustini sonata more prestissimo than Giustini ever intended, then hammered through another, Frilly yapping his disapproval half a beat behind the time.

"Stop! Enough!" Monsieur Belladroit waggled his hands; the notes stung like hornets. "Very illuminating, Mademoiselle Everina. I feel for your harpsichord."

"Feel for it?"

"Feel for how busy you must keep it," he said. "Can you hear a difference between it and this pianoforte?"

She giggled. "You can go just as fast on either."

"That's not what I asked. Can you hear a difference?"

"What does it matter, Monsieur? Once you've finished playing, the sound's over."

Monsieur wondered what Cantabile would do if he were suddenly in the room. He might chop Everina's fingers off. At this moment, Monsieur would help him. He closed the lid over the keyboard. "Do you read books, mademoiselle?"

"Of course," Everina said. "Every parlor boarder at the Misses Lees' Academy reads books."

"And do you like them?"

"I found Mr. Richardson's *Virtue Rewarded* very instructive." She had learned this response from her teacher.

"And is Mr. Richardson's story the same as every other story?"

"Of course not."

"But all stories are made of words, so why are they not all the same?"

She wagged a coquettish finger. "I see what you're doing. You're saying words are like notes. They're not. Words aren't notes. Books aren't music. How am I to go on with the lid closed?"

Monsieur gave her a look that was not benign. "I shall reopen the lid if you promise to do as I ask."

"And what will you ask, Monsieur?"

Her tone was so arch that it flashed across Monsieur's mind that this pudding had already been tasted. He did not have to wait until the end of the lesson to know this would be a relief.

Luncheon arrived: three lamb patties, a hunk of bread, and some weak ale. He picked with distaste.

Alathea's lesson did not start well. The lamb patty repeated on Monsieur, and in this dismal room she seemed completely ordinary, her skin dull, her hair lusterless. A quick glance revealed thick stockings. He was disappointed. This girl was not intriguing.

"Good afternoon," he said as she settled herself at the

keyboard. "Please accustom yourself to the pianoforte and then play something. I hope it will not be Giustini." The fire had been banked up again. Mrs. Frogmorton was rein-stalled. Monsieur stifled a yawn.

Alathea did not look at the pianoforte. She looked at him. A twitch in her cheek—Monsieur could not tell how it was done—splintered any sense of ordinariness. "I think Herr Bach is a very good choice," Alathea said. "The *Clavier Übung* will challenge us all. You'll have to give us a great deal of help."

"You know this work?"

"Prepared for the soul's delight of music lovers," she said. "You told us yourself."

"And you count yourself among their number?"

"Music lovers?" She stressed the "music."

"Music lovers," he repeated without taking his eyes from her.

"Would you?"

"Count you or myself?"

"Whichever you like."

He relaxed. She was playing a game. He could play too. "How do you know the work? It is not printed in London."

"Sir John Hawkins has some of it in his history of music. The rest was not hard to find. My father has Leipzig contacts and it's not a secret work, only a work containing secrets."

A peppercorn scorch in his throat. "And you know these secrets?"

"Monsieur, we waste time."

His brows flattened and he resisted an urge to loosen his collar. "You have played a pianoforte before, mademoiselle?"

"I have one at home," she said.

"You never said so."

"You didn't ask me."

I'll test this girl, he thought. He reached into his case and pulled out the aria and variations. "Very well," he said crisply. "Begin."

"We'll play together," she said, moving along the piano stool. He was aware of a scent—musk, he thought, yes, musk, smokily beguiling, with animal undertones. Unusual perfume choice for a young girl. He was not sure he liked it. From behind the screen Mrs. Frogmorton cursed as she pricked her finger, and Frilly yapped commiseration. Monsieur curled his lip. The dog needed drowning. He caught Alathea's eye. It was clear she was thinking the same—an unexpectedly murderous connection. Alathea pointed to the music.

A change now. Mrs. Frogmorton and Frilly were left behind. Monsieur and Alathea sat completely still, completely silent, and from the silence, in this ugly room, something marvelous emerged: G, G, A-trill to B, A, grace note to F-sharp, grace note to D. So sure was each note, so confident of its place, the ornaments so neat and the sequence so clean, that Mrs. Frogmorton was hardly aware the silence had been broken.

Monsieur played with questioning delicacy. Musically, he was prepared for anything. Alathea played with complete belief. She knew this music. She did not flirt or tinker with it. It was a beam she drew directly from the instrument. Monsieur's top lip fluttered. *Quelle merveille.* He and this girl were perfectly in time, sympathetically phrased, drawing the beam together. Though a music master from an early age, Monsieur did not reckon to feel like a musician when he taught. His pupils sometimes had talent, yet never this kind of intelligence. Usually he wondered why his lessons were called music lessons at all.

Lessons in mechanical reproduction would have been more apt. Naturally, he corrected and instructed but his mind always strayed, and the years had blunted his sensibility. He knew this and regretted it. Yet in this unlikely place he experienced a taste of what might have been had he not needed to earn his daily bread. Melancholy threatened to overwhelm him.

Taking the aria as a duet, Monsieur's unused right hand and Alathea's left rested on their respective knees. They both kept their feet from the pedals. Occasionally their hands touched, a touching of music, not flesh. They repeated, then moved over the repeat marks to the second section. They repeated this. Grace note, crotchet, the aria ended, the beam broke.

As if to ask a question, Alathea turned to face Monsieur. He wanted to thank her. He wanted to confide his melancholy. However, before he could say a word, with no change of expression her unoccupied hand was no longer on her own knee, it was on his. It was above his knee. It was halfway up his thigh. It did not rest there. Melancholy vanished. Flesh was very quickly flesh again. Monsieur's gasp made Frilly stir and growl. Mrs. Frogmorton rose and peeped around the screen, where she observed Monsieur's eyes fixed glassily on the score and Alathea looking much as Alathea always did: irritatingly amused, as though enjoying a private joke.

Alathea smiled at Mrs. Frogmorton. Such a strange thing, a smile. Alathea knew as much about them as she knew about tongues. She knew how the pull of the cheek, one, or both, and the releasing of the lips to expose just this or that amount of tooth, or no teeth at all, or no teeth to start with, could alter the thing entirely. She knew how to keep Mrs. Frogmorton looking at her smile (at the moment, both cheeks drawn back, lips beginning to open) so that she did not look elsewhere. This was essential since things with Monsieur were warming up considerably. When she was ready, Alathea dissolved her smile slowly, first relaxing her cheek muscles, then allowing her lips naturally to relax into their usual position. The whole affair took nearly half a minute.

Mrs. Frogmorton's irritation subsided. The girl was only smiling. She couldn't help being the way she was. Mrs. Frogmorton returned to her seat. Another leaf to embroider.

Alathea turned her attention back to Monsieur. Monsieur, not wanting Mrs. Frogmorton to appear again, swallowed a small gasp, then nearly choked on a bigger one. The luncheon lamb fat refluxed. He turned a gasp into a burp. *Mon Dieu!* When he could breathe again, he smelled like Marianne. Alathea rose, leaving Monsieur Belladroit gripping the pianoforte stool. "Good-bye," she said, "see you next week." She nodded at Mrs. Frogmorton as she passed. Mrs. Frogmorton caught a whiff of musk, and of something else that she couldn't quite place. She put away her needlework and followed Alathea down the stairs.

A full five minutes passed before Monsieur put the music away and ten before he was fit for the street. His shirt stuck unpleasantly to his stomach. He closed the door of No. 23 behind him and walked swiftly in the direction of Tyburn. He had forgotten his surprise at Alathea's music making. He had forgotten his melancholia. All he remembered was that hand. He was both in awe of and revolted by its expertise. Alathea was so young. How had she dared? Never mind the daring. Where could she have learned such arts? He checked his breeches as he walked. He did not feel in control of his legs. He slowed, stopped, and leaned against a wall.

It was the dead hour between three and four. Few people were about. Behind curtains, women drooped. Behind desks, men rubbed inky thumbs and counted the hours still to go. Whores inspected themselves frankly in the glass before applying their paint. Even the sewers were still. Monsieur tried to breathe in some of the deadness. He did not want to blurt out what had happened, not to Cantabile or to anybody else. In his own time, he walked on, trying to notice ordinary things: the way you heard carriage wheels before carriage horses' hooves. The same with Mrs. Frogmorton: the rustle of hoops before the stamp of serviceable heels. A corpse was being manhandled out of a doorway. A little girl was crying. He breathed the breath of ordinary life. Brushing himself down again, he walked more quickly, searching the mud for a lucky coin, as he sometimes did in Paris. Just outside Cantabile's he did find a penny, though it was so dirty he did not pick it up.

The shop was, as usual, closed against the world. Monsieur fumbled for his key and pulled his pistol against a gang threatening to fleece him. The weight of the stock restored him fully to himself. After locking the door behind him, he paused, not because it was dark—he knew his way—but because somebody was playing. Mozart. The second movement of the sonata in C. He leaned against Cantabile's desk. It must be Annie. Her father could not play like this. My, he thought, she must have come on in the—how many years since he last saw her? Five? Six? The movement's little dramas, so often syrup, were individual droplets: simple, understated, with every regard for timing. Monsieur felt the droplets gather and rinse Alathea away. He made his way into the warehouse. Annie had her back to him.

"Annie?"

Annie had been waiting. She dreaded Monsieur's first view of her after so many years. She was no longer a child, with the sweetness of a child's face reducing the calamity of her lip. He would see her as she really was. She needed all the courage Mozart could give her. She hesitated long enough to say "Monsieur," then she grasped the lamp, sparing herself his first reaction by turning so that she was entirely lit and he was still in the dark. "I knew it must be you," Monsieur exclaimed before the light spilled over her. "How well you…" He faltered. Annie held the lamp closer so he would know for certain that what he was seeing was not a trick of the candle. She gave him time. She played Mozart in her head. "It is…" He faltered again.

When she was twelve, Monsieur had found Annie's lip bad. He had thought it might improve as she grew older. Now that she was seventeen, his shock was greater because of the permanence: this is how Annie would always be. The pity of it! She could have been lovely. "It is very good to see you." His reaction was more marked by his attempt to hide it. "It has been a long time. Too long," he finished lamely.

Annie lowered the lamp. The introduction was done. Nothing untoward said. Everything untoward said. "I'm sorry my welcome is a little late, Monsieur." Her voice betrayed nothing. "I've been with my mother. Come, please. You must be hungry."

She led the way to the stairs and took him up into what her mother had once called the dining room, though it was really the kitchen, its furnishings three hard chairs, a small doorless cupboard containing plates and glasses (the doors were burned for heat last winter), a mesh-fronted box they used as a larder, and a table. She poured a glass of the fine port Monsieur used to like and searched for signs of seduction.

Blotches of lip paint? A smudge of powder? A band of perspiration? Monsieur flipped his coattails as he sat. A waft of musk. Annie smelled it at once. She could not name it, but she would not forget it.

Monsieur took a large swig of the port and tried to make conversation. Annie's lip glowed. Never, Monsieur thought, had a man experienced quite such a day as this. "How long since I stayed here last?" He looked in Annie's direction.

"Five years, Monsieur," she replied.

"Five years! And how is your mother?"

"Better tonight, and sleeping now." She refilled his glass. Now that he was actually in front of her and looking at her just as she was, against her will Annie's dream revived. Certainly, it underwent rapid moderations. Monsieur did not need to kiss her and there was no question of marriage. She would be his friend. He would take her into his confidence. In due course, he would share details of the girls' tumblings and he and she would laugh at them together. That would make the seductions and even any marriage easier to bear. She made a great effort to put him at his ease. "People are flocking to hear Herr Haydn," she said, sitting squarely in the light. The more he saw of her, the more he would get used to her. "Have you heard him?"

"No. Have you?" Monsieur picked up the poker and put it down.

"No."

"I would like to, Annie. Perhaps you and I—"

Her heart leapt. She could not stop it.

Mr. Cantabile thrust open the door. "Ah, Claude." Monsieur never finished his sentence. Annie wondered whether her father had chosen his moment deliberately. She got up, fixed the lamps, closed the curtains, and produced the dinner. Monsieur was aware of being good to her in the way men are good to a dog of whom they are fond but wish to keep at arm's length.

When the evening drew to a close, Annie checked on her mother before going to her own room. She undressed, got into bed, and tugged the blankets under her nose. Then, despising herself, she got up and opened the door. Monsieur's room was beyond hers. She heard his footsteps. They were quite slow. She got back into bed and pulled up her knees. Was that a hesitation? She pushed her knees down only when it was clear that Monsieur was not going to put his head around the door to wish her good night. She had known he would not. Nevertheless, it was bitter. Annie decided that Monsieur's girls would pay for his omission. She would select a first target and her aim would be deadly.

SIX

A FORTNIGHT PASSED BEFORE ALATHEA KNEW for certain she was being followed by a new and rather different stalker. March was now April and although winter seemed to have returned for a last blast, she took to walking more slowly, just to be sure. She had fun with most of those set on her trail, leading them for miles, sometimes south toward the river's wharves, sometimes east to the lanes around the law courts, sometimes west to Piccadilly to hover outside the offices of the London Corresponding Society, where she had once, by chance, managed to get her tail apprehended by pointing to him when arrests for treason were being made. Today she was simply squelching her way home from Newgate Street. She knew these two miles well. Three times in the last three years she had required an abortionist and her father had recommended Newgate's Salutation and Cat as where everybody went, everybody, that is, who could afford more than a slurp of poison and a knitting needle.

On her first visit, Alathea thought her father mistaken in the place. Instead of a huddle of miserable women, she found a man standing on a chair extolling the virtues of some utopia to a group of more or less interested drinkers. A pamphlet was pressed on her. She would have left had her arm not been taken by a respectable lady arising from a makeshift office in the corner. Alathea was sent up two sets of narrow stairs. The pamphlet had provided at least some distraction from the heap of instruments to be employed should the administered potion fail. Once, the potion had worked and Alathea had stumbled home an hour later. Twice, there had to be poking, plucking, stretching, sucking, scraping, clamping. On those occasions, she remained in that room for two days, at first unconscious, then, when her eyes could focus, reading the pamphlet steadfastly, turning the phrases "strong tyrannize weak; government of all for all" into bulwarks against bodily horrors. Odd words caught at her particularly: pantisocracy, Susquehanna, the former some kind of society of incorruptibles, the second the name of a river. Even in her distress, she was struck by the irony of the abortionist above and the incorruptibles below, and when the pain was bad, she clung to the name of the river as to a talisman. After she understood that she would never need the abortionist again (nor a midwife, for that matter), she returned to the Salutation and Cat to hear more about utopia and the river. Today she had been expecting a new speaker—a poet, no less—but he had not turned up and his replacement, wretched with cold, had abandoned utopia in favor of complaints about too little sugar and nutmeg in his egg-hot. Alathea had left after half an hour, emerging into the street at just the wrong time. The Thursday market was drawing to a close and it was hard to move for carts parked back to back. From an open cage, six angry geese hissed and nipped at her. She hissed back and glanced behind. Up to now, her stalkers had always been men, which was why, this time, she had taken so long to be sure. A girl.

She pushed through the crowd. The shadow pushed after her. She stopped to haggle over a knuckle of ham. The shadow stopped. She paused to give the ham to a beggar. The shadow paused. When the crush thinned and grand houses gave way to shacks, Alathea whipped around. Even then she caught only a glimpse, what with the rain and umbrellas. Certainly a woman. This made the shadow much more interesting. She rejected her usual practices. She would draw this stalker home and take her prisoner.

Once the road was clear, Alathea set her course and kept steady until she could smell the pickle factory that made all new Soho Square residents sneeze. She looked behind. The stalker was sneezing. Her first time here. At the corner of Charles Street, Alathea glanced back again. The shadow had recovered. Alathea walked briskly past Trotter's warehouses, the academy, the surgeon's house (one of two), and avoided four gentlemen just finished with the whores at No. 12. The stalker avoided them too.

Alathea made for her front door. The house was imposing, though Alathea felt no pride in it. It had not been chosen; her father had acquired it in lieu of a debt. The number plate had fallen off and they had not bothered to learn what the number was, referring to the house only as "Soho Square." It was too big for the two of them, but neither wanted to be cozy. Neighbors often conjectured about the inside, having never been invited in, and in truth, Alathea and her father knew little more about the inside than a stranger, since few covers had been removed from the furniture and other household goods left in their entirety by Sawneyford's debtors. To all intents and purposes, the house was uninhabited.

On the doorstep, Alathea bent to scrape the mud from her overshoes, rain trickling down her neck. The shadow hung back and Alathea was nervous of a quick disappearance. The stalker was too far away to grab. Alathea needed her to come nearer. She took a gamble. She stood straight, got out her key, and let herself in (they had one servant only; he never attended the door). She kicked off her overshoes so that she could run, then jerked the door open again, preparing to dive out in pursuit. She stopped short. The shadow was standing directly in front of her, face hidden behind a veil of unusual thickness, right hand half raised as though to ring the bell. No tail had ever rung the bell before.

Annie was fumbling. Under the loose cuff draping her right hand, she held a small jar of acid. With the other hand, she was trying to pull off the stopper. She must do this instantly. Any kind of conversation and she might lose courage. Come off! Come off! The stopper stuck. Her hands were shaking, her thumbs and fingers slimy from the rain. She should have brought a knife. A quick slash across the face would have been more certain. The moment was passing. Her veil was sticking to her nose. She panicked. She would run away and return another time. She spun around. Alathea darted forward and seized her arm. The acid bottle dropped and smashed, white vapor hissing like the geese. Both girls jumped and Annie cried out. She was still held. After a brief tussle, she was propelled by Alathea's knee over the doorstep into the hall with the door slammed and locked behind her.

The two girls stood, panting slightly, water puddling from

soaked hems. Alathea could sense that the person beneath the soggy veil was young. She wondered, is this girl my father's mistress? She let Annie go. "Are you looking for my father?"

"I'm looking for nobody," Annie said. "I've made a mistake."

"I don't believe you," Alathea said. "You followed me from Newgate Street, and you must have followed me there from Manchester Square. If you want my father, you should have waited for him at your home."

"I'm not looking for your father," Annie said. "I don't know him. I've made a mistake." She contemplated rushing the door.

"Did my father set you to spy on me?"

"Let me leave, please."

"Perhaps you're a stooge of Mrs. Frogmorton's? She likes to know others' business."

"I don't know Mrs. Frogmorton," Annie said.

"You don't seem to know anybody." Alathea shook off her cloak. "Yet you were following me most particularly. I know you were." She threw the cloak over a chair.

Annie seized her chance, slid past, and turned the door handle. Alathea held up the key. "Are you a thief?" she asked. "Did you want my jewels?"

"I don't want anything."

"Why were you going to ring the bell then?"

Annie shook her head. She was shivering, and in the sepul-chral chill of the hall, Alathea began to shiver herself. "Come," she said, and when Annie did not move, she pulled her away from the door, past the stairs and shrouded statues, into what had been a card room. Beneath the mugginess of wet garments Annie recognized the smell of musk. Her gorge rose. She could imagine Monsieur with this girl. If only she still had the acid! As it was, her nails were not long enough even to scratch. Alathea kicked the card room door shut and tried to flick back Annie's veil. Annie resisted strongly. There was enough light from the windows for Alathea to see her lip, and this Annie could not allow. Scorn would be tolerable; pity outrageous. Annie caught her veil with both hands and pulled it tight. Alathea abandoned the veil, locked the card room door, and closed the two sets of window shutters to prevent Annie breaking through the glass. She seemed desperate enough. Alathea struck a flint and lit a small lantern. Annie was again a shadow. "Take off your cloak and remove that veil," Alathea com, manded.

Annie did nothing.

"I want to know what you look like," Alathea said. Annie clung to the veil more tightly. Alathea held up the lamp. "I'll let you go when I know who you are. Take off the veil."

"I can't. I won't."

"You can. You will." Alathea put the lamp down. Annie ran to the door and rattled it. Alathea was after her at once, forc, ing her back around, struggling for the veil. She pulled it right off. Annie reeled back into the room, seized the lamp, and waved it at the sheets covering everything except one sofa, one table, one upright chair, and one oval miniature, a portrait, hanging on the wall. Alathea sucked her lips. If the girl fired the house, she would have to unlock the door. She dropped the veil. They tussled for the lamp, splashing oil. Flames guttered. Alathea stamped them out. A sheet caught. Alathea bundled it into the hearth. Finally, she wrested the lamp from Annie and raised it high. At once, Annie began to curl up. Alathea was quick. She caught Annie's hair, yanked her head back, and spilled light all over her face. Annie stopped struggling at once. Her humiliation was complete. Alathea blinked. "Who are you?"

"This is who I am," Annie said.

Alathea tugged her hair. "What is who you are?"

Annie gritted her teeth. "You can see."

Alathea let go of Annie's hair. "I see your face but I don't know who you are."

"I'm Annie Cantabile," she said. "I'm the daughter of the man who made the pianoforte you're playing."

"The pianoforte in Manchester Square?"

"Do you have another?"

Alathea ignored that. "What on earth do you want with me?"

Annie backed into the sofa and sat down. Her skirt was flabby, her feet soaking, her veil a rag. Alathea kept hold of the lamp and sat in the stiff-backed chair she thought of as her father's. A considerable pause. "I know Monsieur Belladroit," Annie said. "You're his pupil."

"Are you a pupil too?"

"No," Annie said. "I've no need of lessons." Alathea's ignoring of her lip was as insupportable as Alathea gloating over it. She felt like a circus bear waiting for the dogs.

Alathea considered Annie, the whole of her, sitting bolt upright. "You may not need lessons at the pianoforte, but you've something to learn about following people. I've noticed you for a fortnight and today I knew you were behind me before I got to the end of Newgate Street." She got up. "I'm going to ring for some tea and ask for the fire to be lit. If I unlock the door, will you run away?"

"You have the front door key," Annie said. Her lip twitched. She could not stop it. She half bent her head, then decided against it. She would stay upright and hold on to her dignity.

Alathea unlocked the door without looking back. "Crouch," she called. From somewhere, footsteps echoed and an old man appeared in a frock coat dirty beyond cleaning and shabby beyond mending. He, too, had been bequeathed by the house's previous occupants, glad to be rid of him since he was never where expected or doing what was required. "A fire, and tea. Two cups. I have a visitor," Alathea said. She had never before uttered those last four words. She stood for a second. A visitor.

She returned. Annie had not moved, not even to replace her veil. The girls sat without speaking as Crouch shoved aside the singed sheet and lit the fire, shrugging at Alathea and with no interest in Annie, at whom he did not glance. Crouch was interested in only one person and that person was not here, nor ever likely to be. Every day since God had carried off his wife and child, Crouch dreamed of turning assassin and going to Rome to kill the pope, whom, for reasons he explained to nobody, not even himself, he held directly responsible. But life had kept him a footman. Alathea and her father suited him. Their demands were small and they never checked the bills. He had a tidy sum stashed away. He returned with tea, hoping visitors were not going to become a habit. He saw Annie's lip as he deposited the tray, started, faltered badly, and shuffled swiftly out, slamming the door as though Annie's lip were alive and might escape.

Alathea poured the tea. She set a cup on the floor beside Annie and drank her own, standing. The fire sulked. Alathea kicked it several times. Her shoes steamed. "So, you're Annie Cantabile, daughter of the pianoforte maker, and you've no need for pianoforte lessons."

"No," said Annie. She was determined to force Alathea to acknowledge her lip. She must get that over with.

Alathea's face still registered nothing. "Monsieur Belladroit taught you until you reached this happy stage?"

"No. He has never taught me." Annie kept her face raised high. Say something, she willed. Then we can fight.

"I see."

Silence. Alathea looked as though she could remain silent forever. Annie could hardly bear it. She had achieved nothing. She tried something else. She picked up the teacup and sipped, and when a drop dripped from her lip, she didn't dab it. Now, surely, with the lip glistening and the tea dripping, Alathea would at least blench. After people blenched, so Annie had learned, they usually felt the need to say something. Alathea neither blenched nor spoke. Instead, Annie found herself speaking. "Monsieur's living with us while he teaches at Manchester Square. I believe there's to be a concert."

"Monsieur Belladroit told you about the concert?"

"No. Your father told us when he came to buy the pianoforte." Annie made an assumption.

Alathea shook her head violently. "Drigg! That oaf! Not my father." She put her teacup on the table. "We're indebted to your father, though. The pianoforte is remarkable."

Annie's feet were so cold it was hard to be still. "It's just a pianoforte."

Alathea frowned. "Is that what you think?"

Annie did not want to have a conversation about the pianoforte. She huddled into herself. She needed the fire. Suddenly the world moved—or at least the sofa. Alathea was pushing it forward toward the blaze and was now kneeling, her hands untying the laces of Annie's boots. "No," Annie said. Without her boots she could never escape. Alathea was determined and deft. The laces were undone, the boots were off, and Annie's stockinged feet were set on the hearthstone. The flames were more lively now. The heat was wonderful.

Alathea shifted to one side, still kneeling. "You'll ruin your boots without overshoes," she observed. "What neat feet you have. I've neat feet too. Sometimes I look at women with large feet and feel sorry for them, don't you?"

"Sorry for them?" Annie was astounded. She should feel sorry for women with large feet!

"Yes, sorry for them. You can't do anything about large feet. They're there, like dinner plates, sticking out. I always look at feet. It's how I judge people. Yours are fine feet, the feet of a lady." Alathea chose what she said with care. She was not sure, at the moment, how she wished things to continue or end.

"I can't bear this!" Annie burst out, pulling her feet away. "Let me go home."

"Can't bear your feet to be judged? Why not? You came to judge me on behalf of your father, didn't you? He knows what his pianoforte is. He can't have wanted to let it go to people like the Frogmortons."

"I didn't come for my father."

"For whom, then?"

"You know why I came. You saw."

"Oh, the acid. Were you really going to throw it?"

"Why else would I have brought it?"

"Well, I'm glad you didn't throw it, and I'm glad you came.

I've never met anybody else who had no need of pianoforte lessons."

Annie raised her eyes. Before she could snatch them away, a tiny spark. Alathea smiled. Annie stayed very still. "There are five of us learning with Monsieur," Alathea said conversationally. Conversation was certainly not her usual custom, but then having a visitor to tea was not her custom either. "The others have barely an ounce of talent between them."

"I'm sure they've nice feet." Annie meant her voice to sting.

Alathea laughed. "Everina's and Marianne's feet are not hopeless, which is just as well. They certainly can't rely on their faces."

Now, Annie thought. Now she'll say something about my lip. The poker was within reach. She could seize it. She would seize it. She prepared herself. "We're all to be married, you know," Alathea said. "Our concert is supposed to increase our value—not monetary, you understand. Our fathers are rich. It's to make up for our parentage. You've played our pianoforte?"

"Of course." Annie was still contemplating the poker.

"Does Monsieur Belladroit speak of us?"

Annie's voice was clipped. "I do not speak to Monsieur about you."

"But you'd like to know what he feels about us."

Annie fixed her eyes on the portrait. It was too small to see any detail except that it was a child. Her jailer-hostess? Alathea's own eyes flicked briefly to the portrait, then back. "Monsieur's the reason you followed me." She wondered why she had been so slow to guess.

"Of what interest could Monsieur possibly be to me?" Annie made herself stand up.

"The same as for any other girl," Alathea replied. "Monsieur may not be young but his charms are undiminished."

"Monsieur's a friend," Annie said tightly.

"A man like Monsieur can only be a friend to old women, or women possessed of no beauty, and that, Annie Cantabile, is a category to which neither of us belongs." Alathea's response was not remotely thoughtless. She waited for Annie to break.

Annie broke. She collapsed back onto the sofa. "Are you blind? Do you see nothing?"

"I see everything," Alathea said.

"Well then," Annie cried.

"I think we may be quite similar, you and I."

Annie pointed to Alathea's perfect lips and then her own. Not content with that, she pulled her lips wide and thrust them in front of Alathea's. The musk scent was overpowering and Annie's lip pulsed hard enough to hurt. She thought it might burst. She hoped it would drench Alathea in blood.

Alathea grabbed Annie's hands and locked them together, forcing the girl backward. Furious, resistant, despairing, powerless, Annie tried to imagine she had the acid, that she had thrown it, that Alathea's purple pupils, so dense, so cool, were shrinking and shriveling instead of softening and spreading. Annie shook her head. A quirk of Alathea's cheek. A certain unconscious pleading in those lips, those lips whose perfection, if there had been any justice in the world, should have been matched by Annie's. Pleading? Alathea was making fun of her. Annie punched against the spell being cast about her. And something worse. Perhaps it was the warmth, perhaps it was the desperation, perhaps it was even something in the tea, but tears arose. Annie bit them back, wrenched Alathea's hands from her shoulders, and crouched down facing the fire.

Alathea crouched too. "I've always had a strange taste in beauty," Alathea said. At last, an acknowledgment. The relief was intense. Annie remained crouched. From the corner of her eye she saw Alathea pick up one of her boots. "Is your lip painful?"

Annie kept her eye on her boots. "No," she said.

"I'm glad." Alathea put the boot where it would dry more efficiently.

"Are you an idiot?" Annie began to rock. "It pains me every minute of every day."

Alathea picked up the other boot, then dropped it. The singed sheet, toasting on the hearthstone, had begun to smoke again. With a sudden swoop, Alathea bundled it over the logs. The blaze thundered, enormous, threatening the chimney, pouring warmth into the room, and making the other sheets billow. Annie threw up her head. Alathea's own head was thrown back, her throat entirely exposed. Annie could reach for the poker unhindered. She wanted to. She even made a small movement. Alathea turned. She put her hands on Annie's shoulders, the pressure intense as the heat. Annie wondered whether they were both about to go up in flames. She felt half drugged. She wondered again about the tea.

"I think you have two lips," Alathea said softly, "this one"— she ran a finger first over Annie's bottom lip—"and this one." She ran a finger over the top lip, which took a little longer. She grasped Annie's index finger. "And I think that I have this one"—she ran Annie's finger over her own top lip—"and this one." She kept hold of Annie's hand. "Come," she said. "I've something to show you."

She drew Annie to her feet. Annie made to put her boots on, but Alathea would not wait. She picked up the lamp. When they reached the door, she indicated her pocket. Annie pulled out the key. She could smash the lamp, unlock the door, and be free. She should do it. She unlocked the door. She could refuse to climb the stairs. She climbed the stairs. She and Alathea walked past the dead rooms. Outside a large set of double doors Alathea let go of Annie's hand and reached for a bronze key hidden behind a draped Madonna. She unlocked one door and swung it open. She walked in. Annie walked in behind her. Alathea closed the door and locked it.

The room had been a small ballroom. Alathea still called it that though nobody had ever danced in it. Sheets covered three of the four consoles in the four alcoves on the right hand side, with more sheeting covering the sitting out sofas between each console. A large fireplace, clearly in frequent use, divided the four alcoves. The console nearest the door was uncovered and on it were an assortment of lamps, candles, and flint boxes. On the left hand wall of the room hung a complete set of gilt framed mirrors. These were uncovered. To save space, a musicians' balcony had been built above the mirrors. At the far end, the two long windows were heavily shuttered and above the girls' heads six chandeliers shivered. Annie saw none of this. She saw only that in the middle of the room, in lonely polished splendor, stood a pianoforte, a harpsichord set to its right, nose to tail. Two long stools waited. Alathea lit a second lamp and gave it to Annie. "Shall we play?"

Both girls moved forward. Annie could feel the dust under her stockinged feet and in her nostrils. It mingled with Alathea's musk, thickening the air. Alathea set down her lamp and went to light the fire. Annie ignored the harpsichord and sat at the pianoforte. Alathea returned and sat on Annie's right. There was music on the stand. Alathea set it aside and chose music from a pile on the floor. Mozart duets? An imperceptible nod from Annie. Alathea counted them in. Two sets of hands on the keyboard; two sets of eyes reading the script; two investigatory glances and listenings; two intellects phrasing the music, prob, ing, coaxing; two sets of shoulders sinking, loosening. Four hands obedient, powerful, practiced. Occasionally, one girl would stum, ble and correct. Occasionally, the other would tap a bar in the text for a repeat. Occasionally, Alathea would stop and make a suggestion. At first, Annie was content to follow Alathea, then, as the room warmed and the music took hold, Annie made sug, gestions. This was her skill and her language. She was equal here. Together, they filled the room. The last motif. The last recapitulation. The last chord. They turned to each other. Alathea raised her hands, palms out. Annie raised her hands in response. Their fingers gently beat together: one, two, three, four; one, two, three, four. Alathea drew back. Annie was left poised. Alathea opened her arms and from her, like a draft, blew exhilaration, triumph, and joy. It was the joy that swept Annie in. With a long sigh, she tipped forward and clung to Alathea. Without hesitation, Alathea clung to Annie. They clung to each other.

It might have been an hour after the embrace before the girls returned to the card room. The tea things were as they had left them. The fire was almost out, the sheet reduced to ash. What had happened in the ballroom after the music puz, zled them both and it was in neither girl's nature to speak about what they did not know. They could recount their move, ments chronologically. They had clung. They had clung very close. Their clinging had moved them from pianoforte stool to the rug in front of the fire. There had been movements of hands under clothes. There had been skin and hair, strokes of various urgencies, intrusions and exclamations. There had been no kiss. None had been proffered by either girl and none had been taken. When movement ceased, they had lain still until, without a word, both got up and made ready to come down-stairs.

They had not returned to the pianoforte before they left the ballroom, though Annie had touched it as she passed like an explorer touching a marker flag. She had been here. She might not come again. In the card room both girls could see they were extremely grimy. Annie wiped her hands before bending to put on her boots. She stood. They moved to the hall. Alathea was ready with the veil and Annie was glad of its cover, not to hide her lip—how could she care about that now—but to hide her expression. She had no idea what it revealed to Alathea, or what it might reveal to passersby or to her father.

There was no sentimental parting. Annie secured her veil. Alathea ran upstairs. Annie waited. Alathea returned in moments with a score. This was the invitation to return. Annie tucked the score under her arm and prepared for the street.

When the door shut between them, Alathea leaned on it. She had an unfamiliar feeling in her stomach. It was happiness, though she assessed it as one might assess pain. Good? Bad? Dangerous? It was good, and it was dangerous, she decided. She also knew she could not and did not want to get rid of it.

She dined with her father in the card room, Crouch in reluctant attendance as both cook and waiter. Alathea was rav-enous. She was not concerned that Crouch might speak of her visitor. Crouch said nothing to anybody, not even when asked.

As usual, Alathea went upstairs directly after supper. Unusually, she did not look in at the pianoforte. Instead, she lit the fire in her bedroom and sat in front of one of the room's many mirrors, brushing her hair. A sense of shock was part of the happiness. Though Alathea had had no previous encounter such as this afternoon's, the shock was not sexual. What shocked her as she stared at herself, unsmiling, was something new she saw in those elastic eyes of hers, something unlooked for, uncultivated, unarmored. Ridiculous. Annie was a stranger, and a malignant one at that. She had brought acid, to destroy. Alathea did not know Annie well enough to be her enemy, let alone her—her what? Alathea stopped brushing. How could they not know each other? The music they had made! She pulled a guard in front of the fire, got into bed, and waited.

In the most secret hour of the night, her father came to her, as was his habit. As was hers, she accommodated him, tonight very careful that he should sense no difference. As always, he was furtive, scarcely moved. As always, she chose the form, directed proceedings, did the work. She kept her eyes open. His were closed. Neither spoke. This was the way it had always been, only varied if Sawneyford brought jewels. Then, before the other business, she would light a candle and he would place the stones where he liked to place them, admire them, play with them, then slip them back into their soft bag or into a box he had given her and which she kept under her bed. Tonight, no jewels. She was quick and efficient. He arrived as the clocks struck three and was in his own bed before they struck the quarter. When Alathea had washed and changed her nightdress, she reread the pamphlet she had brought from the abortionist's, lay back, and gazed at the ceiling. The foolishness of men. How strong they seemed; how authoritative.

They owned their wives and children. They could start a war with a nod. Yet all the while they were powerless against a reflexive judder that made them ludicrous. No wonder men preferred to rut in the dark. Her smile hardened and broadened. She and Annie would not rut in the dark. In utopia there would always be candles.

ONCE IN the street, Annie was sorry the rain had stopped, since with every step she expected shame to engulf her and rain might help wash the shame away. She wondered whether shame would leap out of the whorehouse, out of the academy, out of Trotter's warehouses, even out of the pickle factory whose hot vinegar made her sneeze again. She wondered whether shame was waiting on the corner of Charles Street or as she turned into Oxford Street, splashing her way westward among the wheelbarrows, dung, livestock, and people, always people, all confronting or avoiding, threatening or persuading, hiding or revealing, meeting or parting. Hats on. Hats off. Deference, contempt, derision, admiration, the lucky, the unlucky, and the shameful, to whose ranks she now belonged. Shame would surely stalk her more efficiently than she had stalked Alathea. But it had not caught her yet.

She hurried into Tyburn's muddle of lanes. Shame might grab her as she picked up some fish from the fishmonger for supper, or insinuate itself as she flung a coin at the local amputee. Nothing. Surely it would stamp on her as she opened the workshop door. She halted in front of her father's desk, ready to be engulfed. Her father was filing ivory. Annie removed her veil. Nothing. Perhaps when she went to tell her mother she was back. Nothing. She went to her own room, hid Alathea's music under her mattress, washed her face, brushed down her skirt, and tidied her hair. For the first time, she regretted a mirror. Not knowing her expression was unsafe. She went into the kitchen and did what she always did: rinsed the fish, peeled the potatoes, unwrapped the bread she had made earlier. She glanced about. Monsieur would be back soon. Perhaps he was already here, in his room, resting. Yes, see. His coat was slung across a chair.

When Monsieur appeared for supper, she kept herself away from him, nervous that he might smell Alathea's musk on her as she had smelled it on him. She did not allow herself to revisit the afternoon, not one second of it, until she was in her bed. Then, to her horror, shame and ridicule flooded through her in the dark. She could no longer hear the music in the ballroom. She heard Alathea laughing and Alathea was not alone. She saw Alathea in Manchester Square with the other girls and they were all laughing and chanting her name. Annie Cantabile! Annie Cantabile! As they chanted, they stuck fingers in their mouths in rude approximation of her deformity, Alathea pulling her mouth widest, turning her lips inside out. Alathea was telling the girls what she had said; she was showing the girls what they had done; turning it into a freak show. "Sixpence to see the lip lady!" The girls were loving it, their mouths slashes of derision. Annie lay rigid. Was that how Alathea had spent her evening?

She heard St. Mary's chime three o'clock. The images of the other girls dissolved. Alathea's alone remained, and she no longer had her fingers in her mouth, she had them quite elsewhere, and Annie was again lying in the music-studded dust with Alathea's pulse beating through flesh, nerve, and sinew. She and Alathea were composers together, conductors together, instruments together. She clenched her fists. This was the way to madness. To Alathea, Annie would be a passing fancy. So many other girls—all perfect. Yet those few short hours had been the crown of Annie's life. How could she live if those hours, already over, were all there was?

She got out of bed, pulled the music from under her mattress, and pressed it against her stomach. The flatness of the paper calmed her. The clefs calmed her. The black printed notes calmed her. She would not have only those hours. Alathea would be expecting her tomorrow. The door was open. The music said so.

She returned to Soho Square late the following afternoon, clasping the music to her. Crouch was standing by the door like a sentinel. Annie lost courage. The day after, she saw Alathea going out. In a deep blue cloak and a hat with feathers, supremely confident and self-possessed, Alathea looked right and left. She might have been looking for Annie, she might not. Whatever the truth, her confidence depleted Annie's. She dared not approach Alathea in the street, in full sunlight, not even in her veil. She could not risk Alathea uttering that telling "Oh, hello," which really meant "Oh, what a nuisance." Annie watched Alathea pause, walk, and pause again. If she looks my way, I'll go to her, Annie thought. Alathea walked swiftly the other way and Annie returned to Tyburn in agony, half revolted at her memories, half longing to relive them.

SEVEN

*L*ESSONS CONTINUED IN MANCHESTER SQUARE.
On Alathea's days, Monsieur took to wearing
a long coat, a garment appropriate for the
chilly early morning walk from Tyburn but
far too hot in the stale air of No. 23. It came
down to his knees, all around. There must be no possibility of
embarrassment. He did not always need the coat. Alathea chose
what she did and when. He wore it more in hope. On the days
he was not teaching, he wandered through the shrill clamor of
the streets, quite contented, a man who had made more of
himself than anticipated by the gray childhood, dull school-
master father, stolid mother, and dreary provincial town
known for nothing at all.

Monsieur did not believe in God, but had he done so, he
would have thanked him for the musical talent that had taken
him to Paris at an early age. A dutiful son, he had sent some of
his first pay back to his parents, who had returned it with a
kindly letter; they had no need of it. That, Claude had taken

some time to admit to himself, had been a curious blow. He had wanted them to need it, just as all these years later he had wanted them to be concerned about his living in Paris, its streets aflame. However, his father had no knowledge, or desire of knowledge, of flaming streets. His little school was still well attended; Claude's brother was taking classes for younger children; one sister was married to a butcher, the other to a baker. There were grandchildren in the offing. When Claude had returned to tell them he was off to London, he found the only shadow cast by the revolution was his mother asking whether the door to Claude's lodgings possessed a good lock and, in an oblique reference to the state of his shirt, whether all the laundries had closed down. In the end, Monsieur had not bothered to say he was leaving for England. Nor did he say he was resolved never to visit his childhood home as long as he lived. Paris was awful, Paris was dangerous, but at least Paris was alive.

On Manchester Square days, he was fully occupied. The girls' technique and the learning of the *Clavier Übung* progressed in line with his seductions—in other words, slowly. Marianne had taken to wearing a sprigged faux-shepherdess dress and ringlets. Was this an English joke at the expense of the dead French queen's rural affectations? If so, the joke was on Marianne. She looked like a sheep decked out for a May holiday. Fat fingers, fat arms, fat brain. "Brace yourself, *mon petit*," he murmured before Marianne attacked the pianoforte.

His scoldings over the music were careful. Everina and Marianne might not know the difference between making music and making a din, but—and apologies to poor Herr Bach's celestial variations—what did it really matter? When the time came, the girls would be deflowered after the manner of their playing: coarsely and without compunction. All the composers they had traduced would have their revenge. Even so, sometimes he could not help lecturing. "My father, who has been Kapellmeister to emperors, told me when I was still a baby that instruments must be coaxed like shy choirboys, not slapped about," he barked at Marianne when her thump, ing hit him directly behind the eyes. He wanted to beat her like a carpet. He would enjoy it.

He worked them all hard and, to his relief, found as much to amuse as annoy. Harriet, for instance, often wore an expen, sively simple rose-colored muslin sack dress, no whalebone, no stiffening, no decoration, her hair loosely bound up. The effect should have been pleasing, but Harriet, nervously uncon, stricted, moved as though caught in the street in her nightdress. Still, as Monsieur coached her through the crossing hands, arpeggio patterns, and finger swapping needed for the concert piece, her garments made appreciation of her lovely neck, downy below the hair line, very easy. "Duckling hair," he mur, mured to himself. "How did la Frog produce such a creature? Nature performs miracles."

He thought about Mrs. Frogmorton more than that lady could have imagined. Principally, he thought how to get rid of her. No seduction could reach its grand finale with a chaper, one hovering. But sometimes, when she came over to exchange a word, he found himself amazed that there was one word for both her flesh and Alathea's. Not that he had experienced Alathea's flesh as yet. A hand is not flesh. Yet Madame Frog, morton's hand would not do. Had la Frog once been like Alathea, he wondered? Take away a chin or two, thin the cheeks, cut away the belt of neck fat, and rake off twenty years, he thought, and yes, la Frog could have passed muster.

She had good round eyes and her one eyebrow had presumably once been two.

Harriet practiced well. Monsieur was pleased with her. "Feel every finger as a cog in a weaving machine," he told her. "Each part has its own job, and together all the parts weave the cloth." He encouraged her to think of their relationship as a contract. "Partners," he suggested after Harriet had told him rather wistfully that had she been a boy she would have been in her father's office. "You will be my little businesslady and I your office manager, your chief clerk, your steward." It had been a good conceit. Harriet had shaken his hand with a twinkle and swished out, leaving him appreciating, through her gown, the slight overflow of flesh from the tops of her stockings.

Then there was the day when Everina turned up sporting frizzed hair and an absurd dress of slashes and frills. "And what book have you been reading today, young lady?" he asked as she tripped toward him.

"Classical mythology," Everina told him.

"Are the stories moving?"

"They're silly. I like flesh-and-blood heroes. Who wants to be loved by a god dressed up as some horrible bird? And I'd be furious if any husband of mine flapped off leaving me with a scrawny baby who was going to grow up to kill me."

Monsieur Belladroit's laughter was genuine. Everina began to drill out some preludes he had given her: small works, easy on the fingers, of no musical importance. She paid no attention to Monsieur's instructions so he seated himself on her right and began, with malice, to copy exactly what she did, two octaves above. The faster and louder Everina played, the faster and louder he played. Everina began to giggle, her tongue protruding, a flash of grayish pink, thin as a hen's. Faster and faster she played. Faster and faster Monsieur played. More and more percussive grew the sound, with Everina working the pedals like treadles on a sewing machine. Monsieur felt the pianoforte cry out for mercy. "Not yet, *mon petit*," he muttered. When the final chord rolled, Everina was sweating like the Stratton Street step scrubber. She mopped her brow with her sleeve. Mrs. Frogmorton clapped. Monsieur tilted. Everina braced, anticipating a scolding. Monsieur surprised her. "Again!" he whispered, his breath like sulfur on her cheek.

The volume increased. Frilly began to whine, and then to howl. Monsieur grinned. This might be the way to get rid of la Frog. "*Continuez*," he ordered Everina, and poked his head around the screen. Mrs. Frogmorton's sewing was abandoned. She was half out of her seat. Monsieur waved and shouted above the din. "Apologies! Mademoiselle Drigg does play a little loudly, dear madame. That is her style. My ears are of no consequence but I worry for you. It cannot be good to sit so close."

Mrs. Frogmorton resented a charge of weakness. "My ears will manage perfectly well," she said, and sank down again. Frilly whimpered.

"But the little dog suffers, no?"

Mrs. Frogmorton eyed Monsieur, picked up her embroidery, and stabbed it. "You leave the dog to me." Monsieur bowed and returned to the pianoforte. A different approach must be taken and taken soon.

Of the girls themselves, Georgiana troubled him most, floating tremulously toward him, a wisp of pale foam amid folds of indeterminate color and texture. At least, after that first lesson, she remained untrammeled by hoops or stays, her hair usually down, a lick of honey loosely gathered by a gauze ribbon. Unlike Harriet, Georgiana was more comfortable in this ethereal state, imagining that floating clothes rendered her almost invisible. To Monsieur's delight, she had no idea that the almost invisible is also the almost visible, and the almost visible shouts "look at me" very loudly. When he sat beside her on the pianoforte stool, Monsieur made the happy discovery that there was more flesh than he imagined within the foam.

He won her confidence with a pretty untruth. "We are both perchers if I am not mistaken," he said at their third lesson, Georgiana still too paralyzed with shyness to play more than simple scales.

"Perchers?"

"Yes, perchers. Birds for whom no position is ever comfortable. I do not know about you, mademoiselle, but perching came to me early. My father died when I was a baby, you see. I never knew him. It was always only my mother and myself, perching together, never sure enough of anywhere to make a home. During our early perchings, I had no instrument on which to play and barely a stool on which to sit. In the end, my mother gave up struggling for a perch. She died when I was ten, with nothing."

Georgiana, wide-eyed, said, "She had you."

"I was not enough, mademoiselle."

Georgiana's eyes filled. "It's not nice, not to be enough."

"Not nice, no, mademoiselle." Monsieur let her droop a moment. "I was enough for another, though, a girl of great talent whom I taught as I teach you. She was taken from me by a fever." Georgiana's tears sparkled.

"I fear my confidences make you sad," Monsieur said.

"We're sad together," she replied.

After that, he got her to play her initials, G and B, in various combinations, then his own, C and B, then put the two sets of initials together. Georgiana was unable to resist. Soon, she was playing music carefully chosen by Monsieur not to frighten, and she proved to have more natural musicality than Harriet, though it was a pity, Monsieur thought, that she would never play like Annie. Annie. What a terrible shame. If only she could offer the world her music out of sight. Monsieur supposed it would be possible, but it would take some arrangement and he did not have the inclination. Georgiana had no need to play out of sight and she would at least do Herr Bach more justice than Marianne and Everina. When he told her that the instrument liked her, he was speaking sincerely.

He remembered little of his verbal exchanges with Alathea, but he remembered clearly the purple satin open robe with the paler under-dress, the cross-over handkerchief covering her shoulders caught at the neck by the nondescript brooch—each individual constituent demure, yet the girl emerging through the green gloom like a ripe plum. Her hair, too wiry for conventional beauty and uncovered by any cap, was a nimbus of Muscovado sugar. Monsieur breathed her in, like brandy.

Alathea never offered any greeting or acknowledgment of what happened between them—or, more accurately, what she did to him. Usually, she filled the hour uttering almost no words at all. But oh! Oh! One day she played Bach's gentle aria again, this time making it peep like a courtesan through a grille. When she spread the chord of the eleventh measure, Monsieur's mouth was dry. Then it was wet. Then it was dry again. The fingers and the beringed thumb now feathering those notes absorbed all his attention. He could not help imagining them feathering a different place entirely. Only Mrs. Frogmorton's infernal presence prevented him from grabbing those hands. At the final Gs, he was reduced to quiet panting. He would never forget what happened next. She turned to him, then turned back to the keys and played Variation 1. He hissed. Then Variation 2. This time, no repeats. She did not begin Variation 3. Instead, "Play," she ordered.

"What shall I play?" he asked, his voice husky.

"Whatever you please."

He began immediately, though he could not have said what he began. (It was Bach's Prelude and Fugue No. 2 in C minor—Alathea recognized it at once.) Without blinking, she undid two buttons of his breeches. His hands shook. He could not think how he kept on playing. She pushed back his coat and undid a third button. He was released. Relief and terror on his part. There he was, Monsieur Belladroit, playing Bach while fully exposed. He thought, "If that dog barks now, I'll have to kill it." Was it the fugue he reached before Alathea bent over? He recalled no sound. He recalled only hair, hand, lips, then lips, hand, hair. At the crucial moment, the fire crackling, the heat rising, his face contorting, she gave him her thumb and he bit down on the ring. As soon as practicable, she withdrew her thumb, thanked him for the lesson, nodded to Mrs. Frogmorton, and left him winded and speechless, his heart hammering, a host of nameless sensations rampaging, and sweat crackling in unexpected places—the backs of his knees, the crooks of his elbows, behind his ears.

After that, she took to missing lessons. Mrs. Frogmorton said she was probably unwell but after her fourth absence,

Monsieur wondered whether she was waiting for him to shift the great mass of the chaperone before she returned. Surely she must return? He must get rid of la Frog.

One sunny Friday in May, as Mrs. Frogmorton was leaving for her lunch, Monsieur seized a candelabra and spilled wax onto the floor. He shouted aloud at his clumsiness. "Oh no! Oh *mon Dieu!*"

Mrs. Frogmorton, alarmed, appeared around the screen.

"So sorry, madame. What a clot. Is that what you say, a clot? Yes? No?"

"For goodness' sake, Monsieur, don't dab at the wax like that. If you leave it to dry, it'll peel off and the servants can polish over the mark."

"Indeed, but I'm sorry. Your beautiful floor in this beautiful room." He got up slowly, picking wax out of his nails.

Mrs. Frogmorton frowned. She thought at first that he was making fun of her. Then she thought he seemed downcast. "The floor will recover, and the girls are getting on well," she said, since it was hard simply to turn her back. He nodded. "I hope your pay has been left for you every Friday on the table in the hall? The servants are honest, I believe, but I trust you still count it."

Monsieur made no comment. The reminder that he was hired displeased him.

Mrs. Frogmorton blew out the candles. She thought Monsieur looked a little overcome. She felt kindly, and kindliness led to confidentiality. "It's a great worry, having daughters to marry," she said. "Do you have daughters yourself?"

"I have—" A heartbeat as he considered whether a daughter might be useful. "I have not," he amended. He made a motion of regret. "The fact is . . ." He looked up, as though gauging her trustworthiness.

"Yes?" said Mrs. Frogmorton. She hoped this was not going to take long.

Monsieur took a deep breath. "The fact is, madame, I am not as other men." Frilly growled. Monsieur narrowed his eyes.

Mrs. Frogmorton caressed her pet. "Of course you're not as other men, Monsieur. You're French."

Monsieur stared at her. What did the old fool mean? Did she seriously think Frenchmen constituted differently to Englishmen? *Mon Dieu*, but he could show her. He clenched and unclenched a fist. Back to the task in hand. "Not just because I'm French, I am sorry to say."

"Oh? Why then?"

You could always rely on women's curiosity. He dangled. "I cannot tell you, madame. The story is too horrible."

Mrs. Frogmorton took the bait. "Horrible?"

Monsieur did not waste his chance. "I was orphaned as a baby, and at five years old was taken in by a choirmaster on account of my beautiful soprano voice."

From Monsieur's emphasis on the final words, Mrs. Frogmorton gathered she was supposed to learn something, although what, she had no idea. "You never knew your parents?"

"No. Had they lived, they never would have allowed what occurred to occur."

"And what did occur, Monsieur Belladroit?"

Monsieur's lips pursed. "That is what I cannot tell you."

She spread her feet. "Monsieur, you've begun, so you must finish. I doubt you can tell me anything I haven't heard before."

Monsieur shuffled his music. "I think I can."

"Let me be the judge of that." She cast a huge shadow over the pianoforte.

"Very well. Perhaps you are right. Perhaps you will not find it so shocking, being a lady of experience. Perhaps it is even common practice among you English. Many odd things are." He coughed. "My beautiful soprano voice made money for the choirmaster. When I reached a certain age, he did not wish to lose his income. Do you follow?"

"He sounds a very practical man."

Monsieur bit his lip. This woman! "He was frightened of my voice, how do you say, cracking."

"Breaking," Mrs. Frogmorton corrected.

"Thank you. Breaking. Do you know how he made sure my voice would not break?"

"I cannot..." A pause as Mrs. Frogmorton's imagination began to grind and her jaw to drop. "Monsieur..."

"Butchery, Madame Frogmorton, nothing less than butchery. One night, during the dark hours, he rendered me deliberately insensible through drugged wine. Then he and a medical man crept into my bedchamber, uncovered me, and used abominable tools against my—"

"Oh, glory!" said Mrs. Frogmorton, and clapped her hand hard on Frilly's head.

"Against my—"

"Enough, Monsieur!" Mrs. Frogmorton trumpeted.

"I hope I have not caused offense."

Mrs. Frogmorton was not sure what Monsieur Belladroit had caused. There was a name for such men. Castrati. It sounded absurd. It was absurd. Nevertheless, she must respond. "I'm sorry for you, Monsieur," she said. "A man without—" She stopped and searched about. "A man without, er, without *parents* is unhappy indeed." She backed away.

"Please say nothing," Monsieur begged. "It is a hideous embarrassment to me. As you may imagine, I am in a constant state of . . ." He looked to her for help.

"Mortification," supplied Mrs. Frogmorton.

"Exactly as you say."

"I'm sorry for you," Mrs. Frogmorton said again. "I think your lunch is about to arrive." She rustled smartly off. Foreigners. What dreadful things they did. Poor Monsieur Belladroit. She wondered whether the same practice went on with those Spaniards over the road. She must watch for her younger servants.

Monsieur brushed his lapels and congratulated himself. That had been quicker than expected. He worried a little that Mrs. Frogmorton had not waited for him to explain in more detail, since it was common knowledge that castrati were not always incapable of the act of sex, even if incapable of fathering children. He had wanted to stress that his butchery had been very complete indeed. No matter. He doubted she would discuss the finer points. To her he would be "unfortunate Monsieur Belladroit," a man but not a man and certainly not necessitating a chaperone. He did not care whether she respected his confidence. Indeed, it might be helpful if the girls believed him incapable. Alathea would not be fooled, of course. She would laugh out loud. Mrs. Frogmorton might tell the servants. He had to remind himself of Cantabile's money to make that humiliation tolerable.

Nonetheless, he was pleased with himself as he packed away his music and let himself out. (Spencer, the footman, did not consider Monsieur's comings and goings any business of his.) In Oxford Street, a crocodile of schoolboys tossed dung at their teacher. Boys were very unpleasant, Monsieur thought. He had never taught one to play the pianoforte and never would. He headed straight back to Tyburn.

"These girls," he said much later, and after Cantabile had been suitably entertained by the recounting of the ruse.

Cantabile poured more wine. "What's the matter with them?"

"Oh, everything with two of them. But there is more to some of the others than you might think."

"So?"

"At least one is worthy of your pianoforte."

Cantabile banged down the bottle, no longer entertained. "Don't speak of that instrument."

Monsieur raised his hand. "Come now, Vittorio."

Cantabile growled. "I don't want details of the girls. Do what has to be done. Bed them and leave them. That's what I'm paying you for."

"What about the one Monsieur is to marry? Isn't that part of the plan?" Annie's voice was cool from the corner. She was mending a nightcap.

Both men jumped. "What are you doing, skulking in the dark," snarled her father.

"Hardly skulking. I've been sitting here for an hour or more and I have a candle."

"You know what I mean. Your clothes are always dark. You might as well be a nun. But she's got a point, Claude. What about marriage?" Cantabile said. He drank his glass in one gulp and poured another while Annie took the cover off a veal pie she had left warming on the hearth. Monsieur sniffed. In the absence of a daughter, he thought about the attractions of a wife. Marianne? *Mon Dieu.* Harriet? Too prim. Georgiana? Too exhausting. Everina? He shuddered. Alathea? He blinked. What would that be like? He tried to imagine her cooking a veal pie. "I do not envy their husbands," he said.

Cantabile snorted. "No husband is to be envied. We don't marry to be envied. We marry because we can't see the future. If we could, well—"

Monsieur said quickly, without looking at Annie, "Annie's pie makes me hungry."

Without a word, Annie laid out plates and dished up for the men before taking a tray to her mother. She returned once the meal was finished, collected the plates, and washed them in a bucket.

She was wiping her hands when Monsieur put down his glass and caught her arm, wanting to make up for her father's unpleasantness. "Play for me," he said. It was the only thing he could think of.

Despite her new longings, Annie's old fantasy (since her father's guessing, this was how she termed it) was not dead. Monsieur had asked her to play. Perhaps she could at least give her concert. Indeed, she could give it right now. She picked up a lamp and went down the stairs, pushing all thoughts of Alathea away. She would have faith in the music. It would lead where it led.

She did not choose a perfect instrument, she chose the carriage horse and, after flexing her fingers, began with Mozart because Mozart said so much with so little. However, the sonata she chose was too symmetrical, the player's movements too restricted, and Mozart could also be trite. He felt trite tonight.

She began to merge Mozart with something of her own until Mozart vanished into music never yet heard in a drawing room, or in the promenade gardens, or at a court amusement. This music recognized the sol-fa but would not settle in one key. Transitions were not orderly; form was not followed. Nor could the music Annie created be labeled sonata, rondo, pre-lude, or bagatelle. It was a kind of spillage; it spilled out and retreated and spilled again. It was not an uncontrolled spillage. Every note, every unnatural (to Monsieur's ear) cadence, every surge and eddy was choreographed to bear witness to some truth that Monsieur could barely grasp. He did not care for the harmony: it was the control and choreography that touched his heart. Annie's music was an uncomfortable wave, but it never crashed. Whether he liked it or not, it drew Monsieur into its swell. Had Herr Haydn heard the music, he would have shaken his head. Herr Haydn would have had a point. So did Annie.

Cantabile stamped his disapproval on the floor above but Annie played on. This music was not for her father, it was for Monsieur and for herself. And it was working. Monsieur came to her, his face alight, just as she had dreamed. She had made him forget the girls. Her faith had won the day. The music was all. She turned to him. This was her moment.

Monsieur ran five quick fingers over the keys. He did not know what to say about Annie's music. He could say that it challenged his notions of construction and execution. He could say that it agitated. He could say that he both wanted to hear more and wished he had heard none. He rejected all in the face of the most important thing, which was to say something that would make Annie feel she was of value.

He began by asking practical questions. Annie showed him the score, explained the counterpoint and harmonies, the balance and the underpinning, how she had not rejected form, just overturned it. He exclaimed in wonder. He nodded his head. More questions. More answers. Annie was voluble. The sparkle extinguished by her father relit. Eventually, long before the music was exhausted, Monsieur was exhausted. He threw up his hands. "You have a talent, Annie. More than a talent. You play better than anybody I have ever heard, better than the late Herr Christian Schubart. Better, perhaps, even than I"—he could not quite allow that—"at least your use of both the sustaining and *una corda* pedal is remarkable. As for your composing—remarkable too. Truly remarkable. Only I am not sure. It is very odd. That is not always an advantage." He dropped his hands. He looked at her directly. He did not want his smile to alter. He could not prevent it.

Annie saw the alteration. She knew instantly that her moment had gone. The sparkle in her eyes flattened and went out. "Herr Mozart wrote oddly sometimes," she said, chasing the moment and despising herself for it.

"Herr Mozart wrote like a man. You write like a woman. Listen." He sat beside her and began to play. "Here is what Mozart does." He bent his head. "Here is what you do." Annie did not disagree. She simply thought, "And is what I do less?"

When at last Monsieur stood up, Annie set him a final test. She lifted her face to him. She waited. Could he muster the courage? Monsieur could not pretend not to know what she wanted, not for a second. Yet not for a second could he contemplate those lips after Alathea's. Annie, face still lifted, watched him spin around. His "good night" was inaudible. She slowly lowered her chin and closed up the carriage horse. Entering her own room, having looked in on her mother,

Annie thought how strange life was. Her concert had not really been a success, yet though disappointed, she was not devastated, though sad, not desolate. Strangest of all, as she lost her dream again, she wondered if the loss was not Monsieur's.

EIGHT

NNIE WENT TO SOHO SQUARE THE NEXT afternoon, hugging Alathea's music to her breast. She would see Alathea today or she would die. She found Alathea sitting on the step. When Alathea saw Annie, she got up and without a word pulled Annie inside, shut the door, and headed upstairs to the ballroom. The fire was already burn-ing. Annie removed her veil. "I came—"

"Yes. But you went."

"How did you know I'd come today?"

"How did you know I'd be waiting?"

Other girls would have smiled, but since Annie never smiled Alathea did not either. Annie set out the music. Alathea lit candles, then came to Annie and put up her hand. Annie put up hers. Their fingers brushed, then they sat down to play together at the pianoforte. They played Clementi, Couperin, and Haydn's Sonata in C before turning to Bach. They played for two hours without ceasing.

"I must go," said Annie. "My mother needs me."

"Go," said Alathea. "But if you don't come back tomorrow, I'll come and find you."

Thereafter, there was no hesitation on Annie's part. She calculated when she could be away from Tyburn without causing her mother discomfort or her father or Monsieur to comment. She prepared food early. She cleaned late. She left things out in the workshop so that her father would believe her still there.

Soho Square was the girls' meeting place, but it was Bach—demanding, thrilling, unforgiving—who joined them, stretching them and sometimes parting them in disagreements over, say, the phrasing of repeats or the best way to transfer music from harpsichord to pianoforte. They argued fiercely about dynamics, ornamentation, and fingering and most fiercely of all about whether the copyist had made an error with an Aflat, or whether it was the composer's intention. In a fortnight they progressed far beyond duets. They no longer played together on one instrument. Both preferred the pianoforte, so they took turn and turn about. Some days they did not play at all, only transcribed for the keyboard quartets, cantatas, or the orchestral parts of concertos—indeed, any music that Alathea bought from printers, stole from churches, or removed from publishers' windows. Annie did not reveal her own compositions but turned her hand to all manner of arrangements, distortions, inversions, perversions, reversions. The sounds the girls made playing in unison, in harmony, playing things never intended for the pianoforte, empowered them. Their bodily unions too, which did not happen every visit, were splendid; it was music, though, that brought the world to light and made them sharp and unafraid. They did not need God, in whom neither placed any trust. They did not need family. The sound they created at the keyboard was enough to make them feel fresh, salty, and utterly free.

Annie could not see how she had lived before this. She did not resent her former life, as she labeled it. In the hours back at Tyburn tending her mother and cooking for her father and Monsieur—and this was still most of her day—Annie recognized that her solitary existence, her father's insults, and her mother's infirmities had been necessary. That life, enclosed in the workshop and burnishing her musicianship, had been preparation for this. It had made her Alathea's match. She could not regret that, not ever.

On a fine day in mid-June, Annie suggested opening the ballroom shutters. Alathea demurred, and for the first time since that rainy day in March, a nonmusical tension rose between them, Annie's fueled by the realization that Alathea had not seen her uncovered in natural light. Annie in candlelight was not the same as Annie in sunlight. Was it possible that Alathea did not know Annie as she really was? Was it possible she did not want to?

Alathea was not thinking of Annie. She rejected daylight for herself: it deadened her. She was a creature of the city, and, like the city, she shone best in the man-made: the watchman's flare, the burst of the brazier, the flash of a flint, the blaze in the hearth. Sun, moon, glare of summer, and crisp winter dawn diminished her and were to be avoided.

Had Annie pressed, Alathea might have explained, but Annie was afraid to press. She simply sat down to play. It was the slight hunch of her shoulders, a hunch of which Annie herself was unaware, that tempted Alathea to allow considerations other than her own to dictate how things would be.

Annie, at the harpsichord, was listening with the exaggerated care of one whose mind is somewhere else when Alathea got up, took a candle, and before she could change her mind tore back a curtain. In a shower of green dust, a deluge of spiders rattled to the floor and a shaggy canopy of bats surged up. Annie screamed and leapt onto the harpsichord stool, hauling her skirt over her head. Alathea screamed too and waved the candle. The bats swirled in a ragged cloud of twitters and chirps, punching out droppings. Floor and ceiling were alive. Alathea dropped the candle and with both hands yanked at the shutter bolts, praying they would not be rusted shut. Eventually they gave way and she wrenched the shutter back, grabbed the candle, and smashed the window with the base of the stick. Sunlight flooded in; the bats did not flood out. Alathea ran to the pianoforte, trying not to hear the crunch of the spiders. "Make a noise," she cried, and began to bang the pianoforte's lid. Annie stamped on the harpsichord keys.

The vibrations confused the bats. They did not want to go out. They could not stay here. Finally, they seethed through the broken glass, whirled around the square's lime trees, and settled unhappily among the new leaves, causing playing children to shriek and flee, nannies shrieking and fleeing after them. When the room was empty, Alathea jumped from the pianoforte and slammed the shutters shut. All the candles had blown out in the stramash and the fire was very low. Everything was obscured. Alathea made her way back to the harpsichord and touched Annie, who screamed again. "They're gone," Alathea said.

Annie crouched, her skirt still over her head. Alathea climbed onto the stool beside her, out of reach of scurrying spiders. Annie shuddered. "I should never have suggested it. I didn't realize. I didn't think."

"Ssssh." Alathea shuddered too. "I didn't think either."

"Do you suppose they're in every room?"

"I suppose so," Alathea said, folding her skirts around her legs.

"How can you bear to live here?" Annie asked.

"We don't live here," Alathea said. Her arms were sticky with torn cobweb. "Uggh. Horrible."

Annie slowly let her skirt down. "You have another house?" She tried not to peer into the darkness above or below.

"I mean we don't live anywhere. This place is simply a shelter. Protection from the weather." Alathea scraped her fingers over her skull, dreading to find something trapped in her hair. "I live inside my skin. It suits me well unless it's invaded by bats or spiders. I suppose my father does the same. I'm going to relight some candles from the fire. You stay here."

"We have a house," said Annie, peering after Alathea's shadow. She did not want, not for a second, to feel alone in here. "It's my father's home, and my mother's, so I suppose mine too, but I feel more at home here than I ever feel at Tyburn."

"Even with the bats and spiders?"

"It's not the place," Annie said, in a burst. "It's you."

This was the first explicit declaration. It hung in the air. Alathea lit five candles. Treading carefully, she placed them on the instruments. "We need brushes, cloths, and water," she said. "All the keys will be filthy. We'll have to swill the floor." She left Annie alone. Annie did not move a muscle. Alathea returned with buckets. She left Annie alone again. She brought more lamps.

"Should we pull down the dust sheets?" Annie asked.

"We'll do only what's necessary," Alathea answered. "I'm not going to touch the curtains. That one can stay open."

Annie took a brush and they cleaned in silence, sweeping and swilling the floor, dusting the instruments and stools and shaking out the music. Occasionally there was a flutter from above. Not all the bats had taken to the skies. The girls shrank down. The fire was dampened enough for a small group of bats to scud up the chimney.

When the cleaning was over and with Annie's declaration still hanging, the girls settled themselves with Handel and studded the room with music once more. The flurries of the bats had disturbed the cornice work. It was flaking. Before the sonata was finished, the girls were white with it. "I believe this house will fall down," Alathea said as she wiped Annie's face.

"We'll find shelter elsewhere." Annie wiped Alathea's face. Alathea clutched her arm. "Listen," said Alathea, an edge in her voice. A warning. A distance. Annie shrank. She should have said nothing. She was about to lose everything.

Alathea gave her a little shake. "We mustn't become dependent," she said. "Never, ever, dependent. Not on each other. Not on anybody. We can depend only on music. Do you see? Being dependent on any other person lets them get right inside you, like a worm wriggling into your core. If you depend only on yourself, there's no worm. You're intact, completely whole. You do see, don't you."

Annie did not see. Alathea's sense of being intact sounded like being alone, and being alone was not powerfulness or wormlessness, it was loneliness. When Annie thought of being intact, she thought of herself and Alathea attached together, dependent only on each other, the two of them an unassailable

circle. She was not Alathea. She knew nothing of the treacher-
ies of Alathea's life, the what should be and was not, the what
was and should not be. The result of Alathea's warning was
that Annie's heart sank beyond her boots. What a fool she was,
she thought. This ballroom life had come quickly and it would
vanish as quickly. Alathea did not want her, or need her. This
could all stop the same way it started: on Alathea's whim.
Annie felt she must leave while her legs would still carry her.
She tried to get up.

Alathea pinned her down. "You must see." Alathea knew
her voice sounded different from normal. It pleaded, almost
begged. She did not like it, but she had to go on. "If you aren't
dependent, all your strength is your own." She set her jaw. "If
you don't depend and aren't depended on, you can never disappoint. How can you disappoint somebody if you're not attached
to them and they're not attached to you?"

"But what about—" Annie couldn't bring herself to cry out
"love."

"What about love?" Alathea gave Annie's shoulders a little
shake. "Love's perfectly possible. We can be together but apart;
we can be in love, without being dependent. That's how to be
happy. I know it." Alathea pressed her palms on Annie's cheeks,
as if her convictions were stamps. "Most people don't understand, so they're never happy, not really. They're too frightened
of being lost or betrayed or hurt in some way. Let's not be
frightened, or lost or betrayed or hurt. Let's not even entertain
the possibility. We can be truly happy. Do you know why?" A
bit of cornice work floated down. "Because we're rare."

"I don't know!" This burst from Annie despite herself. "I
don't feel rare."

"We're bound together by music but we can play separately

- 123 -

as well. What use would we be if we couldn't? Attached yet detached. It's what everybody would be if only they could. And we can."

Alathea was almost crushing Annie's jaw. Annie's lip was halfway up Alathea's nose. Annie caught Alathea's wrists and pulled them away. She did not want life to be the same as music, but there was something worse: the threatened loss of the happiness she found in this shrouded house of bats and spiders. She could not lose it. She laced her hands behind Alathea's neck. She imagined a core forming and a slow tongue of molten silver folding around this core, encasing it. The tongue met around the middle, its soft edges soldering and hardening into a silver shell with no seam, no wrinkle, no escape hatch. She imagined the same in Alathea, in gold. She drew their faces together. Alathea bared her teeth. Annie bared hers. Their teeth clashed, enamel on enamel. Their hands were at each other. There was tearing of cloth, and in this moment of supreme untenderness, with a few baffled bats above and homeless spiders below, detachment bound them together.

Annie remained in Soho Square very late. When, finally, she left, her silver armor molded and bolted, welded and polished, she stalked through the night streets like a queen. Had her father remained up to ask where on earth she had been, she might have killed him.

NINE

OUT OF RESPECT FOR MONSIEUR, MRS. FROGMOR-
ton had kept his secret. Nevertheless, as summer
waxed, she quietly abandoned her chaperoning for her closet and warming stove—it was
always chilly in Manchester Square. There
came a day when, with the cook to pacify and an upstairs maid
to chide, she openly left Monsieur to it. Nobody remarked.
Everybody was used to him. He was no more than furniture.
Mrs. Frogmorton thought she would tell the alderman of Monsieur's mishap soon, and Mrs. Drigg and Mrs. Brass. She did
not wish to be thought careless of her chaperoning duties but
there was no particular hurry and she did not wish Monsieur
to think her a blabbermouth.

Monsieur had used the time it took for Mrs. Frogmorton
to loosen her grip to good effect, warming his seductions every
day—a touch here, a flirtatious remark there, no pushing or
shoving. When not in the room, Mrs. Frogmorton usually left

the door open. In due course, he would close it and she would not notice.

There were irritations. At the beginning of July, Mrs. Frogmorton told him that the concert would not take place until late in the year. The delay was something to do with the room they wanted, some reluctant duke, some squeamish earl—whatever it was, it irked Monsieur. Why not have the concert in Manchester Square? La Frog was implacable about that. Manchester Square had no saloon and the dining room was too small for the supper. (In fact, Mrs. Frogmorton was suddenly nervous of the quality of her furniture and plate.) There was a row. Mrs. Frogmorton told Monsieur that he could leave if he wanted. There would be other teachers. Monsieur replied that Mrs. Frogmorton must understand that he had other calls on his time.

The row was pointless and Monsieur knew it. He did not want to leave. What, after all, awaited him in Paris? Blood; shouting; flag waving. And he would never rescind his decision to cut himself off from his childhood home. Anyway, the weather in London was lovely. The plantings in the middle of Manchester Square had flourished into syringa and roses, with jessamine following on and the promise of peaches and cherries. London seemed generous, happy, even. His berth at Cantabile's was tolerable enough. And there was Alathea. Or sometimes Alathea. She seemed to be playing a different game now. Nevertheless, she could still surprise and the surprise was worth the wait. The row blew away. Mrs. Frogmorton was pleased to note that Monsieur was very gracious when they next met.

Now that he had an accurate idea of the girls' capabilities, Monsieur divided up Herr Bach's variations. For Marianne's and Everina's sakes, two pianofortes would be required for the concert so that he or one of the other girls could play the left hand and they only had to manage the right. His insistence on exercises was bearing fruit. Techniques had improved, fingers grown more dexterous, touch more secure, pedaling less arbitrary. Last week, after giving each girl their allocation of the *Clavier Übung* score, he had prevailed on Cantabile to send an inferior pianoforte to the Driggs at Stratton Street for the girls to practice together. Already, they were reasonably familiar with the form of the work, though the variations' difficulty was a matter of constant exclamation and complaint by Everina and Marianne. Despite improvements, for all except Alathea, at whose musical ability he continued to marvel, Monsieur regretted the music he had suggested. It had been no part of the plan for the girls to make musical fools of themselves, or of Herr Bach. So there was one good thing about the delay: musically speaking, particularly for Marianne and Everina, more time was beneficial.

In Manchester Square, the Frogmortons were delighted with the blooming Harriet. In Stratton Street, the Driggs endured either furious sulks or giggling good humor from Marianne and Everina, but whatever the girls' moods, Mrs. Drigg's daily headaches and the grumbles of the neighbors were testament to the dreadful drumming of practice. In Covent Garden, Georgiana Brass began to speak, occasionally, at dinner, and at the Sunday tea in mid-July to celebrate the start of a three-week holiday (Mrs. Frogmorton's proposal, not Monsieur's), she had even eaten a tiny cake. The following morning she asked for new clothes, which caused Mr. Brass to remark to his new mistress (his long-standing French *belle amie* had been thrown over for a sulky Russian Jewess) that his daughter might make a decent wife after all. The Jewess shrugged. She had no interest in Georgiana. Mrs. Brass, meanwhile, wondered whether she should take up the pianoforte herself.

On the morning of that Sunday tea, Monsieur met with all the mothers in the Manchester Square drawing room to report on progress. No refreshments were served: Monsieur should not imagine this was a social occasion. Mrs. Frogmorton had the drapes thrown back to give the room an airing. If she hoped the room would be transformed by the sun, she was disappointed. The green was still too green, the brown too brown, and the armor too ridiculous. Mrs. Drigg was reminded of a funeral parlor. "What a good room this is, Grace, so bright and cheerful. I've always thought so," she said, tiptoeing to the pianoforte and inspecting it as she might have inspected an incendiary device. Mrs. Brass sat on the stool and touched four notes: A, B, C-sharp, A. Was that the start of a nursery rhyme?

"Elizabeth?"

Mrs. Brass drifted up and sat where directed. Frilly yapped at Monsieur's sudden appearance, making the women jump. "Goodness, Monsieur!" said Mrs. Frogmorton. "Where were you hiding?"

"Madame Frogmorton? Mesdames?" Monsieur tried to catch the women's expressions before they had time to adjust their faces, to see whether La Frog had revealed his secret to her friends. What woman could resist? He searched for a tightening of lips, a hint of teeth set in sympathetic disgust. Nothing. He was surprised, then annoyed. He meant nothing to these women, not even gossip. A rage took hold of him.

Mrs. Frogmorton quieted Frilly. Mrs. Drigg sat down. "Now," Mrs. Frogmorton said.

"The girls make progress." Monsieur snapped his fingers.

"Come," Mrs. Drigg urged. "You'll have to do better than that."

"The girls improve."

"Monsieur!" Mrs. Frogmorton was hurt. Her husband paid this man on time. He had decent dinners between lessons and was never kept late. She had kept his secret. Yet today he seemed disagreeably French, tilting his head and glaring. An English music master would have stood hat in hand and praised his charges, as mothers had every right to expect. "We wish to know *how* they improve," she said. "We wish for details."

Monsieur's voice was sharp as a needle. "The mademoi-selles capture the capriccio and the cavatina, the gigue and the fugue, the overture and the canon. They master the appog-giatura, the acciaccatura, the inverted mordent, the trill with inversions and subversions and occasional perversions—oh, and the shake."

"The what?" Mrs. Frogmorton really was trying to follow.

"The shake," repeated Monsieur. "The shake, madame. The shake. Of course they learn the shake." He walked back and forth. "They also know of portar la voce, accento, tremolo, esclamazione"—he threw his fingers up like knives—"and all manner of cadences, deceptive, receptive, unfinished, finished—no, no—I beg pardon, *nearly* finished. Then there is the staccato, the legato, the bragatto, the ragatto"—he saw a twitch of the lip from Mrs. Brass. He paused. Ah, that one. She knew a flight of fancy when she heard it. He curbed his flourishes.

"Perversions? Deceptions? Exclamations? Ragattos? I'm warning you, Monsieur Belladroit," said Mrs. Frogmorton with rising anger.

"Really!" echoed Mrs. Drigg. "It's too bad!"

Monsieur jerked his head. "What is too bad?"

"All this—all this—"

A weightless voice interrupted. "All this is as it should be," said Mrs. Brass. Six eyes swiveled toward her.

"As it should be? Are you sure, Elizabeth?" said Mrs. Frog-morton, astonished at this unexpected interruption.

The firmest nod Mrs. Brass had ever delivered. "Well then," said Mrs. Frogmorton to Monsieur. Her voice was still testy, but if Elizabeth had actually spoken… "I suppose that will have to do." She wished him a pleasant rest. They would see him in three weeks.

Monsieur did not have a pleasant rest. He spent the holi-day unhappily cooped up at Tyburn with a summer cold and failing to persuade Cantabile to offer him cash in advance. He had his salary, which continued to be paid, but he wanted to spend money, lots of it. He wanted to feel, for once, like a rich man. Annie was a ghost in the house. She kept the place clean, served up the dinners, and tended to her mother, yet even as she went about her work in front of Monsieur's eyes, she was somehow absent. When he asked her to play with him, she agreed, though this seemed more of an indulgence on her part than a desire. She never again played her own compositions, only what he suggested, and there was some-thing new in the sound she created, which Monsieur took some while to identify as joy. Why she was joyful, he could not imagine.

Over this long visit, Monsieur had become used to Annie's lip and grew tired of her father's constant references to it. When he said so, he and Cantabile argued, and the disagree-able atmosphere was rendered almost intolerable by Monseiur's stuffed nose and by the weather: outside objectionably hot; inside, chilled. The music master either sweated or shivered. Never, he thought, had he lived in a city with houses so badly arranged.

At Soho Square, there was also an atmosphere, though this had nothing to do with the weather. Sawney Sawneyford had never had cause for complaint about his daughter before, and though he had no discernible cause now, he felt that something was not as it used to be.

Alathea had been a half-blossomed child of twelve when she first crept to him in the night. They were living at Blackfriars, renting two rooms from an actress whose admirers often fought for her attention. Alathea had been frightened by the midnight din spilling up the stairs. She had knocked at his door. He had allowed her in. The next night, for the same reason, she crept to him again, all round and warm, with a scent like her mama's. Of course he knew it was his daughter, not his wife who was pressing against his side. Nevertheless, if he did not open his eyes, he could pretend. It could do no harm. An innocent comfort. He kept his eyes closed. He shifted. She shifted. He turned toward her. He had expected stillness, but after a moment's confusion, she was actively accommodating. It was over in seconds. The following night, with no din on the stairs, she returned. He never asked why; she never said. After that, though she did not creep in every night, and he never ordered her, he was always waiting. They never referred to it except when Alathea needed the abortionist, and even then, after her first alarmed request for help, only obliquely until the abortionist was needed no more. Nor, though he hoped she would, did Sawneyford ask his daughter to remove his wife's wedding ring from her thumb. In the end, he ceased to think of it as a wedding ring at all.

The actress's admirers called Alathea "beguiling." The actress herself, catching the tilt of Alathea's eyes, called her "unnatural." The lady began to harbor suspicions. Before her suspicions could be aired, the Soho Square house turned up. Overnight, Sawneyford and Alathea were gone, with no forwarding address.

It was in Soho Square that Sawneyford first visited Alathea's own bed. He had not been sure of his reception but need not have worried. She was accommodating as always. In her own domain—she had chosen dark top-floor rooms originally designed for servants—she appeared more adult. That was when he began to bring jewels. Some men might, by this time, have been pretending their daughters were changelings, not their daughters at all. Sawneyford did not bother. There was no need for make-believe since the arrangement suited them both. Sawneyford had never thought it would last forever. He did, however, believe that until she left him for a husband, Alathea would be exclusively his.

Sawneyford was a man who knew things. He prided himself on it. He knew, for example, all the sharp practices of the trading floor and the sharpest practitioners. He knew the name of every member of the Society of the Friends of the People. He knew that Brass's hairdresser had not paid the powder tax. He knew that Mrs. Frogmorton hid Frilly's butcher's bill. He also knew, although it was of no interest to him, that Everina Drigg's new teeth had cost twenty pounds and were, in fact, secondhand. It was troublesome to realize that there was something about Alathea he both knew and did not know. While outwardly nothing had changed, Sawneyford felt a presence. When he dripped his diamonds, he felt another's eyes. When he touched her hidden folds, he felt another's fingers. Her lips were darkened by another's shadow, her scent edged with something unfamiliar. He feared a trespasser. In his own bed, in this state of knowing unknowing, he lay unmoving and uneasy. Alathea, Alathea, Alathea. Daughter, lover, the only person in the world about whom he cared. How to discover what he wanted to know without breaking the silence about such matters that they both observed? He tried several times. He scuffed over words, never sure which ones to use. He grew angry with himself, and then with her. She waited patiently, whatever his mood, never interrupting. They ate meals together. They sat together. He knew they were no longer together. Somehow, without any visible sign of departure she was leaving him, and he could not bear it.

TEN

Lessons resumed and Monsieur rejoiced, at first, when his mornings were busy again. But he, too, had a problem. It was not Mrs. Frog-morton. She had ceased attending lessons. Monsieur could have stripped naked in the drawing room and danced a jig without fear of interruption. It was not even that if he wished for Alathea's services, he must now instigate proceedings. Her lips, hair, and hands were willing, only he must ask. His problem was unexpected, namely that when he thought of tumbling Marianne, everything wilted. Marianne was not a girl. She was not even an animal. She was a vegetable and he could muster no desire for a vegetable. Yet he could not leave her out. Once one girl had fallen, all must quickly follow. Soon Mrs. Frogmorton would give him the concert date and then he must set his date for the deflow-erings.

With some exasperation, he also found himself at a loss with Georgiana, though for different reasons. Georgiana touched him. Apart from Alathea's lessons, which were hardly lessons, the hour with Mademoiselle Brass was the one to which he looked forward most. Her perfect nose occasionally stopped him midsentence. The blue veins tracing her wrists delighted him. The small dip at the base of her neck moved him. And that tiny mole behind her left ear. He had only recently noticed it and thought she was quite unaware.

Monsieur had chosen Georgiana's *Clavier Übung* variations with care. "Variation 2, my dear dove. The tune is wistful if taken slowly, and the left hand—my hand to start with, I will play with you—so steady and dependable. You will imbue it with magic. Then Variation 3, the first canon, no less. Not the best of canons—even Herr Bach nods from time to time—but my arrangement of it and your playing will remedy its deficiencies." Her rapt attention was flattering. And this disconcerted the most: he was not a man easily flattered.

Worse, her innocence dampened his lust. It would be like defiling a child. True, when her skin flushed with effort and the milk-white top of a breast blossomed through the stitching of a gown, if he concentrated hard, he felt reassuring stirrings. But a man needed more than stirrings.

Today, with September well established, he decided he would try to stiffen the stirrings. He wondered whether laughter would help. He could remember instances when it had.

Georgiana arrived wearing green, the end of her nose still charmingly tanned from her week by the sea. Before she sat down, he played Variation 30. "Mademoiselle, Herr Bach called this a 'quodlibet,' or 'what pleases.' And do you know what pleased him?" He was smiling so broadly, she had to smile too. "Folk dances, and comic roundelays," Monsieur said. "He would gather his family together and they would mix up all manner of songs"—his entire being twinkled—"some rather naughty, Mademoiselle Georgiana! How they would laugh, Herr Bach and his family, at those naughty concoctions. And Herr Bach wanted to share his fun, so here, at the end of this work for the soul's delight, is Herr Bach laughing." He played the quodlibet again, with mock solemnity, then played it again, taking liberties with the time, which might not have pleased Herr Bach.

Georgiana obligingly laughed out loud. She was still laughing as she and Monsieur left the quodlibet and practiced the first canon's semiquavers, his fingers playing the bass, hers the treble, their shoulders brushing. "Curve, curve, curve, mademoiselle!" She curved, her semiquavers grew lighter, and there she was, flying and laughing as their hands collided. "My dear Georgiana," Monsieur murmured. He directed his eyes to her bosom, to those thighs, separated for the pedals. A slight flicker. He concentrated on it.

As the variation ended, Georgiana leaned in to look at some fingering, then turned, her face open to his. "When we both play, it's like cat's cradle," she told him with her shy smile.

"A cat with a cradle? What strange habits you English have!"

"Don't you know it?"

"I know nothing about cats."

"It's a game, Monsieur!" She pulled out a ribbon from her hair, tied it, and spread it taut over her fingers. "See! You must take it from me by catching these two strands between finger and thumb and passing them under." Since both hands were occupied, she touched the ribbon with her nose.

"Like this?" He followed her instructions.

"Up and over, Monsieur, and then spread your fingers and thumbs." He spread—the ribbon collapsed.

"No, no, Monsieur Belladroit." Georgiana shook her head. "Let's try again."

They tried again, Georgiana the sweetest of tutors, Monsieur the humblest of pupils, and there, amid the collapse of the cradle, Monsieur reckoned that with Georgiana all would be well. When the time came, he would take her, and he would treat her with the care she deserved.

Mrs. Frogmorton caught him as he was leaving. "The concert day," she said, beaming. "The second Saturday in December."

"The girls will be ready," he said, looking her straight in the eye. "Quite ready." On his way back to Cantabile's, he lectured himself about Marianne and set a date of his own.

In early October, everything damp, all summer's light and heat vanished as though never intending to return (the Manchester Square winter drapes went up smartish), Harriet was the first to notice a change in Monsieur. She noticed it in his mouth. "Are you quite well?" she asked. "Is it the drizzle? It doesn't always rain in October. Sometimes we can have a nice week. Sometimes." She did not wish to raise his hopes.

"It is my father, mademoiselle," Monsieur said.

She stopped playing. "Bad news?"

"Yes." He sighed. Harriet was encouraging. Monsieur feigned unwillingness, then capitulated. "He is dead."

"Oh! I am sorry!" Harriet removed her hands entirely from the keys—she had been about to start, almost at full speed, Variation 17, which she was to play with Georgiana, and with which she still had many difficulties. "Is your mother alone?"

Monsieur considered. "My mother has been alone for some time," he told her. It was useful, a pianoforte stool, for this kind of story. You could turn to face or look ahead at the music. Both seemed natural. "She and my father married for love, but love did not last. Since I was a tiny child they have lived separately."

"That is sad," said Harriet.

"The sadness, mademoiselle, lies in the fact that my father was a wastrel and cared neither for me nor for my mother. He has now been executed as a Jacobin. He was not a Jacobin. It matters little. My father has always been on the wrong side of everything."

"Executed?" Harriet's round eyes grew rounder. She was wearing her bloody shoes today. The stain had never quite come out. She rubbed the toe on the underside of the sustaining pedal. "Oh, Monsieur. That's horrible."

"Horrible? Oh no. Very quick, I think. And my mother did not mind. She has always depended on me, not on him. It is why I give lessons. I do not resent it. Though the sea currently parts us, my mother and I are close."

"The reward you get from teaching us can't be more than shillings," Harriet said, glad to move on from the blood, "and you've no time to teach anybody else. Your mother must survive on very little."

"I send everything I can, and it is sent with love, mademoiselle." He did not hide the fact that his heart was stirred by Harriet's practicality. His expression had precisely the right effect.

"Of course," said Harriet, and touched his arm. "We can't supply love but I'm sure we can supply more money. I'll tell my father."

"Indeed no," said Monsieur, slightly caught out. "I am paid most satisfactorily, and I would be grateful also if you would not tell the others." He could not remember what he had said to Marianne or Georgiana about his parentage. "I do not wish for pity. Let us continue. Your respective papas do not pay me to talk of my troubles. We need to work on your staccato and I would like to hear Variations 11 and 20 before we finish. You are doing well, Mademoiselle Harriet, but both are difficult, and I think, even at the concert, I must help you out. If you are ready, let us arrange ourselves carefully."

Harriet was still concerned. "Don't you want to go home for the funeral?"

"The funeral has been already. So many funerals in Paris over the past years. It is a city of funerals. Gravediggers are richer than aristocrats. My mother could not afford privacy and writes that my father shares a grave with at least three others, two of them without heads." He gave a little shrug. "Gravediggers give no discounted charge for that. Everybody wants to make quick money, even out of the dead."

Harriet did not know how to answer. She played Variation 11 slowly and carefully as the best way to please. The three semiquavers against dotted quavers were tricky. Monsieur chose to play the left-hand notes with his right hand. As was inevitable, given the music, their hands glanced, crossed, and were muddled together. Disconcerted, Harriet withdrew hers. Monsieur carried on without blinking. After a while, Harriet resumed the treble. When they reached the end of the first section, Monsieur gave a small smile. "Mademoiselle Harriet, you have cheered me," he said. She only then noticed that their legs were touching all the way down.

"I'm glad, Monsieur," she said, moving her legs away.

"Again," he said. "If you play more quickly, you may find the timing easier. Remember, though, delicate fingers. Do not press the notes. Drop your wrist. Persuade the notes down. Light, light, light."

Harriet nodded. They began again, the pace increased. Harriet, her tongue slightly protruding, rose to the challenge. "Excellent, mademoiselle," Monsieur murmured into her ear, making the drops in her ears swing. He put up one finger to quieten. Nobody could have sworn, in a court of law, that he brushed the earlobe on purpose. Harriet gave a shiver. Monsieur imagined it the first of those kinds of shivers, an indication of being ripe and ready. He was wrong. Harriet had shivered in such a way several times over the summer when she saw Mr. Buller, shirtless, helping to saw up a fallen branch in Manchester Square's central gardens. She had not spoken to her intended yet. Like Monsieur, she was biding her time. As Monsieur delved deep into the intricacies of Variation 11, Harriet's earlobe pulsed. She thought she might not wear earrings again. She thought she would never forget to put them on. To stop Harriet's left wrist sinking too low, Monsieur placed two fingers lightly beneath her cotton cuff. Harriet continued to play, but the shiver from her earlobe now tingled down her arm. She wondered whether Monsieur had noticed. She thought not. He seemed absorbed by the music, frowning, nodding in time, and humming. Occasionally he removed his fingers; Harriet felt their loss and was aware, for the first time, that Monsieur carried the faintest hint of rosemary on his breath.

The hour sped by and Harriet gave up her place without a word. At dinner, when her father asked how the lessons were going as the concert neared, she nodded, yes, yes, they were going well. Monsieur was an excellent teacher. She hoped he was being properly recompensed. Her parents exchanged glances. How fortunate to have produced Harriet, so thoughtful, so beautiful, so talented, so unlike Marianne or Everina.

The next day, Monsieur eased forward with Georgiana. "Sadness becomes you," he told her as though continuing a conversation started earlier, "yet I think happiness becomes you better and I believe that I, through Herr Bach, am teaching you something of happiness, no?" She was tripping through Variation 19 with gentle melancholy, nostalgic for she didn't quite know what. She continued playing. The music gave her courage. "Are you happy, Monsieur?" Her fingers drew out, not without feeling, the music's pretty tunefulness.

"I am happy at this moment, mademoiselle."

"Yet you must still miss your family; your loving mother, torn from you so early, and the father you never knew," she said.

"Ah," Monsieur murmured. "Yes, yes. Naturally."

"And your homeland. Do you miss France?"

"Oh, France! What is it now? It is your enemy, and I am a poor émigré, which is an elegant word for a lonely state."

A wrinkle appeared in her brow. She reached the repeat marks and began again. "You could never be an enemy, Monsieur," she said, then stopped playing and burst out "It's terrible to be lonely." Monsieur seized the moment, leaned over, and kissed her. It was a light kiss on the mouth, and he had his excuses all ready: her sympathy, the remembrance of his parents, his homesickness for the home he never had. In the event, and rather to his surprise, no excuse was necessary. Georgiana did exclaim loudly but when he withdrew, her face was alight with an expression he could only describe as gratitude.

On Monday, on the pretext of demonstrating the best posture to master the considerable demands of Variation 14, he stroked her neck. Her semiquavers grew no faster, only more delicate, until they matched his fingers on her skin. He moved his fingers into her hair. She sighed. She slowed. Monsieur removed his finger. "Until tomorrow," he said, closing the text. On her way out, Georgiana unfurled the beatific smile of a Renaissance angel and Monsieur, his conscience not entirely easy, nevertheless judged his own performance masterly.

The conquest of Everina was his most methodical undertaking. She continued to batter the pianoforte, and Monsieur, eyes glinting with fury, contempt, or amusement, depending on his mood, continued to chase her up and down the keyboard. On some days their chase became a wild game of musical tag. Today—the chosen day for final completion of the task—Monsieur removed Herr Bach's music—he sometimes felt a sense of shame, allowing its massacre—and sacrificed Signor Clementi, telling Everina she needed to exercise her fingers. Everina, panting hard, finished her third sonata with banging triumph. As usual, Monsieur allowed her no rest. "You chase me!" he shouted, balanced on one buttock as though the stool were steeply cambered, and thundering away in the bass. Shrieking, Everina flung her hands at the keys and caught him up. "How quick you are, mademoiselle," Monsieur trilled. He played faster. She played faster. Oh, the clashing semitones! Oh, the thrashing melodies! Oh, the lusty muddle of pedaling legs! When Everina eventually howled "Enough," Monsieur seized her plump shoulders. "Everina Drigg," he gasped, "you are right to reject the mythical gods of your books. Quite right! You are fully flesh and blood. Happy the hero who gets you!" He was sliding his hands downward.

Everina caught them and grew coy. "I know I'm flesh and

blood, but I'm also a pianist, Monsieur, wouldn't you say? Much better than Marianne. Wouldn't composers die to get me to play their works? So many girls are just water. Am I not wine, Monsieur?" She held him at a distance, cheeks quivering.

She had spoiled a spontaneous seizing of her virtue. All he could see were those terrible shining teeth. He could never kiss her. Yet she was unintentionally amusing. "Die for you, my dear! Indeed! You are quite the kind of pianist to make a composer die."

Everina let go of him and began Clementi all over again. Monsieur was obliged to follow. By the time she had finished, he heard footsteps outside. He could go no further with Everina today. Alathea was going to grace him with her presence.

At Everina's next lesson, Monsieur made her play hunt the tune, and during the hunt, he removed one hand from the keyboard and slipped it determinedly where it should not have been. Everina roared. Monsieur's fingers began a cavernous tickle. She commanded him to stop. Monsieur carried on, confident that pleasure would trump astonished offense. He was right. Everina gasped, gasped again, and bleated when he threatened to stop. Her movements were not subtle. It was clear she wanted to scream and shout, to smack him, to see him shot, to cling to him, to open herself wider, to arch, to writhe, to hang around his neck, to chop his neck in half. An odor arose that reminded Monsieur of the country nurse who had first taken him in hand.

Everina balked only at the final act. He would not force her even though this posed a danger. Wholly undone, her silence would be guaranteed unless she wanted to ruin herself as well as him. Instead, he was obliged to draw her into a conspiracy of pleasure with whispered gothic nonsense about kindling love and overwhelming passion, carefully pressing his suit through scattered mythical references and ardent but meaningless declarations of the kind he imagined littered the favorite pages of her books. When she tried to speak, he raised one of her fingers to his lips and one of his to hers. It was an old trick, always effective. At the end of the lesson, she kept her finger on his lips for a long minute and removed it with a mispronounced stage whisper of "*a demain.*"

On the next lesson day, he hurried the other girls through. Nothing must distract him from Everina now. He heard her, incoming, greet Georgiana, outgoing, on the stairs. He stood up. What were they saying? He could hear only Everina's interminable giggle and the clack clack clack of her teeth. Then she made her entrance. She had dressed from a fashion plate, with a white broad-brimmed gypsy hat tied under her chin with red ribbons. The hat sported a long red ostrich feather, and on either side of the feather her brown hair had been teased into corkscrew curls. Her red gown, almost indecently high waisted and low cut, had sleeves designed specially to display slender arms, though Everina's incipient underhang rather spoiled the effect. Jet pendants dangled from her ears and, sneaking into Marianne's room, she had stolen rouge for her lips. It was as well Marianne had not seen her leave Stratton Street. It was as well Mrs. Drigg had not either. Monsieur would have laughed had he not been relieved. Mademoiselle Everina was clearly open for business.

He greeted her with a bow and a very personal "Mademoiselle," then took her hand and led her to the pianoforte stool. Without removing her hat she subsided, a giggle in her throat, and arranged herself. Monsieur did some preliminary work, as expected, before, once again, offering something more substantial than his hand. This time, no rebuff. Everina's giggling turned to a hiccup and she opened her eyes very wide. "Monsieur! Oh my goodness!"

Monsieur viewed Everina as an excavation. He prepared the ground, levered in, dug about, then withdrew with the least amount of disturbance. He was more delicate than her music making deserved and he was very careful. Children were no part of his plan. He was pleased by Everina's giggle, and even more pleased when for one minute during and one minute after, her haunches upended and her fists clenched, she stopped giggling entirely.

Everina was not a dissembler. She was not displeased. Indeed, now that it was over, she felt she might take to this new activity given a few more goes. Yet all was not comfortable. Bits of her were hot with ache and she longed, more than for any caress or loving mumble, to run outside, take down her drawers, and squat in the cool mud. This was not what she expected to feel and it was not the response suggested in any book. In books, the heroine was affronted, angry, or distressed—the last if she was duped or doped by a villain. But Monsieur was not a villain. He loved her. He had said so, hadn't he, and she was eminently lovable, much more lovable than Marianne. Moreover, last night she had decided she loved him too, and she must be right about their loving each other, otherwise she would have felt nothing, and she had felt far from nothing. Still, what *was* the right response? She shifted from buttock to buttock. Failing mud, an ice block would be nice.

Monsieur helped her to sit. She grimaced. Her teeth felt glued together. Monsieur moved to consolidate his advantage. "Ah, mademoiselle," he said, stroking her as he might stroke a sheep, palm flat, mechanical pace. "You and I—do you see—do you feel?"

"I do, Monsieur, I do."

Monsieur was solicitous as he resumed his role as music master. He had brought a small bottle of water and a handker, chief. The pianoforte must not become sticky. He was finish, ing wiping his fingers when he found his head pressed against Everina's bosom. "Say you love me," she commanded.

He tried to remove his head but she held it in a vise. "Mademoiselle, love," he muttered.

It was not enough. "Say you love me," she insisted. "All the words. Say it now."

She was hurting his ears. "Release me, please, Mademoiselle Everina," he said.

"Not until you say you love me."

"I'll hear myself damned first," he muttered, not quietly enough.

She let go, her lower lip trembling. "You'll tell me you love me or I'll tell my father and mother what you've done."

He brushed down his hair, checked his ears, and clicked his tongue. "Mademoiselle, you will not, because if you do, they will punish me, then everybody will know and you will never get a husband."

"That's blackmail."

"Do you want to be alone for the rest of your life?"

"Perhaps it's worth it." She was certainly affronted now.

"Really, mademoiselle? I think not. You were not meant to be alone."

Her affront evaporated. She began to snivel, then looked panic,stricken. "What if I have a child, Monsieur?"

It cost Monsieur nothing to be kind. "Dear Mademoiselle Everina," he said, "what we have done does not make babies."

"Are you sure?"

"Making babies is an entirely different process," he said, thinking that not altogether an untruth. "Come now. You are a young and delightful girl and we had fun, did we not? Only do not mistake things. What I give to you is not love and what you give to me is not love."

"What is it then?" She wiped her nose on her sleeve. "All those things you did. All those things you said. They're what lovers do and say."

"Sometimes, mademoiselle. But they can also be said for the pleasure of saying them, and you are a woman who deserves a lot of pleasure. You have a gift for it, which makes you precious. Do you realize how precious you are?"

Her ostrich feather drooped over her face. "But you do love me?"

"Dear mademoiselle! Have you been listening at all?" His patience was running out. "You know nothing of love just as you know nothing of music. In matters of love you are like a goat"—she drew a stinging breath—"my little goat," he reassured hastily. "We are goats together." (Goats, he thought with a groan. It was her smell. Why did it have to be goat?)

Everina tilted backward and forward. "I don't want to be a goat. I want to be a lover, like Ethelinda and Celestina."

"I do not know these ladies."

"They're in my books."

Monsieur controlled his temper. "My dear little goat," he said, taking her hand and deciding there and then that if he were ever to have a daughter, he would forbid her to read novels.

"You want love, yes, but not from me. I am giving you something much more useful than love."

"What could be—"

He talked over her. "Your parents asked Mr. Cantabile very particularly to send a teacher to make their daughters fit for marriage. First I have taught you incomparable music."

She wiped her nose again. "You can't claim credit for the music. Somebody else wrote it and I play what's written."

"Ah, but you do not," Monsieur told her. "You play what is on the page, which is not the same thing. It is I who have turned what you play into music." She threatened to be querulous. He must placate. He patted her hand. "Listen to me, mademoiselle. When you step out of your wedding dress and into your wedding bed, you will play a better tune than ever you could play on a pianoforte. Hush!" He gave her chin a teasing tap. "I have taught you something important. You will surprise your husband—he may even be shocked—but these skills we have just exercised, mademoiselle, if you use them artfully, will marry you and your lucky spouse together far better than God, priest, or even Herr Bach. What is more, these skills will remain long after the *Clavier Übung* is forgotten. Do you understand?"

"But I don't feel I've learned much yet," she complained, though more cheerfully. "I'll need more lessons."

He blew out his lips. A few more tumbles, a few tricks of the trade. He nodded. "And you shall have them."

Everina was flattered. She straightened her feather and wiped her mouth, nose, and eyes on her skirt. "And you do love me."

Monsieur resisted the urge to slap her. He smiled cleverly. "I chose you, did I not, to be my little goat?"

She regarded him, still uncertain. He had said she was precious. He had said she was his. She sought one last reassurance. "And you won't tell the others, particularly not Marianne?"

Monsieur pitched his reply perfectly. He had used it several times before. "Does one ever speak of matters of the heart?" He raised her fingers to his lips, then pointed to the page. "Even little goats must play their Bach. Let us try the right hand of Variation 26 before your mama comes for you."

Everina looked at the music. Apart from Herr Bach, nothing today was as she had imagined it would be. Was it nicer or nastier? Better or worse? She never quite decided. In years to come, what she would most remember of this day was that while playing the right hand of Variation 26, she had longed to sit in the mud.

Monsieur would remember something different. He would remember wishing, not on that day but soon after, that Everina might die. She was not a girl given to suppressing her appetites, and being Monsieur's little goat meant, so she made very clear, that the pleasures of his hand and, on occasion, other parts of his person, were hers whenever required. How else might she learn all he could teach her? Within days, his wrists ached at the very thought of her. He cursed himself for not leaving her until last—or at least until he had conquered Harriet, who was putting up unexpected opposition.

After the first priming, he had stored up Miss Frogmorton for, he thought, an easy uncorking. A week after Everina's first tumble, he had set Harriet more practice of Variation 20, the crossing of hands offering an excellent opportunity to brush against her breasts. At every brush, she flushed and her mouth opened. But then, despite the pulse he saw beating in her neck, she snapped her mouth shut and crossed her hands with such speed and determination that she might have injured him had he not ducked. He was at something of a loss. She preempted him. "I know what you're trying to do, Monsieur," she said, "and I'm not shocked. You're a piano teacher. I'm an heiress. You're a man. I'm a girl. This kind of business goes on. But even if I hadn't decided to be Mrs. Thomas Buller, we couldn't do what I believe you're suggesting. You see, I can't pretend not to know that Georgiana is in love with you. It would feel disloyal."

"No, no, you are mistaken, mademoiselle," he said. "Mademoiselle Georgiana likes me, but I am not of the class that excites the love of young ladies like her."

"That's as may be," said Harriet, resuming her triplets. "I really think she is, though. I know she is. She told me the other day."

Monsieur took down the music and wrote on it unnecessary instructions. "Continue," he said.

"With the music," said Harriet firmly. "I shall continue with the music."

"With the music," said Monsieur. Damnation.

He now viewed Georgiana with some trepidation. Mild infatuation was all very well. Love was no part of his plan. But it was part of hers, as he soon discovered. Boosted by mastery of variations she thought beyond her, by Harriet's down-to-earth advice, and by Monsieur's artful and solicitous care, Georgiana took matters into her own hands. In the afterwash of Variation 10's fughetta, open-eyed and full of trusting hope, she shyly declared her love to Monsieur and, with another of those beatific smiles, clearly expected him to respond in kind. Mon-

sieur's heart thumped, but not with love. It was true that Geor⸗
giana touched him, moved him, and that he cared for her—but
if this was love, it was the love a man feels for a kitten. She
must not think of loving him with real love. Real love brought
snares. When Georgiana raised her face to him, he shook his
head and scowled. This had no effect. She understood head
shaking and scowling as the despair of a man who imagined
their love impossible. "Oh, Monsieur," she said. "Don't be con⸗
cerned. Anything is possible between us."

He saw his mistake and spoke very seriously. "Mademoi⸗
selle, dear mademoiselle, I am flattered, very flattered indeed,
but love is not yours to give nor mine to take."

Georgiana was undeterred. "If my love's not mine, then
whose is it?"

"Your future husband's."

"Yes, Monsieur," said Georgiana, staring deep into his
eyes with unmistakable meaning.

"Ah, mademoiselle." Monsieur's voice was far calmer than
his nerves. "I mean that your love belongs to the man your
papa will approve as the best person to care for you."

"How kind you are!" she exclaimed.

"Kind?"

"Yes, to try and be good to my papa. But how can he judge
who's best to care for me since he doesn't care for me himself?
You care for me, and I care for you."

"You must care for your papa. You must obey him."

She was sweetly candid. "Oh, I do care for him. I think
he'll be pleased."

"Your mama will be horrified."

"You're wrong, Monsieur," Georgiana said without any hes⸗
itation. "If Mama ever spoke, I think she'd say she wants me to

be happy, as she perhaps has never been happy, and I've been so much happier these past months. Everybody's noticed—the other girls, I mean. Harriet asked me about it directly, and I was very glad to answer."

"Mademoiselle Georgiana," Monsieur said much more firmly. He did not want a return to her previous fearful state but he could not allow this to continue. "We shall forget this conversation has taken place. We will continue our work. The fughetta again, please. Left hand only."

"Monsieur," Georgiana said, taking his hands instead. Why, Monsieur scolded himself, had he not removed them out of reach? "I'm not offering only my love and I don't need marriage. I want you to have everything I can give because you have given me everything."

Her eyes were beautifully clear when not filled with tears, and there were no tears today. They glowed at him, hazy and green, not gray as he had first thought, and boasting narrow, flinty rims that could not be new, though he thought they were. More noteworthy even than their color was their expression: open, trusting, and offering, just as she said and without flirtation, the whole of herself. Alathea offering just as much—indeed, offering more—never looked like this. Though Alathea must once have been as innocent as Georgiana, he never would have thought her dovelike. And really, Monsieur was not a bird man, not when it came to love, and if ever a girl was a dove it was Georgiana. He coughed so that he could, without offense, reclaim his hands to cover his mouth. "Mademoiselle Georgiana. Little dove. I am honored. But you must keep all that kind of thing for the husband who will love you and whose home you will grace. Please understand. That husband will not be me; it could never be me. I am not a husband."

"And I don't need to be a wife!" She clasped her own hands together. "With you, Monsieur, I could be anything."

This was too much. His temper began to rise and this, exasperatingly, precipitated the rise of something else. Hell and damnation. Just when he did not want her, he wanted her. He knew he had to have her sometime. But not now. Not now.

"I thought, perhaps, I—I—" She was beginning to disintegrate.

Monsieur felt a brute. He made a final attempt. "What man would not want you? You are a pearl, mademoiselle, a pearl. But pearls must not be sullied by baser stones and I am such a stone. Please, mademoiselle, think of me as such. Let us go back to work. This passage. Variation 17. Sixths against thirds. Left hand, please. It is difficult. I think—yes—shall we try fourth instead of third finger here? It might be easier for the staccato."

She did not move. "You're in love with Harriet."

He was stung into quick denial. "No, mademoiselle, indeed I am not. Come. Variation 17 is waiting."

"But you would have taken her. She told me."

"She told you? When?"

"Last Saturday, when she asked me why I seemed so happy—before I told her I loved you."

"What did she say, exactly?"

"That you had touched her earring."

Monsieur shifted on his seat. "Oh, that. Earrings get in the way."

"You're being kind again," Georgiana said, tears smudging those flinty rims. "You can't help it. I know she's more perfect, more ... more ..."

"Little dove," said Monsieur, rather frantic, "please do not cry. You are perfect. Too perfect. You are like a daughter to me, not a lover. I am twice your age."

"You're twice Harriet's age!"

"Mademoiselle!"

"I thought when you touched my neck, my hair, I thought that meant..." She sat for a moment, fighting with herself. With an effort, she clipped her own wings. "I'm sorry, Monsieur. I've misunderstood. I've embarrassed you. I've embarrassed myself."

"You have embarrassed nobody," Monsieur said with some relief, "nobody at all."

There was a pause. Georgiana twisted her hands. "So you don't love Harriet?"

"No, mademoiselle."

"Or any of the others?"

"No," he said.

Georgiana wiped her eyes. She looked straight ahead. "I'll always love you, Monsieur, and I see that you can't love me. If I've spoiled everything, I apologize. I'm ready for work."

It was her tone that undid him. She was not self-piteous or manipulative, not whining or depressed: she was Georgiana. Perhaps he should have her now and put a smile back on her face for the weeks they had left. His hand found hers. At first, she thought he was correcting the angle of her wrist. When his hand remained, she murmured—tender, no triumph—turned, and drew him to herself. There was time to withdraw. He should withdraw. The danger was obvious. Yet they were kneeling behind the pianoforte stool, then lying, that dear little mole behind her ear, Georgiana drawing up her skirt, neat leather ankle boots, a golden sheen of hair beneath the stocking, the shocking whiteness between top of stocking and

frill of drawers. Rather unexpectedly, her garters were mis-
matching. She had not noticed. A child's mistake. Now he
could not help himself. She wanted him. He wanted her. He
made ready. He made her ready. He took her. Three thrusts,
one grunt, and it was over.

The experience was a disappointment. The blond flesh had
not been solid as Monsieur hoped. She was only foam after all.
The peculiar rush he got from being the first vanished in seconds. He had not even squeezed a breast. With a surgeon's
detachment, he wiped her clean of blood and hoped, with
alarmed and chilly hope, that he had been careful enough.
Closing her legs, he could not imagine his desire of only three
minutes before. When he murmured her name, "Sweet Georgiana, sweet, sweet Georgiana," fulfilling, as he imagined, a post-
tumbling womanly need, he might have been reciting a luncheon
menu. Still, he had done his duty for Cantabile. He never need
take her again.

Georgiana had anticipated exaltation. When all she got was
pain, she blamed herself. She had expected too much. She was
a fool. Careful to show no sign of her disappointment, she comforted herself that Monsieur's animal spasm was ecstasy enough
for both of them. She heard no alteration in tone as he muttered her name. For all his selfless denials, she felt certain that
Monsieur did love her. This was what a man's love was like. She
was a most fortunate girl. When righted onto the pianoforte
stool, without a word she began Variation 17 and her rendition
was ecstatic, her ornaments birdlike chirrups. At the end of the
hour, when she had taken her radiance down into the Brass carriage, Monsieur leaned against the drawing room door. What
an idiot he was. Idiot, idiot, idiot. He slammed the lid of the
pianoforte, shouted that he was taken ill, and returned to

Cantabile's, where he shut himself in his room for the rest of the day.

He emerged at dinner. Rested and away from Manchester Square, he convinced himself that the experience, being so underwhelming, would pale for Georgiana and that when they next met, if he made no mention of it, things would be as they ever were. He must believe this because this is how things must be. Annie poured him a third glass of wine. As she raised her arm, he caught a distinct and powerful scent of Alathea's musk. He was puzzled. The scent must have come from himself, although Georgiana did not smell of musk and he had not seen Alathea either this day or the day before. He felt Annie looking at him. He looked at her. A drip coursed down the neck of the wine bottle. She allowed it to roll over her fingers, then raised her hand and slid her fingers into her mouth. Monsieur winced. Horribly, he was reminded of Cantabile's oyster taunt. Equally horribly, he could not look away. Finger in mouth. A childish habit. It was still childish in Annie. Yet nothing of the child was here. He swallowed and swallowed and swallowed.

Annie removed her fingers, wiped both them and the wine bottle, and fetched the bread. Monsieur gazed anywhere but at Annie. She did not, could not, know Alathea. She certainly could not know her like that. Yet the fingers in the mouth. The unmistakable scent. He followed it around with his nose, like a hound.

Cantabile shuffled upstairs. "Give me wine, Annie." He pulled out a chair. "All done, Claude?"

Monsieur twitched. "Not quite done."

"How many?"

"Three," Monsieur answered. He would not say that Alathea had taken him.

"Only three?" Cantabile stopped tearing at the bread. "The year marches on."

"It takes half a minute, Vittorio. Less. What difference does it make if I take the last girl now or the day before the concert?"

"No difference," Cantabile said. "But don't dally; it doesn't become you."

Annie served the dinner and, as always, left the room. Monsieur hardly ate. He felt the scuff of Everina beneath his nails. Georgiana would not forget. Alathea was playing tricks. He was weary. He was an instrument as much played upon as playing. It was a novel experience. He could not recommend it.

ELEVEN

NNIE'S PLEASURE AT TEASING MONSIEUR was matched by the pleasure of her days. There was always music, and there had been three outings too, three sunny after-noons when she and Alathea, wearing matching veils, had walked together. It mattered little to Annie where they went or what they did. With Alathea beside her, she was happy to stroll around markets, to shiver outside Newgate as Alathea described how the stone arches on the dead man's walk got narrower and lower as he approached the drop—how did she know these things?—or to sit for an hour or two in the Salutation and Cat, up the street from the prison, listening to men she did not know using words she did not recognize to describe a world that could never be. Over this last, Alathea disagreed. "If a world is possible to describe, it must be possible to organize. What's so difficult? Everybody equal, everybody free, everybody owning everything in com-mon."

"If it's so easy, why isn't it done already?" Annie posed the question gently, more for the delight of conversation than for an answer.

Alathea had an answer anyway. "Men. It doesn't suit them."

"It's men who are suggesting it," Annie pointed out. They had left the Salutation and Cat. She stopped and uncrumpled her leaflet. "'Pantisocracy and Aspheterism,'" she quoted, "'will minimize greed amongst men. They are antidotes to the corruption of power and the problems of property.' It's written by a man."

"A poet," said Alathea, curling her lip and walking on. "Can't you tell? What woman would talk of pantisocracy and aspheterism when all they mean is equality and the abolition of property rights. Would you?"

Annie, catching up, had to agree that she would not. "Women could bring about such a world?" she said. "It could happen?"

Alathea nodded emphatically. "It will happen."

"Here?"

"In the New World," said Alathea. "Anything's possible there."

A chill in the sun. "You're going to join them," Annie said.

"I might."

Annie waited for an invitation. None came. Alathea talked easily of other things. Annie did not mention the New World again. When they arrived at Soho Square, Annie expected to go straight to the ballroom. Instead, Alathea led her past the waiting pianoforte, upstairs to her attic bedroom. Annie prepared for something awful: trunks filled and labeled; a traveling cloak laid out. What she got was her first full-on-the-mouth kiss. It was a huge affair of lips, tongues, spittle, suckings, blowings, leakings, nippings, subtle and unsubtle tilts, forces, pressings, and pressures. Taken by surprise, Annie's lip exploded in spasms over which she had no control. This frightened her. She did not know such sensations existed, the biggest sensation of all being that Annie of the harelip was being kissed, kissed, kissed as she had never, ever expected to be. She wanted to cleave to Alathea, to shout her love aloud. She did not say a word, for even as they struggled for breath, she read the warning in Alathea's eyes: together but apart; love but no attachment. This was why there had been no invitation. There would never be one. Were Annie to complain, the door of Soho Square would be closed to her.

On her way home that night, Annie purchased a pocket looking glass and that night burned two candles right down to the stumps as she scrutinized herself. Surely, surely the kiss had transformed her. Yet there was her lip, obscene as ever. Then she was seized by a dreadful thought: perhaps the transformation was the other way around. Perhaps her lip had rendered the kiss itself obscene. And there was another question. If Alathea had been afflicted with a harelip, could Annie have kissed her? The question nagged.

The kiss changed the pattern of the afternoons. They never went out again, and after they finished making music in the ballroom Alathea always took Annie up to her bedroom. There were never traveling cases. Annie's alarm about Alathea leaving for the New World subsided to an occasional gnawing worry.

From the dust and dirt in the upstairs passages, it was clear that no servant, let alone Crouch, had been up here for years. Annie relished the sense of complete privacy, yet Alathea always locked the door. Annie wondered whether this was because the girls undressed each other fully, as they never had downstairs. Perhaps Alathea's father, about whom Alathea never spoke and whom Annie had never seen, had been away and was expected home. Perhaps when he arrived, he might come up the stairs to find his daughter. As the weeks drew on, she began to look out for signs of Sawneyford and saw none that were new. Eventually, her curiosity got the better of her. "Does your father exist?" she asked. The girls were wrapped in negligees. Alathea was lighting the first fire of autumn.

"He does exist," Alathea said. She came to brush Annie's hair.

"There's nothing of him in the rooms we use."

Alathea swept Annie's hair up, silent for a while. "There's something of him in here," she said.

Annie glanced about. The room was a plain box, its sole decoration being Alathea's clothes strung on a rope between the window hook and a nail in the wall. On this rope hung dresses, some of which Alathea was altering. Undergarments were set about in piles, some on a chest, some on the floor. The bedstead was wooden and piled high with thick blankets retrieved from one of the house's grander bedrooms. A table with a ewer and jug stood against the same wall as the door and Alathea had brought up a dressing table, two chairs, and a nightstand from the same room as the blankets. The fireplace was set opposite the door. There were no pictures or ornaments, only Alathea's mirrors, a dozen or so, of all sizes, everywhere. It was a room of reflections from which Annie could never escape. This was the only thing about the room Annie disliked but she never complained. "I can't see anything," she said, turning back to the dressing table looking glass.

"There's me." Alathea let Annie's hair slip through her fingers.

Annie crinkled her eyes. Despite the kiss, she would not smile. "That's not quite what I meant."

Alathea strained Annie's hair again through her fingers. "I don't mean I'm my father's daughter." She stopped straining Annie's hair. "I'm his in another way."

The girls regarded each other's reflections. Annie frowned and turned to face Alathea. "No," she said. She turned back to the mirror. "No."

"Yes." Alathea put the brush down.

Annie focused on Alathea's reflected clothes so as not to see either Alathea or herself. She wished she could hide her face. She remained flat voiced. "Is that why you lock the door? To keep him out?"

"I don't keep him out," said Alathea.

"Are you frightened of him punishing you if you do?"

"Not at all," said Alathea. "I don't wish to keep him out. I lock the door because I lock the door."

"But—"

Alathea picked up the brush. "But what?"

Annie had to pinch her voice to stop it from disgracing her. "Don't you mind?"

"I don't think about it."

"I mind for you. It's wicked."

"It's given me my freedom," Alathea said.

"Your father does that and you call it freedom?"

"Why not? I could ask anything of him now, and it was my choice. What harm has it done me?"

"He's your father!"

Alathea seemed amused. "Fathers," she said. "They're just men like any other."

"But fathers are supposed to—"

"Supposed to what? Protect you? Provide for you? Love you? Mine does, in his way. Does yours?"

Annie jolted. "My father would never think of doing to me what your father does to you."

"Because he cares for you?"

"No," said Annie, her voice hard. "Because he would vomit."

"There then." Alathea began to brush Annie's hair. "It's your father who should be ashamed."

"Should your father have no shame at all?"

"Some might think so."

"And Monsieur?" Annie could not help herself. "What do you make of him?"

"Monsieur has been useful," said Alathea, her voice tighter. "I've tested out on him what I've learned from my father. I thought musicians might be different. Not so."

Annie tried to feel as Alathea spoke: passionless, matter-of-fact, detached. She could not. She was raw, not with revulsion but with sickening jealousy. "I don't like to think of you with any man," she said.

"Detachment, Annie, remember."

Jealousy swept detachment aside. "It can't please you, what your father does."

Alathea left off brushing and began to plait. "It neither pleases nor displeases me. What happens happens. Then it's over. I don't think of the act, only the use I can make of it."

Annie persisted. "I'm thinking of the act and I hate it."

Alathea stopped plaiting. For one dreadful moment Annie

thought she was going to be ordered out of the room, out of the house. Perhaps she would have been had she been dressed, which would have made turning her out easy, or if her eyes had been craven, which Alathea would have despised, or, worse, pitying, which Alathea never would have tolerated. Instead, Annie's skin shone and her eyes were filled with venom. It was like having a tiger in the room. Alathea slowly began to plait again. Annie licked her lower lip and sought safety on more practical ground. "Don't you fear a child?"

An easing. The practical didn't bother Alathea. "No longer. At least I don't think so, and if a child did start, there's a widowhag. She's vile. It's a vile trade. If you can stand the"—a hesitation—"if you can stand it, she takes care of everything. She advertises quite respectably in the Salutation and Cat— that's the reason I went there first. Father found her. He pays. I never say anything. He leaves the money in my bonnet. I'm never short of money." Alathea was still plaiting. "You see..." She seemed uncertain whether to continue. Annie barely breathed. Don't let a clock chime. Don't let a dog bark.

"My mother died when I was very young," Alathea said. "I don't remember her." She raised her thumb. "This ring was her wedding ring. It's why I always wear it." She touched the ring lightly with her index finger. "My father could have drowned me, or dumped me, but he kept me. Mrs. Frogmorton and the other mothers helped, I suppose, and my father and I stuck together, except for once." She picked up a ribbon. "I was about ten. We were staying at the Frogmortons', in the house they had before Manchester Square. I forget where it was. When I woke—I must have been in Harriet's bed as the house wasn't big—anyhow, when I woke I went to find him and he'd gone." She finished the plait. "There."

Annie didn't move. "Where was he?"

"Oh, abroad somewhere." Alathea began to make short plaits in her own hair. "I never asked Mrs. Frogmorton where he was. I never asked whether he was coming back. I never asked anything."

"But you must have been so distressed—more than distressed, much more—you must have been beside yourself! Without a mother, and then your father leaving without a word?"

Alathea moved away from Annie and sat on the bed, plaiting, unplaiting, replaiting. "When I saw his bag had gone, I ran downstairs without getting dressed. Mrs. Frogmorton was standing at the front door. She saw me running. She saw my face. She saw it and she waited. The power of that wait. I could see the satisfaction of it in her eyes. She had something I wanted and she was going to make me beg for it, so as she waited, I turned away, walked back up the stairs, dressed, and carried on. She's waiting still." Alathea secured her plait. "The first day was the hardest. I kept listening for the door. But Mrs. Frogmorton made it easy for me because every time I saw her, that eyebrow of hers jibed 'Aren't you going to ask me now?' and I never would. When my father returned, I didn't ask where he'd been. I didn't need to know because I knew something much more useful. I knew the power of not asking. Some people go their whole lives not knowing that."

"Did he ever leave you again?"

"No." Alathea sat on her hands. "There was a time at Blackfriars when a woman—an actress—thought to marry him. It was in her lodgings that I first climbed into his bed. There'd be no point in his marrying anybody if I could provide what he needed. He's never left me since. He depends on me."

"But you don't like dependence."

Alathea's dark eyes were reflected everywhere. "I don't like it with equal people." She got up and went to the window, her back to Annie. "My father and I aren't equal. I'm indispensable to him but he's not indispensable to me. I survived his leaving me without a word, letter, or message. He couldn't survive if I left him, even if I told him where I was going. I know it. I've made it so."

"What will happen when you marry?"

"I may choose not to, but if I do marry I'll feel quite sorry for him. It will torment him."

"It will torment me!" Annie cried inside, but she said only "I suppose that will be his punishment."

"Yes," said Alathea, turning. "Punishment's interesting, don't you think?"

Annie suppressed a quiver, half fear and half something else. Alathea left the window, picked up the hairbrush, and traced Annie's features with the handle. "Those condemned men at Newgate. That death walk is far worse than the execution."

"Don't criminals deserve what they get?" Annie said.

"And your father?" Alathea kept up her tracing with the hairbrush. "Isn't he a criminal of sorts? Doesn't he deserve the same?" She ran the hairbrush downward from Annie's chin. "And Monsieur?"

Annie took the brush and ran the bone handle from the point of Alathea's chin, down her neck, downward, downward, downward over the contours loosely covered in silk, then suddenly inward, taking a roll of silk with it. Alathea bit her lip. Her eyes were purple diamonds. The mirrors reflected all. Annie could see a dozen Annies, a dozen Alatheas, a dozen hairbrushes. The hairbrush handle remained where it was. She controlled it. Alathea lay back, lips apart.

"I've punished my father already," Annie said. "He never wanted to sell the pianoforte you play at Manchester Square. I sold it. It was to punish me for that that my father sent Monsieur to you. When I first came, you guessed I cared for Monsieur. You were right."

"And you came here to punish me for having him."

Annie twisted the hairbrush handle.

"Ah!" Alathea's face melted. "I'm punished."

The mirrors played tricks with Annie's lip, sometimes turning it into an artist's blot, other times making it vanish altogether so that she was a normal girl, with hair and a nose and a slightly oddly shaped mouth. She moved her head. New angles. Her lip was now a bruise. Now it was—God help her—a flat line. How had she ever dreaded the mirrors? They painted things that weren't with what there was. She watched herself. She watched Alathea. "Do you want Monsieur now?" She tapped the hairbrush handle lightly with her index finger. "Or now?" She heard Alathea hiss. "Or now?" Annie circled the handle like a conductor's baton. "Tell me." Alathea arched and Annie lost her reflection as the girls clashed together, Alathea grasping Annie's plait and slowly pulling Annie's head back. Annie remained in charge of the brush handle. She would not give it up.

"Who needs Monsieur?" Alathea said.

"Not me," Annie answered. She twisted the handle and opened her mouth.

"Not *us*," said Alathea, russet flushing up her neck and into her cheeks. She rolled Annie over. She still held her by the hair, their noses almost touching. "Poor Annie," she gently mocked. "Monsieur was to teach us girls to get husbands and you weren't to have one."

Annie's mouth quivered. "Poor me. And you poor girls, with Monsieur's lessons not stopping at music."

"I rather think I taught him." Alathea flicked her tongue at Annie's chin.

"And he taught the others," said Annie, catching Alathea's tongue with her lips.

After a muddle of tongues, Alathea said, "What do you mean?"

"Monsieur's taught the others some of what you taught him." Annie rolled them both right over again. "That was his job. He was to pick all the cherries before your husbands got a chance. My punishment, for selling the pianoforte, is that Monsieur should take all you beauties and not take me. Your punishment for having the pianoforte is to be ruined by Monsieur."

Alathea let go of Annie's hair and laughed. "Well, I never! Harriet, Marianne, Everina, and Georgiana! The old goat! And to think I never guessed."

"It gives my father a thrill."

"Yes, I see that." Alathea was still laughing. "Why didn't you tell me before?" Annie removed the brush. Alathea rolled back. "What a triumph for him!"

Annie thought of her father's past triumphs. Her throat silted up. "Why should he triumph."

"Because it's a perfect plan."

"That's not what I mean. I mean why *should* he triumph."

Alathea smoothed her legs and untangled her robe. "You want the girls to collect husbands and live happily ever after?"

"I don't want my father to win. I want——" Annie sat up. "I want to show him he counts for nothing."

Alathea finished the untangling. "You do want to punish him. And the girls?"

"I don't care about the girls."

"And Monsieur?"

"I'd like him to feel something..."

Alathea searched Annie's face. "You'd like him to feel trumped," she said.

"Trumped?"

"Outmaneuvered." Alathea sprang up and stood by the window. Annie remained on the bed and pulled her legs under her chin.

"Your father is your business," said Alathea, "but Monsieur..." She gazed over the rooftops. "If, somehow, we could show that Monsieur is the puppet, not the puppet master."

Annie hugged her knees. "Could we do it in public," she murmured, "so that everybody could see?"

Alathea, walking about, hovered midtread. "The concert's public," she said. "Perhaps the music could tell a different story from the story Monsieur expects."

"Not the *Clavier Übung*." Annie found a piece of ribbon to secure her plait. "It's so precise and the audience will be stupid. Any story would have to be clear as speech."

"The pianoforte speaks a looser language than the harpsichord and will be on our side. Still, you're right. Making everything clear would be hard. We'd have to break a great many rules." She began to dress. "It could be done, though. Let's go downstairs."

Annie peeled herself off the bed with some reluctance.

Alathea was still talking, and Annie dressed more quickly as the idea took hold. By the time she pulled on her shift, she was nodding, experimenting in her mind, her fingers itching for the keyboard as, most of the day, they itched for Alathea. "The girls," she said as she tugged the strings of her chemise. "Would they agree to join in? Could they join in? And what would happen to them afterward?"

Alathea lowered the candle for Annie to find her shoes. "I'm sure I can persuade them to join in," she said, "and do you care what happens to them afterward?"

Annie tied her laces. "Don't you care?"

Alathea considered. "It will be good for them. Girls shouldn't be puppets, though I can't think of any other use for Everina and Marianne. But a little sedition might be the making of Georgiana. As for Harriet, she may even thank us."

The girls' names and the familiarity of Alathea's judgments were a small sting, a reminder that Alathea inhabited worlds closed to Annie. Annie wanted to be rid of those worlds. There should be only one world for her and Alathea. She would never say so. She hardly dared even feel it lest Alathea should guess.

Halfway down the stairs, Alathea stopped. She was gleaming in the dark. "I know what will happen to us, though. And you know too."

"I do?"

"We're going to the New World, you and I. We're going to make that world as we want it."

Annie's heart leapt. Not an invitation, an order!

Alathea was lit with excitement. She gripped Annie's arm. "We'll be free of everything! I can take money from my father, I have a box of diamonds and we can make a living through music."

Annie was swept away. She and Alathea at the dock. She and Alathea boarding a ship. She and Alathea in a cabin on the high seas, tossed toward a new shore. She and Alathea giving concerts. Annie and Alathea, bound together in a new life with music at its heart. Then a terrible thought. Her mother. How could she leave her? Detachment. That is what Alathea would say. But would Annie be detached enough for that? She knew what she hoped. She hated her hope but could not escape it. She hoped with all her heart that her mother would die before the day came for the ship to sail.

Alathea was already opening the ballroom door. Annie hurried after her. They sat very close on the pianoforte stool, Herr Bach's variations open in front of them, and for the next two hours they played, planned, discussed and argued, tried things out, rejected, accepted, marked up and crossed out. Love would be their engine, detachment their creed, and music their passport. When Annie got home, she went straight to her mother. She would tell her everything. Her mother was asleep. Annie wanted to wake her. She didn't. Later, Annie thought. Later will do.

TWELVE

*T*HE VIRGINIA AND BALTICK, NOON, THE
last day of October, the four fathers
seated again at the small table rather
than the long trestle, Mr. Spence's
weekly still wedged under the leg. Three
discussed their daughters' progress. Sawneyford, as usual, was
silent. The day was the hot finale of a late week of Indian
summer. The heat made little difference in the V & B, where
the coffee required a constant fire. Wood swelled, legs ached,
heads throbbed. Nowhere was comfortable. Everything was
sticky.

Dinner had been ordered at the long table but a squabble
over the wisdom or otherwise of French abolition of slavery
had blown up, two shipmasters declaring money would be
lost and three fur traders declaring money would be gained.
Boiling coffee had been thrown in an abolitionist's face and
there was general sneering at the fools more concerned with
the rights and wrongs of slavery than the threat to profits of

drawn-out war. Outside, the burned abolitionist was spraying his blistered face with water from the Threadneedle pump. Inside, uneaten pies leaked gravy onto the *Morning Herald* and a coffeeboy was trying to mop up the slop with a likeness of "the late Queen of France taken from life in the year 1789." Eventually she disintegrated and the boy used the tail of his shirt instead. The argument reflared. More coffee was thrown and the atmosphere was increasingly ill-tempered. Still, as Mr. W. remarked to Mrs. W., a good rumpus livened the place up.

The fathers had not ordered pies. Nor had they gotten involved in debate. Small glasses of port had replaced their coffee cups, and Brass and Frogmorton had drunk more than one glass already. In a fit of sunny generosity, Mrs. W. had provided a wax candle. The generosity had one good effect and one bad: the men could see one another; they could also see that their skin, despite the wash of blue sky outside, glowed without health, like London itself. They had pushed back their wigs. Only Gregory Brass still had a full head of hair and it was glued to his scalp like paint.

The fathers prickled gently, palms sweating, feet swimming in their boots, fingers leaving tacky pads on the table. The concert was a month and a half away. They spoke with no direct knowledge of either the music or the arrangements. Since setting this venture in motion, Frogmorton and Drigg confidently left everything to their wives. Brass knew Mrs. Frogmorton and Mrs. Drigg would steer his own wife and they could steer her to perdition for all he cared. Only Frogmorton had met Monsieur Belladroit. This caused no worry. Mrs. Frogmorton had assured her husband, and he had assured the others, that Monsieur was doing what they had employed him to do.

Drigg basked in Mrs. Frogmorton's approval. The image of Annie Cantabile had faded. These days he never allowed his companions to forget that it was he who suggested the whole idea of the pianoforte. The concert looming, the competitive spirit was hot as the room. "Mrs. Drigg tells me that when she gets home, our Marianne rushes straightaway to practice, exactly as the music master directs her," Drigg boasted, "although I don't believe there's any need. She plays naturally, you know." He irritated even more by repeating, as though from the Book of Revelation, what Everina said about the move-ments of the *Clavier Übung*.

Brass broke in, banging his fist. "For the love of Christ, Drigg! Do cease your babbling." Brass's mistress was cranky. Her acting skills had not gained her membership of a Drury Lane company and as a consequence, she would not be grac-ing the new stage at the Theatre Royal. Brass had laughed at her. She had slapped him and cried. He had slapped her back. She had screamed for the neighbors. There had been a scene. "What with this and those school prizes, your girls are turn-ing into clever misses. Marriage to hell. They'll be writing pamphlets next."

"Really, Gregory." Drigg looked to Frogmorton, who was barely listening.

For nearly five months Frogmorton had been carrying Monsieur's little secret. There were two reasons he had not shared it. First, it seemed faintly improper for Mrs. Frogmorton to have been told such a thing by a tradesman like Monsieur. He did not wish his friends to imagine his wife having such a conversation. The second reason he described to himself as "delicate," although where Mrs. Frogmorton was involved, it was hard to imagine delicacy.

The delicacy, nonetheless, was this. Mrs. Frogmorton had told him of Monsieur Belladroit's mishap as they were lighting candles for their nightstands. She had actually blushed and that, combined with the thought of a eunuch in the house, reminded the alderman of parts of himself that routine worries and his wife's bulk had reduced to an occasional itch. He itched that night. He had assessed the itch. It was enough to need satisfaction so he abandoned the bed in his dressing chamber and, for the first time in several years, climbed under the marital canopy without an appointment. His intrusion was remarked on but not resisted. A eunuch, it seemed, was not only a male aphrodisiac. Heavy flesh met heavy flesh. He remembered his way. She remembered hers. Directly afterward, the alderman removed back to his own bed, where he slept with astonished soundness. Dressing, he wondered what his reception at the breakfast table would be. It was more than pleasing. Mrs. Frogmorton not only poured her husband's coffee with her own hand, she sent Frilly to the kitchen instead of feeding him at the table, a habit she knew her husband disliked. An hour and a half later, on the stairs to his office, Frogmorton passed a spittoon boy he had recruited from the V & B. The boy winked at the roses in his employer's cheeks. The wink was insolent. Mr. Frogmorton growled but his pleasure increased.

He did not push his luck. He took to visiting Mrs. Frogmorton twice a week. She did not pour his coffee again; however, she evinced no revulsion he could sense. As a result, Frogmorton harbored a certain gratitude toward Monsieur Belladroit and kept Monsieur's secret, though it weighed on him. Such a secret to share! Should he? Shouldn't he? When Drigg pondered aloud, for a second time, whether the girls' concert gowns should be splendid, to show off their wealth, or simple, to show off their taste, Frogmorton only grunted.

With his chair drawn slightly back from the table, Sawney-ford was also preoccupied. The suspicions raised in the summer over a trespasser in Alathea's garden had not abated and he had come to suspect Monsieur. Suspicions bite harder than knowl-edge. Some days they bit hard indeed, yet the tails he set on Alathea reported no clandestine meetings. Alathea traversed, for the most part, only between Manchester Square and her home. A woman visitor was recorded, nothing else, and the pianoforte lessons were chaperoned. Other days, after he had visited Alathea, he scolded himself. Even if Mrs. Frogmorton nodded at her chaperoning duties, his daughter knew her worth. She would not lower herself with a music master. Then there were days when business took over and he had scarcely time to think of anything but bills and speculations. In the V & B, though, with the daughters the subject of the meeting, Sawney-ford's suspicions were biting harder. Alathea. Was she still his alone? He had given her everything: money, freedom, and above all, himself. He would never marry again and she was the rea-son. She must know he would never allow her to be usurped. The world might not understand fathers like him and daughters like her, but by some miracle she and he understood each other.

Frogmorton cracked under the weight of his secret. "I'll tell you something about Monsieur Belladroit that might sur-prise you," he said, interrupting the squabblesome seesaw devel-oping between Drigg and Brass. "The man's a gelding."

"What?" said Drigg.

"A gelding," Frogmorton repeated. His companions stared at him.

"Who?"

"Monsieur Belladroit," said Frogmorton impatiently. "The music master."

"You mean . . . ?" said Drigg, his eyes wide.

"I mean," said Frogmorton, "that he's castrated, de-balled, and a eunuch. What else could gelding mean?"

"Well, blow the bridges," whistled Brass. "Our French Monsieur not such a monsieur. How on earth do you know?"

Frogmorton blushed slightly. "Grace told me."

"Grace? Heavens, man! During what kind of conversation?"

"Oh, he thought she ought to know," Frogmorton said airily, not wishing to dwell. Brass raised a thicket of eyebrow. Frogmorton felt obliged to go on. "For goodness' sake, Brass, they're alone together sometimes, and I expect he was thinking of Grace's reputation." Brass snorted and grinned and Frogmorton found himself grinning too. "Those Frenchies don't just chop off heads with that National Razor."

All but Sawneyford sniggered. They shifted about, their imaginations in their breeches. Brass openly gave himself a stroke. "All present and correct," he said. The weight of the secret lifted, Frogmorton sent a coffeeboy for champagne. When it arrived and was poured, he raised a glass. "To the parts of a man that matter," he said. They laughed so loudly that the men at the long table, assuming some great financial success, raised glasses and coffee bowls too.

Sawneyford drank without tasting, his face blank with shock. What fools his companions were! What dolts! No man who had really been cut would volunteer such information about himself. His suspicions roared at him, scoffed at him, and jeered that they had tried to warn him. Monsieur Whatshisname was a fox, his suspicions had bellowed, the girls, including Alathea, unprotected chickens. Sawneyford gripped his glass, unable to suppress the image of the music master's papery skin scratching against skin that was his own—God help him, he had created it, nurtured it; he owned it. A husband for Alathea, he could barely accept. A music master's fumblings? An abomination. "How long?" he said, trying to keep his voice steady.

"How long have I known?" Frogmorton was caught a little on the hop. "I can't say for certain. A few months—"

"A few months?" Sawneyford could not disguise the outrage.

Frogmorton bristled. "What does it matter?" he said. "You know now." The others drowned Sawneyford's silence with jests.

Sawneyford sat perfectly still. From long habit, his face registered nothing but his rage grew. He cursed himself. He had known. He had *known*. He should have acted. And he knew his daughter. She was no victim. Did she think that having chosen her father as the keeper of her body—chosen, mind; he had never forced himself and he had accepted the guardianship in good faith—she could open herself up like the lock gates of a canal? They had had a bargain and she could hardly accuse him of not fulfilling it. He had forbidden her nothing, not even a husband. He was doing his duty. She needed reminding of hers.

He smacked down the glass, shoved back his chair, and made no apologies for leaving. Since he was adding nothing to the gaiety of the gathering, nobody tried to stop him. He ran down the stairs and slammed the street door behind him. There was not enough air, even outside. He leaned heavily on a beggar and was conscious of having his pocket picked. That made him stand upright. He sliced at the thief, retrieved a few coins, and pushed into a crowd bidding for sheep. He thought he could smell Alathea on everybody—and smell her on the sheep too. He struck out and once the street cleared strode blindly down it, down any street, picturing himself in Manchester Square, grasping Monsieur's scrawny neck and wrenching down his breeches to reveal his scrawny balls. "Here," he would shout to Mrs. Frogmorton and the others. "Here's your damned eunuch. Look! Look!" He pictured what he might do next to Monsieur. Fists curled like a boxer's, he strode and strode.

An hour or more on, he found himself out of the city, on a path flanked by uncultivated fields. Two cows wandered slowly, tended by a ragged grasshopper of a boy. A platoon of cavalry in half uniform was drilling half a mile away. Thin plumes of smoke rose from the squat chimneys of squatter cottages set higgledy-piggledy around a pen. The sun, hanging low, seemed balanced on the bare bones of a chestnut tree. He could hear birdsong and a stream. His forehead puckered. The blindness of anger cleared. He shielded his eyes from the sun, turning slowly, the City man, always the City man, jostling the injured father.

"Christ," the City man said aloud, "what a waste." The idleness of the land disgusted him. There was London, barely, what, three miles away, its mouth agape for food, and here was this, this—he wrinkled his lip—this desert. This land with its desultory cottages, tethered goats, and three pigs was an affront, that grasshopper boy chewing grass like his charges worse than an affront. The boy would be better off being press-ganged. In Sawneyford's view, the press-gang wasn't slavery, as he'd heard argued. Far from it. Sawneyford disapproved of slavery, since it deprived men of aspiration and any desire to work. The press-gang, on the other hand, if you could survive a couple of voyages, offered prospects, and what prospect was here, in these acres of nothingness, for a boy enslaved to cows? The shouts of the cavalry drifted over, the swearing, sweating men, the steam from flanks, the thump of hooves. War was escalating. Sawneyford screwed up his eyes. The City man took over completely.

War was tricky. It forced restrictions and opened doors, taking with one hand and giving with the other. It gave generously to fathers with no sons to lose. Damn his daughter, but thank God he had no son. He needed to make a list. Leather, cloth, buttons, swords, sabers, belts, muskets, gunpowder, bridles, saddles, bits, horseshoes—millions of horseshoes—timber and fodder. His eyes quartered the land. How much of it was there? To whom did it belong? How much ready cash had he? He'd need money to invest in plows, rakes, men, horses, barns, workers' dwellings. Cattle enclosures. A sawmill. A proper road into town. He saw the acres transformed, the carts rolling in. He saw the grasshopper boy up the rigging, learning a trade. He smelled the smell of production and as he breathed opportunity in, he assigned the elements in his list to business in the making and business yet to be made. He inspected the stream for the possibility of a navigable channel. Not until the City man was fully satisfied did he turn and retrace his steps.

Sawneyford's domestic problem did not fully revive until he was once again negotiating the outlying urban sprawl and then it revived more coolly. His contemplation of Alathea became more clinical, only a twitch in his cheek and a tightening of the lips betraying the occasional lurch of his stomach.

The creature, as he called Monsieur, would have realized that Alathea was no virgin. Might Alathea have confided in him? If so, how would the Frenchman use the confidence? Would he try some kind of blackmail? Alathea. Monsieur. This unconscionable concert. Himself. What to do. What to do. What to do. There was no heat in the sun now. Sawneyford shivered and dodged the mail coach. The road broadened. Wooden shacks gave way to sturdier timber. Timber gave way to stone. He padded toward the City: Hackney, Stepney, Whitechapel. The bells rang four, or was it five o'clock. He would confront Alathea. They would have it out. He should have done it earlier. Monsieur could be dealt with. All could be made well. By the time he padded down Leadenhall Street into Bishopsgate and down Threadneedle Street, his blood was calm. He did not pause at the V & B. He needed his daughter, he needed a land agent, and above all, he needed a piece of paper on which to write his list.

As soon as the champagne was finished, Brass left the V & B and made for his mistress's house. Scarcely bothering to close the door, he tumbled her with a straightforward boyish enthusiasm that surprised her, since Brass usually favored diversions. Afterward, he told her of Monsieur's physical infirmities, then tumbled her again. For a moment she forgot her Drury Lane disappointment and was happy. When Brass lay snoring, she rose, fetched a pair of embroidery scissors, and set to work. Brass snored on. When he woke, he pulled on his trousers, slapped her behind, and left. It was some hours before he urinated and noticed that the hair of his nether regions was now tufted into a heart. He guffawed. He'd get her onto that Drury Lane stage yet.

After draining a second bottle, which Frogmorton also paid

for, Drigg and he stumbled down the stairs and into the street. Frogmorton hailed a cab. Drigg waved him off and wandered slowly west. The sheep were gone, the crowd too. With a cloak pulled about you, walking was quite pleasant. It was even more pleasant when you thought of what you had and another man did not. Music! What a world it was.

Frogmorton headed straight home to inform his wife that Monsieur's affliction was now known to Brass, Drigg, and Sawneyford. Mrs. Frogmorton frowned. Although she had been tempted many times—sorely tempted after the insolent delivery of the progress report—she had not told the wives. What with one thing (her husband's visitations) and another (the embarrassment of anybody sniffing out her husband's visitations) and the fact that whenever she thought she might venture it a servant threatened interruption, it had never happened. Oh well. "I expect Agnes and Elizabeth know by now," she said. "I wonder, Archibald."

"What, Grace?"

"I wonder how the operation is done."

The alderman did not pursue this. Mrs. Frogmorton was wonderful in many ways, but she never knew where to draw the line.

THIRTEEN

A T TYBURN, SITTING AT THE CAPRICIOUS piano with which she had entertained Mr. Drigg, Annie toyed with the score of Maria Barthélemon's sonatas, signed, "To my very dear Vittorio, whose instrument has given me such pleasure." Annie did not need the score; the sonatas were lodged in her muscle memory and mind. She traced the dedication with her right index finger and contemplated murdering Mrs. Barthélemon's music. She had not been to Soho Square today or yesterday. She had been with her mother. Her father had refused the doctor entry, not because of the money but because on the previous visit, the doctor had tried to prepare them for the worst and her father feared the man would, if allowed to come again, pronounce there was no more hope.

It was impossible for Annie not to feel relief at the diagnosis, though she had hidden her relief from herself as well as from her mother. Her father, on the other hand, did not hide his futile and despairing rage. According to Cantabile, the doctor was both a Jewish poisoner and a murderous Jacobin; also, an incompetent, a corpse botherer, a grave defiler, a quack, and a misanthrope. When the poor man fled, Vittorio Cantabile declared his wife better. She would soon be up and about. The last twelve years of infirmity were a passing malady. Nobody had given the infirmity a name, therefore it did not exist. Then he turned on Annie. Had she nursed her mother better, Mrs. Cantabile would have been up years ago. It was Annie's fault. She was always out these days. Did she think he hadn't noticed? Had her deformity deprived her of a heart? What kind of a daughter was she? Her mother needed her day and night. Annie was forbidden to go out again.

Annie had seen the sonatas' dedication many times, but with her father's tirade ringing in her ears, his admiration for Maria Barthélemon riled as never before. She stopped tracing the letters and tore the score carefully into shreds. This shredding was not the murder. Murder came through Annie's playing of these sonatas, one by one, in her own particular way. It was only what her father and Mrs. Barthélemon deserved. The sonatas were not great revelations. Nevertheless, they had been carefully composed, so where the articulation was precise, Annie smudged. Tight runs were spread. She pedaled over phrase endings, slurred through pauses, expanded or reduced the rests, and overdid the syncopation. These murders delighted her. She stopped only to open the pianoforte's lid for a more public execution.

As she murdered, she sensed her father pausing, lever in one hand, wedge in another. She sensed him breathing. Her playing dripped whimsy. How her father hated whimsy. She rejoiced in every note she extended, every pause she milked, every bar line she strained. Her enjoyment was limited. She became conscious of something else: she was not an efficient music murderer. Whatever she did, the music failed to die of shame. Instead, Maria Barthélemon's sonatas began to speak a different language. Annie frowned. What language was it? With awful dismay she realized it was the language of revelation, and that she was not murdering Mrs. Barthélemon; Mrs. Barthélemon was exposing her. Disconcerted, she raised her hands, lowered them slowly, resumed her playing, and listened. She could hear it. She was telling the story of herself.

An unwanted hope surfaced. Might this music open her father's heart to her, just a crack? She scoffed at herself. Music would not dissolve his scorn, his derision, his implacable ill will. There could never be a change. Yet as she cleared the music of whimsy and allowed it to resume its proper shape, she found herself reminded that his life had not flowed easily. Blighted by a wife who was no wife and a daughter with a deformity, would she have acted differently? Alathea would condemn these thoughts as weakness. But Alathea was in Manchester Square, in the world that would never include Annie. This was Annie's world: her sick mother, Maria Barthélemon, her father, and herself.

Cantabile was as familiar with the Barthélemon music as was Annie. His skin tingled and his nerves grated as he heard Maria's sonata pulled, squeezed, elongated, and squashed. It was sacrilege. How dare Annie? Then, as Annie left the whimsy behind and played the music as it was meant to be played, he saw his wife a dimpled girl behind the counter in her father's pastry shop and in her wedding dress, her hair coming loose on that windy Milanese day when his own mother had danced and his father had sung. He recalled the hopes. He recalled their dashing. His throat knotted. Annie was manipulating him. It was an outrage.

The Allegro ended; a Largo began. Cantabile pressed his lever into his palm as the melody floated toward him, an echo of another's work—Maria had never been very original. Why his wife had been drawn to him, Vittorio had no idea. All he knew was that her smile had once warmed him and here was smileless Annie, daring to tease him with the memory. He knew what Annie wanted. He could hear it. She wanted love, and her need of it was a rope pulling at his insides. Why couldn't she stop? He dropped the lever onto his toe. The pain was acute and triggered some upsurge in his windpipe. His breathing grew loud; his throat was blocked, his mouth filled, his nostrils widened, his whole face swelled, and all accompanied by a heaving of his heart fit to burst his frame. He knew what was happening. He was going to weep. He, Vittorio Cantabile, who only wept for his pianofortes, was going to weep for himself, for his wife, and for his daughter. Well, he would not weep. He staggered to his desk and clung to his stool. He would never weep for himself. He would never weep for his wife and he would never weep for the daughter who sold his pianoforte. He unpeeled his hand, stumbled to pick up his lever, and hurried into the back workshop. "You're a wicked creature," he said. "That's not how music is. That's not what it's for."

Annie carried on playing. "What do you mean, Father? What's music not for?"

"Not for this!" he gargled, hitting his own face to bat the tears away.

Annie stopped playing. Hope had not quite vanished. "Music can be for anything. We who know music know that."

"You know nothing," he roared. "You're no musician. Not musician, not daughter, not wife, not anything." Annie began to play again, this time something of her own. "Stop that!" shrieked Cantabile.

"Why?" Annie raised her voice. "Herr Mozart wrote things like this. He knew what music was, and what it was for."

Cantabile crashed the main lid over the strings. "How dare you speak of Herr Mozart. He would have spat at your playing today."

Annie played more loudly. "He would have spat at your Maria Barthélemon. He would never have spat at me."

"Enough!" Her father raised the tuning lever. Annie did not blench. Hope of any paternal warmth or even a glimmer of understanding was ridiculous. She felt completely detached. Whatever Cantabile did to her, it would not hurt. He had not the power anymore. Cantabile dropped the lever and made for the keyboard lid. Her fingers would pay, those menacing, wheedling, treacherous fingers. Annie played on. His breath came in rasps. There were no tears now. He reached for the lid. She never stopped playing. He fumbled and looked down. The lid was not there. Annie had removed it. It was lying on the floor amid the sonata scraps. Cantabile roared again and crouched, scrabbling to get his lever back. Annie spread a chord. Cantabile found the lever and raised it again, his thin arm quaking.

"Do you know, Father," Annie said, as her father tensed to make the blow.

"Do I know what?" His voice was high as fever; there was thunder in his ears.

"Do you know that I am happy?" she said, and left him, lever still above his head, with nobody to strike.

FOURTEEN

AWNEYFORD GOT HOME WELL AFTER EIGHT o'clock and let himself in. He had had no dinner and did not want any. Crouch gave no proper response to his inquiry about visitors. Sawneyford picked up the lamp. He had prepared a speech. Alathea was not in the card room so he climbed the stairs. No light in the ballroom so he climbed again. Her door was closed but not locked. He went in without knocking. She was sitting by the window, an amber smudge in a loose green gown, reading, her book slightly tilted. The place was awash with candles. Sawneyford hesitated. He had never before seen this room in complete light. He had no idea it was filled with mirrors. They caught him every which way, like set builders testing different aspects for a bedroom scene. Musk, strong as beef gravy in a cooking pot, rose from the bed's rumpled linens. Sawneyford swallowed. Crouch was a liar. Monsieur had been here. That was clear.

"Downstairs," he rapped, his reflection caught amid ribbons, silk scarves, and stockings. Alathea was reflected too, her toes peeping from the bottom of her gown. She was regarding him over the top of her book. The piece might have been labeled "A Man and His Mistress." Sawneyford stumbled out.

He collected himself, at least physically, in the card room, leaning on the mantelpiece. His legs were tired, his hands sticky, his palms rough with dust, and he wanted to wash. There was, however, no time. He wiped his hands on his breeches as Alathea glided in. Over her nightgown she had a brocade jacket, all the buttons secured, tight as a breastplate. Christ in heaven, Sawneyford thought. What on earth is she expecting? Faced with her, he found he could remember only random phrases of the speech he thought he had prepared. He should have written it down. Failing his speech, he waited, hoping she might ask about his day as she usually did if they met downstairs. Perhaps once she had spoken, his speech would return to him. She sat down demurely on the sofa. Tucking her feet underneath her, she raised her eyes to him as though she would answer any question in the world, as a good daughter, on an ordinary evening—fire lit, supper eaten—should. Sawneyford knew at once that if the silence was to be broken, he would have to break it. His nerves jangled. How had he let City business intervene? This was far more important. If he was not careful, he could crack their whole world in two. He rubbed his hands on his coat and reconsidered. He should not speak. It was too dangerous. He should send her back upstairs and they should just carry on. He would have to learn to share her soon enough. He was a fool to work himself up over a music master. Yet he could not bear it. He clasped his hands. "Alathea."

"Father?"

"Alathea, I need"—now he had spoken her name, he knew what he needed: he needed to revive his earlier anger. A revival of that red-throated blindness would see him through. Yet no. Anger would confuse. Think, Sawney, think. What did he know? What did he want? He clenched his teeth. It's just business. Yes, business. Treat it as business. Identify the problem. Identify the outcome. Identify the risk. Identify the plan of action. A few phrases of his speech floated past. He opened his mouth. "Frogmorton tells me the music master's a eunuch," he said before he could stop himself. "I don't believe him." This was not a part of his speech. He could not take it back.

"He's not a eunuch."

Sawneyford heard himself breathe. Steady, steady. "How can you know that?"

"Same way as I know you're not a eunuch."

Her candor almost knocked him over. He abandoned any attempt to formulate a plan of action. Speech came now but he could barely open his lips. "Alathea. If you're that man's whore, well and good. But just you remember. What happens in this house remains in this house. If you ever speak of it, I'll deny it and throw you into the gutter." He was appalled at his words. Where had they come from? They were nothing like what he meant to say. He did not want to beg forgiveness—what for? He could not speak of love. He could, though, have spoken about the duty a daughter owes to a father. Yet here she was, with her suit of armor, and now her face was armor-plated too. Too late, he knew what he really wanted. How simple it was. He wanted her to acknowledge that she was his, just as he was hers. He desired that more than anything and he had botched it.

Alathea twisted her thumb ring. "It's not long since we were out of the gutter so it'll not be far to fall," she remarked.

Her tone was so normal it helped him. This was business. Business could be rethought and plans of action rearranged. The botched could be unbotched. "A music master!"

"He doesn't have your diamonds, it's true," she said, twisting and twisting her mother's wedding ring. "He plays well, though—at the pianoforte too."

Sawneyford grimaced. She sat, twisting and watching. She seemed amused.

"Don't you have any pride?" he said, slumping into his usual chair.

"I suppose I don't," she said. "Pride's not useful, you see, not like power."

"You have no power. I own you entirely."

"No you don't. It's not your fault. I'm not an ownable kind of daughter." She never raised her voice. They might have been speaking about the weather.

He had to ask her. "Do you speak of . . ." He could not go on.

"Do I speak of you to him? Do I speak of what we do?" She stopped. He knew why. She was going to force him explicitly to acknowledge what had never been openly acknowledged before. He nodded. He felt too tired to do anything else.

"You're not a subject he's raised," she said.

His heart fluttered. "Have you spoken of me to anybody?" She glanced from beneath her lashes. "I speak of you often."

"To God?" Christ Almighty! What was he saying?

Alathea stopped twisting for a second. "To God? Of course not to God. There isn't a God. You know that perfectly well.

You must, or you wouldn't do what you do. Even I can't be worth eternal damnation."

Ah, that tongue. Proficient in all its purposes. "You're the devil, Alathea! Who do you speak to?"

She resumed her twisting. He wanted to grind that ring into dust.

"I have another lover," she said. "I speak to her."

"Her?" That brought him up short.

"Yes. Her."

Her? Her? What was she saying? "Are you talking about Monsieur—we both know he's not been—"

"Why should I speak about Monsieur? I have another lover. She is a woman."

Sawneyford paled. He wondered whether he was losing his mind. A girl. *A girl!* She must be one of the others' daughters. He could not guess which one. He had never bothered to look at them.

Alathea stopped twisting for a second. "She has a father too, you know. She's not close to him in the way that we're close, although she may confide, I suppose. That's what daughters do, I think. Indeed, that's what we do, isn't it? The deepest kind of confiding?" Her tone was pleasant and her demeanor cool, but her eyes were like powder pans. She flashed them up and they lit a charge in his. Overwrought and overcome, mad with weariness, with frustration, with fear, with love even, Sawneyford rushed at her, all control collapsing. "Alathea!"

She caught him, held him, soothed him, goaded him. "I do what I want, I am what I want, and I take what I want. You've taught me how." She tried to stand, to ease from under him and glide out of the room as she glided in. She was strong but he was stronger. They struggled. He floored her. She cried out.

She hammered at him with her fists. Sawneyford heard nothing but his own snarl. His fingers ripped at her nightgown. Damn that breastplate. Off with it. Off. He had diamonds but there would be no scattering tonight. She thought she could play him like she played that damned pianoforte? He would show her that he had her absolutely. He pulled and he pushed. She was spread-eagled. If there were any boundaries left to breach, there were none now.

IMMEDIATELY AFTER her father had left, Alathea got up, adjusted her clothes, and picked up a candle. She walked slowly, clenching her legs together. She stopped to look at the portrait of herself. The child in the picture stared out, almost smiling. Had that ever been her? She put her candle down, took the picture off the wall, threw it into the fire, and watched it burn, then made her way to the stairs and felt for the banister. She leaned on it. She did not feel sorry for herself; she did not feel anything. She decided something, though. Her father would never have her again. Her choice had been everything in the matter. He had removed the choice; she would remove herself.

A week passed. She did not tell Annie what had happened. The act itself could have been admitted—Alathea could have spun that any way she liked. Inadmissible was Alathea's urgent longing to be consoled. Consolation was the thin end of a crumbling detachment. It rendered the impermeable permeable. Yet her hunger to be reassured, to be held, and to be comforted would not subside. She ached with this hunger, and it was at its most potent when she and Annie were making music.

Alathea had never seen music as the enemy: it became the enemy. When she played, the intensity of her longing shocked her. And more shocking than the longing was the need. More shocking still, it was precisely the kind of need Alathea despised.

Two weeks passed. She and Annie were working on their variations of Herr Bach's variations—the variations with which the other girls would, if Alathea could persuade them, astound the concert audience. Today they were studying the cavern, ous sonorities of Variation 25. Annie was frowning, brown head bent to study, fingers of the right hand absentmindedly testing the keys, left hand forefinger tapping the paper. She was humming. The circle of absorption, so self-contained, so focused, melted something in Alathea. She felt her core warm and soften and the next thing she knew, jabbing its way into the warmth, was that need, and the need was ordering, beg, ging, and compelling her to wriggle her way into Annie's core and seal it up with both the girls inside. Alathea could not be without Annie. Annie was mother, father, sister, lover. Her father's physical assault was nothing. His real crime was to have fatally undermined her.

Annie continued to work. The *Clavier Übung* was a series of small seas and she was a diver mining with fierce intensity. She counted. She calculated. Occasionally, she made a silent suggestion. Surely, a quicker resolution. No, no, said Herr Bach to Annie. You have not understood. Mine deeper. Count again. Work it out. Annie counted and worked it out. Yes. If we lose a finger here, we can use it here. But how to make it smooth? Both hands flitted over the keys, crossing, testing. Herr Bach held up his own hand—a strong hand, capable of good business. Even if you are using my music for your own purpose, you must observe the rests, he said. Observe them to the end. Silence is a note. Annie worked on, her fingers under, standing; her muscles taxed; her intelligence grasping the destination, faltering only on the journey. Every sequence, every cadence, every modulation, every nuance was scrutinized, dissected, executed again and again. Everything must fit together.

Alathea, holed beneath the water, joined Annie on the piano stool. Annie moved along. Usually, when they touched at the keyboard it was entirely professional, but now Alathea pressed against her, her whole length shaking. Annie felt the shaking, its strength betraying Alathea's weakness, though Annie had no idea what had brought this weakness about. For a moment she allowed the pressure. For another moment she returned it. This was what she had longed for. Alathea was not detached at all. She needed a prop and Annie was that prop, offering everything again, though Alathea had everything already. But an inner voice whispered "Beware." Alathea was changeable. Before Annie's arms had opened, she might be withdrawing, detaching; then Annie would be left exposed. And there was something else. Annie could still see her father's hand raised to strike her. Her detachment had beaten him, left him standing with the lever raised, helpless as a baby. She understood detachment's power now and she understood more clearly than ever before that she would be a fool to give up such power. Neither she nor Alathea were fools. She moved away. "The gigue," she said. "Variation 7. I'll play, you dance." She gave Alathea a small push.

Alathea got off the stool. Not knowing what else to do, she danced.

FIFTEEN

HE GIRLS WERE SURPRISED TO RECEIVE an invitation from Marianne to come to Stratton Street. It was Sunday—the second Sunday in November—there were no pianoforte lessons. The weather had deteriorated and the day was miserable. The Frogmorton carriage called for Georgiana, and she and Harriet arrived together. Georgiana was cheerful—like a real friend, thought Harriet with pleasure.

Alathea arrived on foot, the bottom of her skirt clodded with mud. She had debated, right to the door, whether she would go. She could tell Annie had not wanted her to. They had agreed, though, that Alathea might discover how far Monsieur had got in his seductions, and introduce the idea of turning the tables. If the girls liked the idea, they would have to get practicing. Nevertheless, Alathea wished the invitation had not come. She did not feel up to it. Worse, she no longer quite trusted herself. She might give away her weakness. She walked fast to try to drum up some energy and was at the front door more quickly than anticipated. "Goodness me, you never walked!" admonished Marianne as Alathea dragged dirt over checkered marble. Marianne was bristling. She had hardly been able to wait for today. She had something very important to say.

The previous Wednesday, after dressmakers' fittings (all conducted separately, even Marianne's and Everina's, since sisters as well as mothers wished to surprise, or possibly outdo, each other on the concert night), she and Everina had been practicing Variation 8, which they were to share. Everina could not keep up with Marianne. Marianne refused to slow down. They never ended up together. Frustrated by the music and fed up with being queened over, Everina had blurted out that she didn't care about the music: she was doing other things with Monsieur.

"What sort of other things?" Marianne immediately asked.

"Things that are usually very, well, very nice," Everina said. She could not think of the best word. She tried again. "*Lover-like*. Special things, just for us." She wanted Marianne to feel left out.

Marianne's long jaw dropped. "Are you saying he treats you like a wife?"

"Oh no!" said Everina. "Not like a *wife*. Like a lover."

Marianne closed her jaw. "That's disgusting."

"Not at all. It's to help with my marriage."

"Is that what he's told you?"

"It's true."

"For goodness' sake! Have you told Mama?"

Everina stopped crowing. "Of course not, Marianne, and you mustn't say anything either." She backtracked slightly.

"The thing is, I'm not absolutely sure what he does. It's certainly not disgusting. In any case, please don't tell Mama."

Marianne demanded details. Everina refused. Marianne insisted. She almost begged, and in the end, Everina, unable to resist, embroidered and fantasized through a panoply of euphemisms. Marianne was a perfect audience. By the time Everina had finished, Marianne was speechless and Everina for once felt superior.

At nine o'clock on Thursday morning, Marianne accosted Monsieur. Why was she being done out of these special things, these loverlike delights, these throes of ecstasy, these fields of bliss? Was she not as pretty as Everina? She certainly had better teeth. It was too bad, and unless he showed her these things straightaway she would tell their mother and father.

Monsieur expressed shock. What had Mademoiselle Everina been saying? What could she mean? He became coy. Had mademoiselle not heard of his, his er, his affliction? She looked blank. He tried to explain. She laughed. What nonsense. Monsieur regarded her. He swallowed. Well, now was a good a time as any. "Mademoiselle," he said. "Can I be frank with you?"

"Frank as you please."

He picked his words. "You wish me to . . ."

She had the grace to blush slightly. "I only want what Everina had—is having."

"You wish that from me?"

"Look, Monsieur Belladroit. I know what's to be done when I marry. Mama has told me about the making of babies. But Everina says what you do is different. She says it's not about making a child. She says it's French."

"The French are your enemies."

"Not in everything," said Marianne. "We drink French wine. Harriet has some French shoes. And you're not our enemy or you wouldn't be here."

"Mademoiselle—"

"I know I'm to marry an Englishman. I just want to feel this French feeling first and I don't see why I shouldn't have what Everina's having. After all, I am the elder." She stood, a lumpy shadow among the lumpy furnishings, hands on lumpy hips. "I'm waiting, Monsieur."

Monsieur sighed. Never again would he agree to seduce a gaggle of girls. Marianne had nothing, not even Everina's earthy humor. He did not want to take her now, with weeks still to go, in case, like Everina, she demanded repeat performances. He had planned to do her on the Thursday before the concert, once only. But here she was, immovable. Nothing for it. He got up, faced her to the wall to avoid her breath, planted each of her palms against the green flock, and raised her skirt. "Brace yourself," he said. He undid himself. His fingers performed a perfunctory exploration. There? Or there? There. Serve her right. A maneuver. A jerk. Another. Over.

It was not as her mother had described, it was not as Everina had described, and it was certainly not as she had expected. She gave a shriek and turned around, her jaw clenched. "That was horrible."

"I'm sorry. That's how it is."

"Are you sure?"

"Quite sure. Maybe marriage will not suit you, mademoiselle, for I am sure your husband, particularly if he is a wise man, will do exactly the same as I."

She began to cry. Everina must be deranged to enjoy such

a thing. She could not resume her lesson as she could not sit down. She hobbled down the stairs. Once home again, she brooded. On Friday, she wrote to summon Harriet, Georgiana, and Alathea, and here they were.

Ordering a maid to clean the marble and fearful for the carpet, Marianne nevertheless hurried Alathea up the stairs and into the sitting room. The room had been turned into a wedding store. Two trousseaus of dresses, chemises, undergarments, nightgowns, jackets, gloves, hats, shawls, feathers, shoes, and stockings were laid out. On a table under the window, silk-threaded needles were ready to embroider whatever initials might be required—an abundance of scarlet, in case of coronets. Two empty chests had already been marked "Small Wedding Presents."

Everina, in maroon, had plumped herself on top of a traveling hatbox near the fire. Alathea, brushing the last of the mud from her plain black skirt, settled on a chair strung about with stockings. Marianne eyed Alathea's skirt anxiously and removed the new stockings. She rang the bell. Georgiana, sitting next to Harriet, surprised herself by observing, only half joking, that the laundry aspect improved the room.

As they waited for tea and fancies, Harriet remarked on the trousseaus, surmising that Marianne wanted to talk about what they would wear for the concert. The girls respected their mothers' secrecy, but their dresses, still in the early stages of construction, were a source of anxiety. What their mothers thought suitable and what the girls thought attractive might not coincide and the dressmaker would always side with the mother.

"I'm set on gold, though Mama says no," Harriet confided. "Mama thinks gold is too old but I think it suits me."

"I don't know," said Everina, envious of the bridal night-wear their mother had ordered for Marianne and determined hers would be a match. "Gold can be fetching." It would not hurt Everina if Harriet looked older than her years.

Marianne did not join in; nor, when the tray arrived, did she serve the tea. Instead, she motioned the servants away, stood before the fireplace, and prepared to scandalize. "I've asked you here to discuss Monsieur Belladroit's behavior," she said.

"What?" said Harriet.

Everina giggled. Marianne glowered. "It's not funny."

"Tea?" Alathea rose and busied herself. She would take charge of spirit stove and kettle. It would settle her.

"I didn't ask you to do that," said Marianne sharply.

"Cake?" Alathea said, pressing a plate on her.

"Can't you sit down?" Marianne barked.

"In a moment." Alathea made the tea and handed it around. She then handed around the cake, offering more to Marianne, who refused with a violent shake of her head. Finally, Alathea set her own cup and plate on a table.

"If you're quite finished acting as maidservant," Marianne said with angry irony, "I'll tell you that Monsieur Belladroit . . ." She wanted to gesticulate but her hands were full of cup, saucer, and plate.

"What of him?" asked Harriet.

Marianne dumped her crockery on the floor. She could not think of eating. "Monsieur Belladroit has been giving Everina more than pianoforte lessons."

Everina half choked. She, too, had thought Marianne wanted to talk about dresses. That's what Marianne had told her. Georgiana, whose decision to eat cake had been hard enough, froze, mouth open. Crumbling cake between index finger and thumb, Alathea watched.

Harriet felt Georgiana's shock. Georgiana was aware, of course, that Monsieur had propositioned Harriet, but Everina? Harriet was quite shocked herself. When Harriet turned Monsieur down, it was for Georgiana's sake. She did not realize all the girls were in his sights. He plummeted in her estimation.

Marianne moved away from the fire. "I see you all know what I mean."

Harriet made a vague gesture. "More than pianoforte lessons?" It was hard to think of anything proper to say.

"Don't pretend, Harriet." Marianne glared around. "And it's not only Everina, is it? I mean"—she breathed and flushed slightly, remembering Wednesday—"he's been at . . ."

Everina was still choking. Alathea got up and patted her on the back. "He's been at all of us. Is that what you're trying to say?"

"You too?" Marianne asked.

Alathea hardly moved her head. As with her father, it could have meant yes or no. She felt more herself as she took command. Monsieur had clearly had Marianne and Everina. Had he actually had Georgiana? Alathea calculated from the stunned expression on Georgiana's face that the answer was yes. Harriet? Harriet didn't move her legs. Her mouth didn't quirk. No. Harriet was so far untouched. Surprising. Alathea's estimation of Harriet went up.

Everina recovered herself. "I don't believe Monsieur's had anybody but me. He loves me. He said so."

At the word "love" Georgiana wilted. Harriet squeezed her hand. "Love? What are you talking about?" Marianne filled the room with her noisy complaint. "What Monsieur did wasn't anything to do with love. It wasn't even nice, and not remotely what you said, Everina. Nothing like fireworks, and you never told me you had to face the wall. If that's really what the French like, Harriet's mama's right to hate them."

"You traitor!" Everina was on her feet. "What I told you was private. How dare you! And . . . and"—she was choking again—"all I can say is that if he had you, you must have bribed or blackmailed him. He would never have betrayed me otherwise."

"Betrayed? You think he's in love with you? You must be stupider than I thought." Marianne planted her feet wide.

Everina squared up to her. "Did he say 'I love you' to you? Did he use those words?"

"What does it matter what he said. *I'm* saying he's had us all."

"Do stop shouting," begged Harriet.

Everina ignored her. She glared at Marianne. "Even if he has had us all, you said what he did to you was horrible, which means he doesn't love you. I enjoy myself every time, so that means he does love me." Entirely persuaded by her own argument, she sat back on the hatbox. "And if he doesn't love you, Marianne, you've cheapened yourself."

"Cheapened myself?" Marianne could hardly get the words out. "How cheap does this affair make you?"

"Please," begged Harriet again, but was interrupted by Georgiana, propelled by shock into unexpected life.

"Every time?" she said, her voice high. "You enjoy yourself every time, Everina? You mean you've done it often?"

Both Marianne and Everina turned toward her. "Every time

I have a lesson," said Everina with some triumph. Marianne snorted.

Georgiana clung to Harriet's hand. "Every lesson! Monsieur and Everina do it every lesson!"

"Really every lesson, Everina?" Harriet said, patting Georgiana's arm and, with a distinct shake of her head, encouraging Everina to revise her tally downward.

Everina refused. "Yes, every lesson."

"When did it start?"

"Oh, I don't remember exactly. Weeks ago."

Georgiana raised her head. "After the holiday?"

"Yes, after the holiday. September time, so you can see that Monsieur does love me, can't you, Georgiana?"

Harriet kept a firm hold of Georgiana's hand. "I think Marianne may be right that love doesn't have much to do with it," she said.

"Obviously not with Marianne," agreed Everina. "I mean, he can't love a person if he makes them face the wall. I never do that. He's never even suggested it."

"Perhaps that's because he wants to laugh at your teeth," cried Marianne, scarlet with fury.

"Don't be so cruel! Why do you always spoil things," Everina cried back. "He's using you for practice."

"That's outrageous!"

"Girls!" Alathea raised her hand. "Why are we squabbling?" She launched a comforting smile, first at the pale lake of sorrow that was Georgiana's face, then at all the others. "Don't you know that men love different girls in different ways?"

Harriet, grateful to Alathea, quickly nodded. "Yes," she said, wanting to stop Georgiana's happiness from evaporating completely. "Alathea's right. That's how love is. It comes in different forms. It's possible that Monsieur loves us all in different ways, and each way is just as strong as any other, although some ways of love will be stronger." She looked rather helplessly at Alathea while continuing to pat Georgiana's hand. "Isn't that how it is?" She herself doubted that this could be true. Nevertheless, it would be good for Georgiana to believe it.

"Well, as far as I'm concerned, Monsieur loves me in an exclusive way as well as a different way," piped up Everina, determined to lay a particular claim on the music master. "I'm the special one." She turned again to Marianne. "I can't think what it must feel like, to do it the wrong way around. I didn't know it was possible." She took more cake. "Come on, Marianne. Tell us. After all, we may marry Frenchmen whether our mamas like it or no and it's best to be prepared."

Marianne opened her mouth to snarl.

"Don't be like that," Everina said. "We want to know, and if you don't like talking about it, that's your fault. You asked everybody here. You started it."

Harriet staved off another row with a solicitous "Was it dreadful, Marianne? He shouldn't have hurt you, he really shouldn't."

"It was extraordinarily horrible, what Monsieur did." Marianne's snarl became a whine.

"You poor thing," said Harriet, her sympathy not entirely false. "Are you still suffering?"

"Not now, but at the time it was like sitting on a tree root." Marianne addressed herself exclusively to Harriet. "And then—"

"And then what?"

"There was a kind of fizziness."

"Fizziness!" Everina exploded. Marianne's eyes were dag-gers. "No," hooted Everina, "I'm not scoffing. That's it exactly, Marianne, exactly, except when it's done the other way there's no pain, or at least only to start with, and then after the pain there's a lot of fizziness." In her excitement, Everina spilled her tea into her saucer. "Fizziness." She wanted to be friends with Marianne, to make sure she said nothing to their mother. "That's excellent."

Harriet was concerned. "But don't you worry about conse-quences?" she asked. "I mean, I would worry if—if I'd—"

"Poor Harriet!" Everina interrupted. "I don't believe Mon-sieur has done anything with you."

Harriet shook her head.

"Oh dear," said Everina, delightedly winking at Marianne. It was rare that these two were one up on Harriet. It was at least some kind of a bond between them. "I wonder why not? What do you think, Marianne? Do you think Harriet's too bony? I think he likes to be comfortable, and for your infor-mation, Harriet, fizziness isn't the same as making a baby. At least Monsieur says not and it really can't be," she added a little uncertainly, "because Monsieur wouldn't want that. What he does with me can't ever have any, you know, consequences. It's not that kind of thing."

"Now I understand." Georgiana let go of Harriet's hand, her face lit with relief. "You see, I didn't feel this fizziness either, just like Marianne, but then with me Monsieur didn't do the fizzy stuff. He actually made love to me, which is obviously a little different, and if there are consequences, he'll look after me." Harriet tried to interrupt, but Georgi-ana's radiance silenced her. "No, Harriet, for once I know I'm right. The difference between Monsieur's love for the others and his love for me is that he knows you're all to be married to titled people whereas I"—she grew rather shy— "I'm just for him."

There was an incredulous pause. Everina decided to be blunt. "I don't think so, Georgiana."

Georgiana turned on Everina with some passion. "Monsieur needs somebody just for him. He's so lonely. He's got nobody."

"He has his mother," Harriet said a little tartly.

"His mother died when he was ten," Georgiana said, "and his father when he was born. And he had a love, but lost her too."

Harriet's forehead furrowed. "His father died the other day. He was executed as a Jacobin."

"No," insisted Georgiana. "His father's been dead for years."

"His father's seventy and Kapellmeister to emperors. That's what he told me," said Marianne. "He never said anything about his mother."

"He told me both his parents died when he was born," said Everina. Monsieur had told her the previous week, trying, with an elongated tale of woe, to save his wrist from her demands for endless "lovers' intimacies," as she called them.

Those still holding teacups put them down. "What did he tell you?" Harriet demanded of Alathea.

"Nothing," said Alathea, fingering her hair. "We don't speak much."

Everina took a deep breath and asked what they all wanted to know. "Did you get the fizziness too?" Alathea seemed hesitant. Everina leaned so far forward she almost fell off her hatbox. "Come on, Alathea. Tell us."

"I'll tell you something more interesting and useful," she said, lowering her voice, "if you want to listen."

"Of course we want to listen," cried Everina.

"Make sure nobody can overhear," said Alathea.

"Mama is out."

"Check for the servants."

Marianne went to the door, flung it open, then closed it and locked it. Alathea slid off the chair and sank down in front of the fire. "I'll tell you then," she began with no further delay, drawing the girls into a circle. "There are worlds out there, some of which we know and some of which we have to discover for ourselves. There's the world of men, the City world where our fathers do their business. Women don't go there. Why would we want to? It's a dull world of deals and ledgers and men rattling antlers at each other." Even Harriet smiled. Mr. Frogmorton with antlers!

Alathea held out her hands to the fire. "Then there's the women's world—the world of your mothers and the one for which we're destined. And then . . ." She paused.

"Oh, do go on!" urged Everina.

Alathea dropped her hands and licked her lips. "There's the world neither your mothers nor your fathers are going to tell you about. Perhaps they don't know much about it themselves. It's a world where men and women don't live only for business or domestic things. It's a world of pleasure given and pleasure taken. It's a private world, but it's the best world there is."

"When you say 'pleasure,' are you talking about the fizziness?" asked Everina.

"I am."

"But isn't the fizziness what a man gives to a woman?"

Alathea blinked. "Don't men want the fizziness too?"

"Of course, but don't they get it themselves?" Everina was genuinely puzzled. "What's their fizziness got to do with us?"

Alathea drew up her knees. "Why do you think men go to whores?"

The girls were taken aback. They had never thought about it.

"They don't want to," explained Alathea, "but what's the choice if their wedded wives just lie back, spread their legs, and screw up their faces? If there's no fizziness at home, they'll go out looking for it." She scrutinized the girls each in turn. "Don't you see how kind Monsieur is being?"

"Kind?" Marianne echoed. "*Kind?*"

"Yes, kind," said Alathea. "Our fathers want to marry us into good positions in society. That's commendable. Monsieur wants that and more. He's introduced us to the fizziness so that we can be happy and know how to make our husbands happy too."

"That's precisely what he told me," said Everina in triumph.

"But our parents want us to be happy," said Harriet, ignoring Everina.

"Of course," said Alathea, "but can you imagine your father talking to you about how to keep your husband from the whorehouse?"

Harriet blushed.

"Exactly," said Alathea.

"I only feel happy when I'm with Monsieur," whispered Georgiana. "I could never be happy with anybody else."

Harriet hugged her. "I'm sure you'll be happy."

"We'll all be happy," said Alathea, "but only if..." She paused.

"But only if what?" Everina's eyes were round. "Only if what, Alathea?"

"Only if we marry men who appreciate what Monsieur has taught us about the fizziness."

"I thought you said all husbands would appreciate it," said Marianne quickly.

"Not all," said Alathea mildly. "That's why we must make sure we marry those who will. If we make sure to do that, then we'll be happy forever."

"But how can we make sure? We won't see any future husbands until the concert," Everina said, "and we can hardly send out a letter telling them what we want them to know."

"And we're playing music at the concert, not making speeches, even if we could find the right words, which we couldn't," added Harriet.

They looked to Alathea for an answer and she was ready. "Music can be more than music," she said. "Herr Bach's variations can show off everything we've learned, including the fizziness."

"How?" said Marianne, disbelieving.

"If you like, I could teach you."

Marianne was scornful. "You may be an accomplished player, Alathea, but I don't believe you're much better than the rest of us, and Herr Bach doesn't seem very fizzy. Indeed, he's not fizzy at all."

"I've been practicing already, just to be sure," Alathea said smoothly, "and I've found Herr Bach to be perfectly fizzy. That's his genius. If we try, we can play him any way we want." She was shining brightly enough to shine away any misgivings. "Believe me, we can play Herr Bach so that any man worthy of us recognizes *all* our talents."

She sat back. The girls sat back too, their heads—even Everina's—full of doubts that, in turn, they spilled out and Alathea deftly mopped up and swept away. It still wasn't right, what Monsieur had done. Perhaps not strictly right, agreed Alathea, but he only wanted what was best for them. And what about their virginity? (This from Everina, on whose mind the question had been preying, since virginity was so prized in the books she read.) Virginity, Alathea explained much to Everina's relief, was old-fashioned. The men they would marry would care not a jot for it. At length there was only one puzzle left. How could it work at the concert? "We can hardly hitch up our skirts in front of the audience," Harriet observed.

"Oh, there is no need for anything like that," Alathea replied. "There'll be no impropriety, no exposing of flesh, nothing at all shocking. As I said, we'll reveal our magic through our playing. The pianoforte will speak for us."

"But we don't play how we speak," Marianne persisted. "Monsieur insists on strict time."

"That's true," said Alathea. "But honestly, Marianne, it can work. Let's see. The concert is five weeks away yesterday. There's time for me to show you everything I know about making the pianoforte say what each of us wants it to say. We can meet after our ordinary lessons. There would be just one thing. If we decide to make ourselves and our husbands happy in this way, I think we should keep it secret from Monsieur so that the concert is a marvelous finale for him—a kind of thank-you." She put a finger to her lips and met their eyes, pair by pair. The girls' hearts beat quickly. There is always something delicious about a conspiracy. Even Georgiana was cheered. Her face lit up once again. "My playing could speak to Monsieur himself!"

Alathea nodded. "Through Herr Bach you can shout of love and Monsieur may hear you."

Georgiana rose, tall and full of joy. "Oh, he will," she said. "I know he will. I'll make him understand that he needs me and loves me. Thank you, Alathea. You've shown us what we were too blind to see." She leaned down and kissed her. Alathea did not want to be kissed by Georgiana, but she did not move.

Harriet stood up next. What if Mr. Thomas Buller, seeing she was deficient in any knowledge of the fizziness, chose one of the others? She took a deep breath. "I've not yet had Monsieur," she reminded them.

"Don't concern yourself, Harriet," Alathea reassured. "There's time. Be determined. He'll not resist. What's more," she added, "all of you must get Monsieur to teach you everything he knows. Now he's begun, he can't deny you."

"We must practice hard, at everything," said Georgiana, ready to start at once.

The girls agreed, even Marianne.

"The invitations go out on Monday," Harriet said.

"Yes, so we should meet every day from now on. Our mamas will be pleased we're doing extra practice. Nobody will suspect," said Everina.

"Only we'll have to fit practice in with the dressmaker and shopping," Marianne reminded, gesturing around the room.

The girls' eyes flitted over the trousseaus. Something struck Harriet. "Who's going to get your trousseau ready, Alathea? You can't do it on your own."

Alathea's smile was fixed. "Thank you. I'll manage very well." She got up and moved to find paper and ink to draw up a schedule of work to be done. Exhausted as from some great challenge, though duping the girls had hardly been that, she

wanted to go home, yet it was another hour until, after copi-
ous good-byes laced with whispered plans and arrangements,
she could set off for Soho Square. Her skirt dragged and was
soon muddy again. The distance seemed great. At Holborn,
she bought a sprig of berries—to reassure? To cheer? Just to
hold? Men might be fools, but girls were fools too, she thought
as she made for her own front door. Once, she would have
excepted herself, but since the day of the incident—she never
called it rape, since that would make her a victim—the only
person she excepted from the list of fools was Annie.

In the Stratton Street parlor, Alathea's musk scent lingered.
Mrs. Drigg smelled it when she returned from Mrs. Brass's,
and despite the chill, she opened the window to let it out.

SIXTEEN

IN MUSIC, THERE ARE REPEATS. THIS IS A MIS-nomer. The notes are repeated but music is not a parade of notes. A repeat offers subtle or not-so-subtle differences in phrasing, in tone. A fourth finger instead of a thumb can change a mood entirely, and a wrist carried higher or lower shifts the hand's balance. Such nonrepetitious repeti-tion is observed in a court of law, where two witnesses observ-ing the same phenomenon never tell the same story. And so, in Soho Square, events unfolded.

FIRST PRESENTATION

Sawney Sawneyford was in the card room, lamps and fire lit, wine untouched as yet, and two glasses on the table. He was waiting for Alathea. They had seen each other every day since the disagreement—Sawneyford never called it rape, since that would make him a rapist. They had passed on the stairs. They had sat at dinner. They had not, however, spoken, not a word.

Sawneyford spent the first part of the night after the disagreement in turmoil. What had she done? What had he done? She
had been insolent. He had been angry. She had come toward
him. He had taken her. He did not shy away from that, only
the manner of it. It was not a good manner. For some hours he
wondered whether the manner had been bad enough for Alathea
to run away. He should stop her. He should post Crouch at the
front door. He did nothing. If she wanted to go, she should go.
By dawn, when the front door remained closed and there was no
sound from above, he was reconfiguring. What had she really
said? What had he really done? She had purposefully annoyed
him. He had taken her, and certainly his manner had been
hasty, which was not their usual manner. But nothing really
untoward, he thought. After all, she had not screamed. Had she
screamed he would have stopped. The best thing would be to
draw a line, as he had learned to do over bad deals, and move
along. He would not speak of it.

This had seemed enough at breakfast the following morning. It had seemed enough at dinner that evening. But as the
days had gone by, it was not enough. Silence had long been a
feature of Soho Square, but silence was now hard where it had
once been soft. Despite all his rationalizations, Sawneyford
could not stand it. His temper shortened. What he wanted, he
told himself, was entirely reasonable. It would suit them both
very well for things to be as they were before—not just before
the disagreement, but before the marriage talk at the V & B.
Alathea should return to being as she was on the first night she
had come to him. He would accept her and be as he had always
been. After all, for years that arrangement had contented them
both. Had Alathea not been content, she would have spoken
out, and had he not been content, he would have spoken out

too. It was fair to say that in the absence of any speaking out, they had been content together, and in her contentment he was happy, and in his contentment, presumably, she had been also. He was willing to turn the clock back. She should be willing, too.

He heard the front door latch. Alathea would see, from the lamps, where he was. He heard her remove her overshoes and brush down her skirt. He heard her foot on the stair. He spurred himself out of the card room. "Alathea." She stopped. She was holding berries. A spray of red. Who were they for? He swallowed and made a gesture. "There's a fire and wine." She did not argue, just glided before him, bringing her scent with her. "You've been quite a time at the Driggs'," he said. It sounded accusatory. He had not meant it to.

"We took tea and spoke of the concert," Alathea said. She sat down. The dust sheets billowed.

Sawney breathed a little more easily. Alathea sounded the same as always. He had been worrying about nothing. Perhaps she had already forgotten. His anger abated. "And are preparations going well?" It was what any father might ask.

"Yes." She began picking off the berries and throwing them into the fire. They hissed.

"Wine?" Sawneyford poured two glasses and went to give her one. Both her hands were occupied with the spray, so he put the glass on the floor beside her. Raindrops sparkled in her hair and dripped onto her shoulders. The diamonds in the lining of his coat scraped against each other.

"Did you walk all the way home?" he asked. She nodded. "Well, I suppose it's not far." He was like an actor practicing a part. How could silence hum when they were speaking? He coughed and moved about. "I've been thinking," he said. Alathea kept on picking the berries. "I've been thinking," he said, more loudly. "I don't see why you should marry." She stopped picking. Good. He drank. It took only a moment for the silence to hum again. He kicked at the fire, for the noise. "That's a better blaze." He kicked it again. "Drigg, Brass, and Frogmorton need their daughters to marry. I don't need you to marry. You can stay with me." Humming silence. "What do you say to that?"

Alathea put the shorn spray down and picked up the wine. She was in shadow, hard to read. Still, she was drinking.

"Would you like that, Alathea?"

She did not answer at once and anxiety rose in him again. She had not forgotten. He drank some more.

Alathea put her glass down. "I don't want to marry," she said.

"Well then," said Sawneyford with forced cheeriness, "you won't. We'll carry on here together." He paused. "Just as we were before." He wanted Alathea to nod. If she would just nod, the slate would be clean.

She did more than that. She rose and came to him, exactly as she used to before the disagreement, except things were quite different. Before the disagreement, all her movements fueled his desire. In his present relief, he felt no desire at all, at least not that kind of desire. What he felt, as she stepped toward him, was an ache for the world as it might have been, the world, indeed, as it had been before that night of the din in those lodgings, the world where she had been only his daughter and he had been only her father. And she understood. Here she was, coming to him and standing before him, a daughter in front of her father. He greeted her as a father. She gave a half smile. She raised her hand and touched his cheeks. A considerate daughter, apologizing for a disagreement, comforting a father after a hard time and a long day. She ran her fingers over his face. He dropped his wineglass and heard it smash on the hearth. Her fingers probed and soothed the knots in his forehead, the knots in his neck, probed and soothed, probed and soothed. Her hands were cool and clean. How did she keep them so clean? He stood quite still and allowed his relief to flood upward, right from his toes. He closed his eyes. Probing, soothing, her fingers asked his eyes to open. He obliged. Her face was turned up to his, so close that her hair, some rain diamonds still persisting, brushed his nose. Her eyes, black tonight, drew him in, offering entrance to the core of her being. This was new, and the novelty combined with relief was so great that it turned into something else—love, Sawneyford thought with thankful recognition. Love has survived. I love my daughter. It's love that welds us together. These past months have been leading to this, not a parting but a tighter binding. So what if Monsieur has had her. He is nothing to her whereas she and I are one flesh. I've always known it and she's always known it too.

The silence still hummed, but the hum no longer threatened and he did not want it broken. This hum could go on forever. He wrapped his arms around her. Her scent caught in his throat. She was smiling. The fire spat and blazed and he saw her in flashes. Her hands moved from his face, those expert hands with that wedding ring glinting. She licked his lips with her tongue. Ah, now he was moved beyond words. She was forgiving and giving. He could see it. He could feel it. He had no fear of her. There was no need, nor ever had been. His ache for the world of only father and daughter evaporated. This was the world he wanted, the familiar world where she both was and was not his child, both was and was not his wife, was more than either, was Alathea, just Alathea, that was all, and what an all it was. He was conscious that the door was not entirely closed.

She slipped from his arms and ran to close and lock it. She could read his mind! She was a miracle. Then she was back, undoing buttons, hers and his, sinking him to the floor, unrolling her stockings, removing her skirt. He was breathing with difficulty. This was not as it had been. This was in the light, where before it had always been dark. This was gloriously abandoned, where before it had been clandestine. This was two lovers, equal in passion, where before it had been not quite that. He was lying flat. She was above him. She paused. Every part of him reached up for her. He could smell her. He could feel her. She leaned down. "Now?" she asked. He groaned. He didn't want her to speak. He was powerless to stop her.

"Now?" she asked again.

"Now," he said. "Yes, now."

She crouched over him, then quick as a fish, her hands were on the hearth, then behind her, and a burning pain shot from his groin along his legs and up into his throat. At first he mistook the pain for pleasure. His hands thrust upward to her shoulders, pressing her down. But something was amiss. The pain seared. Alathea was no longer crouching. She was standing above him. She was still half-naked but she was watching him, just watching. His hands flew to his groin. His fingers were soaked. Everything was soaked. He felt himself. Nothing was as it should be. "Oh Jesus!" he cried. "What have you done?"

"I've turned you into a father," she said, and pulling on her skirt, she walked to the door, opened it, and shouted for Crouch to get the doctor.

REPEAT

Alathea closed the door behind her and removed her overshoes. She saw, from the lamps, that her father was in the card room. She brushed down her skirt and headed for the stairs. The speed of her father's appearance was unexpected, as was his calling of her name. She stopped and turned before she thought. He was eyeing her spray of berries. He couldn't possibly imagine they were for him? She saw him gesture. "There's a fire and wine." She could still have gone straight up the stairs. She chose not to. He could come after her and she did not want to run. She went to the card room.

"You've been quite a time at the Driggs'," Sawneyford said.

She felt it an accusation. "We took tea and spoke of the concert," she said warily. She sat down because she did not want to admit to herself that she was frightened. Some of the dust sheets billowed. She thought, this room's like a warm mausoleum. These sheets could be my winding sheets.

"And are preparations going well?" It was what any father might ask.

"Yes." She wished for Annie. She began pulling berries from the spray and throwing them into the fire. The hiss brought Annie nearer.

"Wine?"

She said nothing and when her father came over, she kept pulling berries from the spray. The glass was put beside her. As Sawneyford turned back to the fire, she could see the outline of the diamonds in the lining of his coat. The coattails swung.

"Did you walk all the way home?" Sawneyford asked. She nodded. "Well, I suppose it's not far."

Her father seemed unusually uncomfortable. She wondered whether he was going to beg her to forgive him. What would she say? He coughed and moved about. "I've been thinking," he said. Alathea kept on picking the berries. "I've been thinking," he said, more loudly. "I don't see why you should marry."

The surprise made her stop picking. Was this supposed to be an apology? Or a reward for her silence? Or, to make her sweet again, tacit approval of her taking a woman as a lover, since he didn't see a woman as any threat? She watched him knock back his wine and kick at the fire. Was that a warning? Since she didn't know what to say, she said nothing.

"That's a better blaze," he said. She watched him kick the fire again. Yes, a warning, she thought. "Drigg, Brass, and Frog-morton need their daughters to marry. I don't need you to marry. You can stay with me. What do you say to that?"

Alathea put the shorn spray down. She picked up her wine. She needed it.

"Would you like that, Alathea?"

It did not seem a question so much as a statement. Her father drank more. She did not know how much he had consumed. She had better answer now. She put her glass down. "I don't want to marry," she said.

"Well then," said Sawneyford, "you won't. We'll carry on here together." He paused. "Just as we were before."

As we were before. That was when she looked at him properly. Of course there was no possibility of an apology. Sawneyford had already put the incident behind him. He had drawn a line, as he did under soured business deals. He had no idea what he had done to her, no idea what he had shattered. He had recalibrated what had taken place. Yet he needed an acknowledgment of "just as we were before," an explicit willingness to wipe the slate clean. Realizing this, a little power returned to her, a little confidence. Her edges hardened. She could wipe the slate clean or she could not.

She told Annie afterward, and it was true, that she had no idea what she intended to do. She only knew that despite the incident, her best power over him was always going to be physical. She went to him and when she reached him, she ran her fingers over his cheeks, his neck, his forehead, wondering whether to gouge out his eyes. When he dropped his wineglass, the musical tinkle made her think of Monsieur's tinkling laugh. That was when it came to her. She would not gouge his eyes out, she would make him keep them open. This time, he would see her so close that he would never forget the face she turned up to his. Two more strokes down his cheeks, and then to begin. When she turned up her face, she saw the relief in his eyes. All was as it was before! Her eyes said as much to him and she made them say more, opening them wide to draw him in. She saw desire melt him, felt it as he wrapped his arms around her. Men. When they weren't destroying you, you could do what you liked with them.

Her hands moved from his face, those expert hands with that glinting wedding ring. She licked his lips with her tongue. She would give him the full works. She would be and not be his child. She would be and not be his wife. She would be more than either. She was conscious that the door was not entirely closed. She needed to close and lock it. It was hardly a risk to slip away for a second unless he thought her about to run away. She was quick, turning the key and then back undoing buttons, hers and his, sinking down with him to the floor, unrolling her stockings, removing her skirt. She heard his breathing thicken. It was the first time that he had actually seen her at work. It restored her power completely. He was hers. She almost laughed. Indeed, she could have laughed. She knew he would not have heard her. She knew he could hear only the din of his own desire. He was lying flat. She was above him. She paused until every part of him reached up for her. She knew he could smell her, could feel her. She leaned down. "Now?" she asked. He groaned. She knew he didn't want her to speak. She knew he was powerless to stop her.

"Now?" she asked again.

"Now," he said. "Yes, now."

She crouched over him, then quick as a fish, her hands were on the hearth. There were shards everywhere. Any one would do. Her hands were behind her. She had no wish to kill him— far from it—but she must get this right. His desire made every, thing easier and all those years of practice had made her more than familiar with the external geography. Shaft, hair, two pimpled, wrinkled sacks, the weight, the dampish underside. Despite her study of anatomy books, she wasn't so certain of the internal layout but she didn't fumble, only calculated. It must work like this. Wasn't that what the book suggested? She organized both hands. Lift, hold, two deep slashes, easy as slic, ing cloth. His hands were on her shoulders, pressing her down. What was he doing? Had she made a mistake? Couldn't he feel? She pulled herself up. A quick look behind reassured. No mis, take. He was no longer pressing her down. His hands were at his groin, his fingers soaked. Everything was soaked. He was feeling himself. "Oh Jesus!" he cried. "What have you done?"

He was helpless between her legs. An inspiration came to her. "I've turned you into a father," she said, and pulling on her skirt, she walked to the door, opened it, and shouted for Crouch to get the doctor.

CODA

Annie came to Soho Square as soon as she could. Alathea's message had been cryptic, suggesting a development of some kind, nothing more. Annie thought Alathea wanted to tell her about the tea party at Stratton Street, so when she arrived at Soho Square, she was surprised to find the place unusually busy—that is to say, the door was open and a boy was helping an elderly man whose bag proclaimed him a doctor into a trap drawn by a lop-eared cob. Crouch was standing in the street. Neighbors were peering.

Annie clutched the railings. Alathea was ill. She was dying. She was dead. She didn't care who saw her run to the front door. When Alathea's arms drew her inside, Annie kicked the door closed, leaving Crouch on the outside. "Alathea! Are you ill? Why was the doctor here?" Annie tore off her veil.

"It's my father." In some agitation, Alathea hurried Annie up the stairs to her bedroom. She did not lock the door. In the forest of reflections, she turned preternaturally calm.

Annie scrutinized her, still very nervous. "What's the matter with him?"

"Here," Alathea said, "this is for you." She presented the almost naked spray. Annie took it and was baffled. "Tell me. What's the matter with him?" So many pairs of reflected eyes, all burning. "What is it? Is it catching?"

Alathea laughed harshly. "Why? Are you frightened?"

Annie had never seen this mood before. She suspected something dreadful. "Not for myself," she said. "I'm frightened for you. What is it? Please tell me."

"Nothing to tell," said Alathea. "It's an injury, not an illness." Her eyes flashed. "He'll recover."

"Oh." Annie did not bother to hide her disappointment about recovery. "What kind of injury? Will he need nursing?" Her heart sank. She had nursed her own mother long enough to know what this might mean.

Alathea shone in all the mirrors. "He will need nursing," she said.

"And you'll have to do it?" Annie could not read Alathea at all. The mirrors made her dizzy. "Did he fall?"

Alathea laughed gaily. "I suppose he did, but not down the stairs or from his horse. It was a different kind of fall." She stopped laughing. "Didn't I tell you detachment was the most useful thing in the world?" Annie nodded. "That's what I used, that and a broken wineglass." She was looking at one of Annie's many reflections. "I thought of Monsieur."

Annie turned Alathea so that they were face-to-face, no reflection. Her hands were on Alathea's shoulders. "You're making no sense at all. Tell me. What did you do?"

"I cut him."

"On his face? On his arms? Was he hurting you?"

"No. I cut him as you cut a horse."

"What?" Annie was quite still. "You mean, you—"

"I mean that I have catapulted him into the ranks of the castrati." All the blood drained from Annie's face. "That's what I did. I did it yesterday evening after getting home from Marianne and Everina's."

The tea party! That other world. Now this world, which was beginning to spin. Annie kept her hands on Alathea's shoulders. "Are you telling the truth?"

"Do you doubt me?"

"No—only why now? I thought—"

"You thought I didn't mind?" Alathea tossed her head in case a spasm should reveal what she would rather keep hidden. Even now, she wouldn't tell Annie about the incident. Nobody would ever know except herself and her father.

"You said it gave you all the power in the world."

"It did," said Alathea. "Then I decided it should come to an end." She shrugged. "That's all."

"And your father?" Annie did not know what to ask.

"He lost blood. The card room floor looks like a butcher's shop. I don't expect Crouch will clean it. The doctor patched my father up and oh, Annie, his words when he explained to my father what he must expect when he's recovered. So blunt."

"Didn't he ask how it happened?"

"That was the funniest thing. Crouch blamed you."

"Me?" Annie let go of Alathea's shoulders. "*Me?*"

"Yes. I sent him for the doctor directly after I'd"—a momentary shiver at the memory of glass on skin—"directly after I'd done it. My father fainted, so I stanched the blood with his shirt. The doctor found me and was quite horrified, fussing about the unsuitability of a girl of my class tending a man, even a father, in such an intimate way. He never looked at me. He assumed I was in a state of silent hysteria, I suppose. He spoke only to Crouch and Crouch didn't care at all about my father. He wanted the doctor out of the house. But when the doctor asked him directly who might have done such a thing, Crouch said he had seen a veiled woman come and go who, he assumed, was my father's mistress. He thought my father had probably thrown you over and you'd taken your revenge. When the doctor asked your identity, Crouch said 'a Catholic, I'll be bound' and the doctor couldn't get any more from him."

"Crouch saw me come in just now," said Annie, highly alarmed.

"There's no need to worry. Crouch is probably on your side. A funnier thing is that this morning, in his fever, my father kept shouting my name and the poor doctor kept exclaiming,

'Don't call for your daughter! It's not right, Mr. Sawneyford, that she should see this.' He kept patting my shoulder." She took Annie's hands. "Forget all this. My father will recover perfectly well, and quickly. He'll be back in the City in no time. It makes no difference to us. As for the girls, they were easy to persuade about the concert. The evening will certainly be startling. The moment it's over, we'll fly."

Had her eyes been completely frank and sparkling, Annie might have worried about Alathea's sanity, but there was a strain, a continuous tic, a suspicion of panic that reassured. Alathea was trying to make things normal when they were not normal at all.

"When your father's fever has abated, you're sure he still won't say anything about you? Shouldn't we go now, just in case?" Too late did Annie think of her mother. Whatever the circumstances, Annie could not simply walk out and leave her.

Alathea's shake of the head was, for this reason only, a relief. "I'm as sure as I can be that my father will say nothing. Admit to being a gelding? He'd rather die."

They perched on the bed, neither sure what to do next. Gradually they sank down and Alathea drew the covers over them. They held each other. Alathea pushed against Annie. They pressed together when awful images of Sawneyford intruded. Eventually, Annie sat up and asked about the tea party. So they sat, still pressed together, with Alathea describing her afternoon with the girls—even laughing sometimes—for all the world like any two young innocents on the dizzy brink of womanhood, only Alathea could not quite let go of Annie's hand and Annie kept seeing that shard of glass.

SEVENTEEN

PREPARATIONS FOR THE CONCERT WERE FAR advanced. The Earl of Allemonde, who owed Brass money and Sawneyford gratitude for discretion (the earl still kept a slave or two in the country), had agreed to lend his house for the performance. To the Countess of Allemonde's fury, Mrs. Frogmorton, Mrs. Drigg, and Mrs. Brass had already been to the Pall Mall house to plan winter flowers, supper tables, and where, exactly, the pianofortes should be placed to show off the girls to best advantage. After Mrs. Frogmorton complained that the kitchens were dirty and the vases inferior, the countess took herself and her children out of town. They would not grace this concert. The Allemonde heir, however, would be parted from his horses for the duration of the aria and variations. When he objected, he was shown the stable bills. He, sensibly, asked how much money each girl had. The four fathers, sensibly, supplied the answer. The guest list had been easy. It included all peers, down to baronets, secure in their title (wealth was not required) who had an eldest son (or second son, if the elder was sickly) of marriage‚ able age. Any peer not fulfilling the criteria was excluded. Sworn to secrecy, the printer responsible for the invitations quickly alerted Pall Mall, Westminster, and St. James's. The aristocracy laughed.

"Why bother with thick card?" the Marquis of Poderum remarked, having heard of the concert from his tailor. "Why not parade the creatures at Smithfield, after the cows?"

"With the wedding settlement tied around their necks in bags," chortled his son. "I'd rather go to Smithfield than endure some poxy concert."

"You'll go to that concert," his father said sharply, "and we'll make an offer. Choose the one who takes your fancy. I hear the fortunes are more or less the same."

Similar conversations were heard in similar establish‚ ments, though not in all. Some fathers looked at their own children and wondered what kind of City men these were, who sold their daughters for a title. They did it themselves, of course, but that was old blood trading with old. New trading with old was different—necessary, sometimes, if old blood had run out of old money, but that was for old blood to decide. This concert was crude. What was more, City girls were ugly girls. Everybody knew that. The fathers reassured their sons that duty done, husbands were free to roam.

At the V & B, Frogmorton, Brass, and Drigg also laughed. The printer had blabbed, just as they expected. The aristoc‚ racy had laughed, just as they expected. When the invitations were delivered, nobody refused, just as they expected.

The mothers took to meeting at ten o'clock every morning so that Mrs. Frogmorton could update them on the acceptances.

So far, they were pleased with the list. They were less pleased with their daughters' new practice arrangements. "Do you think it healthy, Elizabeth," Mrs. Frogmorton asked, seated in the Drigg parlor, legs splayed to the fire in the hearth, cup of chocolate at her side. She sat between stockings and handkerchiefs, the room still decked out with marriage clothes a fortnight or so after Marianne's tea party. "I mean to say, do you think it healthy that our daughters spend quite so much time at their music?"

"Whatever can you mean? What's health got to do with it?" Mrs. Drigg shifted to toast her other side.

Mrs. Frogmorton clicked her tongue. Agnes could be obtuse. "The point was not to turn them into pianoforte players, just into girls who can play the pianoforte. I'm happy enough with their lessons from Monsieur. He doesn't tax them too much. Indeed, sometimes there are long gaps when, I gather, they speak about the music without playing so that they shouldn't tire themselves. But I don't know why they need to practice so much when they're not with him. Harriet spends more time here than she does at home. It's not at all convenient for the dressmaker."

Mrs. Drigg tried not to blench when she heard Monsieur mentioned. Since her husband had revealed what he had learned from Frogmorton about Monsieur's unfortunate history, this was hard. The knife. *Down there*. She twitched. "Do we really need to worry? Marianne says this air and variations are so spectacular, they need the extra time."

"That's as may be," said Mrs. Frogmorton "But why does Alathea always have to be with them? I saw her when I left here last week. She had that smile. You know the one."

Mrs. Drigg and Mrs. Frogmorton both grimaced. Mrs. Brass made a small moue with her lips.

"I agree, Elizabeth," said Mrs. Drigg. "I wish she would keep away, but Marianne says that Monsieur has suggested she practice with them. For all her faults, she's a fine musician and the concert's so soon. Can it harm?"

"I suppose not." Mrs. Frogmorton picked up a pair of brand-new stockings and began, absentmindedly, to roll them as if for a journey. Her hands were slightly chocolate stained but Mrs. Drigg did not like to stop her. "And perhaps you're right. I expect they spend most of the time talking nonsense and comparing clothes. You know what girls are like."

"Indeed we do, don't we, Elizabeth," said Mrs. Drigg. Mrs. Frogmorton finished rolling. Mrs. Drigg quickly took the stockings from her and removed all others within reach.

Mrs. Frogmorton hardly noticed. She sighed. "Why can't Alathea be like our daughters?" She sat musing for a moment, then blinked back into the present. "Don't you think she's been worse lately?"

"In what way worse?" asked Mrs. Drigg, setting both knees to the blaze. There was guilty enjoyment in gossiping about Alathea.

"There's a sort of excitement about her," Mrs. Frogmorton said. "I saw her after her lesson the other day. She seemed—I want to say sly, only Alathea isn't sly, not like"—she was about to say Everina, whom she suspected of encouraging Marianne to greater and more unfortunate efforts with the rouge, and halted only just in time—"not like some others, none of ours, of course. Anyway, not sly. She was"—Mrs. Frogmorton sought the word she needed—"I'd say, fizzing. Yes. Fizzing."

"Fizzing?" Mrs. Drigg tried to imagine what Mrs. Frog-morton meant. "Like a bottle of fizz? I've never connected Alathea with champagne." Her brow creased. The connection seemed dangerous.

Mrs. Frogmorton poured herself more chocolate. "Don't look so worried. It's an expression fashionable with the young. I've heard Harriet use it several times. I thought it rather pleasing."

Mrs. Drigg did not want to be thought unfashionable. "I expect it's because her father's ill," she said, in a bid to regain ground. "Drigg told me this morning that Sawneyford hasn't set foot in the City for over a week."

"Oh?" said Mrs. Frogmorton, startled. "I hope it isn't seri-ous with Sawneyford?" The awful possibility of having to offer Alathea a home under the Frogmorton roof if she was left an orphan and didn't marry made her grip her knees together.

"I did make inquiries as soon as Drigg had gone," said Mrs. Drigg, her pleasure at being the imparter of news mixed with disappointment that she was going to learn nothing fur-ther from Mrs. Frogmorton. "According to the servants, the doctor's been at least four times, only he's saying nothing, not even for half a crown."

Mrs. Frogmorton became agitated. "What can it be? Could it be catching?"

"I don't think so," Mrs. Drigg said quickly. An agitated Mrs. Frogmorton was as disconcerting a sight as a dependably solid edifice displaying suddenly tremulous foundations. "If it was catching, wouldn't Alathea have been sent away?"

"You never know with Sawneyford," said Mrs. Frogmor-ton, half rising. "He's a queer fish, and—"

"But he's fond of his daughter," Mrs. Drigg reassured. "He wouldn't wish her ill."

"I suppose not." Mrs. Frogmorton subsided. Her motherly instincts surfaced. "I wonder whether he's got somebody to help with her concert dress? But I wish we knew what was wrong."

"I'll send Sam again this afternoon," said Mrs. Drigg. "He's a great one for prying. Now, we were going to decide about flowers, and we've never discovered if the Allemondes will allow our guests to use their water closets. I can't see any reason why not, can you, Elizabeth?"

At Manchester Square, Harriet was sitting in the footman's chair, huddled in a cloak and gazing through the window into the communal garden. Severely hampered by fat winter outer garments, children were attempting to play hoop. Harriet fought an urge to join them. She could, she thought. After all, there must be some advantages to being still a child, by which she meant still untouched. Though she had swung her earrings every day at Monsieur, he kept his hands firmly on his lap and Harriet was faced with having to force his hands, a concept she found insulting. Nevertheless, it must be done and, she had already decided, it must be done today. She would not return to her bedroom in the same state as she left it.

She swung her legs. Why didn't he want her? Marianne said she was learning new techniques from him almost every day and even facing the wall had become quite enjoyable. Yet she, Harriet, was far prettier than Marianne. She decided that despite her best efforts she was being too coy. Monsieur must think she was still concerned about Georgiana's feelings. She would have to be less coy. She tweaked her cloak. Underneath, she wore the loose pink tea gown she had debuted at Marianne's the previous Sunday, only today, after the dressing maid had gone, she had removed the gown's underpinnings. Between dress and specially scented skin remained only a gossamer shift, pale stockings, and a pair of silk slippers with bows. She shivered. The fire was some distance away. Her feet were cold. She pulled them under her and admired her ankles. From upstairs she could hear the same phrase being played again and again, left hand only, right hand only, hands together. Marianne might be good at the fizziness. She was no good at the pianoforte.

A noise in the street. Mr. Thomas Buller emerged from next door, evidently waiting for his horse to be brought around. On impulse, Harriet jumped up. She had been waiting for an opportunity to see Thomas. How infuriating that she was not more suitably dressed. Could she really go out in these shoes? She knocked on the window. Mr. Thomas Buller, fresh-faced, round-faced, red-faced, of little brain and endless good humor, gave a faux salute and grinned cheerfully. Not being the son of a peer, he had not been asked to the concert. Not yet, Harriet thought.

Harriet and Thomas were not well acquainted and Harriet suspected that the Buller parents had aspirations for their son beyond marrying a Frogmorton. It was true, however, that Thomas liked her—at least he always seemed pleased to see her—and she calculated that he would be more than obliging if she could persuade him that the feeling was mutual. Commendably self-deprecatory, she did not think her charms her best weapon: she thought her best weapon would be surprise. The Bullers, like the rest of Manchester Square, must know that the Frogmortons had a title in mind for Harriet, so Thomas must believe that Harriet was not for him. Now might be a good moment to shock him into imagining how nice it would be if she was. She knocked on the window, then smiled and waved.

Thomas waved back without embarrassment. Harriet was right: since he thought she was not for him, he was perfectly at ease. Even if he had to speak to her, he thought with relief, it mattered little that he was neither interesting nor clever. Harriet was destined for another.

Harriet pulled her cloak about her and opened the door. The shoes would have to be sacrificed. She went into the street, her warm breath wafts of steam. At once, Thomas was full of concern. "You'll get cold, Miss Frogmorton," he exclaimed, "and your feet'll get all wet in those slippers." Exuding heat, he bundled his own cloak over hers. He's like a large dog, Harriet thought. Once they were married, she would pet him and stroke him and give him plenty of treats. She looked forward to it.

"I've something for you, Mr. Buller."

"Thomas, please."

"Thomas." She twinkled at him. "I've something for you, Thomas. I'm inviting you to a concert. It's on Saturday next in the evening, at the Duke of Allemonde's saloon in Pall Mall."

Thomas fidgeted with his gloves. "I think he's an earl," he said.

"Earl, duke, what does it matter? I want you to come to the concert."

"That's very kind of you, Miss Frogmorton," Thomas said, "but I've heard it's only for those with titles."

"Ah," she said, twinkling more, "you've heard that."

He blushed. "Everybody's heard. Well, obviously not everybody. I mean, snake charmers in India won't have heard."

Harriet laughed kindly. "You mean everybody who matters has heard."

"Yes, that's exactly it. Everybody who matters."

"Your father could buy a title, you know," said Harriet, hoping her nose was not turning red. It really was cold.

"Even if he did, Miss Frogmorton—"

"Harriet, please."

He flushed beetroot. "Even if he did—Harriet . . . I'm not . . . well, you know, I'm not . . . I'm never going to be—"

"Never going to be the type of person my parents want at the concert?"

"Yes. I do like the way you say exactly what I mean." His flush deepened until Harriet wondered how much deeper it could go.

His horse arrived, a pleasant creature, large, solid, and dependable, much like its owner. Harriet formed an enchanting O with her lips and blew on its muzzle. It blew back in friendly fashion and lipped a stray oat from a whisker. "But Tom—can I call you Tom?"

He swallowed. "Please do. It's what my friends call me."

"Well, Tom, it's me who has to play at the concert"—she turned from his horse to himself—"just as it's me who'll have to get married after it." Would that be direct enough?

It wasn't. Thomas kept fiddling with his gloves. "Yes, indeed. But you want what your parents want."

Harriet gave a feathery sigh. "Do I, Tom? Do I?" She looked him straight in the eye.

A slow computation. "You mean you don't want what your parents want?" Harriet didn't blink. "You mean," Thomas said, his Adam's apple shooting first up, then down into his stock.

There, Harriet thought. Now he's getting it. The horse stamped a back foot. Harriet blew on its muzzle again. "Come to the concert, Tom," she said. "That's what I want. Will you promise?"

He looked stunned. "Really?" he said.

"Promise?" Harriet prompted. "Please promise." She twin, kled. She purred. She folded herself more neatly into his cloak. "I want to see a friendly face—somebody who might care for—well, you know—more than my father's stock of gold in the bank."

"Only a fool wouldn't care for more than that," Thomas said.

Harriet touched his arm. "Promise to come?"

He stood to attention, puce face, ramrod back. "I promise."

"Excellent," said Harriet. Her task accomplished, she began to take off the cloak. "That's all arranged. Now you'd better get on before— What's the horse's name?"

"Gallant."

She smiled. "Gallant. Like you, Tom. Better mount up before Gallant turns into an icicle, or I do. Have a pleasant ride." She returned his cloak and skipped back through her own front door.

Thomas Buller remained transfixed. Had the groom not broken the spell with "Ready, sir?" he might have spent the rest of his life gazing at the place where Harriet had stood. As it was, the groom nudged him and the horse nudged him too. He put on his cloak, found his stirrup, mounted, and, with a loud "I will have a pleasant ride, Miss Frogmorton, I certainly will," headed out into Oxford Street.

Harriet tossed off her shoes—yes, ruined, she thought—and looked out the window. For all that his heavy cloak accentuated his roundness and dogginess, Thomas looked quite fine on a horse, properly martial, even, with his spurs shining. Harriet was glad. It was good to marry somebody who looked nice. More important, though, was her certainty that with Thomas she would have a life of her own choosing, and once they got over their annoyance, her parents would be content. After all, her parents were happy together. Why shouldn't she and Thomas be equally happy? It was only after Gallant clattered off that Harriet realized she was herself being looked at—more than looked at. Harriet was being inspected.

Annie was well wrapped against the weather, her whole face, except for her eyes, covered. She had come through the square on her way to buy iron wire for strings. Manchester Square was not a direct route and she did not want to be here. She came because she had seen Alathea only rarely since the day after Alathea had told her what she had done to her father, and she missed her. Annie knew she was not being deliberately ignored. She knew that time must be spent at Manchester Square or at Stratton Street practicing with the girls if the concert was to go as she and Alathea had planned. Nevertheless, on the rare occasions Alathea was with Annie, she now spoke of the girls, imitated the girls, was always so full of the girls that Annie could not help wanting to see the girls in the flesh. Alathea told Annie she despised them, and Annie did believe her, certainly from her descriptions of the Drigg sisters. She was not so sure about Harriet and Georgiana. Alathea had some regard for their dedication. She had even commended their playing. This last had shaken Annie. It was why she needed to see the girls. It was why she was here.

At first, to Harriet, Annie was a black distortion through the glass. Then, when Annie was clearly a person, a female person at that, and not simply looking at the window but studying it, Harriet wondered what business a woman could possibly have at Manchester Square. Perhaps, under the veil, she was one of those old crones who pestered for money. Yet she seemed disinclined to ring the bell. Harriet called for the footman. "There's someone hovering at the railings, Spencer. See what she wants."

Spencer went outside and addressed Annie without deference. He saw from her cloak that she was not a lady. "Madam?"

Annie backed away.

"Wait." Harriet was hopping in her stockinged feet on the cold doorstep. "Who are you looking for?" she called.

Annie focused on Harriet's pretty cheeks, her pretty hair, her perfect mouth. Alathea had never described these. On impulse Annie said, "I've come from Mr. Cantabile's."

"Mr. Who?"

Annie raised her voice. "Cantabile."

"Who's he?"

"The pianoforte maker. He sent me to ask if you're happy with your instrument and the teacher he sent with it."

"I happy?" echoed Harriet, puzzled. "Yes, of course we're happy with the pianoforte and with Monsieur Belladroit. If we weren't, we'd have complained long ago." It seemed to Annie that Harriet's lips involuntarily twitched into a small kiss.

Annie moved forward. She couldn't look away from that mouth. How slim it was! How elegant! How could Alathea resist it? Here in Manchester Square, with Harriet alive in front of her, Annie felt as though a cataract had been removed.

In the space of a second, the past months took on a different aspect and all Alathea's talk of America struck a false note. Until she saw the reality of Harriet, Annie had accepted without question that Alathea's lessons, the lessons that were going to show the girls as tainted goods, were being learned by the girls only through music. But of course Alathea had never said so explicitly. She never said, in words, that music was her only connection with Harriet or the others, and knowing what she did of Alathea's appetites, knowing what she did of Alathea's impulses, Annie realized that she had been too trusting. Alathea could have been doing anything these long afternoons when Annie was at Tyburn with her sick mother and surly father. After all, Alathea never suggested that Annie join her to help with the practice. Why not? If she chose, Alathea could make the girls see beyond Annie's ruined face. It must be that she did not want to do so. Annie thought of that shard of glass. Once Alathea no longer wanted her father, look what she had done to him. Once she no longer wanted Annie, what might she do to her?

Harriet was still on the doorstep. "Would you like to come and inspect it?" She peered at Annie, who, almost unknowingly, had moved closer. The veil disconcerted. Harriet wanted to see beneath it. She lifted her arm as though to touch it. It was purely in Annie's imagination that Alathea's musk scent cut up her nose as the glass shard really had cut into Sawneyford. Harriet smelled of the dried rose petals the maids scattered on her sheets every night. Yet to Annie's heightened sensibilities, the scent turned animal and conjured up images of Harriet and Alathea sitting together, playing together, the pale and the dark perfectly contrasted and lit up for the world to admire. She could feel Alathea's hands on the warm porcelain of Harriet's flesh. And those lips. Those lips. Harriet touched the veil and Annie whizzed around and fled, slipping in the frost, sliding into children, baby carriages, dogs, and all the domestic paraphernalia of Manchester Square families, seeing nothing except that her own lips, those very things about which poets wrote and lovers dreamed, were absurd and always would be. Alathea could kiss them and set each nerve athrob, but they were still absurd. Alathea knew that. Monsieur, though he spoke kindly to Annie and admired her playing, knew that. Her mother knew that. Her father was the only person brave enough to tell Annie the truth, that Annie was a joke, somebody to be toyed with or played with, but not somebody to flee with to America. There would be no new life. Annie had been dreaming, just as, before Alathea, she used to dream about Monsieur and the concert she would give. She rushed into Oxford Street and back to Tyburn. When she arrived, fumbling for her key and crashing through the door, her father could have destroyed her completely with a word. Luckily, he was out.

At Manchester Square, Harriet shut the front door and told Spencer to lock it. There seemed something ominous about the veiled girl and Harriet did not like ominous things. Marianne tripped down the stairs, humming. She winked at Harriet, the first of the leery winks for which she eventually became known. Harriet murmured something, then made her way slowly up the stairs, collected some new shoes, came down, and quite forgot to make the beguiling entrance into the drawing room that she had planned.

It hardly mattered. Monsieur was not looking. "Ah, Mademoiselle Harriet," he said from the depths of the pianoforte when he heard the door click shut. He was fiddling with one

- 241 -

of the dampers to calm his temper. What was the matter with Marianne that she wouldn't rest until he had her again and again? She could not enjoy it, for he took no trouble, not even to enjoy it himself. And the questions she asked, as though his person were some new kind of musket. How did it fire? How did it recharge? English girls of her sort were vulgar vulgar vulgar. He finished his work. "Are you ready to play?"

Harriet pulled herself together and wafted over. "A girl was here," she said. "She came from the pianoforte workshop and needed to know if we were satisfied with our instrument."

Monsieur started. "What did she look like?"

"I don't know," Harriet said. "She was heavily veiled. I wanted to see her face but she ran away."

"I expect that was Annie." Monsieur wondered whether he should tell Harriet about Annie's lip. He decided against it. He sat next to Harriet. "She is the daughter of Vittorio Cantabile, the pianoforte maker." He opened the music. "She is a fine player herself," he explained, though he could not, and did not try to, explain what business Annie could possibly have in Manchester Square. He tapped the music. "Variation 27. Begin."

"Annie," said Harriet, not beginning.

Monsieur tapped the music again. "Annie. That is her name. Come along, mademoiselle. We have not long until the concert and you are not yet ready."

Harriet opened her mouth, nearly saying "Oh, but I am, Monsieur, you've no idea how hard we all practice when we're not here," but Alathea had been insistent on the pact of secrecy over the extra hours they put in. Harriet stopped thinking about Annie and thought instead about Thomas, then about Monsieur. She must concentrate on what must happen within this allotted hour. She began Variation 27, the ninth canon, proficient enough to set the semiquavers tripping and the ornaments adding intricate vivacity. She shifted her knees so that her dress fell between. Everina had suggested that. She raised her chin to expose her smooth neck. Georgiana had sug- gested that. Her hair was already bound up. Her earrings danced. "Come on, Monsieur," she thought. "Come on. I've already caught Thomas today. What's the delay with you?"

Monsieur could tell that Harriet was not concentrating on the music. He himself was finding concentration hard. He was slightly sore from Marianne and it was not just she who irritated and alarmed. All the girls' behavior had altered. Like Marianne, Everina had turned questioner, asking how she might improve her technique, by which she did not mean at the pianoforte. He preferred her giggle to her questions. Then there was Georgiana. No matter what he said or did, she worshipped him, and when he took her, which he found himself obliged to do just often enough to spare her the indignity of begging, the whole operation moved him less than washing his hands. Harriet was still untaken, though he could see from her dress today that for some reason she was no longer unwilling. And Alathea. His brow furrowed more. Still irresistible. Still sensational. Monsieur wondered whether she was some kind of a witch, since sex with her drained the pleasure from sex with any other. His frown turned into a sigh. Perhaps he would never tumble Harriet. Perhaps he would hand back a fifth of Cantabile's money and leave her be. Perhaps, for his next assignment, he would go to the East, where girls were kept in harems and never let loose on music masters.

"Monsieur?" Harriet had finished.

"That was good, Mademoiselle Harriet, very good."

"I'd like to practice Variations 4 and 5 now," she said.

"Ah, your great entry."

"Yes, and my hands get in such a muddle in 5. You must help me."

"You must try on your own." Monsieur edged away.

"Very well." She began. Her left-hand G was confident enough, but she faltered over the right-hand run and put the wrong finger of her left hand on the treble B. She stopped to correct, started again poorly, and everything collided in the last six bars.

"Try again," Monsieur encouraged.

She tried again. The same. "Can you show me, Monsieur?"

He did not want to. There was a small battle of wills, which Harriet, by easing along the pianoforte stool and sitting determinedly expectant, won. Monsieur touched the keys. Harriet at once set to work trying to drum up the pulses she had felt at least once before in his presence. That she felt no such pulse today did not alter her determination. Business was business. Tightening her lips, she leaned down, straightened the pink bows on her shoes, and made her move. She went first for Monsieur's ear, into which she breathed, as Alathea had suggested. No response. She breathed harder and placed a hand on his knee. Still nothing. She tried a more direct approach. She seized his left hand and placed it on her breast. Monsieur snapped it away and continued playing. Harriet took a deep breath and plunged both hands into his lap. At that, Monsieur leapt up and flung her hands back, knocking his knees against the pianoforte frame. She expected him to shout and was perfectly prepared for that. She could shout too. She deserved his attention, just as the others did. He said nothing. Harriet stood. They were about three feet apart.

"Monsieur, is there something the matter with me, or is there something the matter with you?"

"What can you mean, mademoiselle."

"Come now, Monsieur. You know what I mean." Harriet knew she sounded like her mother.

Monsieur folded his arms. "Mademoiselle Harriet. Do you want to be married to Mr. Thomas Buller?"

"Of course."

"Then let us concentrate on the pianoforte."

"But, Monsieur, that's exactly the point. Thomas won't care about the pianoforte, not now, not ever. He will care about other things, though, and I know you've been teaching these things to the others. Don't I deserve to know them too?" She blazed a little. "You wanted me badly enough before, and I hardly think it boasting to say that I'm more of a beauty than Everina or Marianne. What's the matter with me? Do you hate the color of my hair?" She loosed it to drift over her shoulders. "Isn't my skin soft enough?" She seized his hand again and pressed it against her cheek. "Am I too thin or too fat?" She ran his hands down her body.

Monsieur pushed away. Those stupid, blabbing girls. He must think quickly. "You are very pretty, mademoiselle," he said, "every part of you. Teaching you these . . . these things, would be a pleasure. But it is for Mr. Buller to be the master. I am sure he will be an excellent guide." He was astounded at this statement, which he had never imagined himself making.

Harriet grew cross. "Thomas Buller only knows about horses."

"I only know about pianofortes."

"Monsieur, you're a liar." Harriet's color was high, and she had never looked more delicious, with her dander up and her defenses down, and all barely enclosed in that rose-pink dress. Yet he must put an end to this. "Mademoiselle," he said, "please. Please. We are business partners, are we not?"

"Business partners must be honest with each other. Trust, Monsieur, is at the heart of business."

He sat down and, for safety, took both her hands in his. "Mademoiselle Harriet. My dear business partner. Listen to me. I do not deny that my lessons with the others have not been restricted to the pianoforte, but those lessons are over."

Harriet removed her hands from his. "Oh, Monsieur," she said, a little world-weary. "You think it's as easy as that? You think that because we're young and a few of us are silly you can give lessons, withdraw lessons, teach some and not others?" She shook her head. "You can't. What you give to one you must give to all."

"Mademoiselle Harriet."

"Stop repeating my name. Why should you have the others and not me? Lord above, I've made it easy. Look at me!"

He looked at the floor. "And what will you do if I refuse? Call your mama?"

"Of course not." Harriet was effortlessly equal to this. "I'll tell Georgiana you laugh at her and that all your kind words, all your cooing and my-little-doveing, have been false. It would finish her."

A flash. "You would not do such a thing, mademoiselle. You are too kind."

"I am kind," Harriet said, sensing victory, "but I also like to get what I want. Come along." She gripped his left hand and ran it between her legs. "Is this a good way to start?"

"Mademoiselle," said Monsieur rather pitifully. "I am tired. I have just had Mademoiselle Marianne." He regretted the words as soon as he said them.

"You see!" cried Harriet. "Those lessons aren't finished at all. You can rest afterward. From what I gather from Alathea, it doesn't take long."

Ah, Alathea, Monsieur thought. She knew how to hurt a man. "That entirely depends," he said, trying not to sound injured.

"Well, it can't take long today," Harriet said, "because we've wasted so much time already. I suppose the time it takes is something to do with age?"

"Is that what Mademoiselle Alathea says?"

"I think she said something about age, and you're no longer young."

Monsieur was nettled. Harriet thought this a lively sign. She moved her hands. "Is this right?" she asked. "Or this?"

It was extraordinary, to Monsieur, to be taken by an untouched girl, as though he were the virgin. Extraordinary and, he could not deny it, arousing. He shifted slightly to allow Harriet to place his hands, and her own, where she would. He mumbled answers to her questions in a tone as polite as her own. "A little to the right, mademoiselle." "Perhaps a little softer." "Yes, undoing the buttons would be a good idea now." "No, this is quite usual." (This last after the buttons were undone and Harriet gave a gulp of surprise.)

"What next?" she asked.

"This," he said, guiding her fingers.

"And for me?"

"This," he said, guiding his own.

"Oh," Harriet said. "Oh. Oh. Oh. I see."

For the finale, he carried her to the sofa though she, in effect, was carrying him, since she was far from passive. Concentrating hard, she followed his movements. Occasionally, her murmurs gave way to brief groans or yelps, once an "ouch." She persevered. When Monsieur felt the oncoming full cadence, he withdrew into his handkerchief, and when all was over, he stood, did up his buttons, and tossed the handkerchief into the fire, where it spat and smelled unpleasant. Despite the previous chafing from Marianne, he had enjoyed this.

Harriet tidied herself more slowly. "Thank you, Monsieur," she said, as though they had just signed a contract.

"Mademoiselle," Monsieur replied.

Harriet went straight to her room. The whole affair was messier than she imagined, and more peculiar. She was worried about stains on her dress. She supposed she could tell her mother it was her monthly courses. She had had two shudders (she had counted) and suspected these were not the fizziness Everina had described. It would be galling if Everina turned out better at this than she was. Still, even now, with this first session under her belt, she had something to show Thomas on their wedding night. She hoped he would appreciate it.

EIGHTEEN

ITH ALL THE GIRLS NOW TUMBLED, and with their constant tumbling demands, Monsieur's days were exhausting. He returned to Cantabile's barely able to manage his supper. He forgot entirely that Annie had been to Manchester Square and even had he remembered, it was hardly important. December came. Only the short time left until the concert—a week—and Cantabile's failure to pay the fee Monsieur felt he deserved twice over stopped the flagging music master from feigning illness (hardly feigning—some days he really did feel quite sickly) and vanishing in the night. He had never gritted his teeth so often.

Dress fittings for Harriet, Georgiana, Everina, and Marianne took up the hours not spent at the pianoforte. Alathea kept their practice going with unremitting intensity. In Manchester Square, work began directly after Monsieur left. In Stratton Street, there was a strict timetable, which Alathea ran with the precision of a Bach cantata, angry if the girls were late or said they must leave early. She left it to them to placate, confuse, and mislead the parents. It was she who must be accommodated, not they.

Very occasionally, if they could snatch an hour in the early evening, she and Annie sat sewing Alathea's concert dress in Alathea's bedroom. After so much practice with the girls, Alathea declared herself too tired to play, so they came straight up to the top floor and remained there, door locked. Annie never saw Sawneyford. She never said she had been to Manchester Square and spoken to Harriet. She did listen very carefully when Alathea spoke of America: how they would get there (Alathea assured Annie that passages were cheap and plentiful); how they would live (Alathea gave Annie the much-thumbed Pantisocratic Society pamphlet she'd brought from the Salutation and Cat); how life would be. Alathea spoke of this new life with a passion Annie had not seen before. Alathea gripped her needle, but Annie did not grip hers because above all Alathea's grand protestations and plans hovered Harriet's perfect face, and this face was a question mark. "You really think Alathea will stay with you? You really think she loves you?" Alathea's new lack of reserve, far from reassuring Annie, fueled her doubts further. This chattiness did not seem genuine. As she sewed, Annie began to strengthen and reinforce her own armor. Her silvered core would protect her when the American dream came to nothing. With her armor on, even with Alathea hammering at the door, Annie could be queen of her own castle, drawbridge up.

It took Sawneyford ten days to recover physically from Alathea's assault. The doctor assured him nobody would know what had happened to him. After all, there was nothing to see.

Sawneyford believed him. It was that, or kill himself. A fortnight later he was back in the City, yet not quite. Perhaps nobody could see his deficit, but Sawneyford knew, he knew and he could not forget. So clerks, stewards, office boys, tradesmen, journeymen, jaggermen, naval spies, military spies, agricultural spies, builders, speculators, banking men, Lloyd's men, opportunists and hangers-on, crooks and enthusiasts—all his usual acquaintance—were avoided. He did not visit the barber to be shaved. He went nowhere near his office, with its flicking thumbs and clicking abacuses. He went nowhere near the V & B. Instead, he hunched in alleys and crouched in corners, scuttling like a rat amid the City's jingling heave and ho. Scuttling was his distraction from the horror—more than a distraction: it was his lifeline. He had to scuttle. He had to scuttle in the City. The City was his place of safety.

In his bed he lay awake. It was not true that nobody knew of his gelding apart from himself and Alathea. The doctor himself knew. Crouch knew. He contemplated killing the doctor. He contemplated killing Crouch. He did not, however, contemplate killing Alathea. An irrationality gradually took hold of him. What Alathea had taken away, she could return. With her, he would still function as a man: her arts, her lips, her fingers would restore him. Alathea could stop this scuttling. He waited until she was practicing at Manchester Square, then made a wax impression of the lock on her door. On his way out to get a key made, he left a folder of money for Crouch, enough for a one-way ticket to Rome. He left a note for the doctor. If Sawneyford found he had gossiped, he would know where to find him.

After the shard, Alathea avoided the card room. Since she had not planned her assault, she had not thought how things would be afterward. And now she was frightened, for she thought her father as capable of murder as she was herself. It was fear that made her garrulous with Annie, both fear of her father and fear of seeming fearful, because fearful people were the kind of people for whom she had no respect. She scolded herself. Her fear was needless, just a reaction. It would pass. After all, her father would surely be frail for some time yet and the concert was so close. She and Annie would be gone in a week. She did take precautions, though. Whether Annie was with her or not, she was doubly careful to lock her door and kept the key with her, sleeping with it under her pillow. Several times in the night she thought she heard the pianoforte twang. She imagined Sawneyford cutting the strings. It was not the exhaustion of practice with the girls that made her avoid playing with Annie, it was fear of what they might find in the ballroom. Sawneyford's missing coat told her he was up and out again. Trays of half-eaten street food left in the hall told her that Crouch had abandoned the house and they were now without a servant. She left the trays where they were.

On the Thursday night before the concert, she woke from a half sleep. At first she thought her room ablaze and started up. It was ablaze, though with light, not a conflagration. Candles were reflected in every mirror. Next to the bed, leaning over her, stood Sawneyford, hair awry, dry skin powdering hollowed cheeks. He was wearing a dressing gown loosely knotted and it was clear he wore nothing beneath. Alathea lay perfectly still. She could feel her key under her head. What a numbskull. She should have changed the lock. She hardly breathed. She kept her eyes almost closed. The lamp beside her bed was heavy. She could hit him with that. But he was above her, and gazing at her. He would hit her first. Be still. Be still.

Sawneyford unknotted his dressing gown and climbed onto the bed. Alathea would not look at the scene of her destruction. She closed her eyes fully. Sawneyford lowered himself until he was resting on her thighs, then pulled down the covers. Be still, Alathea, be still. His stubbled cheek scraped against her nose as he tilted forward, then up again. His breath rasped. He felt in his pocket for seven diamonds of different sizes, all cut and polished, drew up her nightgown, and dripped the jewels onto her belly. One rolled into her belly button, the rest he slowly rolled downward until they were half-lost. He took her hand in his, her fingers so soft and unresponsive that he himself had to fold them around where they were needed. All the while he kept his eyes fixed on her face. She was beautiful, his daughter. She would see that after destruction came restoration. Restoration was her duty and she had always been dutiful. His lips were working. He moved her hand. It was smooth and cool. A nice feeling. That was all. His breathing hardened. He clenched her hand and winced. He clenched it again and rejoiced in his wince. Pain might help. His pain. Her pain. Clench, wince, clench, wince.

Nothing worked. He abandoned her hand and pulled her arms above her head, pressing both down with one of his. He shuffled the rest of himself up the bed, his knees at her shoulders. He raised himself. He lowered himself. Alathea, still as the dead, felt wetness on her eyelids, on her cheeks, on her lips. No, she begged silently, though her face never changed. No. It can't be possible. Not that. I've finished him for that. She heard her father groan. Her arms were no longer trapped. The bed creaked as Sawneyford clambered off, leaving the diamonds where they were. He was at the door, fumbling for the key. He was gone.

The second he was out, Alathea tipped her head sideways. She sat up and touched one cheek with a finger. She could have cried with relief. The wetness was light, not heavy; salty, not sticky; clear, not cloudy. She had done her work properly. Making both hands into fists, she used her knuckles to wipe away her father's tears.

On Friday morning, Cantabile went with Monsieur Belladroit to supervise the removal of the pianofortes to Pall Mall, where the final practice would take place. When Monsieur had made this request, Cantabile had at first refused even to listen, then declared point-blank that his pianoforte was irrecoverably tainted, infected inside and out with the girls' mediocrity and inanity, and nothing would make him break his vow to have nothing to do with it again. Monsieur spoke of what would happen to the pianoforte after the concert. Once the girls were exposed by their husbands and returned, disgraced, to their homes, the instrument would be a scandal. "It will be passed from house to house like a blighted child," Monsieur said. "Only its value will prevent its destruction." Could Cantabile not hear it call out to him? Did he want to abandon it in its distress? "It is not a blighted child, it is your child, Vittorio," Monsieur said, hard-eyed for all his sighs, "and whatever the faults of the girls, it is the finest pianoforte I am ever likely to play. Come, do. Come where you can comfort and save it. Must I go down on my knees on its behalf?"

It was not pleasant for Monsieur when Cantabile shrieked and shouted, flying first into a rage and then into a frenzy. Yet Monsieur persisted, not for the sake of the pianoforte, fine as it was, but for the sake of Annie, the blighted child Cantabile would never comfort. She who had so little should have the pianoforte. It was the only thing he, Claude Belladroit, could offer her. Once he had gone, whatever erupted in that awful workshop, there would be beautiful music.

Monsieur's persistence was rewarded. Having been determined not to think about his pianoforte, Cantabile opened his ears and heard it calling, and not just calling: he heard it howling. He did want it back. He wanted it back so badly he could not sleep. He said nothing directly to Monsieur, giving his answer only through hiring the undertaker's cart again and sending an inflated bill for transportation to Mr. Frogmorton. The pianoforte would go from Manchester Square to Pall Mall, and shortly afterward to Tyburn. Cantabile underlined Tyburn twice.

The two men walked to Manchester Square dressed against the weather.

"You're very quiet, Claude," observed Cantabile, swinging his bag of tuning and regulating tools.

"I have the aria and variations going through my head," Monsieur said untruthfully, for going through his head was the joy of the end. There would be no more girls, no more unwanted advances, no more sex. At Pall Mall, thank all the gods in all the heavens, he and the girls would never be alone. Servants would already be busy in the saloon preparing tables and flowers. The doors would always be open. There would be no privacy, not for a second. He recollected with a wry shake of the head his desire to get rid of Mrs. Frogmorton in the spring. Truly, there had been times in the last fortnight when he would have given ready money to have her back in her chair with that odious dog barking. Fancy, he thought. Claude Belladroit in need of a chaperone. *Mon Dieu.*

The cart was already outside No. 23, people gathering

around waiting for a body. Neither the undertaker nor the hired muscle had corrected them. Cantabile rang the bell. It never crossed his mind to use the servants' entrance. Mrs. Frogmorton was already in the hall, Frilly tucked in. She had been waiting for Monsieur, and she berated him at once. "Do you still have no understanding of English taste, Monsieur? An undertaker's cart again? You should have consulted me. And who is that?" Mr. Cantabile was already on the stairs.

"It is Vittorio Cantabile, the pianoforte maker." Monsieur gave a quick apologetic bow.

"What is he doing in my house?"

"He is necessary for the removals to the concert saloon, madame. Come now." Monsieur smiled his most charming smile. "Soon we will be out of your house and the undertaker's cart will be turned into a marriage wagon, yes?"

"Wagon?" Mrs. Frogmorton swelled with vexation. "You think Harriet will leave this house in a wagon? Really, Monsieur, you don't—"

"No, madame," said Monsieur Belladroit sorrowfully. "I expect I do not, but what matter now. After today I will trouble you no more." He smiled again, ruefully this time, then made for the stairs.

Mrs. Frogmorton deflated slowly as she followed Monsieur. "Foreigners!" she said to Frilly. "Music is awash with them."

Monsieur found Cantabile greeting his instrument as a mother greets a child released from a kidnapper. When his greeting was over, he methodically wiped down every inch of its frame, every key. "Fetch the men," he ordered Monsieur. "Let's get my precious out of here. The concert saloon can't be worse than this—" He broke off, unable to find a word insulting enough.

The hired muscle found the instrument an awkward corpse and were duly cursed and bawled at as they detached the body from the legs. It was an odd procession down the stairs: three men maneuvering the bulk; two men manhandling the frame; one man clutching the pedal mechanism. The removal left a considerable gap and several stains on the floorboards that only poor light and the quick shifting of the harpsichord kept from Mrs. Frogmorton's notice. She closed the door on the room's green gloom, patted Frilly on the head, and remarked with some satisfaction that it was nice to have things back to normal.

At Stratton Street, Mrs. Drigg was glad to see the second pianoforte go to Pall Mall, since this meant that Alathea would no longer be a constant visitor. The concert could not come soon enough, Mrs. Drigg thought as the instrument was trundled away, nor the moment when Alathea would be married, saddled with a dozen wailing children, and holed up in the country, preferably with a husband too poor to have any decent carriage horses. Mrs. Drigg felt guilty at the unchristian quality of this thought, though guilt was quickly overtaken by relief at being able to dedicate herself completely to the subject of Everina's concert corset.

The fathers, minus Sawneyford, were also in good heart. Frogmorton, Drigg, and Brass arrived at Pall Mall at noon to see the instruments installed at the far end of the Allemonde saloon. The earl had graciously provided two long stools from the servants' hall and carpenters had been summoned to make certain they were the correct height. Drigg was not pleased to see Cantabile and avoided him. They all ignored the undertaker's cart, at which the Allemonde servants sniggered.

This was the first time Brass and Drigg had seen Monsieur Belladroit, the castrato. Drigg glanced surreptitiously. Brass openly smirked until Frogmorton reminded him that Monsieur was French and Frenchmen were notoriously huffy. If Monsieur walked out now, where would they all be? Brass growled but stopped smirking. Anyway, there was not much to smirk at. Monsieur was exactly as their wives had described. He did not, on the face of it, look like a eunuch. But what did a eunuch look like? Brass found it more useful to inspect the saloon furnishings and wandered around calculating and assessing. The marble and gold consoles he considered French and without merit. Nonetheless, though he had never seen the Allemonde son, he could imagine Georgiana mistress both of this house and the one fifty miles to the north that he had had independently valued. He would tell Georgiana what he expected of her.

Mr. Cantabile and Monsieur Belladroit cared nothing for the fathers and took no notice when Brass, having finished his inspection of the room, came over to inspect the pianofortes at close quarters. Frogmorton was similarly engaged. "It's a pity they don't match," Frogmorton said.

"And a pity that they seem to insist on the brown one being in the front," said Brass. "It's an ugly piece."

"Oh well," said Frogmorton. "The Frenchman knows best, and once the girls are playing, nobody will look at the instruments." Something struck him. "You," he said to Cantabile. "Mr.—"

"Cantabile," said Monsieur, when Cantabile did not reply.

"Mr. Cantabile," said Frogmorton. "You'll be on hand during the concert to keep the pianofortes well tuned?" He turned and called Drigg over. "Didn't you say tuning was necessary, Drigg?"

Drigg approached unwillingly. "Well, I suppose—"

"Let's not suppose," Frogmorton said. "If tuning is important and we've two pianofortes, we'll need two pianoforte tuners. There must be no delays while the girls are playing. What do you say, Cantabile?"

Cantabile, lever in hand, grinned at Drigg. Drigg looked at his boots. "I'd say two tuners would help the smooth running of your show. I'll send my daughter." He spoke to Frogmorton but never took his eyes off Drigg. "Would that be acceptable?"

Drigg paled.

"I don't care if you send your mother," said Frogmorton, "so long as she can tune properly."

"Oh, my Annie can tune properly," said Cantabile, "and I'll have my pianoforte back after."

Brass snorted at him. "Have it back? We paid good money for that instrument."

"Is that what he told you?" Cantabile jabbed a finger at Drigg.

Frogmorton was immediately suspicious, not of Drigg but of Cantabile. "We paid what we paid," he said, narrowing his eyes.

"What you paid was rent," Cantabile said. "No money in the world could come close to my pianoforte's true value, even after your children have . . . have . . . have . . ."

"Drigg?" said Frogmorton.

"Oh, er, I don't . . ."

Cantabile snarled his lips in fearsome imitation of Annie.

"Don't you remember, sir? Wasn't that our agreement, sir? I didn't want to sell. You must remember, sir."

"Of course I remember," snapped Drigg. He had nothing, really, to be ashamed of, or to hide. He had not told any lies. Not really. Why did he feel like a criminal?

Cantabile kept going. "And I wanted to send Annie as teacher. Do you remember that?" Much to Frogmorton's surprise, the snarled lip was snarled up some more. "You'd have done well with Annie," Cantabile said. "Really very well."

"We've done very well with Monsieur Belladroit." Drigg moved to block Cantabile. "I think, Archibald, that perhaps there was some equivocation. The quality of the instrument may have been . . . the day may have been . . . the arrangement may have been—"

"Oh, for goodness' sake, Tobias! It hardly matters. If the man wants his instrument back, let him have it. What else are we going to do with it? You should just have made it clear at the start. You can return some of our money if that makes you feel better. Add it to the money you owe for the Frenchman's lessons."

Cantabile was back at the pianoforte. After twenty minutes, with pressing business in the City, the fathers left.

The mothers arrived soon after, Mrs. Frogmorton and Mrs. Drigg bickering gently over the number and setting of the candles, Mrs. Frogmorton wanting more light, Mrs. Drigg rather less. With the pianofortes in place, they were nervous. The concert, so long spoken of, now lived and breathed on its own. The sale of their daughters was about to begin. As they fussed, Mrs. Drigg knew with depressing certainty that one candle or a hundred, Marianne and Everina would be outshone by Harriet and Georgiana. Mrs. Brass wished everything were over: concert, marriage, life. Mrs. Frogmorton, confident of Harriet, worried about details. The ordered hothouse flowers had arrived. She sent them back. "Midday tomorrow," she scolded. "They must be perfect." She made sure to inspect the kitchens, cleaned at her own expense. She had hired the cooks herself. For the fifth time, she counted out the plate bought specially for the occasion. It was bad enough they had to borrow a room; their china must not be found wanting. Mrs. Drigg's father provided the fish free of charge. It was in the larder, packed in ice. Mrs. Frogmorton smelled it. Good fish. Excellent fish. It had been nice of him.

In the later afternoon, Cantabile returned to Tyburn, his heart filled equally with disgust and delight. The City men were frightful. Their daughters would be frightful. The concert would be torture. But the concert would soon be over and his pianoforte returned to him. He pushed open the shop door and pricked his ears. Was Annie here? He could never be sure these days. He heard the click of a lever in the back and smelled something bubbling on the stove upstairs. She was here. He moved warily. Since Annie had tried to murder Maria Barthélemon's music, she and he had padded around each other, alert to the possibility of bloodshed. "Those City people," he said aloud, going through to the back to find her. "Hyenas."

Annie did not look at him. "I expect the girls are pretty."

"The girls weren't there. If they're anything like their mothers, I should have paid Claude more. He'd have been better off with you."

Cantabile knew that these days his jibes were wasted, his barbs blunt. He was unclear exactly how Annie had rendered him impotent, physical hurt the only punishment left to him, and he no longer cared. From now on, he would think solely of his pianoforte. It never had and never would disobey or challenge. It bent readily to his will. It would never leave here again. He went farther into the warehouse. From a tall cupboard he collected the axe, took it to the front, removed his coat, and there, in the workshop, set about destroying his current project. Like his daughter, it was unworthy of him.

Monsieur Belladroit returned to the workshop directly after collecting his last pay pouch from Manchester Square. He considered not collecting it. It always made him feel cheap. However, money was money. He weighed the bag—he never counted it—and put it in his pocket. For the first and last time, and only because he was ordered to do so by Mrs. Frogmorton, Spencer opened and closed the front door for him. The footman and the music master exchanged glances containing not an ounce of camaraderie.

The evening sky was cloudless, the stars bright pinheads. It had already begun to freeze. Nevertheless, Monsieur stopped to look back at the house in which he had spent so many hours. How tightly the windows were shuttered, or curtained, or both, to keep the winter out. All that fuss about dangerous air when real danger was warmly wrapped and came through the front door. His skin tingled. He wound his scarf closer around his throat. A wig would be good tonight; he did not like a cold head. He thrust his hands into gloves. Where next? Where had he not yet been? The possibilities should have excited him: he could go anywhere, but the whole concept of anywhere suddenly seemed very bleak.

He was almost out of the square when, through clouds of steam and showers of sparks more suited to a return from the battlefield than a canter in the park, a man clattered by on his horse and a groom ran out from the back of No. 22. That would be Mr. Buller, thought Monsieur, and nodded. Thomas did not nod back. He was already searching the upper windows of No. 23. The shutters meant there was nothing to see, yet his cheeks reddened with more than the chill. Ah, thought Monsieur, Mademoiselle Harriet has made her move. Poor Thomas Buller. He will not escape now. He chided himself. Why would Thomas Buller want to escape? Mademoiselle Harriet was a nice girl—much nicer than Marianne or Everina. He wished young Mr. and Mrs. Buller well. Banging his hands together, Monsieur made his way into Oxford Street. In the gloaming, stonecutters were still at work. Buildings going up, buildings coming down. Shouting boys had tipped bricks out of a cart to make an ice slide. The bricklayers, half-annoyed and half-indulgent, pelted the boys with mortar from above. Clamoring, belligerent, and constantly battering the ears and nose, London was never so lovely as when you were about to leave it.

NINETEEN

SATURDAY, 13 DECEMBER 1794

MORNING

ONSIEUR RETURNED TO ST. JAMES'S early. In anticipation of the concert, the Allemonde servants had lit fires at either end of the saloon. The shutters were still closed, also the curtains, and despite its size, with six lamps and twenty candles blazing, the room was warm. Monsieur ran his hand over the brown piano-forte. The sound, in here, would be rich as plum cake, as any-body discerning would appreciate. Of course, the audience would not be discerning. He tested each note again. When he was satisfied with the brown instrument, he moved to the black. Again, he sounded the notes carefully, occasionally two notes together, A, A-sharp, B, C, A, and C together, C-sharp, and on, methodical as a workman testing the rungs of a ladder. Two young servants hoping for a dance returned to their duties disappointed.

Monsieur wiped his hands and appreciated the saloon. The major furniture had been cleared and the room was free from the larger elements of concert clutter. The walls, predominantly sand colored, were lightened by white stucco cornice cherubs of unusual daintiness that Monsieur found graceful and pleasing. He bowed to an imaginary audience and sat down at the brown pianoforte. First, a scale. The scale became an arpeggio, then back to a scale in thirds and sixths, then finally scales and arpeggios decorated, ornamented, syncopated. He checked the clock. There was time. He took off his coat and played as he had not played for months: for himself. The toccatas, sonatas, fugues, and inventions of Bach, Handel, and Haydn stretched his fingers, wrists, wit, intellect, and technique. Oh, he had forgotten! In teaching the girls, even Alathea, he had been denied the joy of music *toute seule*. It was glorious here, just himself and Cantabile's miraculous instrument. After two hours, he was as refreshed and reinvigorated as a man starved of books let loose in a library. He put his coat back on and relaxed. The girls would arrive soon, with no danger of even the mildest flirtation. He was in charge again. It would be quite like old times.

Mrs. Frogmorton and Mrs. Drigg arrived at Pall Mall before their daughters, each preceded by a cart bearing flowers, fruits, and large silk balloons containing the girls' concert dresses. During the course of the morning, the graceful saloon was transformed into what Monsieur could only describe as an overblown village market. *Tant pis.* He happily tinkered with the instruments, checking the pitch for the sheer pleasure of it. A little later, the girls themselves arrived ready for their final practice. They would not go home before the concert, hence the dresses in their traveling covers. Alathea arrived last. She brought her own dress, also covered. She did not bring any flowers or fruits.

Monsieur set out the scores. The girls, apart from Alathea, studied them with alarm, all the familiar variations seeming, on this morning of mornings, as unfamiliar as something entirely new.

"I can't remember anything," moaned Everina. "I'm sure to go wrong."

"Why did we have to play something so complicated?" whined Marianne.

Harriet and Georgiana were white and silent. They would forget. Their fingers would freeze or grow clumsy. The con-cert would be a disaster. They kept looking at Alathea.

Alathea was calm, though her heart beat faster than usual. She had not seen her father since Thursday night. On Friday morning, taking the diamonds he had left behind on that last dreadful visitation, she had sped out of the house, first to a jeweler who had given her ready money for one of the dia-monds and agreed to cut the others, then to the Salutation and Cat, and from there to the Pool of London armed with the name of the captain of a merchant ship. The Pool had been chaotic. It was almost impossible to see the water, so closely were the ships crowded together. She had been determined and not left until she had solicited a paper guaranteeing her-self and Annie a berth on the *Maidenhead*, due to edge out at first tide tomorrow. Alathea had given a wry smile at the name. From the Pool, straight to Stratton Street where the girls had gathered at Marianne's harpsichord, the pianofortes already removed. She would have preferred to go to Tyburn to show Annie the passage papers but she had promised the

girls this final practice, so she entrusted the papers and a letter to a courier. She would collect Annie from Tyburn directly
after the concert. By Sunday noon, they would be on the high
seas. Before she sealed the letter, she took her mother's ring
from her thumb, kissed it, and slid it inside. It was still a wedding ring. It would always be a wedding ring. After finishing
at Stratton Street, she had returned to the jeweler. Once back
in Soho Square, she spent most of the night working on her
dress. This morning, she was tired but exultant. She smiled
confidently and confidentially at the girls. Everina and Marianne stopped wailing. Harriet and Georgiana hugged themselves. This is our day, Alathea's smile said to them each in
turn. Enjoy it.

Monsieur rattled the score to get their attention. "Now,
mademoiselles. To work. This is how the morning will go." He
would hear each girl's particular variations first. Afterward,
they would run through the whole performance. During those
variations where he was to help out, the girl should always
play the brown pianoforte and he would play the black. The
five chairs behind the pianoforte stools were where the girls
should sit when not playing. Did they understand? They nodded. Practice began and after a while Everina and Marianne
were hammering away as always, Harriet and Georgiana
offering something more sonorous. Alathea's sound was rich
and—what else? Safe? Yes! For the first time since that first
lesson Monsieur was not wondering what was going to happen
next.

The room filled with servants, tradesmen, concert chairs.
Occasionally, the instructions of Mrs. Frogmorton and the
twitterings of Mrs. Drigg, both resplendent in aprons and
working caps, drowned out the music. There was tension over

the lighting. Mrs. Drigg moved candles. Mrs. Frogmorton moved them back. Mrs. Brass arrived. She whispered. Monsieur barked. The noise—human, musical, mechanical, domestic, congratulatory, admonitory—surged until by one o'clock, all was prepared.

Even Monsieur was content. He shut the pianofortes' lids. The girls made to leave the room. "Wait!" Monsieur said. "Sit." The girls sat obediently in the front row of the seats arranged in two banks, six on each side of a center aisle, not pressed together since the skirts of the lady guests' dresses were expected to be full.

Monsieur walked up and down. He had not intended to give the girls a lecture, but his morning's playing urged him to remind them of their duty to Herr Bach. He cleared his throat. "As you know, mademoiselles, the *Clavier Übung* is a serious piece," he said. "To be able to play it at all marks you out as young women of distinction, and it is, of course, this distinction that will attract the future husbands sitting in these rows. I have one last instruction." He sought their eyes. All were wide, wide, wide. "You must perform the music exactly as Herr Bach wrote it," he said, "exactly as we have practiced. Do not allow yourselves to be distracted. Place yourselves in Herr Bach's hands. He will be your guide. That is all." There was no hint, as he spoke, of the man who had taken them and tumbled them. At this moment, Monsieur Belladroit was musician and music master only. Mrs. Frogmorton and Mrs. Drigg, grappling with ferns and oranges, nodded their approval. How silly their misgivings had been. The castrato was a serious man who had done a serious job. Mrs. Frogmorton thought she would tell the alderman to tip him.

Four of the girls tripped out of the room. Georgiana

remained seated. Monsieur went to her. "You must go and have a little food, and then submit yourself to the hair setter with the others," he said. She did not move. "Mademoiselle Georgiana, do not fear. You are well rehearsed," Monsieur reassured, "and I will be here, playing my part, as we have arranged. You will not be alone, little dove. The concert will be a success, and afterward, you will never be alone again." Georgiana squeezed his hand with ferocious intensity. Monsieur had not called her "little dove" since their real intimacy began. Monsieur squeezed back and propelled her after the others.

EVENING

Dressing the girls was a long affair, begun in the light and completed in the dark. An upstairs room had been made available, with fires lit and bathtubs provided. Troops of maids trudged to and fro with hot water and cinnamon oil, slicks of gentian cream and warmed towels. The girls did nothing for themselves. The mothers whisked soap and flanneled backs, patted shoulders and rubbed feet. Only Alathea demurred, asking for privacy. After some discussion, she was shown another room in which a fire was hurriedly, and rather resentfully, lit and another tub brought. "Call me when you're ready for the hair setter," said Mrs. Frogmorton, "and I'll help with your dress."

Alathea was already shutting the door. "I can manage myself."

"Will your father be coming?" asked Mrs. Drigg, wedging the door with her foot. "Is he quite well? We heard—"

"He's quite well, thank you," said Alathea. Mrs. Drigg had to move her foot or have it crushed. Alathea called for hot water but once her tub was filled, she locked the door and bathed herself slowly. She had no idea whether her father would come. If he did, how would he be? Wrapped in a towel, she curled up in a chair and closed her eyes. She wanted neither hair setter nor face painter. She must hear the music. That was the thing now. Only the music.

Marianne had ordered a low-cut, short-sleeved polonaise-style dress of midnight-blue velvet over a satin under-dress, sky blue with silver spangles. Her arms were bare. The tight boning of the bodice made sitting difficult. Nevertheless, Marianne was firmly encased in the dress before she sat for the hair setter, a sensible precaution given that she refused to wear a fichu, and the freckles on her neck, on her shoulders, and at her cleavage required almost half a pound of powder to disguise. To ensure Marianne would be blue and white in the right places, it was best not to disturb the powder. A dust sheet provided the necessary protection. Mrs. Drigg trimmed the hair in Marianne's armpits and hung small pomanders from her shoulders to nestle in the remaining tufts. Marianne would smell, as well as look, delicious. Mother and daughter were pleased with the dress. It really was magnificent, its only disadvantage being to accentuate Marianne's miserable ringlets. No matter. With the dress settled, the hair setter tipped out the contents of his wig bags, and after some discussion Marianne chose a chalk-white, highly structured creation, creamed with pearls and silk lily of the valley and topped with an ostrich feather. In moments, the rattails were in a knot, the wig bearing down. Marianne opened her mouth to whine that the wig was too tight, then saw her reflection and was silent. The long feather shortened her long jaw. The pearls obscured her open pores and cast a peachy luster over her skin. For the only time in her life, from the top of the feather to the tip of her blue velvet slippers, Marianne could have passed for a lady of sophisticated distinction. Mrs. Drigg almost wept. And this before the face painter had even begun.

Everina had wanted the natural look currently fashionable. As soon as she saw Marianne dressed, she regretted it. Her frock, unboned light gray silk with embroidered roses in pastel colors and crimped up at the back, was certainly pretty, and its floating train added a touch of fairy dust. But against Marianne's midnight blue, Everina's dress seemed insipid—a dairymaid in the court of a queen. Everina's chin began to wobble. With the inspiration and bravery of panic, Mrs. Drigg quickly reassured that though Marianne looked fine at the moment, everybody knew that wigs came off, and that Everina's unpowered arms, spotted with fresh scented petals, contrasted favorably, very favorably, with Marianne's arms, which, without powder, were not things to be left uncovered. Also, so Everina comforted herself, Marianne's décolletage was too low, as though she were a married woman already, and there was nothing even the powderer could do about that incipient mustache.

Georgiana emerged as a goddess, sprays of white buds peeping from a long, loose cascade of golden, newly washed hair—all her own. She had chosen the polonaise style like Marianne, but hers was a milky waterfall of pure white silk, no ruching, no decoration, the long-sleeved under-dress of equally pure white lace, delicately patterned with white pimpernels. When, the day before, she had described the dress, the other girls secretly thought it too simple. Now they saw what simplicity could do. Once ready, Georgiana sat by herself, studying her pure white slippers.

There was nothing simple about Harriet. She had won her

battle for gold, and Mrs. Frogmorton, having given in, chose gold upon gold upon gold: a high-waisted under-dress of heavy gold silk, then lighter gold speckled net, then, from directly under the breasts, a flutter of floor-length gold ribbons with tiny gold stars echoing similar stars on gold-brocade shoes. On her head, a golden turban, its folds secured by a large emerald, all the more dramatic for the plain gold setting. The effect was imperially Eastern. With her lips painted to a pout, Harriet was magnificent.

Alathea did not appear. The mothers conferred. Mrs. Frog-morton knocked on her door. There was a polite rejection.

It was nearly six. With the hair setters and face painters gone, the girls' everyday clothes tidied, the mothers also in their concert attire and running out of conversation, they were all aware of the arriving guests. Mrs. Drigg opened the door, the better to catch snippets. "I'm only here because the duke insisted," drifted one voice. "And I because my son's interested in music," drifted another. "Let's hope it doesn't go on too long," drifted a third voice. "I've heard the girls are frights," drifted a fourth, or it might have been the first again. "Frights with fortunes," the second voice declared—no drift needed. Mrs. Frogmorton got up, drew Mrs. Drigg away, and closed the door.

Monsieur waited downstairs. The arriving guests glanced briefly at the pianofortes before searching for the supper tables. Mrs. Frogmorton had foreseen this and wisely instructed that the supper should be firmly locked away. No food until after the concert. Nobody should get a free dinner and then slip off. Only champagne was offered and graciously accepted.

The Duchess of Oxford put her finger on it. Asked why she was here since her older son was already engaged, she replied, "Because everybody else is." And it was true. Every-body was—everybody who was asked, that is, and one other. Thomas Buller arrived alone, refused champagne, and chose an unobtrusive seat. Only the Frogmortons would have recog-nized him, and they were otherwise engaged. Cantabile arrived promptly, pushing his way past the dresses, jewels, velvet coats, and embroidered cloaks. Once he and Monsieur had opened up the pianofortes, he sat glaring from the stool of his treasure. Drigg was relieved to see him and not Annie.

The fathers greeted aristocratic creditors and noncreditors equally, their tone polite, not obsequious; deferential, not toadying. This evening, the City was ascendant, the fathers running the market. Only Brass's badgerish leer threatened to lower the tone. He enjoyed setting some of the ladies simper-ing and enjoyed it more when their husbands scowled. Frog-morton nudged Drigg. "Remind Brass that he's looking for a son-in-law, not a mistress." Drigg, however, was not listening. Mrs. Drigg had emerged from upstairs, fussing away and won-dering, even at this late stage, whether she should go home and get more jewels for Everina. What if people did not realize how expensive the gray satin and gauze had been, with each embroi-dered flower individually stitched and different in design? What if the Driggs were thought poorer than the Frogmortons or Brasses? Drigg was angry. "That side of things was your domain," he barked. "I'll not forgive you, Mrs. Drigg, if you've let me down." Mrs. Drigg vanished upstairs again. Frogmorton smugly went to have words with Brass. His wife would have made no such mistake.

There was a kerfuffle as the final guests arrived and every-body took their seats. For people who despised this concert of nobodies, the guests seemed uncommonly anxious to get a good view. And indeed, it was a fine show, with the candles, the flower and fruit arrangements, the two instruments, all overlaid with the scent of money. "Almost as good as a fox hunt," so a son obliged to give up a day in the field conceded to his father. "Tallyho!" his father replied.

Mrs. Frogmorton, Mrs. Drigg, and Mrs. Brass appeared all together, bowing stiffly to their few acquaintances and making for their appointed places on the ends of the first three rows, Mrs. Frogmorton and Mrs. Drigg on the right, Mrs. Brass on the left, the adjacent chairs reserved for their husbands. They had dressed with careful formality and had dressed their husbands similarly. All gowns were unyielding, all coats were new, all breeches spotless, all boots clean. Nothing ostentatious. This was the daughters' show. Parents were strictly scenery.

"Is Sawneyford still not here?" Brass said to Frogmorton as the fathers gathered at the back. "Surely he's not going to miss this?"

Frogmorton frowned. "I've been trying to locate him for days. Where can he have got to? And Cantabile was going to send his daughter to help Monsieur with the tuning. Is she here?"

"Cantabile's here himself," said Drigg. "As for Sawney, none of us has seen him, and not for want of trying. Anyway, we can't wait for him. He knows the place. He knows the time. The concert must start."

Monsieur rose. The guests turned from their neighbors to face the front. Monsieur raised his arms. There was a hush, as in a congregation expecting a bride. The fathers clapped one another lightly on the back and separated, Frogmorton and Drigg up the right-hand outside aisle and Brass up the left-hand. They could not worry about Sawneyford now. The footmen, primed by Mrs. Frogmorton, blew out the candelabra on the consoles, leaving only dozens of tiny floating flames (Elizabeth Brass's suggestion) and the candelabra on the pianofortes. Cantabile vanished to a bench set behind both the instruments, out of sight.

There was a small commotion, a slight altercation. Sawneyford appeared, no wig on his head and his hair untied. The footmen would have ejected him had not Drigg turned and raised a hand in an admonitory though relieved greeting. Sawneyford did not return the greeting. He did not see it. Nor did he want the glass of champagne thrust into his hand. He wanted to feel only the stock of the pistol hidden in the top of his breeches.

The girls, minus Alathea, gathered outside the door. "Do you think she's fallen asleep?" Marianne was whispering. The audience was waiting. The door was opening for their entrance. "What can we do?"

"You," said Harriet from under her turban to one of the footmen. "Go upstairs and knock on Miss Alathea's door." They could hear the saloon's expectant hush. Harriet gripped hands with the others very briefly. "We've got to go in. She'll be here."

"But—"

"Go, Marianne. By the time we've all walked in, she'll be here. She will be. Go."

The door was wide now. With a tiny push from Harriet, Marianne entered, head up, eyes down, just as they had discussed. Any concerns over Alathea vanished when she heard murmurs of surprised appreciation.

As she walked, the murmurs grew louder, the appreciation

deeper. The blue was gorgeous. The richness and fine cut of the cloth, expert hair, and clever powdering had successfully transformed Marianne from potato to full-blown hyacinth. She could, at that moment, have had her pick of the room. Harriet next, her pretty face rendered royally beautiful by the turban, the emerald, and the gown glowing like golden coin. "A living bank," exclaimed Lord Rathbone. His son was speechless. The concert had not even begun and already the audience's expectations were far exceeded. Two dozen heirs wondered why their mothers had scoffed. A blue bloom in Marianne! A golden bank in Harriet! And more to come.

Thomas Buller, too, was agog, though his heart was sinking. This glowing girl could not have chosen him. She was mythical queen and he was fleshy mortal. She would never be his. It was cruel of her to suggest it. As others gawped, he slumped.

Georgiana walked fastest up the aisle, a slur of untouched snow, the train of her silk overdress rippling behind her. Only she was not snow. Her face was warmly alight with girlish hope and joy. Her father's jaw dropped further than anybody else's. His daughter seemed barely his daughter. Against the white of her gown, her flesh was bright with love. Brass did not recognize this look as love. How could he? Love like Georgiana's was not something with which he was familiar.

Next, Everina. The panic had been justified. After the blue, gold, and white, the gray was almost invisible, the pastel flowers unremarkable, and Everina's arms were just arms, even under their petals and bows. But the spell had been cast already. In this atmosphere of surprise and thrills, the floating flames rendered her ghostly and mysterious, a gauzy enigma—not what was intended, but it worked. Moreover, the shadowy color and smudged outline hid her ungainly gait. Far from looking underdressed, Everina looked tastefully understated. Nobody ever would have guessed that her mother had started life in a fish stall.

Mrs. Frogmorton and Mrs. Drigg sagged with relief, as far as their bolstering corsets would allow. What did it matter what the girls played? The job was done already. The audience was delighted. Frogmorton leaned forward. "A triumph," he whispered. Drigg nodded. Only Alathea to go.

There was a pause. Where was the girl? A dull clinking sound. The audience turned and a different silence fell, the strange vacuumed silence that precedes an earthquake. If Gregory Brass's jaw had dropped at his own daughter, it gaped now.

Alathea was studded from top to toe with diamonds. Sewn onto the thinnest flesh-colored, limb-clinging, lucent silk flowing up to her neck, down her wrists, down to the floor, each stone exploded with brilliance against her rich skin. All the light in the room was sucked toward her and she reflected it back in splinters and shards. Apart from the stones, she seemed quite naked. Harriet, Everina, and Marianne gasped. No wonder Alathea had hung back. She had outshone them all. For one uncharitable moment, Harriet saw the diamonds as winks of malice. Should they clap or hiss? Only Georgiana was oblivious, her mind firmly fixed on something else.

Alathea began to walk. The diamonds rippled. None was strategically placed over any part of her and it was obvious to everybody that she had been at work with the tweezers. Apart from the hair on her head, the sculpted eyebrows, and eyelashes thick as pelts, she was completely shorn. Against those deep, suggestive shadows even the diamond fireworks played second fiddle. Her hands were bare of jewels. Around her neck she had a diamond-spiked choker, as a fighting dog might have, and this served to complete her nakedness. "Ye gods," said Brass. "*Ye gods.*"

A sixth sense made Alathea aware of her father. She did not acknowledge him. She was beyond him. She moved slowly up the center aisle, looking neither right nor left. When the fathers and sons breathed again, they did not meet each other's eyes, nor the eyes of their wives or mothers. Those hard stones; that yielding flesh; the submission and the arrogance of that choker; those dagger flashes and—throttled throats—those shadows. Footman and duke were as one: they all wanted her; she was all they wanted.

ANNIE HAD found it hard to open the note delivered by the courier, convinced it was the rejection she dreaded and expected. It stood to reason that Alathea's treasured detachment and the separation of the past weeks would have made the note easier to write. She had tended her mother with the letter still unopened, then sat on the chair beside her mother's bed and propped the letter against the candle. She comforted herself. She could never leave her mother and rejection would mean she did not have to. In the circumstances, rejection was the best thing. She focused on that. She picked up the note. If she opened it here, her mother's presence would ensure detachment, or at least some self-control. She broke the seal. The ring fell out. She read the written words. She could not control herself. She folded over.

"Annie?" Her mother whispered. "Annie?" Mrs. Cantabile tried to sit up. Fear injected strength. Her waxy face grew waxier still. "Annie? What is it? Tell me."

Annie did not know how. She must go with Alathea. She

must. She could not ask Alathea to wait until her mother died. It might be months or even years. Alathea would go alone, and if she did that, Annie would lose her.

"Annie?" Her mother's voice was frailly insistent. "You must tell me."

Annie moved the candle and handed her mother the letter. Her mother tried and failed to read it. "Read it to me."

Annie read it. When she looked again, her mother was staring at the ceiling. For one wild moment, Annie thought the shock had killed her. Her mother's lips moved. Annie leaned over in a dreadful confusion of hope and despair, each muddled and tainted.

"Go," her mother said.

A great weight descended. Annie knew she could not go. "We'll take you," she said. How ridiculous.

Her mother's fingers found hers. "Annie," she croaked, and fixed her daughter with eyes empty of everything but pain, rheum, and broken veins. "I can go with you," she mouthed. "But not like this. Release me, Annie, as I release you. Let my soul fly from here. God brings death, I know, but sometimes he needs a little help."

"I can't!" whispered Annie.

"Don't lie to me, Annie. You can, and why not? You want it. I want it."

"No," Annie said out loud.

"Yes, my sweet girl. Wishing me dead and wishing I was dead—they're not the same. Not for us. You know that. Don't deny it. Don't. There is no need."

Annie was silent.

Mrs. Cantabile lay back on her pillow. "Your father won't help me. Only you have the courage and the generosity."

"Generosity?" Annie burst out. "Ah, Mother! Not generosity."

Mrs. Cantabile's fingers curled around Annie's hands. She smiled. "Generosity, Annie. Yes, generosity, because it won't be easy. The body struggles for life against the wishes of the soul. My struggle will haunt you. But you'll bear it for me. You'll do it."

"I don't know how, Mother."

"I would say laudanum," Mrs. Cantabile said. "Drifting off while you were playing one of your own compositions would be like being in heaven already. But it must be quick." Her breath was shallow. "The pillow," she said. She did not let go of Annie's hands until Annie repeated "the pillow" and both knew the decision was made.

Now Mrs. Cantabile looked directly at Annie and Annie looked directly at her. Both were afraid, but the strength of purpose in both faces cut through the fear. Mrs. Cantabile placed her own hands over her breast. Annie kissed her mother's forehead—a real kiss, the first. She kissed her mother's hands, a real kiss, the second. Then she slid a pillow from under her mother's head and with all the force of love held the pillow down. Ten minutes later Annie left the house carrying her small bag with her. Alathea would not have to come and fetch her after the concert. Annie arrived at the Pall Mall saloon doors as they were closing.

ALATHEA REACHED the top of the aisle and sat in her allocated chair. Monsieur, blinking, got up from the stool of the second pianoforte. He fiddled with his lapels. "We are going..." His voice was high. These girls. They were wonderful. And Alathea. Alathea. He tried again. He must bring himself and the audience back to the music. He dispensed with the proper greeting for such a gathering. "Ladies, gentlemen," he said, his omission of titles gaining the titles' immediate attention. "We are going to play for you today the last part of Herr Bach's *Clavier Übung*." Uttering Herr Bach's name helped Monsieur, though what Herr Bach would have made of this spectacle, he had no idea. "We shall play this work in its entirety for the first time ever in London. It is a very particular work. It is a work those of you with taste and discernment will not forget and a work only those of very particular accomplishment can offer. These young ladies have that accomplishment. It is rare. As you can see"—he gestured at the girls—"they are rare. Please save your applause until the end." He sat down.

Alathea's nakedness moved to the brown pianoforte. She did not open the score. She did not need to. She sat until expectation tightened to suspense. Had this diamond vision forgotten the music? Was this naked girl ever going to start?

Only when she was completely ready did Alathea pick up her hands and, into the silence, drop top G, G, A ornamented dotted quaver, to B. The tender run. Then the lower G, orna-mented twice and the running semi- and demisemiquavers measured into the steady cadence of the bass. The aria was begun, so economical, so clean, so clear—so slow, Monsieur thought at first with alarm, then with increasing and wonder-ing admiration. His buttocks unclenched. Of course. Slow, slow, slow. It was quite right. Alathea made no fuss, no unto-ward movement, no pedal. The aria was played straight as a die, just as Herr Bach intended. That it could sustain such a deliberate pace was Alathea's miracle. Monsieur had tears in his eyes.

The astonishment of the audience was palpable. This

sound, so rich! How could it be coming from this brown thing that most had assumed, not having read their invitation properly, was a harpsichord. Plum cake indeed, even to the uninitiated.

Sawney Sawneyford heard as through a cloud and saw as through grit. He was sweating. His daughter, his lover, as he only should see her, a blur of sparkles and skin, on public view displayed. Jesus Christ. How could silk cling so close? And those fingers, those fingers that were his, creating this beautiful, truthful sound. Sawneyford pinched his forefinger nail into the mound of his thumb.

On the side opposite Sawneyford, Annie never took her eyes from Alathea. She waited through the aria's second section; the long lines, the gathering tension. Half a bar before the resolution, Alathea turned her head. Through the heavy gauze of her veil, it should have been impossible for Annie to see. What need had she to see? She felt that turn. She felt Alathea feeling her presence. This was the trumpet welcome Annie longed for. Why had she ever doubted? Her veil billowed in, out. Breathing was the only movement she made.

Behind the pianofortes, almost out of sight, Cantabile was sitting bolt upright, his hands gripped together in furious astonishment. His pianoforte had never sounded like this. How dare this naked girl confound him? It was impossible that she had talent. It was unforgivable. It was not what he had expected, and what he did not expect could not be. The aria came to an end. Alathea, shimmering, left the pianoforte stool to Marianne.

Marianne rustled the score and rushed into Variation 1 like a horse out of the stalls. Monsieur winced. Cantabile relaxed. This was more like it. Marianne fluffed the hand crossing. Monsieur tutted. She had often missed the G. She was going far too fast. Marianne gulped and slowed for the second part, keeping her eyes glued to the music. This was utilitarian, a respectable marshaling of notes. Monsieur nodded his head. Good. However long he might have had with her, Mademoiselle Marianne could never play better than a tolerably efficient automaton. He glanced at the audience. The initial speed of the variation, such a contrast with Alathea, had impressed. Frogmorton, Drigg, and others were tapping their feet. What idiots, thought Monsieur. Still, the variation did have something of a swing to it. Marianne banged to a halt, returned to her seat, and patted her wig. Monsieur gave her an encouraging nod.

Now Georgiana. Variation 2, a duet of echoing melodies over a steady bass. She began with obvious nerves, her timing careful, the tune taking its turn in each register, a walk after Marianne's gallop. She remained at the pianoforte for Variation 3, the first canon, introducing it with the same care. Only when the bass quavers erupted into semiquavers did she surprise both the audience and Monsieur by directing a light smile into the air suggestive of girlish elation.

Harriet made the most of her great entry, playing Variation 4 like a businessman constructing a letter of serious import. Pay attention. No slacking. Hint of whip crack. Yours sincerely. The audience liked it. This golden girl had spirit. Thomas Buller remembered just in time not to clap. Taking a deep breath, and glancing briefly over her shoulder at Alathea, Harriet began Variation 5. Over the first three bars, a nervous metamorphosis took place. She was no longer the businessman. Now she was a tease. Her face registered only concentration— the variation was technically difficult—yet what was it about the set of her shoulders as her left and right hands crossed and recrossed that made every man in the room feel as if her hands might, if he was lucky, land in his lap? As she gained confidence, Harriet's mouth turned up at one corner. The semiquavers, that deliberate fingering, turned Variation 5 into something sensational in the literal sense. Monsieur sucked in his cheeks. He clicked his tongue at Harriet. In the audience, Frogmorton tensed, although Mrs. Frogmorton was clearly enjoying herself. Harriet was marvelous. The alderman scolded himself. He had been upset by Alathea. She made everything seem peculiar. Anyway, this variation would end soon. It did. Harriet stood, imperial once more, turban intact, face slightly flushed.

Everina rose. The contrast with Harriet was appreciated, and the scent released by the arm petals wafted pleasingly toward those in the front row. Monsieur nodded to her. She emanated panic. Monsieur frowned. He gestured to the pianoforte stool. She sat down, adjusted the score but did not start. Monsieur was annoyed. Everina could play this variation alone. He had heard her. Yet if she was nervous, it was unjust to be angry with her. He slid onto the stool next to her. They could play this variation on one piano without impeding each other. Everina, happy now, eased into the music, a picture of unspoiled, childlike maidenhood. Mr. and Mrs. Drigg pressed together. Oh, this was lovely. Everina was lovely. The dress was lovely. Everything was lovely. Mrs. Drigg knew, without even looking about, that every mother in the room wished her daughter were sitting up there at the pianoforte, just like Everina. Only Monsieur was annoyed as Everina mistimed the runs and forgot the accidentals. It was good, though, he thought, to reassert control.

Everina started Variation 7 so quickly after Variation 6 that Monsieur was trapped beside her. Under Alathea's instruction, Everina had learned this variation by heart, and how to make it naughtily provocative. She accentuated the gigue, and showed her teeth, touching Monsieur's shoulder with her own and smiling at the audience from under her lashes. Mr. Drigg's stomach lurched. That was not so lovely. He felt his wife stiffen through the stiffness of her gown. Both were glad when Everina was back on her chair. Marianne again. Monsieur moved to the black pianoforte. Marianne patted the seat beside her. Unless he was to cause a scene, Monsieur had to join her. She played cat and mouse with the music master, shimmying a little as their hands muddled and crossed. Monsieur tried to pull her back to earth, moving down an octave so that their fingers did not touch. Marianne moved down an octave too. The audience had no idea whether this was in the score or not, but the pantomime effect made the fathers and sons grin and the wives and mothers fan themselves disapprovingly. Funny it may be, but for all Marianne's velvet and powder, it was not ladylike. Mrs. Drigg gripped Mr. Drigg's knee.

Alathea next. It was difficult to pinpoint exactly how she turned a stately melody of dowager propriety into an erotic invitation. Yet this is what happened to Variation 9, Herr Bach's third canon. With clustering diamond dewdrops between breasts and legs and that tantalizing, breath-throttling tan where there should have been dark cover, she played the audience as she played the keyboard, painting a picture of slow pleasures in which she was clearly well versed. Come, join me, Alathea said, see how pleasure can be found in unexpected places. Cold diamonds challenged; warm lips enticed. Above, a halo of hair; below, smooth as a glove.

Mrs. Frogmorton's palms had not yet begun to sweat, though she was no longer sitting easy. Harriet would have none of this, surely. Mrs. Frogmorton remembered business‑ like Variation 4 and pinned her hopes on that. She was only gradually aware of Variation 10, Georgiana's intense fugetta, during which this vision in white never once looked at the keyboard, but leaned with passionate and, so the mothers could see clearly from the gentle sway of her head, intimate intent at Monsieur. Brass refused to believe his eyes. Georgi‑ ana was simply showing character! This was all to the good. He felt his wife sit up. He nudged her. She began to rock.

Harriet again. Mr. and Mrs. Frogmorton held their breath. Variation 11 began innocently enough, and it was difficult. That was the trouble. Through that painted pout, Harriet's tongue appeared, and those hands still seemed capable of playing more than ivory keys. Harriet kept her eyes on the keyboard, demure but, so that tongue suggested, hardly inno‑ cent. Her legs, outlined by the fall of the ribbons to the side and down the middle, seemed far apart. And then, at the end, her tongue still poking through, she wrinkled her eyes at Monsieur and then at somebody in the audience.

Mrs. Frogmorton whipped around. Who? She could not see. "Archibald!" she whispered. Her palms were sweating now.

Onward. Everina was back at the keyboard, playing Varia‑ tion 12 with gusto, shaking her shoulders at the little orna‑ ments not, so her mother realized with horror, to assist in their execution but to advertise her embonpoint—the dress seemed lower cut than it had at the start. The embroidered flowers were rollicking as though drunk. Monsieur was again sitting next to her and Everina, working the pedals with all her might, manufactured a stage wink. One or two of the sons in the audience gave low guffaws. They had seen such winks before, and not in places their mothers would take them. Everina nodded to Monsieur to pick up the left hand. For the sake of the music, he did. Now free, Everina's left hand ran up and down her own thigh, occasionally tipping toward somewhere more intimate. Those who could not see properly, strained. Those who could see had to look away. Mr. Drigg was one of them. Mrs. Drigg, who could only manage tiny, shallow breaths, drummed Mrs. Frogmorton's shoulder. Mrs. Frogmorton could not turn around. She could not admit that something untoward was happening. It was not possible that it was. Their daughters were not in Paris, in the low quarter, playing banjos. They were in a saloon in Pall Mall playing Herr Bach's holy music.

For a moment, as Alathea unfolded Variation 13, all seemed normal. She played only for Annie, glowing through the sarabande doublée with no pretense of detachment. On this public platform, ignoring the other girls, ignoring the audience, ignoring her father, Alathea spoke openly of a pure love, a real love, a love that acknowledged, albeit wistfully, a dependence Alathea could not, and no longer wanted, to deny. Annie's silver core dissolved. It was no longer needed and she let it melt away without regret. The audience, though, was disappointed. After Alathea's last performance, they had hoped for something with more spice. There was a bit of muttering. They felt cheated. Not Sawneyford. He was sickened. Like Annie, he heard Alathea clearly. The girl was parading her love to someone in this room who was not him. Had she no pity? Had she no love left for him, who had so much for her?

Georgiana beckoned to Monsieur. He was to help with

Variation 14. He remained firmly on the black pianoforte stool. In a gesture so extraordinarily bold that her father exclaimed out loud, Georgiana abandoned her own stool, sat beside Monsieur, placed his hands on the keys, and gently forced him to begin. He began. Their hands crossed and Georgiana ensured that they sat closer and closer together. Monsieur could not move down or the lowest notes would fall off the end of the keyboard. Yet Georgiana was practically sitting on his knee. Worse, she kept looking at him, and her look was not just a look, it was a proposal. And the truly dreadful thing was that at this moment, in her white gown, the little brown mole beneath her hair known to him and him alone, Georgiana was absolutely delectable again.

In the audience, Brass was actually choking. "Hell and damnation, Elizabeth!" His wife was still rocking. These girls were, in a most uncanny way, running wild.

At the end of Variation 14, Monsieur pulled himself together and virtually shoved Georgiana from the pianoforte stool. He would play Variation 15, the fifth canon himself, on the brown pianoforte, and restore order. After that, Cantabile could retune the instruments while Monsieur had severe words with the girls. When they resumed, it would be like starting again. Variation 16 was, after all, an overture. Everything before would be forgotten. He turned his face into a stone and played Variation 15 with utter sobriety. The audience did not enjoy it—not, that is, until the girls rose and began to process around the pianofortes, stately (as far as Everina and Marianne could manage) and mesmeric. Monsieur, doing his best to restore the music's more respectable wonders, pretended not to see them. The Driggs, Frogmortons, and Mr. Brass gripped their chairs. Surely this was the end. Mrs. Brass never stopped rocking.

It was not the end. Variation 15 had barely floated away when Marianne knocked Monsieur aside with a cheeky hip and rolled Variation 16's opening chord. The audience cheered. Everina, suddenly jealous of the cheer, rushed to sit beside Marianne. At first, Marianne was cross. She could manage this variation on her own. She began the overture again, trying to push Everina out. Everina gave her a sly nudge. The audience whooped. Marianne's mood altered. Sly met sly. The two girls pushed so close together that the buckles on their slippers clashed. Giggling—even Marianne had a giggle—they slid their slippers off. Two pairs of silkily stockinged feet were exposed to public view. When Georgiana and Harriet, seated at the black pianoforte, took over in perfect staccato, Everina and Marianne, slipperless, danced and flirted. Marianne's wig came adrift. She righted it, almost.

And so it continued, Monsieur unable either to stop the girls or control them. When he tried to shut the pianoforte lids, they flipped them open. When he silently implored Cantabile to help, he was met with a cackle. Cantabile thought the girls were monsters, but he did not want this travesty to stop. His pianoforte was making clowns of them all and in less than half an hour, it would be his again.

Monsieur contemplated running away. All that prevented him was the knowledge that the girls would pursue and catch him and then the fathers would kill him. He sat or stood, played or did not play, he hardly knew which.

During Variation 18, Marianne and Everina were conspirators with a secret so naughty they challenged the audience to guess it. There were more guffaws. Georgiana, coming next, did not care about the audience. The nineteenth variation was for Monsieur, every note declaring Georgiana the model wife, gentle but glorious, undemanding but dedicated, externally soft with a core of white ivory. Georgiana shared secrets with Monsieur, her music said, and she did not care who knew.

Monsieur was supposed to play Variation 20 with Harriet, for it was fiendishly complicated, but Harriet set off on her own. It was a most inaccurate performance, leaving the pianoforte vibrating. Marianne and Everina, not waiting for the vibrations to die down, transformed the lament of Variation 21, the seventh canon, into alehouse sentimentality before picking up their skirts at the end and skipping back to their chairs. One of Marianne's underarm pomanders loosened, dropped to the floor, and rolled away.

Variations 22, 23, and 24 turned into a game of "tag," the girls pulling Monsieur down, then pushing him up. They were all getting hot, except for Alathea. Even Georgiana was pink. Marianne's wig came entirely off her head and flapped down her back from a small rope. Her powder crumbled into a shoal of white pimples. Everina's underarms were dark with spreading sweat. One of her stockings was laddered. Harriet's lipstick was smudged to a bruise, but being more careful, she kept her turban intact and her shoes on. Monsieur, living a nightmare, pinned his hopes on the intense chromatic pathos of Variation 25. Nobody could pervert that.

Variation 25 was Alathea's. She played it as Herr Bach intended except that the pathos was so sinuous and sensual, the audience might have been watching a very slow, very melancholy, and very indecent ballet. Cantabile did not know whether to laugh or scream. Sawneyford, a small lick of spittle on his lips, pulled out his pistol.

Momentarily bonded as sisters, Everina and Marianne had ideas beyond anything Alathea had suggested during practice. They whispered together, then set Monsieur between them for Variation 26. The stool proved too crowded for them to play. Perfect, though, to show off arms and calves as they leaned over him. Eventually they pushed him off the stool and treated the variation as a romp. Who cared about mistakes now? Marianne's wig bounced and with her tongue right out she was a perfect bawdy house madame counting the evening's takings. This was when her marriage prospects vanished and her real career began. Most of the men who eventually became her clients were sitting in the Allemonde saloon that evening.

The sight of Marianne sobered Harriet. There was a boundary that must not be crossed. She played Variation 27, the ninth canon, alone and without fault. I am not like these others, Thomas Buller, she said. Hear my left hand. Hear my right hand. Hear how I marry everything together. That's what I will do for you.

Everina desperately wanted to steal Variation 28 from Alathea. All those patterned, synchronized demisemiquaver trills! She tried to play it. She failed. Alathea waited, then rose, as arranged. Not as arranged, she caught Georgiana's arm. "Come," she said. Georgiana, reckless, obeyed, so they sat together, the swan goddess and the diamond dagger. Every now and again, Georgiana threw her head back in joyous abandon and her goddess's drapes shivered. When she got up from the stool, she flew over to Monsieur, eyes shining, and stood beside him, the music she had made ringing in their ears.

It had been clear since at least Variation 7 that Monsieur

had been more than a music master, but only now did Frog-morton turn on his wife. "You said the music was holy. You said he was a eunuch." He hurled both accusations through gritted teeth. "You *said*."

"*He* said." Mrs. Frogmorton found she could not stop blink-ing. It was the shock. She could think of nothing to say about the music, but as for the other: "He told me how. He told me when. Of all the tricks, Archibald!" She would have sagged had her clothes not made this impossible. Frogmorton, seeing that his uncowable wife was cowed, controlled himself. Argu-ments were for later. They must decide immediately what to do. It was far too late to stop the concert. They must let these ghastly variations run their course. Frogmorton clung to one hope: that the brilliance of the girls' arrival might wipe out everything that had followed. He clung to that hope so hard it was a moment before he was aware that silence had fallen. He looked up. Four of the girls were sitting on their chairs. Monsieur was standing alone. Cantabile had stopped cackling. Alathea was back at the pianoforte. What now, thought Mr. Frogmorton. What new circus could there be?

Alathea raised her hands. Top G, G, A ornamented dotted quaver, to B, then that falling, falling. The aria again, exactly as it had been to start with. This was Alathea's final miracle. After the mayhem, through sheer force of touch, desire, and focus, she recaptured the clarity, dignity, and purity of Herr Bach's holy creation. She did not need to recapture the truth, for the music, from Variation 1 to Variation 30, had told noth-ing but the truth. Through the music, the girls had presented themselves exactly as they were. Alathea raised her eyes to the back of the hall. Annie moved into the aisle. Under her veil, she may have been smiling.

Sawneyford clapped his left hand over his left ear. Why was everything so loud? He must speak to Alathea. She must listen. He knew she was going to leave him and he could not allow it. Father and daughter. Lover and loved. Loved and lover. He saw Annie. He had no idea who she was. He moved out behind her and past her. She saw him and she saw the pistol.

Alathea also saw her father and the pistol. She played on. The men nearest the aisle began to rise, some expostulating and raising their arms, some pushing, some pulling their wives out of Sawneyford's way. Nobody dared tackle him, not with the hammer cocked. Sawneyford reached the front. Alathea played on, the tender aria unhurried and unflinching. Sawney-ford stood in front of her. Did he love her? Did he hate her? He could hardly tell. He only wanted her to stop playing. She played on. She had no fear of Sawneyford. Herr Bach's aria would protect her. She knew it would. Her father would not shoot her. Despite what she had done to him, he had come to her and he had cried. The pistol was not for her. She knew it and he did too. She watched him angle the pistol so that the barrel was under his chin, pointing up through his head. Their eyes met, hers steady, knowing, encouraging—it's the right thing, the decent thing, the best thing—his searching and clouded with despair. Still she played: G, G, A ornamented dot-ted quaver, to B, then that falling, falling, and rising to D, the perfect pattern again.

Annie was behind Sawneyford. She could not see much through her veil, but she saw him raise the pistol. She saw him wait. She saw his arm twitch. No! She flicked up her veil and launched herself at him. The pistol jerked, tilted, then went off with such a dull retort that at first Annie thought it had not gone off at all. But it had. The girls were screaming. Their parents were screaming. The room was an uproar of over-turned chairs, and screaming, fleeing titles. Cantabile crouched under the brown pianoforte. Alathea was no longer playing, she was tipping forward, and Monsieur was no longer sitting at the black piano, he was already out the door.

The room emptied before the screaming stopped and in a very short time another sound was heard. It was laughter. Great peals of it, echoing down the street. The audience had come. They had been amazed. They had been amused. For a moment they had even been alarmed. All in all, it had been a splendid entertainment. Now they were going home. There would be no supper. There would be no weddings. The concert was well and truly over. Thomas Buller alone stood quietly in the void. When he saw his opportunity, he took Harriet's hand and proposed.

TWENTY

ON A DANK AND CHILLY MORNING TWO WEEKS later—Boxing Day, as it happens—we find Alderman Frogmorton, Mr. Brass, and Mr. Drigg walking solemnly behind a cart set for Kennington Common. Sawney Sawneyford is not with them. He is in Soho Square, nursing his daughter. That jerk, that tilt, propelled the pistol ball intended for his own brain forward and it is now lodged next to Alathea's heart. The damage is containable, the surgeon says, if the ball remains exactly where it settled. Any movement or attempt to remove it will most likely be fatal. If Alathea wishes to live, she must remain still. Alathea does not wish to live. Her father wishes the opposite, and he controls the laudanum with which she is made too drowsy to resist.

Alathea's astonishment as the ball embedded itself where it had not been aimed was obvious to everybody. Everybody heard Sawneyford's appalled howl—the most unequivocal sound Sawneyford had ever made. Only Annie saw Alathea's incredulity. This must be a dream, because how was this possible? The music was an unbreachable shield! Then wild disbelief directed not at her father but at Annie. *Annie!* It was impossible, surely, that Annie, the girl who needed no lessons at the pianoforte, had not shared Alathea's faith in the pianoforte's power. Impossible that she had not trusted the aria's perfection. Impossible that she had not understood how Herr Bach would protect them both. Christ! Oh, Christ! *Annie!* Alathea's shattered incomprehension was a trauma beyond the trauma caused by the wound. It blistered Annie's soul long after Alathea's forehead hit the keys, creating discord after discord as she rolled sideways to the floor, blood flowing in streams over and through the diamonds.

Cantabile stepped over the blood, noting with distaste that the blot on Alathea's face came from Annie's lip, bitten when she fell to her knees. "Why did you do that, Annie? Why did you destroy this girl? Were you jealous of her? Was that it?" He gazed without emotion at Alathea. "Now there would have been a daughter." He flicked Annie's veil back over her face and began shouting that if Frogmorton or any of his City fiends touched the brown pianoforte, he, Vittorio Cantabile, would strangle them. He was seized from behind. The fathers threw him out and set an armed guard on the door.

Today, as they walk, Frogmorton, Brass, and Drigg, thick booted and thickly clothed, are still being threatened by Cantabile. He, in his thin working jacket, is hopping along behind, restrained by two of Brass's heavies. Cantabile has buried his wife. He is trying to forget his daughter. His only concern is his pianoforte. The men take little notice. They dream they have Monsieur in the cart. In truth, Monsieur is in Paris.

Worse, Georgiana has gone after him, fleeing from Covent Garden, still in her white gown, not even a cloak against the winter night, clutching a bag of jewels that Elizabeth Brass, with rare energy, bundled up for her. When Mr. Brass discovered Georgiana had fled, his fury had been loud and coarse, yet he did not send after her. Let the ruined daughter go, and the stinking jewels. Brass has another plan. Monsieur might have fooled idiot wives about his nether regions but he would soon fool nobody. Brass has dispatched a very particular man for that job. The contract is never fulfilled. On his way over the channel, the man dispatched is afflicted by conscience: he would happily kill Monsieur, but this other thing seems too drastic. He never finds Monsieur. Monsieur is, though, found by Georgiana, and dogged by a sense of irritated responsibility, he remains with her until her death, twenty-five years later. She bears him three children and sends for her mother to help look after them. Her father would be welcome but he never comes. He spends what would have been her fortune on fighting dogs.

In the cart is the brown pianoforte. With no Monsieur to lynch and Herr Bach already dead, the fathers turned on the instrument. Absurd, of course, but the pianoforte is the one thing on which they can take physical revenge. Drigg had been for breaking it up even before Alathea was carried away. Calmer counsel prevailed. In the event, it had taken only twenty-four hours to decide what to do and, with Christmas intervening, today is the designated day.

Like a criminal, the instrument is tied by the legs. The procession reaches the common, empty except for a group of boys supervising a cockfight. The carter asks, "Where now?" Frogmorton gestures to the gallows in the middle. The wheels crunch over the half-soggy, half-frozen dew and the men stamp after it, breath steaming. They all help lever the instrument down. They take care. As with a traitor brought for hanging and evisceration, they want their prisoner intact. The strings twang gently as the frame is placed on the base immediately in front of the gallows platform. If the pianoforte had a stool, it would be ready to play. The stool, though, was judged not guilty, and the same judgment was made of the inferior piano. Both are still in the Allemonde saloon. The carter tosses out fagots and kindling. Drigg raises the pianoforte lid and places fagots inside the body while Brass stacks fagots around the legs.

Cantabile is brought to a halt a little way off. He is crying like a baby, cursing Drigg, cursing his daughter, cursing Claude Belladroit. Drigg wants to shout "Curse yourself," but since the other men are silent, he is silent too.

The carter asks if he should light the kindling. "Yes, light the thing," Frogmorton snaps. For a moment, he can hear Harriet playing. Past pride heightens present humiliation. Burning the pianoforte. What a sign of impotence. Had Cantabile stopped his cursing, Frogmorton might have halted the whole charade. But Cantabile curses on and Frogmorton stands, feet apart, recalling the forced calm of his wife in the carriage home, a calm that broke behind her closed bedroom door without even Frilly as witness. The tempest lasted ten minutes. Afterward, Mrs. Frogmorton emerged and carried on as usual, except she was deflated, diminished, unstitched. When Harriet announced she was marrying Thomas Buller, her mother registered neither pleasure nor displeasure. She would recover, the alderman thought. She would find some stuffing and stitch herself together. But it wasn't right that she should have to, not right at all. The carter strikes a light. Cantabile shrieks. Frogmorton wishes they could burn him.

Drigg suffers more acutely than Frogmorton. The sight of both his daughters flaunting themselves like tipsy heifers will never leave him. The servants knew before the Drigg carriage brought them all home. Mrs. Drigg has told him to put the house up for sale, and her first act the morning after the concert was to dispatch the girls' entire trousseaus to a City charity for unmarried mothers. (In the curious way things often turn out, Marianne herself became an unmarried mother, though her new career rendered charity unnecessary.) Mrs. Drigg then drew the curtains, pulling one down as she blundered about. She could not face the neighbors. She could not face the girls. She could not face her own mirror. In the face of all this not facing, Drigg can do little. The girls, on the other hand, and for reasons unfathomable to their father, are in a state of high elation.

Everina took an early decision: she decided Alathea had been right. After all, despite the concert's unhappy end, it had been followed by propositions pushed through the Stratton Street door on a daily basis. Men had seen what the Drigg sisters had to offer and wished to offer for it. She showed the propositions to Marianne and scoffed when Marianne wept at their crudity. True, these were not the offers their parents had hoped for, but look! The concert was barely over and already money, servants, houses were being paraded—all for them! "We can do as we like," Everina said. "We only have to decide."

"But there's nothing here about marriage," Marianne sobbed. "Propositions aren't proposals. Harriet's had a proper proposal."

Everina made a face. "Only from a plain mister." She tossed her head. "We don't need proposals. Look how much fun we had. I don't think our mother ever had fun like that. We're celebrated all over the newspapers, Marianne. We're more famous than anybody in a story, and we're real." She giggled. "The expressions on people's faces! They loved us!" She thrust out a handkerchief. "Come on, wipe your nose. We should thank Alathea, and"—she gave Marianne a sly nudge—"she's never going to upstage us again."

This last, at least, cheered Marianne. The sisters did not have to disguise from each other that they went to see Alathea because they were sure she would not want to see them. Marianne made suitably pitying noises. They were both shocked by the house. On the way back to Stratton Street, they wondered what had happened to the diamond dress, and Marianne openly conjectured that Alathea was in a partnership with the underworld. "It would be just like Alathea to have conjured up a demon," she said, referring to Annie, whom she had briefly glimpsed unveiled. Everina had hardly been conscious of Annie at all. They never spoke of her again.

The sisters grew closer. Instead of squabbling, they began to frequent taverns, playhouses, trinket shops, and the parlor of a man offering tattoos—places to which they were guided by new friends. A world of novelty opened up, and it was productive. Offers continued to flow in abundance. The girls encouraged competition. When their mother returned to her father's fish stall, Marianne and Everina opened the Stratton Street drawing room in which, intoxicated by their newfound freedom, they held bawdy court until the house was sold and they moved, together, to lodgings paid for by the sons of three peers. Things progressed from there. Luckily for Drigg as he watches the execution of the pianoforte, he cannot see the future.

THE KINDLING is smoking. The carter takes his guinea fee and leaves. The cockfighting boys truss their birds and wander over, diverted by the sight of four men rooted around a burning pianoforte, a skinny devil screeching in the background.

The men are silent. With flames licking its underbelly, the pianoforte tries to remain silent too, and also upright and dignified. It refuses to buckle, wishing to sink gracefully, not like a cow with foot rot. It knows its worth, even if its murderers do not and never have. It has been sublime. The flames leap. The pianoforte cannot help itself. Its strings give voice as they melt: short, high hums, then snap snap snap with brave twang and stuttering cadence. The sounding board's hisses are gentle, its cracks apologetic. The pianoforte would like to die to the strains of Herr Bach's aria, if only somebody would help. Where is Alathea? The keys begin to drop away. First the white, then the black. The pianoforte is being stripped. The lid, not yet alight, slips, to cover the nakedness. There is wood and soft iron, ivory and leather, brass and steel, and a tarnished soundboard rose. There is nobody to comfort the instrument in its distress. Cantabile certainly cannot, having neither the practice nor the gift. He can only watch and grind his teeth. The end comes in a heap of charred fragments, blackened coils, brass screws, and mangled, tangled strings pointing every which way, as though unsure from which direction help might come.

The boys are quickly among the smoking heap, scrabbling for loot. At this point, Brass's servants let Cantabile go. He rushes at the boys. They tease him and, once they have nudged out anything of value, kick the remains of the piano forte's guts in Cantabile's direction. He gathers the pieces as a mother gathers the bones of a child. The boys hold up their birds, beaks firmly tethered shut. "Want to see some real sport, old man?" they shout, friendly enough. Cantabile does not answer. His hands are full. He cannot even shake a fist.

Frogmorton, Brass, and Drigg make their way to Thread needle Street and into the V & B, their first visit since the concert. They have been at home and in their offices. They have been in Pall Mall trying to rectify matters with the Alle mondes. They have met at Manchester Square, whose hall was the pianoforte's condemned cell. In the V & B, the famil iar fug envelopes them. Mr. W., emptying coffee grounds into a measure, nods. Frogmorton nods back. Mrs. W. offers the comment "Chilly day" and wipes the men's usual table. There is some whispering, but few City men have heard about the concert and fewer are interested. Trade is king, and trade is threatened by war, not by pianofortes or concerts or daugh ters' marriages. The tallow dips splutter. The water urn, dirtier than it was this time last year, swings and gurgles. A new cat is warming its behind. The last copies of *Spence's Penny Weekly* have long since been thrown in the fire, except for the one still stuffed under the table leg.

Two noticeable changes. Mr. W.'s lewd pictures have been exchanged for patriotic song sheets, and there is a new awk wardness among the men. They remove their hats, push away the chair that might have been Sawneyford's, and sit quietly until coffee arrives. Frogmorton shakes his head at the coffee boy. No, they don't want pipes.

"Well," Brass says.

Drigg interrupts. He just needed somebody else to start. "How did Grace not know?" he says quickly to Frogmorton. "I mean, how could she not *know?*" This question has been asked before, many times, during these two weeks.

"Monsieur was convincing," Frogmorton says wearily. This answer, too, has been given before, many times. "I told you what he told her. You were convinced."

"But she was acting chaperone!"

"She did what she thought was right." Frogmorton puts down his coffee bowl with unaccustomed care. "As I keep saying, nobody could be more sorry."

"Agnes has collapsed," says Drigg. "Marianne and Everina are out of control."

"I heard Everina say that the creature who jogged Sawneyford was a witch," says Brass. "I hardly saw her. Did you?"

Drigg takes a breath. "She's Cantabile's daughter. She was there when I bought the pianoforte."

"His daughter?" The notion seems to tickle Brass. "Well whadaya know. I'm glad she isn't mine."

"Have you found Georgiana?" Drigg asks.

"No," says Brass, "and I don't intend to." He wonders whether to keep his contract on Monsieur's offending parts to himself. He does not. There is strained laughter. It seems the only response. Brass stretches his legs. Drigg stops fidgeting. More coffee is poured.

"How's Sawneyford?" Frogmorton asks. "Has anybody seen Alathea?"

A glance, flickering around. Alathea. Brass whistles. "Wasn't that something." They know he is not referring to the shooting.

"I reckon the diamonds in the choker alone were worth at least a thousand pounds," Frogmorton says. They cannot talk of the other thing. They cannot even think about it. They must not. Even Brass must realize it is forbidden.

"More than a thousand," Drigg declares.

"Did you count them?" asks Brass.

"Fifteen," says Drigg. The laughter is more genuine.

"More valuable than that damnable music," Brass says. "Didn't Grace say Monsieur described it as holy?"

"Wholly unsuitable," Drigg chips in. "We could try and get it proscribed?"

Frogmorton shakes his head. "No need. It'll go out of fashion soon enough." The men nod.

"I think I will have a pipe," Frogmorton says. "You, Drigg?"

"Why not."

Pipes are brought. A clerk from Frogmorton's office appears to consult Frogmorton over an account that does not tally. Frogmorton and Drigg lean over it. Brass leans back and thinks of his new squeeze—a perky London miss. He has had enough of foreigners.

"So Harriet's to be Mrs. Thomas Buller?" Drigg says when the account has been dissected and the miscalculation identified.

"She is," says Frogmorton, and shrugs. "His father has interests in India: indigo, salt, cotton, that kind of thing." He sucks at his pipe. He starts to say "It won't be a bad match" but realizes the tactlessness just in time. There will no matches at all for the others. He says, "We should help Sawney out. I don't know what got into him. It's hardly his fault everything went wrong."

Mr. Drigg and Mr. Brass agree. They will set up a fund. They may not like Sawneyford, but he is one of them. The fund will be generous. It does not need to be. Though Sawneyford nurses Alathea assiduously and with all due propriety, her wish to die is too strong, even for the laudanum. In a month she is gone. Sawneyford sells his City businesses and leaves without a word, vanishing into the fog of revolution and war to float or sink, as fate decrees.

The men linger long in the V & B, and even as they discuss the fund for Sawneyford and his daughter, in the hold of the *Maidenhead*, newly slipped from the Port of London, the hangman is working his passage to the New World. With not even one hanging from the November treason trials (treason in itself), he has thrown in the rope and will try his luck in America. The first job given him by the ship's captain is to lash down a pianoforte, bought in London for a New York family of musical girls. His familiarity with knots is turning out an advantage.

In the hold is a veiled girl, waiting for him to finish. Annie boarded early. She already knows she will find no utopia in the New World since the Pantisocratics cannot get themselves past Bristol. Nevertheless, she will make the voyage. Throughout the entire crossing, she never leaves this pianoforte. At first she cannot bear to play Bach, then she cannot bear to play anything else. The dreadful storms of the Atlantic are welcome. The pianoforte groans while Annie howls, clutching Alathea's ring.

Disembarking in New York, she grips her veil and does not speak. It is left to the captain to explain her attachment to the pianoforte as best he can, which, since he has no idea of Annie's story, is no explanation. The mother of the New York girls, making far too prosaic an assumption about the wedding ring on the chain, senses tragedy. She takes pity and a risk. She invites Annie to their home. There Annie remains, silent for the most part and nearly always veiled, until people no longer ask where she came from and must content themselves with the one thing they do know about her: that she belongs to the pianoforte that she plays for the greater part of every day. The family come to believe that Annie blesses them through her music, and through their unquestioning, continued welcome, Annie believes they bless her, so far as blessing is possible.

Annie's heart never heals. Music is just enough to keep her sane. When she dies—a sudden stroke—the New York family bury her in their own plot, her veil secured, her secrets intact, the wedding ring still on its chain around her neck. At her funeral, at her own request, the aria from the fourth part of Bach's *Clavier Übung* is played. Her tombstone is plain and the inscription simple. It reads *Annie 1777–1843*, and underneath, *Pianist.*

Acknowledgments

All novels benefit from the following: an enthusiast, a generous expert, a poet, a keen agent, a meticulous editor, and the provision, by a kindly agency, of time. *The Marriage Recital* had all of these. The enthusiast is my husband; the generous expert, musician Keith Jacobsen; the poet, Michael Schmidt; my agent, Georgina Capel; my editor at Henry Holt, Barbara Jones; and the kindly agency, the Royal Literary Fund. I couldn't be more grateful to you all.

Any mistakes readers find in the text will be mine, and not the fault of any of the people or agencies above or of the many sources I consulted. If you do spot a mistake, I apologize, and hope it doesn't spoil your enjoyment of the book.

32953012462679